# Domestic
# VIOLETS

*A Novel*

## Matthew Norman

HARPER  PERENNIAL

NEW YORK • LONDON • TORONTO • SYDNEY • NEW DELHI • AUCKLAND

HARPER ● PERENNIAL

HarperCollins books may be purchased for educational, business, or sales promotional use. For information please write: Special Markets Department, HarperCollins Publishers, 10 East 53rd Street, New York, NY 10022.

FIRST EDITION

Library of Congress Cataloging-in-Publication Data is available upon request.

ISBN 978-0-06-206511-7

11  12  13  14  15   OV/RRD   10 9 8 7 6 5 4 3 2 1

*For Kate & Caroline*

## A Note on Timing

As you've already been told in the fine print above all the copyright information, this book is a work of fiction. However, many people, places, and things mentioned throughout are very real—particularly the movies. Because I've been so flagrant in my blending of the real and not real, I should probably mention that I've taken some liberties with timing. I tried to make things chronologically accurate, but sometimes things just don't line up right, and so you're forced to blur the edges a little. I appreciate your understanding.

—M.N.

*Part I*

*1*

*I splash cold water* on my face.

This is what men in movies do when they're about to fly off the handle, when shit is getting out of control. I do this sometimes. I react to things based on what characters in movies would do. That's kind of ironic, considering I've always thought of myself as a book person.

At least I think that's ironic. That word gets misused a lot.

The water isn't refreshing like it's supposed to be. It's ice-cold and I gasp. As it swirls into a little cyclone on its way down the drain, I look in the mirror, ashamed and angry at myself.

There's something wrong. With my penis.

It's been an unpredictable thing for a while now, my shlong, all flighty and unreliable like some stoner uncle who shows up hammered at Thanksgiving and forgets your name.

The guy I see in the mirror, Tom Violet, the same lanky, moody bastard I've been looking at for almost thirty-six years now, looks . . . old. The fact that I'm naked certainly isn't helping. Like most men who are not Brad Pitt, I could do without the sight of my own nudity. Back in the day I was a long-distance runner, all streamlined and put together. Now I'm flabby-thin, the way a fat guy might look after a year in an internment camp. Worse, the hair on my chest is overgrown and dark against my pale skin and I wonder if I should be one of those guys who shaves his chest. Maybe that would help.

Of course it wouldn't help. That's not the problem. The problem, still, is my broken wang.

I look at it in the mirror, *really* look at it, and it, too, appears ashamed. It's shriveled up into itself, like an infant's thingy. I close my eyes and touch it, and then I squeeze it, just to try to get something going. I think of my wife. She's lying in bed, not twenty feet away, in a red thing from Victoria's Secret—just "a fun little thing" she picked up. I actually think *that's* the problem. Lingerie screams of effort. It screams of forced intimacy and the fact that we both know she's probably ovulating. We did the math this week. What I need to do is to sneak up on sex. For some strange reason, thinking about getting an erection makes it fucking impossible to get an erection. I tried to explain this to Anna a few weeks ago, but she didn't get it. I don't blame her. It's a very abstract concept.

Maybe it's the economy. Personal and global financial ruin could cause boner problems, right?

Sadly, no. This all started happening before the world ended. I'll have to come up with another excuse.

And so I stroke on, like a fool, like a caged monkey masturbating in front of a horrified troop of Cub Scouts at the zoo. There's a sensation, like a phantom tingling somewhere in my stomach, but then there's nothing again, and I begin to think about the cruelties of aging. In my carefree youth, sitting in Catholic school, I couldn't go more than twenty minutes without popping a painful, trouser-lifting boner. Now, with the prospect of actual sex in the other room, I've got nothing. Zilch.

How many perfectly good hard-ons have I wasted in my short, stupid life? Hundreds? Probably thousands if you count college. It's just not fair.

Finally, I turn off the faucet and give up. In the silent bathroom,

I give my lifeless manhood one last pleading look and then open the door.

Anna is still in her Victoria's Secret thing, but she's de-sexed it a little by putting on her reading glasses. She's stretched out on our bed reading a *New Yorker* by the light of one of the candles she's set up. I've been trying to jerk myself back to life. She's been reading "Talk of the Town."

The stereo is still on, too. It's playing some CD of classical music fused with nature sounds. It's supposed to be relaxing or soothing or God knows what. But, of course, it's just more effort, more unnatural things added to what's supposed to be the most natural thing in the world.

Our dog, Hank, is skilled at sensing anxiety in a room. He's sitting on the floor on one of his dog mats. He's one of those dogs that always seems to be bracing himself for the worst.

Anna smiles and sits up. "Hi," she says. Her legs on our powder blue sheets are long and toned and treadmill-ready. She's beautiful, my wife, I recognize this, but my body is somehow rejecting this fact along with all of its sexual implications. If the nineteen-year-old version of Tom Violet were here in this room, he'd slap the thirty-five-year-old version of Tom Violet across the face in utter disgust.

Three nights ago, after our last failed attempt at this, I woke up in the middle of the night to Anna moaning quietly next to me. At first I didn't know what was going on, and then I realized that she was having a sex dream. In eight years of sleeping beside her nightly, I'd never heard anything like that. As I listened to her whisper her way toward a soft, muted little orgasm, I realized that we had a *real* problem.

I put on a pair of boxers and slide into bed next to her. She rolls over onto her side and looks at me. Her small breasts are vivid against all that silk or satin or whatever those things from Victoria's Secret are made out of. "You OK?" she asks. Her voice has taken on this funerallike tone, which feels absurd and completely accurate.

I sigh and listen to the music and the sound of some whale or dolphin in the ocean. "No," I say. "I'm obviously not."

"It's not a big deal, you know. It . . . happens."

This is what women say in these scenes to the men they love. Her eyes and her face are sweet and concerned for me, but there's enough tension in her voice to know that she's just reading from the script. It might not have been a big deal the first time, or even the sixth time, but it's a big deal now, and I wonder what the man in her head looked like who inspired those little noises the other night. Like me with a shaved chest, perhaps—or, at the very least, like me with a fully functioning penis?

"I don't know what's the matter with me."

She takes off her glasses and sets them on the nightstand. Over the sheets, she rubs my knee, and then she inches a little closer. "Maybe you're just—" but she leaves this hanging. Like me, she doesn't seem to know exactly what it is that I am. I look down at her feet, and her toenails are painted red. This is something new for her. Her feet are typically very functional things, but lately they're lotioned and cared for. This simple act of pure femininity would probably be enough to turn the nineteen-year-old version of Tom Violet into a sex-crazed idiot. But here I am, dejected and lustless.

I don't want to talk about my penis, but I don't want to blow out the candles and roll over, either. I'm vulnerable, yet simultaneously guarded. I want Anna to hold me and tell me that she loves me, but I also want to sleep in the guest room. I'm like a six-foot-tall version of my own flaccid dick, wanting yet pulling away from my only real ally in the world.

Anna's an optimist, though, to the bitter end, and so she forges on. Like her ancestors, great, blond Swedes from Nebraska, she'll continue plowing long-dead fields, even as the locusts converge.

"We haven't been to the Caribbean in a while," she says gently, smiling at me. Her face goes flush.

"Anna," I say, but then I stop. She's right. We haven't.

"Maybe that's where we should go then," she says, and then she tucks her hair behind each ear. "You like it there, right?"

Two days after we were married, we were on our way to the Caribbean, stuck in the very back row of some medium-size plane from Washington, D.C. We'd had drinks at the airport bar and wine after takeoff. The alcohol, the altitude, and the weird joy of it all were enough to motivate my wife to go down on me as the cabin lights dimmed and a rerun of *Frasier* came on the little drop-down televisions.

She kisses my neck and then my chest and then my stomach, working her way downward. My heart is running and I'm nostalgic as I touch the back of her head. "Just relax," she whispers.

I close my eyes as she goes about the little routine of swirling kisses and harmless bites.

Then she puts me in her mouth and I hold my breath and concentrate on the rush of sensations. I think of dirty, pornographic things and grit my teeth. I think of swimsuit issues and those creepy phone sex commercials that come on when you can't sleep. A minute later, I should be as hard as that stupid, ungrateful thirteen-year-old looking down white blouses in Catholic school. But I'm not—not even close.

"Anna," I say.

"Just *relax*." She draws the word out, trying to hypnotize my penis. I'm determined to will an erection out of thin air, so I squeeze my eyes shut and concentrate some more. Aside from the lovely wetness of Anna's mouth, though, there's only this odd, rubbery little thing that I've somehow become.

I say her name again, but she doesn't stop. It's so small in her mouth and I feel a fresh wave of that awful humiliation that sent me scrambling to the bathroom ten minutes ago.

"Anna, please!"

Finally, she pulls away, startled, and I cover my stupid penis.

"I'm sorry. I can't. Shit. I just . . . I'm sorry."

She wipes her mouth and lies down again to stare at the ceiling. "Tom," she says. But before she can say anything else, there's a knock at our door, three small taps.

"Mommy? Daddy?"

Anna sits up and shakes out her hair. "I locked the door," she whispers, and that somehow makes it even more embarrassing. She's planned all of this down to the finest details. I briefly wonder if our daughter has been listening to this entire episode, and if so, how badly will she be scarred? I wish I could sink down into this mattress and disappear.

"Mommy? Daddy? Can I come in? Please! Pleeeassse!" She sounds scared.

Anna takes a breath and clears her throat—a mother again. She hops up and opens the door and Allie runs into the room, her eyes noisy and wide. "You guys," she says.

"What's up, Allie-Cat?" I say.

Her lower lip is shaking. "There's a burglar downstairs."

"A *what*? No, baby. You're just dreami—"

"Nu-uhh. It's *not* a dream." She's on my side of the bed clutching our comforter, and Anna crouches beside her, smoothing her wild bed-head. "He's taking away all of our stuff. He's *stealing* it. I can hear him. And then he's gonna try to hurt us because robbers can't leave witnesses. If they do then we'll be able to pick them out in that room with the glass."

Thank you, *Law & Order* reruns.

"Sweetie," I say, but then Hank stands up, the shittiest watchdog in North America, and growls at the door. There are footsteps and then rustling, and my daughter is right. There's somebody downstairs.

"See," she says. Tears are about to spill from wide eyes. "I told you."

"Shit," I whisper.

I wonder what someone does in a situation like this—all those actors in movies. And then for a moment I do absolutely nothing, as if the situation might simply resolve itself while the three of us sit here in this bedroom breathing. Then I realize that despite what both of them must suspect about me and my abilities as a man, Anna and Allie are looking at me. They're waiting for me to do something. Waiting for me to protect them. Even Hank is looking at me now, perfectly still, the rigid statue of an ugly little dog.

"OK," I say, which seems like a good place to start. "You guys stay here. I'm gonna go check it out."

God help us.

## 2

*I* **creep down the** stairs holding my nine-iron, which is the best weapon I can come up with. This seems like a better option than Anna's hair dryer or, for that matter, it's better than leaping from our bathroom window and fleeing off into the night by myself. I've got some clothes on now, a T-shirt and pajama pants, and Anna is at the top of the stairs in her sexy outfit with her cell phone.

"Who is it?" she whispers. Apparently she believes that I can see through walls and ceilings.

I'm nervous, but, more than that, I'm annoyed with the cosmic order of things because there isn't an adult here to take care of this—a *real* adult, instead of an impostor like me. At this moment, I'm clearly fooling no one.

At the bottom of the stairs I turn through the entryway. Our front door is standing open, but it's unscathed, and I wonder if I've forgotten to lock it. After all, this pretty much *has to be* my fault, the violent death of my family and the theft of our meager possessions and DVD collection. The refrigerator is open and there are bottles clanking. Our house is long and narrow, and so I can see through its length all the way into the kitchen where there's a man rummaging through drawers. Despite the drama and this idiotic golf club, I take a breath and relax. There's the familiar shock of graying hair and the tweed blazer that should have gone to Goodwill years ago. This burglar who has frightened the women in my life and exposed my questionable status as the man of this house is Curtis Violet, my stupid father, and he's pouring himself a glass of wine.

"Jesus Christ, Dad."

He spins around smiling and nearly spills his wine. "This is the only red you seem to have. I've never heard of it. Is it any good?"

"Have you ever *heard* of a doorbell?"

"I have. It's a fantastic invention. Yours, though, doesn't appear to be loud enough."

As I close and lock our front door, I think of Anna's sexifying music/animal sounds and the rushing of the sink and the deafness of impotence. I didn't hear the doorbell, and so my dad let himself in. He has his own keys, because, technically speaking, this is his house.

"Well, you're lucky I don't have a gun then," I say.

"I think we all are, son. You and I aren't the sort of men who should be armed. Oh, you're not still playing with those old Callaways, are you? Let me get you the new PING irons. Pure graphite. You'll never hit a ball straighter, my hand to God."

He plays golf about twice a year, badly, so I ignore his bullshit. From upstairs, Anna yells down, welcoming Curtis as if it's the middle of the afternoon.

"Hi sweetie," he tells the ceiling. "Sorry to barge in."

He pours me a glass of wine, which is no easy feat considering he's obviously drunk. His overnight bag is sitting on the kitchen table, but I ignore it, certain that I'll be hearing about it soon enough. He gives me a lurid smile and his eyes are red and a little glassy. "I wasn't interrupting anything, was I?"

"No, Dad, not tonight."

We've exchanged a few phone calls and an e-mail here and there, but I haven't seen him in a month or so, and when I flip on another light I see that the time hasn't been kind. He hasn't shaved in a while and he's lost some weight. Some men can pull off a few days without shaving, but it tends to make Curtis look like a domestic terrorist.

With the coast now clear, the dog storms the kitchen with gusto, completing a quick victory lap and then landing at Curtis's feet. He's leery of strangers, this little dog, but he's hopelessly devoted to the people he knows. His weird, curly little tail is wagging in a blur.

"Well hi there, Hanky Panky." As he crouches to pet my dog, Curtis has to catch himself on the counter to keep from pitching forward onto the floor.

"You're drunk, Dad," I say.

"I very well might be. But I'm not afraid to be drunker. In fact, I'm determined." Hank rolls over, flashing some skin, and my dad laughs.

I take a long sip of my wine, which is ridiculous on a random weeknight. Or maybe it isn't. Maybe alcohol is exactly what I need—buckets of it.

"Have you talked to your mother lately? How's she's doing?"

This is my dad's default question, one asked simply to fill space in a room. Whenever he asks, I consider asking him why he's so much more interested now than he was during the handful of years they were married three decades ago. But I never do. "Not bad. She's teaching *Catcher in the Rye* again this year. I guess her kids love it."

Curtis shakes his head. "Well of course they do, Tommy. The only people who can actually get through that self-indulgent tripe without throwing up are teenagers and the criminally insane."

Thankfully Anna and Allie arrive to save me from my dad's lecture on Salinger's shortcomings. Allie is in *Sesame Street* pajamas and Anna has changed to shorts and a T-shirt. In her glasses and sensible sleepwear, she's the bookish version of the sultry harlot I failed only moments ago, and her mere presence embarrasses me.

Allie crashes into her grandpa's trousers, wrapping her arms around his legs.

"Well there's the prettiest girl in town."

"I thought you were a burglar, Grandpa. I got scared because you were either going to take us hostage or shoot us."

"Well, you should be scared. I *am* a burglar."

"Burglars wear masks," she says.

"I left it in the car. It's very itchy. I never said I was good at being a burglar."

Anna notices the overnight bag on the kitchen table and gives me a look. I shrug just enough to tell her that I have no idea and then she rolls her eyes at my perpetual lack of knowledge. It's the silent language of marriage.

My dad sets Allie on one of the stools along our counter and touches the top of her head. "So tell me, Allie. Would you like a glass of wine? Or maybe a cigar? I'm buying."

She finds this hilarious, and her laughter fills our little kitchen.

"It's very late, sweetie," says Anna. "How about you go back to bed?"

"Are you going to be here tomorrow, Grandpa? You should have a sleepover party!"

"My plan is to go wherever the night takes me, darling," he says, and then he tips his glass.

"Allie," says Anna. She's stern now.

Our daughter looks at me, hoping that I've got some sort of veto power here, but she quickly resigns herself to defeat and begins a slow march up the stairs.

"I'll come tuck you in soon, honey," I say. "And no spying. Lights out."

I can see by her expression that she'll do whatever she damn well pleases until she hears me coming up the stairs. By now she's old enough to know that we're not going to beat her, so she's pretty much got the run of the place.

When she's gone, Curtis turns his attention to the wine, sniffing the rim of his glass like we're in the south of France. "Is this from one of those little vineyards in Virginia—over in the sticks?"

"I have no idea, Dad. I bought it at the Giant because I like the picture on the label."

He squints at a cartoon kangaroo bounding across the bottle. "You're right. It's cute, isn't it?"

"So, are you just dropping by, Curtis?" asks Anna.

I could have stood here all night sipping wine without asking him what he was doing here, but my wife has gone and blown it, and for some reason I feel like we've just lost a battle of wills. Women don't understand these things. The bag itself was really just a prop to get one of us to ask him if he's OK.

Classic Curtis Violet.

He sees his opening, of course, and embraces it. "Not exactly. I have some news. *A lot* of news, as a matter of fact." He looks out from our kitchen at the rest of our ground floor, assessing things. We still hardly have any furniture, and most of what we do have was put together by me, incompetently, from a box.

"What is it?" asks Anna.

"Well, first off, I'm sad to report that Ashley has asked me to move out. Well, to be more clear, she did more than ask. She was pretty adamant about it. *You know how she can be.*"

"Oh, Curtis. That's terrible."

"What happened this time, Dad?"

Anna's glare is sharp and sudden. Perhaps "this time" wasn't completely necessary, but it's late and I've had a shitty night.

He returns to the morose study of our kitchen, touching a shriveling orange that's sitting on our countertop. "A lot of things, I guess."

Anna pours herself a glass of wine, too, and I sip my own, and now we're both drinking, waiting to see what my father has done now.

"It's a little embarrassing. But I've become involved with someone else," he says. "Another woman. I didn't intend for it to happen. It just did. It was an accident. It's something I simply couldn't control."

"Of course," I say.

Anna touches his shoulder, giving it a little squeeze. The fact that she can be acting both surprised and concerned by this inevitability is worthy of an award from the Screen Actors Guild.

He frowns, showing a row of deep-set lines above his eyebrows. He's about to say something, but suddenly he's gotten distracted. "Anna, dear, my God. What have you done? You look absolutely wonderful."

My wife blushes and tugs at the bottom of her old T-shirt. "Oh, shut up," she says.

"No, I will not shut up. I've never seen you like this. You didn't have surgery, did you? You're too young for surgery."

"I wish. That'd be a lot easier. The gym, five days a week. It was a New Year's resolution." She pats my stomach. "Actually, it was *our* New Year's resolution."

"Well," he says, "it seems one of you is more committed than the other. I urge you to keep it up. You're doing mankind a great service. Look at your calf muscles. I didn't even know that calves could look like—"

"What's your other news, Dad?" I ask.

"What?"

"You said you had *a lot* of news. So far you've just told us one thing."

"Thank you, Tommy, you're right. I have some gifts for the two of you." He sets his wine down and digs around in his overnight bag for a while, finally removing a bright yellow T-shirt. Across the chest it reads, "WWCVD." Beneath that, "What Would Curtis Violet Do?"

"What does it mean?" Anna asks.

"I'm not entirely sure. One of my Advanced Fiction students

came up with it. I guess he made dozens of them, and he's been selling them around campus. Apparently it's a satire on some religious saying, 'What Would Jesus Do?' I guess when Republicans or God people are confronted with a challenge or some sort of existential dilemma, they're supposed to think about what Jesus would do and then use that as a guide. I thought you might like one."

"Of course," I say. "I don't see how comparing yourself to Jesus could cause any problems."

"But that's not all." He's on too much of a roll now to be baited by sarcasm. Next he takes out a thick, hardcover book. There's a black-and-white picture of a much younger version of my dad on the cover. He's sitting at his old typewriter, a sweater around his shoulders, looking all square-jawed and WASPy. I've seen it many times—it's *The Stories of Curtis Violet.*

"Dad, we've got like five copies of that."

"But look, I've signed it for you."

On the title page, I see that he's written: *To my son and his beautiful wife—Curtis.* Next to his name, he's drawn his trademark violet, twisting and looping through his messy script.

"Thanks. But you signed the other ones, too."

"Oh, I know, Tommy. But I thought you might like another one. I imagine they're going to be pretty valuable someday. Maybe you can sell it and buy some furniture."

He's smiling at us in his academic way, and beneath the bloodshot eyes and the patchy growth of hobo beard, I see a familiar arrogance, one I haven't seen in a while. "OK, Dad, I'll bite. Why's that?"

"I'm no expert, but from what I've seen online, signed first editions of Pulitzer Prize winners can bring in a lot of money."

Anna gasps into her hands and a chilly path of goose bumps runs up my arms like electricity. "You're kidding me," I say.

"Sonya called this morning. A lovely surprise, at long last."

Anna hugs/tackles him laughing and they nearly fall over the kitchen table together. "I thought Nicholas Zuckerman was gonna get it again this year," I say. "That's what everyone was saying."

With my wife in his arms, Curtis Violet rolls his eyes like he's smarter than all of us combined. "Don't be an ass, Tommy. That boring old Jew couldn't write his way out of a paper bag."

It's easy for me sometimes to forget who my father is, especially when he shows up drunk and reeking of pot. But the world has a way of continuing to remind me.

"We need another drink," my wife says. She's smiling and a little flushed. It reminds me of the first time she met him, back when we'd just started seeing each other. I was so ridiculously in love with her then after six dates that I pretended not to notice how flustered she got when he kissed her hand.

"I agree," says Curtis. "I don't think this one bottle is going to do it, though. What else do we have in here, Tommy? You don't have any dingo champagne do you? Koala, maybe?"

## 3

*I*t's nearly 1 a.m. by the time I manage to get my dad settled in our office/extra bedroom. We hug, but we're both a little drunk, and so we almost fall down. "I've missed you guys, Tommy," he says. Alcohol has always brought out the many different sides of Curtis Violet, and tonight he's sentimental.

"Where the hell have you been, anyway?" I ask.

"Here and there," he says. "New York mostly. But I'm here now. I'll just stay for a night or so, if that's OK? Maybe I can spend some time with Allie tomorrow. That might be fun. What kind of things does she like to do?"

"She's got school tomorrow."

"School? What? She's like four years old."

"Close, Dad. She's seven."

As promised, I look in on Allie before heading to bed. I find her half dozing against a stuffed panda the size of an acoustic guitar. Her reading lamp is on, a picture book across her chest. It's about a boy who helps a lost penguin get back to the North Pole. It's one of those books that if you read in a certain mood you'll end up whimpering in front of your confused daughter like a mental patient. She senses me there at the door and cracks her eyes. "Hi, Daddy."

"What are you doing up? It's tomorrow already."

"Is Grandpa still here?"

"Yep."

"I don't like his beard. It makes him look like an old man."

"I agree."

She pauses, thinking for a moment. "How come Ashley doesn't want to live with him anymore?"

I suspect she's been spying after all. "Well, sweetie, your Grandpa Curtis can be . . . an emotionally tiring man. It kinda wears some people down after a while. Especially his wives."

"Are they gonna get *divorced*, do you think? Grandpa's been divorced a lot, hasn't he?"

"I think he's going for a record."

She looks at her hands, playing a silent tune with fingers. "Can I tell you a secret?" she says. "I don't like Ashley very much. She's not very nice to me."

I pull the covers up over her chest. "Well then, you're definitely your mother's daughter."

"I'm your daughter, too."

"That you are," I say, turning off her lamp. With just the night-light in the corner, the room is all shadows. I stand up to leave her, but I'm not sure I want to yet. There are responsibilities outside this little yellow room that I'm not quite ready for.

"Mommy said that you guys will never get a divorce. She said you love each other too much."

"Oh yeah, when did she say that?"

In the dark I see the whites of her eyes as she thinks. "I don't know. A while ago."

"Well, she's right. And we love you very much, too."

She nods, acknowledging this fact politely. She's very blasé about our love for her, which I suppose is a good thing. I can tell that she's trying to come up with something to say, a topic to keep me here. She hates bedtime, and if it were up to her, she'd roam the house all night, a wide-eyed little girl specter fiddling with the television and reading about penguins. "Are you still writing your book, Daddy?" she asks.

"Shoosh, honey," I say. "Remember what we said about Daddy's book, right?"

"Yeah. It's a *secret* book?" she whispers. "It's a secret from Grandpa."

"That's right."

"I can hear you typing sometimes after dinner. You're a fast typer, you know. Does it have pictures in it? Your book?"

I'm walking backwards, inching away. "No. But maybe you can draw some for me."

"Maybe. I'm pretty busy with school though. Are you as good a writer as Grandpa Curtis?"

"Good night, sweetie."

"I bet you are. Probably even better. I bet you're the best writer in the world."

"Hey, thumbs aren't for sucking, remember?"

She takes her hand from her mouth and hides it under the covers. "I wasn't. I don't do that anymore."

"Don't let the bedbugs bite."

"Do bedbugs suck blood, like vampires?"

"Good night," I say, closing the door behind me.


In our bedroom, Anna is lying beneath the covers, and I go look out our window at this street, tucked away in Georgetown. It's a neighborhood that Anna and I would never be able to afford in real life. A few blocks over is the townhouse that John F. Kennedy lived in while he was here for law school. He probably couldn't have afforded that house on his own, either, at least back then. Thank God for wealthy fathers.

In our thin little driveway sits my dad's Porsche, parked at a drunken angle, one tire run up onto the grass. It's the same silver

911 that he's had since his third novel, *The Time of Their Lives*, won the National Book Award. It's pristine and beautiful and subtle and classic and it elicits a physical response in me, like it always does, glowing in the streetlamps, watching the front of our house with its frog's eyes. If a car can represent something, this one represents contradiction. For most of his life, my dad has been able to have any woman he wants. In response, he's gone through as many as possible, betraying each for someone younger and more absurd. Conversely, for most of his life he's been able to have any car he wants, too. In response, he's remained married to this, a 1982 Porsche with a tricky clutch.

I can hardly blame him though. It's as cool a car now as it was when I was a kid and he'd let me shift gears from the passenger seat as we cruised down the GW Parkway like we were being chased.

"Maybe you should get one of your own," Anna says.

I strip back down to my boxers, and I feel all dreadful and ashamed again. "Maybe someday."

For a while we lie together in silence. "The Pulitzer Prize," I say, because that's the first non-penis-related thing that comes to mind. Perhaps she was waiting for me to say something, because the moment I do, she rolls on top of me, her strong legs hugging me from either side. Her finger, more thoughtful than sexual, runs up my chest, stopping firmly on my mouth. "Hush," she says. Anna's hair falls, hanging down from the sides of her face. "I ran six miles on the treadmill today, you know." She takes my hand and sets it on her left thigh, which is smooth and long. Her muscle is grainy and hard just below the skin. "And then I did my abs class. Look." She slides her T-shirt up, stopping below her breasts, and there's her bare stomach. "Do you like it?"

"You know that I think you're beautiful," I say. "I think maybe there's just, I don't know, something wrong with *it*."

"Or maybe there's something wrong with *this*." She taps my forehead between my eyebrows. I can smell the slightest traces of wine on her breath. She has questions for me, I can see them scroll-ing across her eyes like a teleprompter, but she doesn't ask them. She doesn't ask why things are difficult now when they weren't before, or if I realize that by tomorrow she won't be ovulating be-cause that strange biological little window will have closed again.

"Maybe," I say.

She touches my forehead again, more tenderly this time, push-ing my hair away. "Sometimes I wish I could see in there. I just wish I knew what you were thinking."

I ease her off of me, and she settles back under the covers. *No you don't*, I think, and we turn our backs on each other for the night.

## 4

*The next morning,* I'm at work, and, thanks to my dad, I'm hungover.

Most people would be afraid to research erectile dysfunction at the office—but not this guy. My penis complications are more important right now than the stack of arbitrary tasks piling steadily in my in-box, and I rarely do anything constructive before 10:30 anyway.

We had a "lunch 'n' learn" about the proper use of our computers a few weeks ago, during which Janice Stringer from HR reminded us that our online activities can be monitored at any time without our knowledge. But I'm not scared. The team of mouth-breathing goons in IT couldn't monitor the broad side of barn. I could be buying plutonium from the Libyans on www.jihad.org right now and no one would know the difference as long as I kept staring straight ahead like a good, hardworking employee.

There are six hundred thousand initial hits for "erectile dysfunction" on Google. The first one that gets my attention is for a device called a PenizPump. I click on a more official-looking link halfway down the page and a drug company's site pops up on my screen. There's a handsome man with gray hair in a denim jacket standing next to a motorcycle.

YOUR PROBLEM DOESN'T HAVE TO BE A PROBLEM ANYMORE, reads the headline, as if the man himself is saying it. But he's not real. He's a model, maybe a part-time actor, hired to pretend to have boner problems, and I find myself picturing him having sex with Anna right here in my office. This is one of the benefits of no longer working in a cube. Let's face it, there's just not enough room in a cube for you *and* your wife *and* the guy she's having sex with in her dreams.

My phone rings, and I cringe. Ringing phones often lead directly to one having to do work, and I'm in no mood for that today. "Tom Violet," I say, all impatient and short, because this is how people answer phones in offices, like we've all been interrupted in the middle of performing impossibly dangerous surgery on a toddler's brain.

"*Tom Violet*, you sound so official on the phone, like a *real* professional."

"Hi, Sonya. I *am* a real professional. I have a BlackBerry and Post-it notes and everything."

Sonya Ross is my dad's literary agent in New York, and I've known her for as long as I can remember. She's got this great voice, all urban and sophisticated, like Meryl Streep. I scroll down the page a bit and read that erectile dysfunction is often caused by health problems, like heart disease and colon cancer. That's just what I need right now.

"Isn't it a little early?" I ask. "I didn't think literary agents got to work before noon."

"Well, normally you'd be right, dear. But it's a big day for us. I'm sure you've heard the news about the prize. It hit the press this morning, and the phones are ringing. Everyone wants to talk to the man of the hour."

*The prize*. Only a person truly used to accolades would refer to the Pulitzer as *the prize*—in all lowercase letters.

"Yeah, he told me last night. I thought Nicholas Zuckerman had it in the bag."

"Nicholas is one of the finalists. But it was Curtis's year—finally. I thought I was going to have to start boycotting."

The handful of people on earth who still sit around comparing writers are often comparing my dad and Nicholas Zuckerman. Zuckerman's about fifteen years older, but neither is young, and they're both very white, male, and experienced at failed marriages. As much as Curtis hates to admit it, Zuckerman is more famous. He puts out something new every eighteen months, at least, and his most recent is a brilliant, devastating little masterpiece about an old man reunited with his teenage love who is now dying of a brain tumor. To make matters worse, Zuckerman's a recluse—like cabin-in-the-wood recluse—which makes him more interesting than my cocktail-party-loving father.

"Can I ask you something?" I ask. "Isn't it a little weird that they're giving him the Pulitzer *now*, for his collected stories? He's written what, sixteen novels? The newest story in that book is more than seven years old. Not to sound harsh, but I always kinda thought the book was just a way to distract everyone from the fact that he hasn't had a new novel in five years."

There's a pause and I can imagine Sonya in her long black skirt and sensible shoes looking out over Union Square. "Think of it like any other big prize, Tommy. Like an Oscar. Sometimes it goes to the best of the year, and sometimes it's like a makeup award for past slights. Remember when Russell Crowe won it for that *Gladiator* thing? Besides, collections win all the time, like Cheever in 'seventy-nine."

"But Cheever was a short-story god, Sonya. Dad hasn't even been in the *New Yorker* since the eighties."

There's a phone ringing in the background, maybe even two, and I can hear people chattering in Sonya's office. "I don't think I need to remind you of the extraneous circumstances at the *New Yorker*, dear. Your father isn't even allowed in the building, and it has *nothing* to do with his writing."

I concede her point, glancing at another online penis testimonial. "But enough about Curtis," I say. "I've actually been meaning to call you. I wanted to ask you about your kid."

"Brandon? Oh, you should see his new boyfriend."

"A new one, huh?"

"The boy looks like he just got out of prison. Tattoos running up each arm, like sleeves. I swear, he finds these guys to spite me."

"Our little Brandon. He's always liked the rough ones. Is it true he's an agent now, too?"

"Yes. And a damn good one, if you can believe it. He just sold a big memoir last week. It's by a refugee from Afghanistan. Whole family was killed by the Taliban and now he's an artist in Soho—designs scarves and blankets. Already sold the movie rights."

My head spins at all of this, memoirs and movie rights and the Taliban. My novel is finished, although I've told virtually no one this—including, for some reason, my wife. I could give it to Sonya, of course, who happens to be one of the most powerful agents in New York. But then that would derail Operation Secret Novel.

"So, where in the hell is Curtis anyway?" she asks. "CBS called this morning. Letterman's people want him for a Top Ten List. Top Ten Perks to Winning the Pulitzer. Sounds kind of funny, right? It could be, anyway."

I tell her that my dad stayed with us last night and update her on his most recent marital troubles. I relish this, knowing, if just for a moment, something about the state of Curtis Violet that Sonya doesn't. Sadly, it's a fleeting moment.

"Well I know *that*, Tommy, of course. That whole arrangement was a ticking time bomb. I just figured he'd have checked into the Fairmount by now. He practically lived there during his last divorce."

"Is he doing OK? He looked a little . . . I don't know, rough last night. Granted, he was pretty drunk, but—"

"I wouldn't know," she says. "He was up here staying at the loft for a while, then I think he was back there in D.C. And, not for nothing, but he has every right to be pretty drunk, Tommy. Pulitzers don't come along every day. I got a little tipsy myself when I heard."

"Yeah, I suppose. So, who do you think the new girl is?"

"What?"

"The new one. His latest train wreck. God, I hope it's not Veronica Stewart again. I don't think I could handle a Thanksgiving with that woman. Ashley has been bad enough."

"Oh don't be an idiot. Your dad's smarter than that, whether *you* believe it or not."

Veronica Stewart has been my dad's on-again-off-again girlfriend/mistress since the early nineties, which would be otherwise uninteresting if she didn't happen to be married to Alistair Stewart, the fiction editor at the *New Yorker*. My father has never been one for making things easy on himself.

"Well, I'm sure it's someone lovely," I say. "I hear Madonna's single again?"

"I just handle the book business, Thomas. Now I've gotta run. The *Today* show's on the other line. Don't work too hard over there."

I try to assure her that I won't, but it's too late. Like a typical New Yorker, Sonya's hung up without saying good-bye.

For a while I stare at my computer screen and complete an online survey about whether or not I have erectile dysfunction.

How Often Do You Have Trouble Achieving an Erection?
Infrequently? Occasionally? Often? All of the Time?

The first three seem vague, and I find the word "achieving" very distracting, like a boner is on par with landing a big promotion or running a 10K for juvenile diabetes.

Just then, my office door swings open and I close my browser as fast as I can as a girl flops down in the chair across from my desk.

I say "girl" not because I'm some horrible, ass-grabbing male chauvinist, but because that's what she is, a girl. Katie is our twenty-three-year-old assistant copywriter and probably the most beautiful person in this office. Most mornings when I see her, I find that I go a minute or so without properly breathing.

"Hey, boss. What's shaking?" she asks.

I look at my screen, ensuring that my browser is gone. Now it's just my wallpaper, a picture of Allie chasing Hank in Rock Creek Park. "Nothing," I say, but I say it too quickly because I'm an idiot.

She narrows her eyes. "What were you just looking at?"

"What? Nothing. The Internet."

"You closed that browser pretty fast. This isn't my first rodeo. I know what guys do with their computers."

"Due to my prestigious position here at MSW, I'm privy to highly classified information. I'm a very important person, Katie. You know that."

"So, porn then, right? What is it with guys and porn? It's all so objectifying and poorly lit."

I lean back in my chair, which squeaks. "I find it relaxing. I come in, have my coffee, check my e-mails, and then I look at porn until lunch."

As usual, Katie is dressed like a college kid at a job fair—like a girl pretending she's ready to take all this bullshit seriously.

"Did you know that dolphins are the only animals other than humans that masturbate for pleasure?" she says.

"Well, this seems like an appropriate conversation for the office."

"You're such a square. It's just science." Katie grabs a random something off my desk. It's a trade show giveaway, a squeeze ball shaped like a heart with our company's logo on it. She's a perpetual-motion machine, this girl, tossing the heart back and forth from hand to hand. It's a combination of youth and a raging ten-Diet Dr Pepper-a-day drinking problem.

"You see CNN.com today?" she asks.

"Haven't made it to the news sites yet. Just the porn so far. Are there still lots of pictures of stockbrokers frowning at computers?"

"Well, yeah. But there's another story up you might find interesting. Apparently your dad won some minor literary award."

I reopen my browser and head to CNN.com. Sure enough, poised between news of global financial despair and an outed televangelist, there's a story about my dad. I click and there's his picture. It's the jacket photo from one of his earlier novels.

"So that's all of them then, right?" she says. "The National Book Award. The PEN/Faulkner. The National Book Critics. And now the Pulitzer."

"I see you've been hitting Wikipedia again."

"I was an English major, too, jerk. I know what's up." She's standing now, leaning across my desk to look at the screen. Her dark brown hair, still a little damp from the shower, clings to her cheek for an instant and then falls across her collarbone. She smells like rain and cinnamon and Diet Dr Pepper and whatever that glossy stuff is on her lips. The crush I have on this girl compares only to the one I had on Leslie Davidson in fifth grade. That particular affair ended with me throwing up one day at recess after she dared me to eat a worm.

"Wasn't he one of *People*'s Fifty Most Beautiful People? Like back in the nineties or something?"

" 'Ninety-seven, I believe. His picture was between Julia Roberts and Gloria Steinem. It was his proudest moment."

"It's scary how much you look like him," she says. "You're better though. You've got the cool-nerd thing going on. Girls like that. Your dad knows he's hot, which negates the hotness a little. It's a very complex formula."

Katie's breasts exist now at my eye level, but I don't stare at them like all the other dipshits in our office. Instead, I accept their presence as a given, allowing only the slightest glance at her ever-present corduroy blazer. She wears it almost every day, even in the summer. It is, somehow, the exact brown of her eyes and has been a character in the sexual fantasies of, I can only assume, every straight male in this building. A few months ago I saw one kind of like it at Nordstrom, and I picked it up for Anna, who accepted the random gift with wifely suspicion.

"Shouldn't you be working?" I say. "I've found that during economic meltdowns it's good to at least *appear* busy."

"Speaking of . . . have you heard anything? Are they gonna do another round?"

The word "layoffs" is avoided here. People talk around it, like one of those complex French words that's difficult to pronounce. I used to manage two people, Katie and a nice kid from Baltimore named Stevie Tanner. But now it's just us. Poor Stevie got laid off two months ago.

"I know nothing," I say, cheerfully.

"You never seem to. Have you ever wondered why that is?"

"It's very deliberate. I've found that knowledge is usually a burden. I prefer to be surprised and then eventually horrified."

"You're a born leader, Tom Violet," she says. "I would follow you into hell."

I've been a longtime appreciator of a good exit line, and this one—solid—lingers for a few minutes after she's gone, making me forget that I'm at work, and that I have carpal tunnel syndrome, and, according to a recent online survey from seven minutes ago, "mild" erectile dysfunction. In fact, she's left me so giddy that it takes me a moment to realize that she's stolen my heart-shaped squeeze ball.

I swoon for a moment. I'm like some dumb kid with unfortunate skin at his locker. But then I see my dad on my computer screen, smiling at me below the headline VIOLET WINS PULITZER FOR FICTION. He's looking at me all smug and accomplished like he's so smart, and I think of that stupid T-shirt. It's a good question. What Would Curtis Violet Do?

## 5

*I*n most companies, no one really notices you until they need you. And even then, when someone wanders into your office or IMs you and finds that you're gone, they just assume you're doing something constructive. Sitting in some horrible, pointless meeting. Stealing office supplies. Weeping gently in a bathroom stall on the fourth floor. Once you've established yourself as reasonably competent, you can pretty much come and go as you please.

And so, as the day wears on and on, I've decided to go.

There are few things as exciting as going over the wall in the middle of the afternoon. On the other side, the air is fresher and the sun is a little more brilliant in the blue sky. There are always people walking around, driving places, and I wonder if they've gone over the wall, too. Are there currently hundreds—thousands—of unmanned cubes and offices in D.C. right now while we all do whatever it is we're doing here on the outside?

I worked at MSW for a full six months before I even knew what MSW stood for, which is Management Services Worldwide. I'm not entirely sure what that means, but, in a nutshell, my company helps other companies be better companies. We have courses and expert speakers and pie charts and business models and acronyms and PowerPoint presentations that throw around ear-splitting words like "synergy" and "best practices" and we have Webinars and binders of information and it's all designed to help your organization work more efficiently. My job, as director of marketing copywriting, is to write ads and press releases and brochures about how if you don't use MSW your company will sink into bankruptcy, your wife will leave you, and you will die alone beneath a bridge.

It's all very fulfilling.

Like most people who have jobs like mine, it was all meant to be temporary. I would write and publish my novel, and then I'd retire from corporate purgatory and become a member of the Community of American Letters.

That was seven years ago. In a climate in which simply having a job is an accomplishment, mine represents failure.

When I arrive at my doctor's office, I stride toward the reception desk where a woman named Glenda sits. Glenda is an elderly black lady who's worked for my doctor for as long as he's been my doctor, but she never seems to recognize me. I can't blame her though, considering I've never made an actual appointment and every time I'm here I claim to be someone different.

"Can I help you?" she asks.

"Yes. I'm Paul Hewson, here to see Dr. Mortensen."

Paul Hewson is Bono's real name, incidentally. Last time I was here, I was Gordon Sumner, otherwise known as Sting.

Glenda looks at a giant desk calendar. Dr. Charlie shares his practice with two ancient doctors, and so everything here seems like something out of an issue of *Life* magazine.

"What time was your appointment?"

I look at my watch, which says 3:45, and so that's what I say.

"Well, I'm sorry, Mr. Hewson, I don't seem to have you down."

"Oh, no worries. I can wait awhile."

As she jots Bono's name down, I walk by the waiting room and through a door leading to the examination rooms. An old woman

reading *Highlights* looks up but doesn't seem concerned that I'm bla-
tantly cutting in line. As obnoxious as this all sounds, it's actually
authorized. Dr. Charlie was my college roommate, and he's too nice
of a guy to tell me that I'm not Barbra Streisand and that maybe I
should actually make an appointment like a normal person.

A few nurses smile at me, assuming that I'm someone else's
problem, as I sneak glances into rooms. One of Charlie's partners
dozes at his desk over a file while listening to Rush Limbaugh. A
young mother sits in an examining room with a little boy dressed
in only socks and tighty-whitey underwear. She's ignoring him as
he drums on her thigh with tongue depressors. I round a corner
and see a poster on the wall diagramming the human respiratory
system, which looks very much like the D.C. Metro map. Then I
hear Charlie's voice. He's yelling, but not in an angry way. I follow
the shouting to find my friend standing in a doorway, hollering
into a very old man's ear.

"Two pills, Mr. Halgas! One in the morning, and one at night
before bed!"

"Twice a day? But I only took the other ones *once* a day. I don't
like all the pills. I'd prefer just one."

"I'd prefer to have more hair and a Bentley, Mr. Halgas. But sometimes we can't get everything we want. Those last pills weren't working, that's why you're here now. You'll feel better, OK? I promise!"

"Well fine then," he says. He's wearing a green cardigan sweater
and Velcro sneakers. As he shuffles down the hallway toward reception, he puts on one of those hats that only old men and Samuel L.
Jackson can wear.

"Say hi to Lorraine for me, Mr. Halgas!" says Charlie. "I'll see
you next month!"

The old geezer grunts good-bye, waving his prescription in the
air. And then I find myself thinking of Mr. Halgas having sex. His
saggy, old-man body is entwined with Lorraine's, who I can only
assume is his wife but who looks like Barbara Bush in my mind.

Mr. Halgas's penis is fine, at least in this scenario I've made up. So, what in the hell's wrong with mine?

Charlie's writing something in a file. "How'd you get by Glenda?" he asks me.

"I hit her over the head with my shoe. Don't worry, she'll be fine in a few hours."

Mr. Halgas exits through the door, and now we're just a couple guys looking down an empty hallway. "Is he gonna be OK?" I ask.

"Mr. Halgas? Shit. He'll outlive us both."

"Damn, I need to find a new doctor. I'm only thirty-five."

Charlie does some more scribbling and drops his pen into his shirt. "So, have you knocked up your wife yet?"

I suspect that Charlie speaks more casually with me than many of his other patients.

"Funny you should ask. You got a second to talk?"


"It's weird. It feels like it goes . . . dead."

I'm scanning Charlie's diplomas, sitting across from him. He's looking at my file, and I'm flattered that I even have a file, considering my insurance company only has the vaguest proof that I've ever even been here. His face is stoic and professional. "Dead? What do you mean by that exactly?"

"No feeling. Nothing. Anna will be right there waiting for me, and it's like a complete failure. Sometimes it even shrinks. An antiboner." Even as I say this, I can feel my penis going numb, like it can hear me.

"You know, that would be a good name for an all-lesbian punk band," says Charlie. "The Antiboner."

"You think maybe we could focus here?"

"You're not eighteen anymore, Tom. Have you and Anna ever tried, you know, *manual* stimulation? Maybe switching things up a little? Being creative?"

There's another quick scene in my head, thrown together suddenly. Mr. Halgas isn't there this time. It's me and Anna and we're in an awful hotel trying to role-play. She's dressed like a slutty maid, but she's got this overly thoughtful look on her face, like she thinks this is all a really bad idea.

"The thing is," I say, "that actually makes it worse. It's like, if we ever try something out of the ordinary, I'm *thinking* about it then, you know. And that's the fucking kiss of death. Thinking. It's like thinking about a two-foot putt. You're screwed."

Charlie nods. "That's a good analogy."

"It might be a simile. I can never remember the difference."

"Seven years," he says, "that's a big age gap for kids."

"I know. On the bright side, it'll give them both something to be mad at us about."

He worries the end of his stethoscope like a doctor on television with a prop. He's gained some weight since I saw him last month, and his hair seems to be receding before my very eyes. "Do you ever get morning wood?" he asks.

"Excuse me."

"Morning wood? Or, if you'd prefer, morning missile. This is actually a medical question, I swear."

I think about the morning version of my penis. That would also be a pretty good name for a band: the Morning Version of My Penis. "Sometimes, I guess. Not like when I was twelve, but, you know. Why?"

"When you're sleeping, you're unconscious, obviously, and you're totally relaxed. So, if there's action downtown when you're asleep, it's proof to me that your problem exists in your stupid head. You're just psyching yourself out. That's all. Anxiety manifests itself in weird ways. I've got this little boy, a patient. He has this rare form of narcolepsy. Whenever he gets stressed, like if his parents are having an argument or he's got a pop quiz at school, he just goes to sleep. He doesn't faint or pass out, he just falls asleep, on the spot. That's what your johnson is doing, falling asleep to cope with stress. Your cock has narcolepsy."

God bless my dopey friend in his white coat. This is his favorite part of being a doctor, wowing people with all the shit he knows. When someone in the dorms was super hungover back at school, he'd sit with them all morning and explain exactly why they felt so shitty. "There's ethanol in alcohol, and that causes dehydration. When you're dehydrated, your brain actually shrinks and pulls away from your skull. Here, have some more Gatorade."

"Don't you need to, like, look at my prostate or something?" I ask. It dawns on me that that's the first time I've ever asked someone that.

"Well, as nice as that sounds, no. We'll worry about that in ten years. Right now, your malfunction isn't in your ass, it's in your brain. There's a lot of stress in the world. Watching the news is stressful. Trying to get pregnant is stressful. Your body is reacting to that. Anna is stressed about it, too, I'm sure. But the girls don't have to worry about rising to the occasion. They have it easy. Well, aside from actually having to carry and birth the babies. Some of them find that difficult."

I tell Charlie about hearing Anna's sex dreams. This information seems to cement something in his mind, and he begins rummaging through his desk drawer until he sets a little box of sample pills on his desk. I recognize the logo from the commercials that come on whenever I watch sports.

"Fortunately, the good people at Pfizer are looking out for guys like you."

"You just keep those in your desk, like Skittles?"

"Take one forty-five minutes before you're ready to go. Works every time. Trust me."

"Umm," I say, but humiliation claims the rest.

Reading my mind, Charlie leans forward, resting his elbows on his desk. "It's just to get you back in the game, man. You need to be out of your own head. That's what these babies are for. When you've got your confidence back up, you can sell whatever you'd got left on the street to teenagers. It's all good."

My BlackBerry makes a little chirp and vibrates in my pocket. It means I have a text message, and there's only one person in the world who texts me. Katie has written:

> Need to get bk here. Ppl r lookin 4 u ☹.

"What's wrong?" Charlie asks.

"Nothing. It's just work."

"You guys gonna survive all this doomsday stuff?"

As I get up to leave, I shrug, because, in truth, I have absolutely no idea.

"What does your company do again? I can never remember."

"It doesn't matter," I say.

"Hey, dumb ass, aren't you forgetting something?" Charlie tosses me the sample box. "Go home, Tom. Fuck your wife. You'll both feel a lot better in the morning."

I think of Mr. Halgas again in his Velcro sneakers. Like him, I'm hating the prospect of medication. But, also like him, I'm begrudgingly beginning to accept it. "You know, I still have a few minutes. You sure you don't want to look at my prostate? Just for a second?"

**6**

*ack at the* office, I head for Cubeland. This is what we call it, Cubeland, where everyone who isn't a manager works. Every floor has one, row after row of tiny little work cells. Each cell is personalized with cat calendars or Dilbert cartoons or coffee mugs, but they're all uniform in their sadness. The tension here today is as palpable as air pollution. Nearly every computer I see is turned to a news site, and articles are up about how we're all spiraling toward a national state of bankruptcy. Lehman Brothers is officially gone, as in, it no longer exists. A girl in a navy blue dress is loading knickknacks from her desk into her gym bag. Another guy a few cubes down is talking on the phone. "Mom, I don't know," he says. "Seriously. We know nothing. No one does."

I suppose I'm nervous, like everyone else, but, in truth, I only half understand what in the hell is going on, or who Lehman Brothers or any of the other floundering and/or destroyed companies are in a practical sense. Terrorism, natural disasters, and little blue erection pills: those things are tangible. But right now, my fear of the economy is like my fear of algebra in high school.

For no legitimate reason, I take a detour past Katie's cube, but, sadly, she's not there. There are a few random files strewn about and an old yogurt carton. The I'm a Pepper sign above her computer is crooked, like always, and there's the picture of Katie and her boyfriend, Todd. In my head, I refer to him as Todd the Idiot, which is a name he earned last year at the company holiday party when he threw up into an arrangement of poinsettias in front of everyone. Next to their picture sits my heart-shaped squeeze ball. If I were a less mature person, I'd steal it back—along with her dancing hula girl bobble head—but I control myself.

In my office, back at my computer, there's an unholy amount of e-mails, 97 percent of which can be deleted immediately. There's one from Katie, buried in the middle, asking if we're going to 7-Eleven today for our biweekly meeting. She's also wondering if she should start looking into food stamps. Another e-mail is from my boss, Doug, the vice president of marketing and corporate communications.

Stop by when you get a second. Need to chat.

I sit down and am prepared to feel the appropriate amount of anxiety, but I'm interrupted by a knock on my door—my *open* door. In my career, I've found that only annoying people knock on open doors. I know that's a generalization, but, using my peripheral vision, I can see that my theory remains rock solid. There's another knock, and for reasons I can't quite explain, I pretend as if I don't hear it. Staring at my monitor, I'm a busy professional man totally unaware of the person lurking in the doorway.

"I know that you know I'm here, Tom, so you can stop ignoring me."

When I look up, I act surprised to see Gregory Steinberg. And then I smile as big as I can. "Hey, Greg, I didn't see you standing there." Gregory is one of those guys who insist on being called Gregory, and so I insist on calling him Greg.

"Yeah right," he says. His face is an unhappy mix of lines and corporate scowls. "So, I suppose you've been in meetings for the last two hours, right?"

"Well, not that it's any of *your* business, Greg, but I was in a pretty important meeting, as a matter of fact. The management team pulled me in to discuss marketing initiatives. You know, with all these little *snafus* in the financial sector, we should probably lay out an aggressive plan. They just wanted to run some things by me. Brainstorm a little."

This is a profound lie, and I'm proud of myself for its boldness and the fact that it came to me so quickly.

"That's not true, and you know it," he says. If such a meeting had taken place, Greg, the director of communications, would surely have been invited, but there's enough doubt in his twitching jaw to give me a little thrill. His hatred for me is strong today, buzzing around his head in swirls and hisses. Greg is my Dr. Evil. He is my one-armed man. Whenever he enters a room, in my mind I hear the Imperial Death March from *Star Wars*. He is my nemesis, yet, whenever I see him, regardless of the situation, I smile like I've just won the lottery. I do this for no other reason than because he hates it. One of the countless complaints he's lodged against me with HR reads:

Dear HR:

Tom Violet insists on smiling and saying hello to me every time he sees me, even in the men's room. However, I know that these sentiments are not sincere, and only succeed in undermining me in front of my team and fellow employees.

These complaints, which I have saved on my computer in a file called "Ass Face," are among the greatest achievements of my career. I read them sometimes when things are bleak or there's a particularly ghastly paper jam in the printer down the hall. They always make me feel just a little better.

"So, Greg, to what do I owe the honor?" My face hurts, but I keep smiling. It's called commitment.

He sits down across from me and sets a stack of papers on my desk. It's copy for a brochure I've written about one of our shitty new products. He's celebrated my hard work by dousing it with red ink, slashing through entire paragraphs and writing suggestions in the margins. There's nothing wrong with what I've written, of course. It's actually pretty good, as far as corporate propaganda goes. He just has this compulsive need to make random changes to everything I write. He's like Dustin Hoffman counting those matchsticks in *Rain Man*. He just can't help himself.

"We need to talk about this," he says, very seriously.

"Well, OK. Did you like it? I wrote it especially for you."

Across the top of the first page he's scrawled, "NO CONTRAC-TIONS!" in big, bold letters. To further articulate his point, he's crossed out every contraction on the page—every "it's" and "who's" and "we've" and "you've." It's a whole new achievement in douche-baggery for him, and I'm almost impressed.

"The tone is all wrong here. It's way too casual for the audience. This is supposed to be targeted at C-levels. *CEOs. COOs. CIOs.* You're talking to them like they're a bunch of interns. These are decision makers here, Tom . . . a sophisticated group."

"Well, certainly. All the executives I know are wildly sophisti-cated. But we're not cutting contractions, Greg. We've been over that. This isn't Comp 101. Have you ever actually tried to read something without contractions? It sounds like it's written by robots."

"They don't have time for casual. All they care about is *WIIFM.*"

I actually close my eyes here for a moment—that's how badly this hurts me. "WIIFM" is one of those bullshit, made-up corporate ac-ronyms, and it stands for "What's in It for Me?" Greg uses it no fewer than ten times a day. Every time it leaves his mouth, I'm convinced that something good and pure in the world—an endangered species or perhaps a rare, exotic flower—is destroyed and Earth becomes that much more hopeless. "I've given them all the benefits, Greg—I've *led* with them, in fact, as I learned in copywriting school. I think these brilliant executives of yours will be able to dumb themselves down enough to figure it out . . . despite the contractions."

The color of his face is beginning to match his burgundy tie. Greg is a tie guy, and I am a non-tie guy. This represents the rift among the males in our office—Business Casual versus Business Formal—and I'm almost certain it will eventually lead to a choreographed dance fight in the employee lounge.

"Seven out of ten people receiving this piece make more than three hundred thousand dollars a year."

"Well, I'm happy for them, but if you wanna start tossing around arbitrary figures, then I can tell you that one out of one Tom Violets doesn't care. We're not cutting the contractions."

Greg sighs deeply, counting to ten in his head. "That's very clever, but they aren't arbitrary figures. It's all in the research that I provided. It's called a customer profile."

"Greg, there are starving children in Africa. And there's this virus out there that actually eats human flesh. But still, you and I are sitting in my office arguing about this . . . *again*."

He drops another stack of papers on my desk, ignoring my plea for social awareness. "Did you even read my messaging document?"

"No, Greg. I *did not*. I *have never* read one of your messaging documents, and I *will never* read one of your messaging documents. I *would not*, if you held a shotgun to my skull."

As he shoots up from my chair, his eyes are alive with anger and his tie whips in a violent arc across his chest. "I can't deal with you anymore!"

"See, Greg. I told you it's annoying when people don't use contractions."

"I know you think this is all hysterical. It's just a big joke to you, right? Ha-ha."

I assume this is rhetorical, and so I just sit there and smile as creepily as I can.

"Well, some of us take this seriously, Tom. This brochure needs to work, because if we don't increase our corporate sales by fifteen percent this year, we're dead. Don't you even understand the world around you? Do you watch the news? People are losing their jobs. But if that's not important to you, then you just keep laughing. Just keep laughing while you still can."

As Greg storms away, his long black cape flowing behind him, I can't help but feel a flicker of respect. I hate to say it, but *that* was a nice exit line.

"Later, Greg," I say, quietly, to my now-empty office.

There's a little light blinking on my phone, and I can see from the caller ID that I've missed two calls today, one from my mother and one from my stepfather, Gary. It seems strange that they'd be calling me separately, but I'm too jazzed up from enraging Greg to be concerned.

"What was that all about?"

Katie, like a cool breeze, is standing at my door with a can of Diet Dr Pepper in her hand. It's late in the day and she looks a little tired and her hair is pulled back in a ponytail. "He looked pissed."

"Greg is in a permanent state of pissed, Katie. You know that."

"Good point. But doesn't it bother you when he yells at you like that? I hate when people yell at me."

"You know how when Rocky gets punched over and over again by guys like Mr. T and Ivan Drago? That's what Greg's rage is like for me—it's energizing."

My *Rocky* reference seems to have no effect on Katie, and I wonder if this girl has even seen any of the *Rocky* movies. Do twenty-three-year-olds know *Rocky*? Perhaps I should do a focus group.

"So, where did you go today, anyway?" she asks. "I had to go to 7-Eleven by myself. You know I hate doing that. There are all those construction workers there all the time."

"Sorry, I was out fighting crime."

She shakes her head at me, which is something that the women in my life seem to do a lot. "Come on, let's go smoke," she says.

"What? I thought you were on the patch."

She shrugs. "That's the problem. I *was* on the patch. Past tense."

I feign a disapproving look, but, in truth, as horrible as it sounds, smoking looks sexy on Katie. It's like that brown jacket; it fits her perfectly. And so as she walks out of my office, I follow.


I don't look nearly as good as Katie when I smoke, which is why I rarely do it. Well, that and all the research about how, apparently, it kills you. I take a measured puff, feel the weird burn in my chest, and blow out, without really enjoying it. There's that little surge, like a shot of espresso, but it only lasts a few minutes, tops. Aside from these secret trips to the roof with Katie, I've quit smoking, but I remember my first cigarette very well. I was an eighteen-year-old college freshman. Like most kids that age, I had romantic ideas of what college would be like. I'd be an English major and I'd shave only sporadically and date girl poets with wild, curly hair. But, more than any of that, I'd be anonymous.

I realized how naïve this was the first five minutes of my first class in college, Advanced Composition for English Majors. The instructor, some kid from the MFA program in a sport coat, began passing out badly Xeroxed copies of my dad's most famous short story, "Macy's." As he read Curtis's prose aloud, he sounded like he was auditioning for something, and I didn't bother following along. Since roll call at the beginning of the class, the other students had been looking at me and whispering about me. They'd heard, of course, that Curtis Violet's kid was a freshman, and there I was. These kids—earnest English nerds like me—knew that the boy in the story, Henry, was based on me. My dad speaks at great length about his inspiration, and that story, which has been reprinted and anthologized more times than I can even imagine, came from a shopping trip one Christmas when I was a little older than Allie. We got separated in the holiday crowd, and so for about forty-five minutes I wandered the store alone looking at mannequins and touching cashmere sweaters until an old security guard found me. I ate a Tootsie Roll Pop in Customer Service while my dad was paged over the loudspeaker.

"That's it," said the grad student when he was done reading. "That's what we're all trying to do when we sit down to write. And until we do . . . we've failed. Case closed."

After class, some kid with a goatee offered me one of his cigarettes, and I took it without hesitation. It was one of those silly acts of rebellion—a rebellion against a man who probably didn't care one way or another if I smoked. It tasted only a little worse than this cigarette I'm smoking now.

Katie exhales toward the sky. "Are you gonna be in trouble for this?" she asks.

I'm not sure exactly what she's referring to. I could be in trouble for keeping my boss waiting, for leaving my office for hours on end without telling anyone, for pissing Greg off, for thinking about this beautiful young girl the way I sometimes think about her. Or, I could simply be in trouble for smoking—of which Anna and Allie would definitely not approve.

"Trouble is my middle name," I say. This seems to cover all the bases.

"Clever."

"It's true. It actually is. My dad lost a bet with Norman Mailer."

There are five or six other smokers milling around on the roof of our building. Some are from MSW, others are from the other random companies that share the building. Most of these people look like they're contemplating throwing themselves over the edge.

"Lehman Brothers went bankrupt, you know," she says. "Everyone's been talking about it. That's our third client to go bankrupt this week." A police car speeds by on the street below, its siren echoing off the pavement. "There's gonna be more layoffs. I don't see how there won't be."

"We'll be fine," I say. "People who aren't *needed* get laid off. They need us. We're copywriters. The company's gotta advertise, right?"

We smoke for a moment, and Katie seems to believe what I've just said, which would make one of us, officially. Advertising and marketing budgets are always the first to go. Anyone who's been in business more than a few years knows this. But there's no sense in letting Katie in on this trade secret, so I just take another drag.

"Do you ever feel like *anyone* could do our jobs, though?" she asks.

"Like a chimp with Microsoft Word?"

"So you have thought about it?"

"Yeah. But, by now a monkey would have choked Greg to death. I'm sure of it."

God, I love the sound of Katie laughing. The other smokers on the roof glance over, men and women alike. She's one of those girls who glows a little, like when you see an actress in real life.

"So, guess what," she says. "I finished your book today."

I nearly drop my cigarette. "Really? I just gave it to you two days ago."

"Yep. I snuck over to the green space after lunch to finish it. I was up till like two last night reading in bed."

I try to keep my composure in the midst of a flash fantasy. The thought of Katie in her night things, lying in bed with my manuscript propped up on her belly, makes me feel like I need to sit down.

"Tom . . . seriously, it's fantastic."

"Really?" I suddenly wish I had another cigarette. "You think so?"

"There's so much there. Like that scene near the end when Danny gets to Hollywood. That's so sad. He spends the whole novel trying to get there, but when he finally does, he realizes he has no idea where he's going. And so he just runs out of gas. That was so . . . I don't know, poignant. It reminded me of your dad's writing—when he was younger. Remember how I told you that your dad knows he's hot? Well, he knows he's a great writer, too, and he kinda writes like it. I think that's why I didn't like his last novel. But you're writing like you're trying to prove it. That's how he used to write. I was actually telling Todd—" She stops here, self-conscious suddenly. Katie and I have developed this unspoken rule that somehow prohibits us from making direct reference to either Todd or Anna. "I was telling Todd that, about your dad."

"Todd's welcome to read it, you know."

"Right. Maybe if it ever gets made into an Xbox game."

I want her to keep talking. I want her to tell me more of the things she liked and to further marginalize Todd, but she doesn't. Instead, she looks thoughtfully—a little sadly—over the roof of our building at the top of the Washington Monument about a mile way. I allow myself a glance at the lovely plunge of skin ranging from her earlobe to her collarbone. There's a line in one of my dad's novels about the most beautiful parts of the female anatomy being the ones that are the most innocent—the ones that have never been scandalized by nudity.

"So the kid in the book?" she says. "Danny. He's *you*, right?"

"I don't know. No, probably not. I don't think so. Just some imaginary kid in a book."

I look down at the street, and I see Danny, the kid I made up, standing at a crosswalk. I'm not crazy, I know it's not actually him and that he doesn't exist. But I've spent a lot of time with him over the last five years, and so I see him sometimes, walking around town in his sweatshirt and sneakers. He never seems quite sure where he's going.

"Well, he's gonna be famous soon. And so are you. You're gonna publish your book and leave me all alone in this place with Gregory."

"Greg," I say, correcting her, and for a moment, I allow myself to believe what she's just said. It's an easy thing to do, because, aside from myself, she's the only person in the world who's read the book. Not my wife. Not my mother, my famous father, or my famous father's famous literary agent. Just this beautiful smoking girl from work in her corduroy jacket.

## 7

*When I finally* do make it to Doug's office, it's after six, and I find him hunched over a glossy proof of an ad that I wrote last week. It's a branding piece for a popular business journal, and it used to be a pretty cool ad. After going through Greg's tractor beam of sucking, though, it's now a typical, buzzword-laden hunk of corporate communications turd.

He looks up at me, weary and gray. Doug is twenty years older than I am, and it shows, particularly this month. Since the bottom fell out of the economy, everyone in charge here looks like they need to go to the hospital. There's a little TV on his bookshelf with the volume down low, and everyone on MSNBC is somewhere between panic and ritualistic suicide. The bold headline beneath the talking heads reads, WORSE BEFORE BETTER?

"Rough day?" I ask.

He sighs, capping his red pen and letting it fall on his desk. "Apparently the roughest since the Great Depression."

"Oh, well that wasn't so bad." I fall down onto Doug's old leather couch. It's one of those worn and tattered pieces of furniture that can remind you quickly of how tired you are. "It's all good," I say. "When Obama wins, he'll save us."

"Yeah, well, I'm voting for him, too, but the president doesn't really have anything to do with any this, I don't care how cute his daughters are. The captain of a ship can run a great ship, but he can't do anything about the tides. My dad used to say that. Did you tell Gregory that you had a meeting with the executive team today about marketing initiatives?"

I pretend to think hard about this. "I'm sorry, Doug, I don't believe I know a Gregory."

"I think you might. Nice hair. Perfect diction. Always wears a tie."

"Oh, you mean *Greg*? Yeah, I know Greg."

"Well, you can congratulate yourself, because I don't think I've ever seen him so pissed off."

I place my hand on my heart. "Well, then the day wasn't a total loss."

Normally Doug would smile here, but not today. He crosses his arms, thoroughly unamused by me, and nods at the television. "You know, it wouldn't hurt you to have a few people on your good side for a change. Comrades are important when corporations start falling to the ground."

"I'd never align with the Dark Side, Doug, you know that. Besides, what do I have to worry about? *You're* on my good side, right?"

He gives me a look that lets me know that he could go either way on this. My rivalry with Darth Gregory has been a pain in this man's ass for years, since the day Greg was reconstructed by evil droids and hired here. Doug is my boss *and* Greg's boss, and, apparently when two of your direct reports hate each other with irrational passion, it reflects poorly on your management skills. Last year, Doug went so far as to take us both to lunch to help us settle our differences. Our latest argument then was about how I'd embarrassed Greg in a staff meeting by suggesting that he no longer be allowed to use the term "low-hanging fruit" to describe easy-to-acquire customers on the grounds that it sounded gross. I'd taken to making a buzzing sound in meetings whenever Greg used buzzwords, which was particularly childish, but very effective. Everything at lunch was going well until I said that I was going to circle back and try to leverage a strategy that would create synergy between my chicken sandwich and my iced tea.

Sometimes it's tiring behaving the way that I do.

"He's also upset about something else," says Doug. "Something a little more . . . well, sensitive."

"Oh?" I say. "Is it the dead fish I left in his locker after study hall?"

Still no smile. Doug is giving me nothing here. "Not exactly. He thinks you've been less than professional with a certain junior copywriter who's currently under your tutelage."

I'm rarely shocked by things said in this building, but here I am, my mouth open. "What?"

He shrugs. "I'm just the messenger here, my friend."

"Katie works for me, Doug, and I'm trying to help her be a better copywriter. And we actually get along with each other, which is probably a foreign concept to Greg. What business is it of his anyway? I don't tell him how to deal with his storm troopers."

Doug rubs his eyes, tired of all this. "Listen, this is Gregory we're talking about, so you have to take it all with a grain of salt. He's probably just jealous. I don't imagine he's had a lot of success in his life with girls who look like that. But let me give you some friendly advice, OK? Off the record. Beware of young, beautiful things."

The awkwardness in the room manifests itself into a burst of laughter from my mouth.

"I'm serious. For guys our age, they bring nothing but pain and hardship."

"Doug, I'm nowhere near your age."

"You're close enough, believe me. When I was coming up, offices were dark places filled with ugly men in bad suits. But now . . . well, you think it's a coincidence that the divorce rate has gone up steadily with the amount of women in the work-place?"

I've never thought of this before, and it makes me wonder how many divorces my dad could have racked up if he'd ever had a real job.

"And *you* need to be extra careful. Remember, I have daughters. I can tell when a girl has a crush on someone she shouldn't. She's not old enough to understand how powerful she is, yet—but *you* are."

"Let's not be dramatic here. She has a boyfriend."

"Yeah, I remember him from the holiday party. Seems like a real winner—reminds me of all my daughters' boyfriends. Just think of me as an old sage, Tom—the voice of experience."

"Duly noted," I say. I glance at the picture on Doug's desk—him and his wife and their five children and a cocker spaniel in a dog sweater. "So, is this why you wanted to see me? Greg's tattling?"

"I wish. Like I said, I don't pay much attention to Gregory when it comes to his opinions on you. Truth is, all this turmoil is making Buckingham Palace nervous. I'm getting some bad vibes."

"Really? From Ian? Is he even in town? Maybe his cricket team lost or something. The Brits are a moody people."

Doug looks out his window where we have a lovely view of a construction site. Every man and woman in this building is afraid of two things:

1. Losing their job
2. Ian Barksdale, our British CEO

"Our clients have lost their asses this week. Some of them don't even exist anymore, as of this morning. If they don't have money, *we* don't have money. Trickle-down economics."

"What's this mean for us then?"

"Ian's been looking to bring over some of his cronies from the Mother Country for years. Those swinging dicks in London would love to shake things up over here. All that bullshit about streamlining. Less is more. That kind of garbage."

I fight the urge to make a buzzing sound. It seems like that would be counterproductive. In the last five minutes I've been told to fear a beautiful twenty-three-year-old girl and all of Great Britain. Doug runs his hand through his gray hair and looks at the television. How Bad Will It Get? the new graphic asks.

"You remember that tsunami from a few years back?" he asks. "Remember how things were all tranquil and sunny in those home videos, like some vacation, and then that big wave came out of nowhere and sucked everything out to sea?"

"Yeah," I say.

He points at the TV again, which has suddenly become the world's most frightening appliance. "I think the wave's coming."

## 8

*I parallel-park my Honda* between a Mercedes and a BMW
SUV. I'm two blocks from the house, but I can already hear
Hank barking. He recognizes the sound of my car, its engine, and
the way the door sounds when I close it. According to our vet,
Hank suffers from something called "acute anxiety." Before Hank
was our ugly little dog, he was someone else's ugly little dog, and
then he was an ugly little dog at the D.C. pound. I don't know how
he ended up there, but when we leave him alone, even if only for a
few hours, he acts like we're never coming back.

As I walk through my neighborhood, I look at all of the expensive
houses, fairly certain that many of their inhabitants are inside suffering from a little acute anxiety of their own. How many of these
people could barely afford these places when they bought them and
now can't at all? The Obama/Biden signs in each of the tiny yards
look uniform and neat, like B-roll footage from a campaign commercial, and I wonder if Doug is right about all of this being bigger than
a president. It seems like one of those pessimistic things that people
say when they've accepted certain things about the world.

Hank's happy yapping borders on mania and I'm surprised to
find my dad's Porsche unmoved in the driveway, one tire still run
up drunkenly in the grass. Like Sonya, I figured by now he'd be

safely tucked away in one of the most expensive suites at the Fairmount Hotel, but apparently he's still here. I touch the car's fender and look inside. My dad's old messenger bag is sitting in the front seat, a few paperbacks spilling out.

Inside, I'm greeted by Hank and Allie together.

"Hi, Daddy!" she yells over all the barking. She's holding her artwork for the day on three pieces of construction paper. I kiss the crown of her head and swipe at the leaping animal, telling him to shut up.

Her first picture is a nature shot—a barn, a big green tree, and a horse. Her sense of perspective is still shaky, and so the horse is comparatively the size of a basketball arena. The next picture is a bicycle, I think, and it's not one of her best efforts. Lately I've been wondering if I'm supposed to criticize her work, or if I'm just supposed to continue telling her how wonderful it is. When I was nine, I wrote a story about a turkey that escapes the day before Thanksgiving. When I gave it to Curtis, he told me it was charming but too overly sentimental to be anything better than emotionally manipulative. Allie's third picture is far and away her best. In silver crayon she's drawn the Porsche and a little Crayola version of Curtis Violet in a green sweater.

"It's Grandpa," she says.

"Heck, yeah it is. I think this one might be fridge-worthy. Well done, my friend."

"Really?"

I make her give me a high five, and then she runs away with the dog.

Anna's in the kitchen boiling pasta and reading the mail. She's dressed in her running shorts and a gray tank top. An oval of sweat marks the spot between her breasts, and I feel fat and lumbering by comparison.

"Your mother called a few minutes ago." she says. "She sounded weird."

"Well, she's a weird lady," I say.

"Oh, and we also got a delightful call from your stepmother."

"Oh Jesus." This is inevitable, but still not good. "What did she want?"

She nods to the answering machine. "Listen for yourself. It's quite a performance. Allie, cover your ears again, honey."

Allie, who's hanging her picture on the fridge with fruit magnets, covers her ears without comment as I push the little button. There's a throat clearing, and then it's Ashley in all her glory. "I know he's there," she says, her voice boozy and sharp. "Hell, you're probably *all* there, listening to me right now, you fucking chickens. Why are you hiding from me, Curtis? You can't just keep hiding. I love you . . . well, I *loved* you. Doesn't that even *fucking* count for anything? Why are you so awful to me? I don't deserve it. And you don't deserve *me*. I hate you now. Hate, hate, hate you. So fuck you, I'm going to New York. Come get your shit before I burn it all in the street." As she hangs up, I can hear the venom betrayed by a sniffle, like a high school girl in tears.

"Well, she seems to be doing well," I say.

"She sounded drunk."

"That's probably a safe bet."

Anna sips from an orange-colored vitamin water. "What do you think the odds are of her killing us all in our sleep?" she asks.

"Nah, even if she tried, she'd never make it past our liquor cabinet."

I take in Anna's body as she stirs pasta. Tight, lean little muscles seem to be appearing daily in new places, like above her knees and the backs of her arms. I guess those are called triceps. I touch one of them with my index finger, poking it with mild fascination.

"Have you been smoking?" she asks.

"Sorry," I say. "Doug wanted to talk after work. Doom and gloom stuff."

"Really? What'd he say?"

"Smoking kills, Daddy," says Allie. "It makes your lungs all black and yucky, like two big sponges all covered in oil."

"I know, honey. That's crooked. A little higher on the right."

Technically, I've just lied to my wife. I've used Doug as a diversion to distract Anna from the fact that I've smoked, and now I'm not sure what to say. I decide to spare her the tsunami metaphor, at least for the time being.

"Is this better, Daddy?"

"Perfect," I say. "He's just worried, that's all. That's what Doug does—he worries. He's got like eleven kids."

"Is it about the . . . *economy*?"

Anna is as helpless as I am when it comes to exactly what it is that's put the world in its current state. At least one of us really should have majored in something legitimate. Our daughter is standing in front of the fridge like Vanna White, presenting her work. "Do you like it, Mommy?"

Anna tells Allie that it's a beautiful picture, but her eyes don't leave mine.

"We're gonna be fine," I say. "I've survived three rounds of layoffs this year alone. I'm untouchable, like Eliot Ness." I flex my biceps, but no one seems impressed. Recently I've begun imagining that other people in my life write formal complaints about me and submit them to imaginary HR departments.

Dear HR:

My husband, Tom Violet, thinks it's fun to mask his anxiety over our potential financial ruin with a series of lame jokes. It's clearly a façade to make me think that everything is going to be OK, but, in reality, I know that we are profoundly screwed. Attached is a long list of the many men I now regret not marrying before I met this smiling fool.

"Grandpa said he's taking me for a ride in the Porsche. He said he'll go super fast, too—way over the speed limit because the cops can't catch him because they all have sucky, American-made engines."

I tell my daughter how fun this sounds, and then I take two beers from the fridge. If this were a different era, the sixties maybe, I'd pour a couple of giant glasses of scotch. But I guess light domestic beers will suffice for now. "So he's still here, huh?" I ask Anna.

She stirs the bubbling pot still. "He's upstairs. I think he's writing."

I open the door and find my dad sitting at my computer desk staring at his laptop and casually smoking a joint. The window is open and he's turned on the ceiling fan, but the entire upstairs smells like the inside of a VW van, and I have to actually wave a plume of smoke out of my face.

"Nice, Dad. Just make yourself right at home."

He coughs and snaps his computer shut with a loud *thwack*. From the sleepy, stoned look on his face, I can't tell if he's been writing or napping.

"You know, there is a child in the house, right?"

He holds the wiry little bud out, offering me some.

I look out into the hallway for signs of Allie or Anna and then close the door. "All right, but I'm doing it under formal protest."

"I'll make sure it's noted in the official ledger," he says.

I take a quick toke, hold, and then exhale. I read somewhere that smoking pot is way worse for your lungs than cigarettes, but it certainly doesn't feel like it. The inside of my skull loosens a notch, and I hand it back to him. "You shaved," I say. "Looks good."

He rubs his chin as if reminding himself. "Allie demanded it. She told me I looked old." He's wearing the same pants as last night and his tweed jacket over a T-shirt. Although he looks better than before, he's still pale, slumping in my IKEA chair.

I hand him one of the beers I've brought with me. He takes a sip with his nonjoint hand and smiles at me. Beer bottles are excellent props for men who don't talk as often as they probably should.

"Your wife called earlier." I say. "She left quite a message."

"I heard it. Ashley's a passionate girl. She swears a lot when she's feeling vulnerable. It's a classic defense mechanism. Her parents are horrible, horrible people . . . or so I'm told."

"Well, I'll be sure to feel sorry for her when she shows up to boil the dog on the stove."

Curtis giggles. He's artfully stoned in a practiced, fully functioning sort of way. He's one of those aged pot smokers who kept at it while everyone else gave it up and got jobs and started quietly voting Republican.

"How's the writing going? You getting some work done?"

"A little. The men upstairs are getting restless. They want this book to be over and done with. It's been a tough road though. Tougher than it's supposed to be."

When I was a kid, I took this literally, and would sometimes sneak into his office when he was gone and look for the "men upstairs." I'd search his closet and under his bed, convinced that they were hiding from me.

"I read about you on the Web today. Even in the middle of a full-blown financial clusterfuck, you're still getting press."

He takes another sip and then the last hit of the joint. "It makes this next book that much more important. I can't follow the Pulitzer with a dog. They'd never forgive me for it. Either way, at least it'll get Zuckerman off my back. Nicholas's been holding the Pulitzer over my head for years, the arrogant bastard. I should take out an ad in the *New York Times* and congratulate him on being one of the finalists. Do you think that'd be too snide?"

"Publicly showing up a literary icon in a major American newspaper? Seems gentlemanly enough."

"You're right. He'd take it too seriously anyway. That's the thing about Zuckerman, he's a talented son of a bitch, I'll give him that, but he has no sense of humor. He still hasn't forgiven me for calling him the most boring writer in America three years ago. *Clearly* I was only joking."

It's been a while since I smoked pot, and things in the room seem misshapen all of the sudden. The pictures on the wall are crooked, and the pattern in the throw pillows is beginning to vibrate. "Jesus, where did you get this stuff?"

"Good, isn't it? It's a special blend from Colombia. Or maybe Peru. I can't remember. Somewhere like that."

I rise to leave, warm and a little giggly. One hit off a joint and I feel like putting on my pajamas, eating an entire bag of Doritos, and watching a Will Ferrell movie. "All right, Cheech. Dinner's in ten minutes. If you're not down there, I'm giving your spaghetti to Hank."

"Yes, sir," he says.

Before I leave to go find some Visine and change out of my work clothes, I stop. "So, who is she, anyway? You're not screwing around with Veronica Stewart again are you? I don't think that'd be a very good idea."

He's smiling at me, this old cad in yesterday's clothes. "What are you talking about?"

"The new girl, Dad? Who are you in love with now?"

Talk of women has brought some color back to his face, and he sits up. "Once again, son, you've managed to expose my tragic flaw."

"Really, there's just one?"

He grins. "Don't you get it by now, Tommy? I'm a writer. I'm always in love."

## 9

*A*nd here *I* am again, looking at myself in the bathroom mirror.

They're like loaded guns, these pills, and my eyes are red and everything in the room that's supposed to be white is now bluish. These are both normal side effects, according to the box, so I shouldn't worry. An abnormal side effect, one that I hope to avoid tonight, is a four-hour boner.

I check my hair and mess it up a little. Then I spray some cologne in the air and quickly walk through it. This is what teenage girls do before the big dance, but I don't want to smell like I've been in the bathroom blasting myself with cologne.

Shirtless, I examine my chest and biceps before dropping to the floor for fifteen quick push-ups. The last five are harder than I imagined they'd be.

The blood, moving through my body now, has added some definition where definition should go, at least a little, and I feel suddenly awake and tingly with sensation.

"You look good," I tell my reflection. "Hot?" But this last part comes out with a question mark at the end. I've never been good at sales.

My heart feels strange in my chest, like it's beating through mud, but these are the risks a man takes sometimes in the name of sexual competence. It'd be an embarrassing way to die, though, felled by a heart attack with an absurd hard-on standing at attention from my own dead body like an Italian baguette.

In our bedroom, the Victoria's Secret outfit is tucked safely into its dresser drawer and there are no candles or music. Anna is lying beneath the covers with her eyes closed and a copy of *Runner's World* magazine open across her chest. I fall onto the bed, landing on my side like some doofus being cute in a movie, but Anna doesn't stir, and for a moment I watch her sleep. Her moisturizer has left a little streak on one of her cheeks and her mouth is just barely open. I used to fuck this woman, when we were younger. It's an ugly word in marriage, "fuck," but that's what we did. We didn't make love or fool around, we fucked like people who didn't know any better or didn't care to do anything else. It wasn't scheduled or worried about or something done when they're wasn't anything good on TV. It was an effortless thing, like breathing, something so natural and fantastic. I don't remember when it became something that I had to think about so much or gear up for in the bathroom.

I nudge her shoulder. "You awake?"

She opens her eyes and says hello, and I rub a streak of moisturizer into her cheek. Just this simple contact, the warmth of her skin, starts things moving in my body—blood flowing and gathering—and I feel kind of dizzy, but not in a bad way. I cross the neutral zone between us and kiss her cheek, finding an earlobe and biting there lightly. I don't know if it's the pill or the fact that I know I've taken the pill, but I feel urgent and affectionate, and these goddamn things really work.

"Did you put on cologne?" she asks.

"What? No, this is what sexy smells like." I slide one hand beneath the covers and find her belly and run my fingertips across the ripples of her rib cage. Her lips are soft and warm against mine, and I feel myself getting harder. The pulse in my head is beating and I move to her neck where things are warmer and softer still.

That's when I realize that I seem to be doing this alone. Anna is completely still. "Are you OK?" I ask.

She looks at me, totally void of anything even resembling desire, and the whites of her eyes, big in the glow of her reading lamp, look blue. I recognize this face. It's the face of an Anna who's been thinking. Thinking too much.

"So, you hate your job, right?" she says.

I look at her for a moment and then I look around the room, wondering if perhaps I missed something while I was in the bathroom doing my push-ups. "Of course. It's killing me slowly, like asbestos."

This is the answer she was prepared to hear, and she sits up against the headboard. "Then, I think you should do something about it. You've been there for years, and you're always talking about how screwed they'd be without you. If that's really true, then they should promote you to something better, or at least give you a raise. And if they won't do that, then you should let them know that you're not afraid to look for something else."

"Umm, not sure if you've been watching the news on a different channel or something, but this might not be the best time to pull ultimatums at the office."

"Or maybe it's the *perfect* time."

I get the sense that my wife's been through this conversation in her head already. She wrote the script this afternoon on the treadmill, and I'm really pretty defenseless here. Forethought is perhaps their greatest weapon against us.

"You're good at your job, right? You pretend like you don't care about it, but if you'd actually apply yourself and take it seriously, you'd be doing everyone a big favor."

"I'm not pretending," I say. "I'm not that good of an actor. I really *don't* care about my job."

"Then why are you worried about losing it?" She takes a breath. "I can tell you're worried about getting fired. You can sneak upstairs and smoke up with your dad like a teenager all you want, it doesn't matter. I know you. You've let yourself get into a position where you're afraid that something you hate is going to go away. You're like those women in Lifetime movies. You're terrified your abusive husband's going to leave you."

Things had been looking up for a minute there, but now, as my wife ventures into the metaphorical, all my blood is diverting back toward the unimportant parts of my body.

"I know that you and I aren't exactly corporate geniuses here," I say, appealing to a sense of commonality. "But I think just about everyone's afraid of losing their paycheck right now. This isn't about having a fulfilling job. It's about being able to afford groceries."

Anna laughs. Apparently I've said something ridiculous. "Tom, Curtis is always trying to give us things. You think he's going to let us starve?"

"Jesus," I say. "He already gave us this house. Is that not at all embarrassing for you? We're almost thirty-six years old."

She takes my hand with both of hers. "I don't want to sound like the type of wife who says something like this, but that's really your fault, Tom, OK? You refuse to ask for a raise, or to make any attempt to get a promotion, or to take on any more responsibility, or, God forbid, to look for a job that doesn't make you want to blow your brains out. You have ten years of writing experience. If you wanted to, you could be making *way* more, and we wouldn't be living paycheck to paycheck and accepting houses from your dad."

"Wow, I didn't realize that it's 1953 all of the sudden," I say. "You make less than I do, Anna. A hell of a lot less. How about you go storming into your office tomorrow and start demanding things?"

She lets go of my hand, and I see Hank's head poking up from the foot of the bed as he studies the tones of our voices. "I help poor children learn to read, Tom. What does your company do again? I always forget? Something really noble, right?"

I lie on my back and so does she, and a long silence fills the growing expanse in the bed between us. I realize that the television is on—the volume turned all the way down. Lately I've been surrounded by muted televisions. Over the anchor's shoulder, there's a graphic of a red arrow pointing down.

"I just don't understand what's keeping you there," she says, looking at the ceiling. "What's keeping you from moving forward? I'm not a Stepford Wife, Tom. I don't want a fur coat and a BMW. I just want to be able to actually afford the baby that we're trying to have. Or, at least the one *I'm* trying to have."

Married couples really only have a few arguments. They just keep having them over and over again. "This isn't my career. You know that. This isn't what I want to do with my life."

"I know that. I'm not saying you have to stop writing, or that you have to give up on your book. I just think you need to start being more realistic about the world. You're an adult. We have a family. You've been working on your book for—"

"I *am* being realistic. The day you take on a *real* job with *real* responsibilities, that's the day you're done writing. You become some poser with five chapters of some shitty novel in your bottom drawer that you're never going to be able to finish because you've got screaming kids downstairs and some bullshit presentation to give about some useless buzzword. You know what my dad was doing before his first novel? Stamping books at the American University library for minimum wage, and he just won the Pulitzer Prize."

"You're not as good as your father, Tom," she says, her voice suddenly loud. "You're not Curtis, OK? I mean, for Christ's sake, wouldn't you know by now if you were?"

In the silence that follows—a silence even longer than the one before, long enough for the lamps to turn off and the room to go dark and quiet—I think of all the arguments we've had and all of the regrettable things we've said to each other since our first silly fights over stupid shit when we were dating. They all seem to have culminated into that.

"It's done, by the way," I say. "I finished it."

I wonder if she's even heard me, if she's simply fallen asleep beside me. "Really?" she asks, finally. "Why didn't you tell me?"

"It's been a long time since you asked."

I've been working on this thing for so long, and now it's done, but it feels stupid now. Years ago, when I'd just started writing it, I used to print pages for her as I went and she'd read them in front of me. I used to imagine bringing it to her, finished, in a box, surprising her with it.

"I'll read it on the train when I go to Boston," she says, and then she says nothing else. Katie read my novel in two days. This girl who shouldn't even give a shit took my book to bed with her and snuck away from work to finish it, and my wife wants to save it for her upcoming work trip.

Anna is absolutely right. I'm not my father. By the time he was my age, he'd published four novels, won two major literary prizes, and left his first wife.

I wake up sometime later, in the middle of the night. My head is throbbing steadily, my stomach hurts, and I'm sweating. I'm thinking of Katie, because, I realize, I was dreaming of Katie. It was as vivid a dream as I've had since I was a kid, so vivid that it takes me minutes to fully accept that it didn't happen, that she didn't come into my office, close the door, and start kissing me.

Beneath our sheets, my cock is so hard that I actually gasp in the dark. My normal, average-as-can-be penis has been replaced with something cartoonish and chemically altered, like a penis from the future. I close my eyes and try to do the impossible, to allow that strange dream thread to continue on again. Katie is there, and she smells like shampoo and her corduroy jacket is the only thing she's wearing. As I kiss the dream version of this lovely girl, my mind wanders.

I've pretended to suffer for my art, telling my wife and even myself that I've suspended my life and stayed at my ridiculous job out of dedication to my book. But that book is done, and I'm lying in bed looking forward to tomorrow because I will walk into that dreadful office and the first person I see will be Katie.

I don't want this dream to be over. I want to stay here where I am, but Anna rolls over, sighing in her sleep, and I'm fully awake. Dream Katie is gone. Anna kicks me, and in the perpetual half dark of our room, sighs again, and one sleepy arm drifts back and rests over her head on the pillow. The other arm soon follows and she kicks the blankets down until they rest on her hips. Her night-shirt is pulled against her breast, crooked and tight on her body, and a shadow falls across her stomach. She sighs again, which becomes a soft moan from somewhere deep in her chest. I sit up, and she's whispering something, but I can't understand her, more sighs and half words. When she moans again, I recognize it and her breath becomes short and fast.

"God," she says, barely a whisper, and she arches her back.

She bites her lower lip and her face is beautiful but from this angle, in the low, shadowy light, it's like the face of a stranger.

"Fuck me," she says, but it's so soft that maybe she hasn't said anything at all.

I am next to her, listening to her. I want to touch her but I can't, because she'll wake up and I'll have to explain this. I want to touch her, but I can't, because I'm angry at her and she's angry with me, and even though I love her, I don't like her as much as I should.

She's right next to me. I'm alone and she's alone. We have never been farther apart.

# Part II

## 10

**I** *watched Letterman all* the time when I was a kid, and then in college, but I can't remember the last time I saw more than his monologue. He's gotten more political as he's gotten older, and he and Paul Shaffer are talking about the election and the economy. John McCain was supposed to be on the show a few days ago, but he canceled at the last minute to deal with the financial crisis, whatever that even means, and Letterman is obviously still pissed.

"Is Grandpa gonna read from one of his books?" Allie asks. She's excited to be up at this hour, even if she doesn't completely understand why. She's wearing pajamas with dolphins on them and she smells like a bowl of mixed candy.

"No, honey," I say. "He's gonna read jokes."

"He doesn't write jokes. He writes books."

"You're right. Someone else wrote these jokes, and now he's reading them on TV."

"That's not fair," she says. "The people who wrote the jokes should be able to read them."

I consider trying to break this concept down for my daughter, but I don't even know where I'd begin. But then Anna is hushing us. "This is it. He always does the Top Ten List after the first commercial."

We're in our pajamas, sitting on the couch, and I'm nervous

for my dad. *Letterman* isn't even live—it was taped hours ago—but I haven't heard from him and I have no idea how it went. He could have fallen on his face or been drunk or accidentally said the F-word on the air. God only knows. Letterman looks up at the audience and raises a blue card over his head. "It's time now, ladies and gentlemen, for tonight's Top Ten List."

Cartoon numbers count down from ten, and Anna and I smile at each other. It's been a week since our fight. That's what one of our fights generally looks like, two people saying hurtful things to each other without raising their voices. Sometimes I think I might prefer movie fighting, where everyone yells and then has sex in the next scene. She technically apologized yesterday, but it was one of those married-people apologies, more of a tactical move than anything else, a way of moving on with things.

"The category tonight, from the home office, Top Ten Perks to Winning the Pulitzer Prize. Have you ever won the Pulitzer, Paul?"

"No, but I'm working on some things." Paul says. He's wearing purple sunglasses.

"Not a lot of people know this about me," says Letterman. "But I actually never learned to read."

"Well, you've done well for yourself, sir. It's an inspiring story."

I've forgotten how much time they waste on this show, just bantering back and forth about nothing. I think of my father standing backstage behind that curtain, waiting. And then I find myself thinking about my mom. This happens a lot, particularly when I'm a little in awe of something my dad is accomplishing—some surreal, famous-person thing. She'll inevitably show up in my head in voice-over format. She's like the Morgan Freeman of my conscience.

*He gets to be on TV, Thomas,* she says. *And I know that's very exciting. But remember who was there for you when you fell off your bike the first time, or when that horrible little girl made you eat that worm and you cried in the passenger seat of my car when I picked you up from school.*

"Oh come on already!" says Anna.

Letterman is making jokes now about some guy in the audience from Canada, and it's going on and on. He keeps asking him if people in Canada are generally able to read. But then he finally clears his throat and gets back on task. There must be a producer off camera somewhere, frantically pointing to an imaginary watch. "Presenting tonight's list is this year's Pulitzer Prize winner for fiction and one of the world's greatest living writers, Curtis Violet. Come on out, Curtis!"

My dad steps out onto the stage in a blue blazer and an open-collared shirt. Anna and Allie clap along with the audience and Allie says, "Grandpa" as if this six-inch version of him can hear her. He waves and smiles.

"Top Ten Perks to Winning the Pulitzer Prize. Take it away, Curtis. Number ten."

The drummer starts a faint drumroll and my dad eyes a spot just above the camera. "I get an exclusive ten percent discount on my next purchase at participating New York area Barnes & Noble booksellers."

"That sounds like a pretty good deal," says Letterman. "Number nine."

"Now maybe I'll be famous enough that people will stop asking me if I wrote those sexy vampire books."

"Number eight."

"I've just been hired as head writer on MTV's *The Hills*."

"Number seven."

"I get to make up my own creepy religion for movie stars and weirdos. It will be called Violetology."

The crowd likes this one, and Letterman laughs. "Number six."

"I no longer have to pretend that I've read *Gravity's Rainbow*."

And just like that, the audience turns and goes completely silent. Curtis looks over at Letterman and shrugs.

"Well, I guess we really shouldn't have expected much more than that, huh?" says the host. "Number five, Curtis."

"I've finally earned enough street cred to have that fruitcake Tom Wolfe whacked."

"Number four."

"From now on, the patches on the elbows of my tweed blazers will be made from one hundred percent *real* endangered species skin."

"That doesn't really seem like something to celebrate. Number three."

"Screw the financial crisis. I have enough money in my wallet right now to buy everyone in the audience a used Dodge Neon."

Television has filled him out somehow, and he looks like a younger, happier man. It's like he's at Politics & Prose bookstore in D.C. for the hundredth time giving a reading and not the Ed Sullivan Theater on national television. One hand is poised in his pocket, the other gesticulates casually as he talks. He is my idol.

"Number two."

"John Grisham and Stephen King have to mow my lawn for a whole year."

"And the number one perk to winning the Pulitzer Prize," says Letterman. The drumroll heightens and my dad smiles at the camera.

"Fabio has finally agreed to do my next book cover."

The band breaks into music, and then, with another quick, professorial wave, Curtis is gone.

"Is that it?" Allie asks. I guess she's unimpressed.

"My God," says Anna. She reaches for my hand and I take it without even thinking—a reflex of love. "He didn't even look nervous. Can you imagine going on TV and being so . . . *cool*?"

"I wonder if he was stoned," I say, but she's right. I couldn't even begin to count the number of times I've imagined what it'd be like to be my father.

Half an hour later, after a series of surprisingly complex questions about how television works, I manage to wrangle Allie into bed.

Her eyes are big and she's jittery from all the excitement, like she's been sneaking handfuls of coffee beans since dinner, and I wish it was legal to fasten children to their beds. We've agreed to skip reading a story tonight, since it's after midnight, but she's demanding two stories tomorrow. Parenting is often about negotiating.

"Is Grandpa Curtis coming back to stay here? With us?"

I tell her that I don't know and that he might be staying in New York for a while, and she just frowns at me.

Dear HR:

I ask my daddy lots and lots of questions. But he hardly ever knows the answers to them. I'm beginning to think that maybe the other daddies are smarter than he is. Seriously, you should have heard him try to explain to me where thunder comes from. It was pretty embarrassing.

When the phone rings, I tell Allie good night and rush out of the room. I can hear Anna drawing a bath on the other side of the house. I already know who it's going to be.

"Did you see it?" he asks.

I settle onto the bed with the phone. "No. Jimmy Kimmel had Carrot Top on, so we decided to watch that instead. I love that guy."

"Did I look old to you? I thought I looked kind of old. They put so much makeup on me. I felt like I was in drag."

"Well, you are pretty old, Dad. But you didn't look *bad* old. You looked *cool* old. Sort of like Mick Jagger."

"You think anyone got that *Gravity's Rainbow* joke?" He sounds quiet and tired. His voice has a cavernous sound when he's calling me from his loft, like he's at the bottom of a well in the Midwest somewhere.

"Hell no, of course they didn't. But I think that was kind of the point, right? I don't think people even pretend they've read *Grav-*

*ity's Rainbow* anymore. They pretend to have read much smaller books now."

"You ever read it?" he asks.

"Of course. Like twice."

"Yeah, I haven't, either. I don't think anyone reads *anything* anymore—unless it's about cutting carbs or fooling the perfect man into marrying you. At my reading today in Rockefeller, it was the same crowd of old people, like always. It's the publishing industry's dirty little secret. Readers are dying off."

Like Allie, I'm restless, and so I get up and pace the room, stopping at the window to look at my dad's car in our driveway. He took the train up to New York, so his keys are hanging from a nail in one of our kitchen cabinets. I could hop in it now and tear off across the Key Bridge like a video game. But, of course, I don't. I hear ice cubes dropping into a glass as he pours himself a drink.

"I think you're being a little dramatic," I say. "Remember your deal last year at the PEN/Faulkner? It was like a Justin Timberlake concert. I saw kids shotgunning beers outside the building."

"Those were just my students. They show up for all those things. It gives them an excuse to not be working on their own writing." He goes on like this for a while, sipping his drink and sighing in my ear. "Do you think they'll read me when I'm gone?"

"Who, your students?"

"I don't know . . . anyone? The way they read the greats? Like Zuckerman. They'll read Nicholas forever. He's really something, the lonely old prick. Maybe *he* should have been on *Letterman* tonight."

I think before speaking, arranging my dad's books across a shelf in my mind. "They won't read all of your books. A lot of them though. It might help if you gave them a few more. It's been five years. Zuckerman's published four since *Stairwell* came out."

The moment this leaves my mouth, I regret it. *Stairwell*, Curtis's last novel, is the only book my dad has published that one could reasonably call a failure, and he rarely ever mentions its existence. The *New York Times* wrote a highbrow, long-winded review that essentially boiled it down to one word: *boring*.

"I really thought people were going to like that one," he says. "Believe it or not, I've never tried harder on a book. It was like giving birth to a cactus every day."

"Well, maybe that was the problem," I say. "You never seemed to be trying before." This makes me think of my own problem, and how things seem to come easier when no one is thinking so hard.

Curtis is quiet for a while, and I know exactly what he's about to say. "Have you spoken with your mother lately?" he asks, his default question again. If for these few minutes a window has been open, that window is now closed.

"No," I say. "I was thinking of her tonight actually, when I was watching you. I need to call her. She's been trying to get ahold of me. I'm having lunch with Gary this week though."

"Well, that should certainly be intellectually stimulating," he says, like some elitist asshole. This is his typical stance regarding my stepfather, a man whose only crime is that he's never harmed anyone in his life.

"Nice, Dad."

"I'm just saying, does the man have any interests besides cars? It's like trying to have a conversation with a copy of Kelley Blue Book."

"Why are you so depressed, anyway? Jesus, you were on TV tonight. This might come as a shock to you, but not everyone gets to go on *Letterman*."

"I'm not depressed. I'm just . . . contemplative."

And drunk, I think.

"Sonya wants me to do the *Today* show this week. Do you think I should?"

"Yeah, why not? But make sure Matt Lauer does the interview. Everyone else over there is bush league."

Curtis turns away from the phone and whispers something, and then I hear a faint voice—a woman's voice, of course. "Dad, are you with someone?"

"What?"

I feel silly for this, for indulging my father while he sits in his multimillion-dollar loft with whatever silly girl he's managed to turn things upside for this time. It's such a strange role that I play in this man's life. He can't walk down the street without someone telling him how brilliant he is, but still he calls me to mope.

"I've gotta go, Tommy. I'll talk to you soon, OK?"

I can only sigh. "Good night, Dad."

## 11

**H**ank and I are walking through Georgetown.

It's early evening and the sun is setting, and we encounter dozens of our neighbors and their dogs. Whenever Hank and I venture out into the neighborhood, it strikes me how clearly neither of us belongs. Everyone in Georgetown, at least everyone outside of campus, is wealthy, and they dress the part. In expensive suits and sweaters from places like Ralph Lauren or Burberry, they walk their pure-bred, well-groomed dogs, often making wide circles around Hank the mongrel and his incessant butt sniffing. My neighbors have all probably lost half their net worth in the last month, but they still exude wealth effortlessly.

With my plastic CVS bag in hand, I bend over to pick up one of Hank's shriveled little turds. I've done this a thousand times, but I still find it humiliating. It's like I should stand on a parked Volvo station wagon and scream, "Yes everyone, I just picked up shit! And now I'm going to carry it around with me in this little baggie!"

I call Sonya's son, Brandon Ross. It's been a long time since we've spoken. For most of my dad's career, Curtis has gone back and forth between his loft in Manhattan and his condo here in D.C. near American University where he's the figurehead of the school's MFA program. During my childhood visits to New York, Brandon and I were inseparable. These sorts of friendships are hard to bridge into adulthood, though, especially when one is married and the other couldn't be further from married.

"Well, I'll be dammed," says Brandon. "Tommy Violet. Are you in New York? Are you stepping out on your wife?"

"No. And no. I'm in D.C. I'm walking Hank. He says hello."

"Lame!" Brandon yells. "There's a club opening tonight in Tribeca. We could have ripped shit up old school. I saw Daddy Warbucks on *Letterman* the other night. Still a hunky old bastard, isn't it? Holy shit, you would not believe the hooker I saw a few minutes ago. She looked like Cher . . . if Cher was a black transsexual."

In a matter of seconds I remember why I like Brandon so much. I imagine him outside somewhere, strolling along in whatever cool outfit he's got on, casually dodging cars and taxis and moving trucks and eight million other people shouting into their iPhones and BlackBerrys.

"Wow," I say. "I haven't seen a hooker in a long time."

"Bullshit you haven't. You know how many hookers there are in D.C.? It's like a cottage industry down there. They just don't look like hookers. They dress like Sarah Palin and blow energy lobbyists. Trust me, you're probably surrounded by hos right now."

Just then, a middle-aged woman in expensive running shoes passes. She's pushing one of those jogging strollers and I'm almost certain that she's not a prostitute, but, who am I to label anyone?

"You still doing any acting?" I ask.

"Jesus, it *has* been a while since we talked, huh? Nah, I'm tired of all that off-off-Broadway bullshit. There's just no call for my particular brand of thespianic brilliance in this town. I was modeling sunglasses for a while, but that got kinda shady. No pun intended. I'm all legit now. This cowboy got himself a *real* job."

"Yeah, your mom told me. Literary agent. Getting into the family biz."

"Oh, don't even get me started on my mother. We're currently not speaking."

"Really? Does she know that?"

"Oh, she'll figure it out. She absolutely detests my new boyfriend, Blaine. For as tolerant as the almighty Sonya Ross pretends to be at fund-raisers, deep down she wishes I'd bring home some nice little Jewish princess to make babies with."

"Wait, your boyfriend's name is Blaine? Brandon and Blaine? When are you guys getting your own show on Bravo?"

"Fuck you and your stereotypes. He happens to be very rugged. He's not even out to his family yet, the closeted motherfucker. He's a tattoo artist—how hot is that?"

When I was eleven and Brandon was nine, he revealed to Sonya and me in Central Park that he sometimes thought about kissing G.I. Joe on the mouth. Even then, ignorant to the many lifestyles a guy could choose from, I remember not being all that surprised. "Me too," said Sonya, sipping an iced tea, not even bothering to look up from whatever manuscript she was reading. Brandon is the sort of homosexual who is exclusive to either coast. While poor, confused boys in Michigan and Ohio and Iowa hid their dark secrets behind walls of self-loathing, Brandon was encouraged to be as in love with himself as any child in history. Even after their divorce, the proud Ross parents would sit together at his ice skating competitions, dance recitals, and lip-syncing contests.

"You didn't get a tattoo, did you?" I ask.

"No. Jews aren't allowed. I'll eat a bacon double cheeseburger the size of a fucking Olsen twin, but I won't allow an ounce of ink to sully this virgin skin. Just call me Jewy Von Irony." Brandon turns away from the phone then, yelling obscenities at someone. "Fucking cabbies. I mean, shit."

"So, an agent now?" I say.

"Word. Mommie Dearest hooked me up with some freaky connection. Hello, nepotism. It's amazing what the Ross name will get a boy in this town. Oh, and speaking of my mother. I thinking she's currently getting laid."

"What?"

"I'm pretty sure she's got some secret piece of ass somewhere in the city. Probably some failed writer or something. She's been all dodgy lately about her whereabouts. That's not the kind of thing you can sneak past a guy like me. I'm like, 'Mom, I wrote the book on secret sex, so step off.'"

As I pull Hank away from a beagle puppy's hind end, it dawns on me that Brandon's conversations with Sonya are probably a lot different than the conversations I have with my mother. When I was fourteen she tried to tell me about condoms and I nearly choked to death on a Nilla Wafer.

"So you know," I say. I'm desperate to change the subject away from Sonya's potentially secret piece of ass. "It's kind of a coincidence that you're an agent."

"OK, Thomas Violet!" he shouts. "Stop being coy with me. You call me out of the blue and act all casual and keep me from my happy hour. What do you want?"

"Well, I was kind of hoping you could maybe read something for me. Something I've been working on."

"Holy shit. Don't tease me. Please God, tell me you've written a tell-all about Curtis and his wives. He's splitting up with Ashley Martin, right? I heard that somewhere. That skinny bitch has had work done, hasn't she? Nobody with two percent body fat has tits like that. It's *muy imposible*. That's Spanish for 'fucking impossible.'"

"No, Brandon. It's not a tell-all. It's . . . a novel."

Aside from the muffled sounds of New York in the background, there's only silence. "A novel? Are you fucking kidding me? A novel?"

I tell him that I am indeed serious and that I've written an honest-to-God novel, and then there's some more silence and a car honking. I consider telling him that the one person who read it—a twenty-three-year-old assistant copywriter—thinks it's awesome.

"You know," he says. "This actually could be even better. Less trashy and lucrative, of course, but *classier*. Son of a literary monster takes his own shot at fiction. We could put your pretty face on the back cover looking all young-Violet. There'd be a ton of buzz. Could be like Oprah-buzz, actually. Shit, your dad's almost done with that new one, right? Dual releases would be off . . . the . . . hizzi."

Before Brandon can begin planning a Violet-themed water ride at Six Flags, I stop him, and I'm only mildly concerned that he's yet to ask what the book is even about. "The thing is," I say. "I was kind of thinking of a pseudonym."

"A pseudonym?"

"Yeah, a fake name."

"I know what a pseudonym is, you asshole. Are you off your fucking rocker? Do you have any idea how hard it is to sell a novel right now—in *this* fucking economy? Especially from some no-name first-timer. Memoirs, baby, that's what the people want. And if they do buy something that's made up, they want it *barely* made up. Former assistant at *Vogue* writes a novel about an assistant at *Vogue*. That kinda thing. Unless your book is about the son of a famous novelist who tries to write a novel and who happens to have a hot, crazy-assed stepmom, I don't want to hear about it."

I stop and lean against a light pole as Hank inspects his favorite fire hydrant. To an eavesdropper, it might sound as if Brandon is angry with me, but he's not. He's no more angry with me than he is with the cabbie he yelled at a minute ago, or the doormen and bartenders and bouncers he'll inevitably yell at later tonight.

"Well? Is that what it's about?" he asks. "You, thinly veiled?"

"Not exactly."

"*How* not exactly?"

"Not at all."

Brandon laughs loudly, and then assures me that this is not a laughing matter. "Is there sex in there, at least? Or maybe some abused teenager or an autistic kid who can talk to dolphins? We need a hook, something hot for the blurb."

"No. It doesn't have any of those things. But my main character gets to second base in the twelfth chapter. That's pretty hot, right?"

"Well whoop-de-do. I think I just blew a load in my pants. Now I have to go home change my boxer briefs. Thank you very much."

Up the street, a kid climbs out of an old car. It's Danny again, my character. I see him in the oddest places. He nods at me and then disappears behind a row of bushes.

"So, you'll read it then, right?" I ask.

Brandon is quiet, letting me sweat it out for a moment. "Fine. But, I should warn you, I'm having my hot intern look at it first. And I'm hanging up now. It's time for me to get drunk with my *real* friends who actually live in a *real* city. Oh, you're coming to that Pulitzer thingy with Curtis next month, right? Wear a blue tie, OK? Blue makes your eyes pop. Now seriously, I'm going. Goodbye, Mr. Fucking Pseudonym."

## 12

*The next day,* Wednesday morning at 11:30 a.m., I sneak out of the Death Star again to meet my stepfather, Gary, for lunch in Georgetown. The fact that he's offered to come into the city is extraordinary. Like many Virginia suburbanites, Gary considers D.C. to be little more than a traffic quagmire full of liberals and morally questionable politicians. Literally, he is the only person I know who plans to vote for John McCain, and he thinks Sarah Palin is both qualified to be vice president and "sharp-looking." I like him so much though that it's impossible to hold these things against him.

As I approach Johnny Rockets, I see his mammoth SUV parked illegally on M Street. The blue Ford Excursion is the size of a New York City studio apartment. It's probably only been sitting here for five minutes, tops, but it's already gotten a parking ticket, and it'll probably get another one before lunch is over.

Inside, Johnny Rockets is crowded and smells like a big French fry, and an Elvis song is playing, "Blue Suede Shoes." I know this place well. It's Allie's favorite restaurant on earth, and it's where we eat when she's in charge. It's always crowded, even more so now, and I find Gary sitting at a red booth sipping from a soda the size of buckets that pioneer women used to bathe their children.

"Hiya, Tommy," he says. Usually, Gary would spring up and give me a bear hug, but he's jammed into his booth pretty hard, and so he offers me one big hand. He looks tired, a little bewildered even, and there's a stain on his Ford polo—a couple of them actually.

"You got another parking ticket, Pop."

He sighs. "What? You're shitting me. I don't understand how people figure out how to park in this damn city. You gotta have a Ph.D. to read all the signs. No parking here on Tuesdays between three and four, except on Thursdays. Like I got the time to figure all that out."

"You parked in front of a fire hydrant."

He studies my face, trying to figure out if I'm kidding, which I'm not.

He's as big as two of me, and he looks cramped in this close, stuffy place. His gray hair would normally be in its military-style buzz cut, but it's grown out like a Brillo pad on his big head, making him look like a more casual, world-weary version of himself.

Our waiter in this ol' fashioned American diner is Asian and incredibly friendly. I order a giant Diet Coke of my own, and we both ask for cheeseburgers and fries. This is one of those lunches that's going to leave me sitting sleepy and fat at my desk for the rest of the day, but seeing Gary always inspires my desires for excess.

"How's the Honda riding?" he asks.

"Good," I say.

"You been checking the oil like I told you?"

"You kidding? Every week."

Gary is the owner of the Mid Atlantic region's third most successful Ford dealership, and my Honda came off his preowned lot. It physically pained him to put me in a non-American car, but he promised that if I checked the oil regularly and took care of it, it'd go for two hundred thousand miles. Gary's grasp of the true depths of my incompetence is shaky though, and I'm not even exactly sure how to check oil, or what I'd do if I found that the car actually needed more of it.

"Saw your dad on *Letterman*," he says. "Never cared much for *Letterman*, but Curtis was funny."

"Yeah, he did all right. I think they put too much makeup on him, though."

"That's just for TV. Whenever I'm in those commercials for the dealership, they pile that stuff on. It's because the camera picks up every nook and cranny. Photo shoots are even worse. You see my new billboard, the one out on I-95. They airbrushed my crow's-feet. Said it made me look more honest, whatever that means."

The waiter drops my gargantuan soda off with a thud, and I stop him. "I'm sorry. I actually ordered the *big* soda," I say, to which Gary and the waiter just look at me, and I can actually hear crickets. This joke never works, but I try it whenever possible.

"Did I tell you I read one of your dad's books?"

He's caught me in mid sip.

"The new one with all those short stories. I liked it. He certainly has a way with words, your dad. Is he still driving that Porsche around? You should tell him about our new Mustangs. What with the economy all hitting the skids, I could probably get him in one pretty cheap."

Most men would prefer that their wives' former husbands simply drop dead and fall off the face of the planet; Gary wants to put his wife's former husband in a bitchin' new ride. "I'll be sure to let him know," I say.

"Your mom told me about that story, 'Macy's.' She said it was about you. Did he really lose you in a store like that?"

"Well, he never won the Pulitzer for parenting," I say.

When our burgers arrive, we eat and listen to classic rock 'n' roll songs. He tells me about the dealership and how my half brothers are doing, Brett and Randy, two far more capable men than I, living in Dallas and Kansas City. And then he catches me off guard for the second time. "So, I hear your dad is having some marriage troubles."

"Well . . . I guess you could say that."

"That Ashley gal of his from the magazines? She's beautiful. How could he let a woman like that get away?"

It takes me a moment to realize that he's not being sarcastic. Gary has made the classic mistake of equating precise cheekbones, perfect breasts, and a vague association with philanthropy as the signs of a good woman. "Gary, my dad has let far better women get away. Did you know that I'm actually four months older than she is? I'm older than my stepmother, Pop. That's just not the natural order of things. The fact that I'm not in therapy is a statistical anomaly."

He pokes at his hamburger, looking under the bun at the half-melted cheese. "Well, I guess he could have just about any woman he wants, what with him being who he is and all."

This is a strange conversation for Gary and me to be having. Curtis is a topic we generally avoid, which I've always liked. He's one of a small handful of people I know in the world who seems to have no interest in my dad. Until now. "You freelancing for *People* magazine?" I say. "Is this why you wanted to have lunch, to talk about my dad?"

"I was just . . . *making* conversation."

"We've never had to *make* conversation before. Why is your shirt so dirty? What, have you been using it as a napkin? Is there something wrong?"

If Gary looked merely melancholy before, that's all come crumbling down now as I really look at him, sinking there in the booth across from me. He rubs his eyes with his fists and sighs. "Well, it's your mom. When was the last time you talked to her?"

He watches me chew and swallow for a while as I think about the four or five missed calls I've had from her. I feel like a dick—classic Child-of-Divorce Syndrome. "I'm not sure. A week, ten days maybe? Why?"

Gary wrings his napkin, tearing at the corners. "Well, I'm sure it's just a coincidence. But, well, it all started about ten days ago, after your dad won that award. They talked on the phone—"

"Wait. My mom and dad talked on the phone?"

"Yeah. I know because I answered. They talked for about an hour actually. And, since then she's been . . . different. And then I hear in the papers about your dad and Ashley splitting up, and I guess I just—" His face begins to flush, and he doesn't want to say whatever it is that he's trying to say.

"You guess what?"

He leans forward, his big belly halved by our table. "Do you think maybe they're seeing each other?"

"Seeing each other where?" Hearing myself say it, this combination of words, I get what he's asking, and I laugh. "Gary. I can't even remember the last time they were in the same room together. There's . . . no way. What are you talking about?"

"OK, that's what I thought, too, obviously. I mean, this is your mom, right? But, well, she's a complex woman, Tommy. I'm not an idiot. I bought your dad's book last week, and it seems like every story in there is about . . . well, *affairs* and people cheating on people and hurting each other. I hate to even think it, but . . . I don't know. I wouldn't put it past your dad is all. Seems like it's probably second nature to him."

As I set my cheeseburger in its little red basket, I tell him that I wouldn't put it past him, either, but that the person we're really talking about is my mother and his wife, but still, the part of my brain that focuses on fucked-up, unforeseen shit begins working through a series of complex probabilities. My dad is in love again— as always—but I have no idea with whom. The smart money would be on anyone else in the world other than my mother. A barista-in-training at Starbucks. One of his students. A longtime enemy's wife. One of the waitresses here at Johnny Rockets. Jesus . . . anyone. "No, Gary," I tell him. "No."

"Yesterday, I was in our bedroom, and I found one of his books in her drawer in the nightstand. I didn't even think we had any of his books—she used to tell people they weren't allowed in the house. But there it was."

"Which book?" I ask.

"A small one, not very long. November something."

"*Tomorrow Is November*?"

"Yeah. Yeah, that's it."

The chilling remains of burger look gross and fleshy in the basket, nestled in fries. That was my dad's first novel, and it's dedicated to her.

"I keep trying to call her, but she doesn't even want to talk to me. Says she wants to think about some things. I'm not an expert on women or anything, but *thinking* doesn't sound like a good thing at all. Because women only think about bad things, I've found."

Gary is right, of course, especially when it comes to women like my mother.

"Wait," I say. "You've been trying to call her? Call her where?"

Gary's eyes fall to the salt and pepper shakers at the middle of the table. "She's been staying out at your aunt Bernice's for a little while now, over in Maryland. She's . . . *sorting* some things out. I don't know what to do, Tommy. What's gonna happen if she decides she doesn't want to come back?"

The waiter returns, sneaking up on us, a ninja waiter. He sets a second Diet Coke in front of me—a bubbling tub of soda. "Another *big* drink?" he asks.

Apparently now he gets my joke.

# 13

**B**ack at work, I'm sifting through all the crap that Greg has jammed into my in-box while I was at lunch. Because he hates me so much, Greg often leaves things for me when I'm gone to save him the indignity of actually having to speak with me. This is an arrangement that actually works best for everyone involved, but I still try to make things as difficult for him as possible. I've been known to sneak things into the garbage and claim never to have seen them. Nothing too important, just random drafts of brochures or press release copy or things that if never seen again would cause no one any tangible harm. Except Greg, of course.

Dear HR:

    I am convinced Tom Violet hides drafts of copy and then denies it. This is not only unprofessional, it also creates a great deal of rework for my team and me and goes against best practices. Not to mention, it is profoundly immature.

Along with Johnny Rockets–induced heartburn/meat sweats, the image of my mom and dad having sex has followed me back from lunch and has managed to thoroughly ruin what's left of my afternoon. If Brandon was here, he'd ask me if my mom had her own secret piece of ass and I'd be left with no choice but to bludgeon him to death with the oddly heavy stapler I stole last time I was in Greg's office.

I dial my mother at her school. Helen, the receptionist, tells me that my mother is currently with her AP English students. Perhaps it's my imagination, but Helen sounds strange, and I wonder if she knows something. I believe this is what mental health professionals call paranoia.

"How have you been, dear?" Helen asks.

I decide not to tell her about the erectile dysfunction, the recent layoffs at my company, how my dad has taken to smoking pot in my extra bedroom, or how my hands smell like French fries even though I've washed them three times. "Oh, you know," I say. "Not too bad."

A few minutes later, I'm pretending to work when my phone rings. I answer, expecting something horrible to be on the other end, but I'm happy to hear Lyle, our media contact at the *Washington Post*'s business section. "Oh. Hey, Lyle," I say.

"I wanted to let you know I got the press release you sent over this morning," he says, friendly, but a little robotic. "Just read it. Solid as always. I'm sending it up to the writers now."

"Thanks," I say. "More hard-hitting news from MSW. I'm impressed you could read the entire thing without falling asleep. You must have had Red Bull for lunch."

Lyle is one of about fifty media contacts I hit up on a biweekly basis with my company's boring press releases, which I am, unfortunately, charged with writing. Sometimes these press releases are turned into news articles by bored staff writers, and sometimes they simply drift off into the cosmos and disappear from existence. I wrote this most recent release about six hours ago, and I can't even remember what it's about. Bullshit, mostly. Whenever bad news is in the air, like a full-fledged economic clusterfuck, for example, our PR guys want us to send out a bunch of upbeat-sounding releases about how great and profitable things are on the Death Star, as if we're somehow above it all. I've never seen Lyle in real life, but we've spoken on the phone or via e-mail a hundred million times.

"That's OK, Mr. Violet. One of these days you're gonna bring me something big. I can feel it—a front pager."

"We don't do big here, Lyle. In fact, I'm not really sure we do anything. How's that for a lead, 'Washington D.C., Company Does Nothing'?"

When Lyle is gone and I've hung up the phone, I'm faced with the grim prospect of having to do my job and write some more corporate propaganda. Perhaps I should get a glass of water first, or look at my *Simpsons* trivia calendar, or curl up in a little ball under my desk and sleep off my cheeseburger. As I consider each of these options, there's a brief crack of static, a click, and then a voice, like a ghost. "Tom, are you there, mate?"

I'm startled, and a little confused. The voice is British and serious.

"Tom? You there then, mate?"

It's the president of MSW himself, Ian Barksdale. I look at the phone on my desk, which, apparently, has speaker capabilities. I really should read the manual one of these days. "Umm, Ian? Mr. Barksdale?"

"You a'ight then, mate?" he says, at least I think this is what he says, because it kind of sounds like one big, long word.

"Yeah. I'm . . . great."

"Are you busy? Why don't you pop up to the top floor for a bit of a chat?"

I pause for a second to translate in my head, and then I wonder if perhaps this is a joke. The voice sounds so British that it's difficult to believe that there's a part of the world where people really talk like this. "Sure. Now?"

"No time like the present. Cheers." There's another click, and then he's gone.

I didn't even know he was in town. No one knows when Ian is in town. He's the president of five other loosely affiliated companies and he seems to be nowhere and everywhere at once. He's like Keyser Söze. My first instinct is to flee, to walk down to the parking garage and simply start driving toward Canada. After all, has anyone in the history of corporate America ever randomly been called into the president's office and had it turn out well?

*Tom Violet, you handsome bastard, you're doing such a good job. Here's one thousand dollars and the keys to one of the company Land Rovers. Carry on then.*

But before I can do anything beyond staring at my no-longer-talking phone, the temperature in my office drops and I hear James Earl Jones's heavy mechanical breathing. Greg is standing in the doorway. "Was that Ian?" he asks. This gives credence to my long-standing theory that Greg is monitoring my office, and I make a mental note to alert HR. He's holding an armful of manila folders against his green tie, which, disturbingly, is populated with little sailboats. It's like someone called a casting agency and requested an actor to play the part someone to annoy me.

But I smile hard, because that's, for some reason, what I do. "Hi, Greg!"

"What's Ian Barksdale doing calling *you*?"

"Believe it or not, we're actually going boating this weekend. He invited Anna and me on his yacht. He probably just wants to go over some things. If you want, I can see if there's room for you." We hold each other's eyes for a moment as he tries to crush my windpipe with his mind. Normally, irritating Greg makes me enjoy being alive, but it's all trumped by this quiet, sinking feeling in my stomach.

When he turns his back on me and leaves, I find myself for the very first time actually wishing that he'd come back. I'd tease him about his tie, make thinly veiled *Star Wars* references, and together we could delay whatever it is that's about to happen to me.

Before I leave, I write Katie a quick e-mail.

In the event of my death, I bequeath you the half bag of
M&M's in my bottom drawer and my three-hole punch. Don't
let the bastards drag you down.

Tom

As if operating metaphorically, the senior executives occupy the
very top floor of the building, and getting to them is a physical
ordeal. It requires an elevator ride, obviously, but also an impromptu walking tour of the entire North American headquarters.
Most of my days are spent looking at or avoiding the same twenty
or twenty-five people in Marketing and PR, but as I venture out of
my cocoon, I'm always amazed at how many freaking people actually work in this horrible place.

I step off the elevator and enter a code to get into a side door.
This code is changed by HR seemingly at random, and so I have
to punch in a bunch of old codes until I finally get it right. There's
another Cubeland—another dreadful little cluster of worksta-
tions like some township in South Africa—and then I'm walking
through Accounting. The Accounting guys are all tie guys and
they look at me suspiciously, as if perhaps I've come to steal their
BlackBerrys. Next, I'm in Customer Service, which is made up of
people who appear to be no older than nineteen. Those not bop-
ping their heads to iPods are wearing headsets and talking to customers all over the world. Although it's the middle of the week,
most of them are wearing jeans. There's a banner on the wall that
reads: OUR CUSTOMERS CAN *HEAR* YOU SMILING!

I pass through a mini-kitchen with a vending machine, a sink,
and a laminated poster demonstrating how to aid a choking victim.
Then I'm in the Legal Department, which consists of three pasty,

sad-looking lawyers. As far as I know, their only responsibilities are overseeing layoffs and reading from a handbook during the occasional Sexual Harassment Workshop.

Did anyone ever imagine that this is where they'd end up, working for a company that none of us can even describe without every other person in the room passing out onto the floor from hyper-boredom? When I was in college I had this sweet old sociology professor with a long beard who insisted that capitalism is an almost entirely imaginary thing. According to him, there are only a handful of jobs that actually fuel the American economy and the rest are wholly orchestrated boondoggles designed to keep people in offices all day or in malls buying shit on weekends and not rioting in the streets. I used to think he was just a pinko academic nut job, but a few years in corporate America have left me reconsidering his theory. Hundreds of us work here—our families depend on it. And yet, none of us is doing a thing to make the world even a little better.

Close to Buckingham Palace now, there's a series of noticeable differences as the quality of my surroundings improves. The carpet is thicker, there are no coffee stains, and the walls are free of Dilbert calendars and hotel-room artwork. Cubelands have become offices and the air is cooler, less close and choking. I peek into the offices of our executive vice presidents. Each of them is hunched over a desk, working, stressed, MSNBC on their televisions, doom everywhere.

Nearly out of breath, I land at the desk of a woman named Lauren, Ian Barksdale's executive coordinator. She's a good-looking forty-year-old with dark, horn-rimmed glasses. "Hi, Tom," she says, smiling efficiently. "It'll be just a second."

I study Lauren's smooth, angular face, analyzing her tone. A few minutes ago, Ian called her and said that I was on my way and that *something* was about to happen.

*Lauren, love, Tom Violet is on his way up. Poor bloke is getting sacked. Call Security and have them ready the Taser guns.*

"Long time no see," I say, going for the charming version of Tom Violet. "How are things on the top floor?"

Back before she was plucked from the trenches and brought up here to assist the royals, she worked downstairs and we were friendly. She'd gotten married about the same time I did, and we compared honeymoon stories. Her ring finger is bare now, though, and rumors are that things ended badly—as if there's any other way. "I'm surviving," she says. "He's on a call with London. You can have a seat over there."

"What?" I say. "Where's the love? Come on, you can tell me. I'm getting a company car right, and a big raise?"

Lauren looks at me, tired and unreadable. "I'm just an assistant, remember?"

"Hey, don't say that. You're an executive coordinator. Own it."

I sit down in a nice leather chair beside Ian's closed door and take a breath, slowing things down a little. I'm probably nervous, and that's why my heart has become an object that I can actually feel working. But I think more than that I'm . . . exhilarated? There's a lot of sameness here, in this hole of a company, heavy, crushing sameness, and so when something that *isn't* the same happens, it's exciting. An admin gets a boob job. An executive gets fired for something vague. The Pepsi machine gets replaced with a Coke machine. In a matter of moments, I will likely be fired along with thousands and thousands of other poor saps around the country, given a cardboard box and an hour or so to gather my shit. I'll have no job—certainly no prospects for a new job—and my family and I will be burning IKEA bookshelves for warmth come winter. But, for the love of God, it will all be very exciting.

Lauren's phone beeps and then a disembodied Ian is talking again. "Lauren, could you send Tom in please?"

I rise and straighten the wrinkles on the front of my khakis with the palms of my hands. "You don't happen to have a tie back there, do you, Lauren?"

To her credit, Lauren pretends to search for one among the efficient clutter atop her desk before shrugging.

"Well then," I say. "God save the Queen."

When I open the door, Ian's back is to me, but he greets me anyway. "Hello, mate." He spins around in his chair, stopping as his shoulders become exactly square with mine. I know nothing about suits, but his is fantastic. By comparison, in my stupid khakis and button-up shirt from the Gap, I'm the homeless guy down the street waving his fist at traffic. The other VIPs have *one* TV in their offices, but Ian has three. He lives in London, but he owns apartments and houses all over the Northeast, including one in Cleveland Park near the D.C. Zoo. Last year, a link to the *London Times* went around the office with a story about how he'd purchased an entire Formula 1 racing team.

With one remote, he turns all three TVs down. Obama is on two of them, giving two different speeches to two different groups of people. "Are you Americans going to actually elect him, do you think?" he asks. Because he's British, everything he says sounds effortless, poetic, and condescending, like someone who really doesn't care one way or the other.

I've never been a spokesperson for my people before, so I think before talking. "Yes we can," I say.

By sheer force of habit, I scan the large bookcase over Ian's shoulder. Among the business texts are a number of real books—a few leather-bound Shakespeares, some hotshot Brit writers, and a copy of my dad's most famous novel, *The Bridge That Wasn't There.*

He rolls backwards, lacing his fingers behind his head. He's maybe fifty-five, but his skin is tan and flawless, save for two serious creases on his forehead. "I'll get to it straightaway then, if you don't mind."

"Certainly."

"I wanted to ask you, how are things going down there? All right?"

For a nanosecond, my brain interprets "down there" as a reference to my fledgling penis and I'm horrified. But then I remember that to this man, everything can be classified as being down there, particularly where I work. "Good," I say.

"More specifically, I'm wondering about Marketing. How are things in the department?"

I have to speak carefully now because I have this strange habit of imitating British people without even realizing that I'm doing it. "Great. Everything's . . . great."

He laughs, running his hands through his wavy British-guy hair. "All right, all right. Fair enough. I've put you on the spot. I guess what I want to know is, what exactly do you do all day?"

I really don't see how any good could come from a question like this, particularly when it's posed by my boss's boss's boss. "Well, I write. I'm a copywriter." I give Ian a muddled ten-second version of everything that I do. "I wrote a letter for you once, a while ago. A letter to our best clients about an end-of-the-year offer on our Requirements Management courses. We sent it first class."

Ian nods. "Is that all?"

"There are other things, too," I say, which clearly means that there aren't. "I wrote a companywide e-mail last month about the annual HR bake sale."

Sadly, he seems unmoved by this. "You mind if I ask you how much you make?"

"Well—"

He holds up his hand and frowns at some papers on his desk. "Actually, I've got it right here." If he's looking at my employee file, then surely I'm fucked. I think of Greg's list of complaints and make a mental note to key his car on the way out. "How do you feel about your salary, Tom? Are you satisfied?"

"I'm not sure what you mean."

I'm suddenly very aware that this would be a strange way to be fired. *Are you happy with your current salary? Well then, how would you feel about no salary at all? Zing.*

He takes a breath, starting again. "There are a lot of people in this organization, Tom. Five hundred and eighty-two, to be exact. We're a worldwide entity—and part of an even larger worldwide entity. Some of these people are content to just do their jobs. They grab a cup of tea and a biscuit, accomplish tasks A through D on their lists, and grab a cheeky pint on the way home. But others . . . others are capable of more. As the leader of this organization, I'm tasked with identifying those people and presenting them with the opportunity to succeed. I'll be frank with you, mate, I suspect that you might be one of those people. I just don't think you've had the chance to realize it. Yet."

There are few things this man could have said that would have surprised me more than this, and I'm tempted to ask where he's gotten his information. "That's flattering, but I don't really know what other things I could do. I'm a director, and there's not a—"

The hand again, and again I stop talking.

"How do you feel about your boss?"

"Doug? I think Doug is great."

"Listen, Tom, it's no secret that some of my vice presidents have grown ineffective—as well as some of my departments in general. I think it's time for some new voices here, and Doug is not a new voice. A financial downturn, even a significant one, can be a terrible thing, or it can be a tremendous opportunity. It can be an opportunity for fresh blood, some new perspectives and energy. A whole new way of looking at things."

"Well, Doug has always been—"

"Do you know what the definition of insanity is, Tom?"

I wish he'd stop using my name so much. I feel like we're arguing. "I . . . *think* so."

"It's when one does the same thing over and over and expects a different result. I don't know about you, but I'm ready for some new results. This could be a tremendous opportunity for you, Tom, along with MSW. You can do more than you're doing. We both know that. Bloody hell, you've certainly got the genes for it."

"Genes?"

Ian nods to his bookshelf. "I saw that you noticed it when you sat down. Let's not pretend that I don't know who your father is. That's one of my favorite books of all time. Bloody brilliant." He removes a Montblanc pen from his shirt pocket and circles my salary on his paper, unimpressive in its little block numbers. "And I'm quite certain we'll be able to do a little something about this. Something significant."

"Oh," I say, hardly sounding like the dynamo that he's mistaken me for, and, for a long moment, we're just sitting in this giant office.

"Right now you've got a job, Tom. Nothing more. You come in and do your job and leave. But this—this could be a career. Something real. That's something you want, right? Don't you? That's what we all want. Otherwise, why would we even be here?"

It's been a long time since someone asked me what I want. So long, in fact, that I'm not even sure I have an answer.

"Give it some thought, Tom. And of course, this should remain between us for the time being. No sense in causing a spot of bother. At least not yet."

## 14

**W**ow," says Katie. "Gregory is gonna shit his pants."

"What, you don't think he recommended me for the job?"

"Right. He's been angling for Doug's office from day one. I think I caught him measuring the drapes last week."

We're in the middle of 7-Eleven, a few blocks from the office, and Katie's holding a twenty-ounce bottle of Diet Dr Pepper and I'm filling a Big Gulp. She's left her corduroy jacket back in her cube, and in a fitted pink blouse and navy blue skirt she's a distraction to everyone in the store.

Telling Katie about my conversation with Ian was fantastically unprofessional, but I had to tell someone. As we wind through the candy aisle, I inspect the Snickers bars, aware of two construction workers near the cash registers eyeing Katie. Like so many beautiful girls, she's either oblivious to this or chooses to be. One guy elbows the other, and the other guy laughs.

"My first action as leader would be to outlaw ties," I say. "And I'd insist that Greg call me Lord Violet, Vice President of Awesome."

"What was his office like?" she asks.

My heart isn't in this. I'm thinking about Gary back in Virginia at the Ford dealership, waiting for the cell phone on his belt to ring, looking out at the vast sea of American automotive metal. I'm also thinking about poor Doug. "Oh, standard president stuff," I say. "Water slide. Gold-plated desk. Little Korean boy fanning him with a giant feather."

She picks up a box of Nerds and gives it a good shake. This is what we always do when we come here for our meetings. We get our sodas and loiter in the candy aisle without ever buying any candy or talking about Katie's projects like we're supposed to.

"What did he do when you told him to shove it?" she asks.

"Shove it? I don't think that translates into British English. He did call me 'mate' a couple of times though, which was nice."

"But you definitely told him no, right?"

Before I can answer, her cell phone chimes. As she reads a text message, I see the two construction guys leave, getting one last eyeful of Katie for the road. "Fuckin' A," says the taller of the two.

Breasts and hips and olive-colored skin must be such a liability sometimes. Men look at my wife, too, but not the way they look at Katie—it's less visceral and raw with Anna. You could see my wife at a cocktail party and not even really notice her at first, until maybe an hour later when you saw her again, petting a dog or looking thoughtfully at a painting, and then you fall a little bit in love. Even their names are different—like opposites. Anna, this graceful sound, trustworthy and classic. And Katie, sharp and impossibly young, curvy and small, clomping around in wedge heels and outfits bought specifically to draw attention to all of it.

"Why are guys so stupid?" Katie asks, and I wonder if I've been thinking aloud.

"That's a complex question," I say.

She jams her cell back into a little purse. "I bought these concert tickets like two months ago and now he's—" But she stops there, fizzling out as we step into line to pay. "Maybe it's just young guys that are stupid. Maybe I should be looking for someone who isn't a twenty-four-year-old teenager."

I think of Todd the Idiot, considering his unique brand of idiocy, comparing it to that of men my age. The only real difference that I can see is volume. Young idiots are louder than their older brethren.

"I know what would make you feel better." I say.

"What?" she says.

She's looking at me seriously, as if anticipating some legitimate moment of insight, and so I feel bad when I point to the slowly rotating hot dogs sweating under their incubator lamp behind glass. "Do you want jalapeño or spicy chili? They come with dipping sauce. My treat."

Outside, it's surprisingly warm, and we dodge a group of Asian tourists. Each of them is wearing sunglasses and Obama T-shirts and they're all thrilled to be here. That's the funny thing about a world crumbling—it often seems as if it's crumbling only on TV. Because out here, everyone seems to be happily going about their lives, and so I consider the ramifications of guiding Katie to the Metro and joining our visitors from the East for a day of sightseeing.

"You're not a vice president, you know," says Katie. "Not by a long shot."

"Ouch."

"That's a compliment, you moron." She shoves my shoulder, a small girl's punch. "You're a writer, dude. You're not a suit. Thank God. You'd hate it. And they'd eat you up with all their buzzwords and bullshit."

"I could be a novelist *and* a VP of marketing. I think that's how Faulkner started out. I would terrorize Greg by day and write beautiful, generation-defining literature by night."

A W-shaped scowl forms across her brow. That'll turn into a wrinkle someday, but not yet. Her feet make little smacking noises as we walk. "You told him no, Tom, right? Come on, you're not gonna break my heart and sell out, are you?"

"Maybe it's more complicated than that. Being poor and tormented is charming when you're young. You can wear flannel shirts and complain about how stupid everyone is. It's hard to be like that when you're older though. Everyone my age is talking about eight-hundred-billion-dollar bailouts and the value of their 401(k). I am thirty-five, you know."

I'm just talking, riffing my way through an explanation, but it's amazing how logical what I just said sounds.

"Man, you're really thinking about this, aren't you?"

"I don't know. Maybe. It's . . . well, it's money."

A teenage boy with a skateboard glances at Katie, as do two mailmen drinking Gatorades. She looks at me, the W gone. "When I was a freshman, I took this drawing class as an elective," she says. "We would spend the whole time sketching like apples or pictures of dogs or whatever and talking about shading. Our teacher was a super-skinny little woman with huge seventies glasses. One day she was talking about how when we're little kids, all we want to do is draw pictures and color in coloring books and write stories about our stuffed animals. And we're encouraged to do all that, because that's what kids do, right? But when we're not kids anymore, that encouragement stops and we're expected to be something practical and worthwhile. The world loses artists all the time because they think they need to be just like everyone else. They let other people determine who they're supposed to be. And it sucks."

I fight back a smile. Her youth beside me—that idealism of being twenty-three and somehow untouched by any of this—gives off a buzz that I can almost feel. "I didn't know you could draw," I say.

"I can't. I'm freaking terrible. But you're not. You're an artist. For real."

The pinky finger on my right hand brushes the pinky finger on her left hand. "Brush" isn't even the right word. They pass, the smallest part of me and the smallest part of her, just close enough to suddenly be aware of one another.

I want to have sex with Katie. But, then again, so do all of the men we've passed by in the last fifteen minutes, and the men she sees every day at the office or on the Metro or at the grocery store. That's a simple, harsh reality tied to hormones and procreation and evolution, and so my wanting to have sex with Katie doesn't worry me at all. It doesn't keep me awake at night or make me afraid for what might be happening. What does worry me, though, is how badly I want to put my arm around her and pull her close to me. It would feel so natural, so simple. The muscles in my arm actually twitch, as if remembering a time when I could.

"So, you don't think I should be a vice president?" I say. "Even if I'd be a super cool one who would abolish the dress code and bring in pizza every Friday."

"No," she says. "But it would be pretty sweet to see Gregory freak out."

A block or so later, the sun on our faces, I ask her finally about her projects and about her job and actually behave like a legitimate boss. We turn a corner, near our office now, and I'm startled to see the same two construction workers from 7-Eleven. They're leaning against a work truck drinking Red Bulls. Up close, covered in a light film of dust from the day, they're just kids themselves, hardly older than Katie, and they notice her again right away.

"Everything is fine with me," she says, still oblivious. "Gregory hates my work, but what else is new?"

"Goddamn," says the taller guy. He has a goatee and a Redskins sweatshirt on.

I look at Katie, who stares straight ahead, not breaking stride. They look at her unabashedly, and it's uncomfortable as hell. "Hey, honey," says the other guy. He looks meaner somehow, less dopey. "Looking good."

"OK guys," I say. "That's enough." I sound friendlier than I'd intended, as if I'm in on the joke, too.

Katie tugs my sleeve, moving me along.

"Oh, don't go," the taller guy says, and they're both snickering. "I didn't get your number yet."

The smaller guy finds this hilarious. "Hey, I called her first. She's mine."

"Good God, look at that ass. You're killing me."

I stop walking and turn around. "Really?" I say.

Their faces don't change, two unconcerned smiles.

"Is that the kind of thing that works for you guys? You have a lot of luck with that?"

"Uh-oh. Daddy's gettin' mad. Sorry, Gramps. Didn't know she was taken."

They're laughing at me, and I feel helpless, because what am I really going to do? They're two guys next to a truck and I'm in loafers carrying a Big Gulp, and it pisses me off.

"That's really original, fellas. Leering construction workers. You're doing a lot for your people."

"Ha. Yeah, nice khakis, Mr. Original. You're a real trailblazer."

Pinpricks of heat erupt along my spine.

"It's not a big deal, Tom," says Katie. "Come on, let's just go."

"Yeah, *Tom*, hustle back to the office. You've got a conference call." It's the little guy—and he *is* little, a smart-mouthed runt.

I'm supposed to be fucking witty, right? I tangle with Greg all day like it's in my job description—but against these grinning assholes I'm plagued with erectile dysfunction of the mouth. "Fuck off," I say. In my own ear it sounds corporate and effeminate.

"Bye girls," says the taller one. "See you next time."

I open the top of my Big Gulp and step toward them to toss it all in their faces, avoiding any thought of the likely consequences. But the toe of my stupid loafer catches a crack in the pavement, and I go lurching forward, stumbling like a drunk. They both step away and I trip right between them, struggling to right myself. My Diet Pepsi splashes across the hood and fender of the dirty truck, and I actually reach for the little guy, not to hit him but to stop myself from falling. Startled, he shoves me away. My plastic cup hits the tire and I face plant against the passenger door. The side mirror, which I manage to catch on my way down, is the only thing that saves me from completely wiping out onto cement.

Katie says my name and the two guys seem stunned at what they've just seen while I die inside from embarrassment, holding the side of my face.

"Jesus, dude," says the tall guy. "Chill the fuck out."

"Yeah, man, we're just fucking with you."

I'd be happier now if these two guys attacked me with wrenches and hammers and I was forced to fight them off here on the street in front of Katie and the various pedestrians now pretending not to be watching this bit of street theater. But they don't. They're not cartoon villains or thugs or criminals. They're just two buddies on their way to or from some construction job who've just watched a physically incompetent, nearly middle-aged man make an ass of himself.

"Dude," says the taller guy. "Are you, like, OK?"

"Shit, man," says the other.

Thankfully, Katie is there to take me away. The two guys don't even laugh. They've become sympathetic characters, the rotten little fuckers. Where's a construction worker stereotype when you need one?

Outside our office building, Katie lights a cigarette and grins like she's trying not to.

"I'm . . . really sorry about that," I say.

"Look at you, tough guy. Defending my honor."

"What was that you were saying about guys being stupid?" My face hurts, which makes sense because I smashed it against a truck. The skin there is all hot and stingy.

She exhales laughing smoke. "That's why you just keep walking. Hulking out doesn't do anyone any good. You wouldn't make a very good girl."

"Is that something you deal with a lot—guys like that?"

She looks at her feet, shy, and I guess it was a silly question. "But that's the first time anyone's ever lost a Big Gulp over it," she says.

She offers me a drag of her cigarette, and I take it. The smoke burns, but the tip is thrillingly damp from her lips and if this is how all cigarettes were I'd take up smoking full-time again.

"Does it hurt?" she asks. "It looks like it hurts."

"A little," I say. "The good news is, I think I dented that jerk's door with my face. So, it wasn't a total loss."

She kisses her hand and then presses it, warm and soft, against my burning cheekbone. "My hero," she says.

We share the rest of her cigarette, and because there's nowhere else for me to look, I look at our reflection in the ground-floor windows of this monstrous building. My hair is a little too long and perhaps my khakis a little too short at the cuffs. And then there's Katie, hugging herself from the chill of our building's shadow, looking up at me and smiling.

## 15

**A**t home, later that night, Hank greets me, but he seems a little distracted. In the kitchen, I find out why. Curtis has returned from New York, and he and Allie are sitting at the kitchen table sharing a box of crayons. Allie is wearing an oversize I ♥ NY T-shirt, and both of them seem to have had a better day than I have.

"Hi, Daddy," says Allie, laughing at something private, something I haven't heard.

"The man of the house returns," say Curtis. "Whoa, what happened to your face?"

"Stockbroker jumped out a window, fell right on my head."

Hank has settled back under Curtis's chair, sitting like a sphinx, and Allie is drawing a picture of some kind of lizard. The entire scene is like a snapshot of an image I've never seen, my dad spending unhurried, undistracted time with a child. An odd, bastardized manifestation of jealousy rises in my throat, and I'm ashamed of myself. Apparently I'm the sort of person who's jealous of his own child. My God, what's happening to me?

"How was New York?"

"Tourists everywhere," he says. "People are still buying clothes and hot dogs. I guess they haven't seen the news about how the world is ending." He's drawing a drooping violet, a yellow sun in the distance.

I open the refrigerator, not even really looking for anything in particular. In the last few months, it's become the sort of refrigerator that's jammed with things like vitamin water and low-fat butter spread and plastic dishes of grapes. Staring at all this health food makes me feel greasy and bloated.

Damn you, Johnny Rockets.

"How'd the rest of your readings go?" I ask.

"I read and everyone listened quietly. Sometimes at those things I get the feeling that everyone is there so they can tell their friends that's where they were. Like church for intellectuals. Does that make any sense?"

"No," says Allie, stealing my answer.

"Who's that person there?" he asks her, pointing to a little man in her picture. I realize that her lizard is actually the Statue of Liberty.

"Umm, duh, Grandpa, that's you. See, I drew your hair perfect."

"Ahh, of course. Look how handsome I am."

"Handsome like my butt," Allie says, and then covers her mouth.

"Your *butt*? Allie, is this how ladies talk?"

It probably isn't, but I give Allie a high five anyway for creativity.

"How come we never colored together when I was a kid, Dad?"

He looks at the green crayon in his hand, dull at the tip. "Let's be honest. You were never very good at coloring. You were better at wrestling and . . . well, knocking things over."

I take a beer out of the fridge, the last one, and notice that Anna's black and white Adidas bag is missing from its usual spot. "Where's Anna?"

"She's at something called Body Pump," says Curtis. "What is that exactly? It sounds like it hurts."

"It's a class Mommy takes at the gym," says Allie. "It makes her all buff and ripped. She's lost fifteen pounds since New Year's. She could probably beat up Daddy if she wanted to."

"Didn't she already work out this morning, before she took you to school?" I ask.

She's filling the space behind the Statue of Liberty with light blue. "She did her running this morning. Body Pump is weight lifting. They're different."

"I'm glad none of my wives have taken Body Pump," says Curtis. "I doubt if I'd have survived this long."

Our cupboards are almost entirely empty; there's just the bottom-of-the-barrel things you can't ever imagine having purchased, the crap you give to high school kids collecting door-to-door for charity. She's leaving for Boston in the morning, and we've got almost nothing to survive on, and I feel weirdly helpless about all of it. "What in the hell are we gonna eat for dinner? I don't think low-fat white rice is gonna cut it."

"Don't worry, Daddy. Grandpa's taking us out. Mommy's meeting us, and they said I can pick—anywhere I want."

Oh shit.

"Johnny Rockets!" she says, clapping.

I almost put my foot down, but then I realize that I'm too tired, and when Allie's smiling like she's smiling right now, no matter how much my face hurts from head-butting a truck, she's difficult to say no to. Curtis exchanges his green crayon for a blue one. "Do I need a tuxedo, or will a shirt and tie be enough?"


I've been a casual reader of *Men's Health* for years, but I don't recall ever coming across an article that recommends Johnny Rockets twice a day. In my youth I had the metabolism of a teenage Ukrainian gymnast, but the day I hit thirty, things began slowly to betray me, turning the perma-lean Tom Violet into something far squishier. I scan the menu, and at the back of my throat, I can still taste lunch from this afternoon. It's sitting in my stomach, equal parts lead and concrete.

"Excuse me, but I actually ordered the *big* Diet Coke."

I look up just in time to see the delighted waiter laugh. Curtis, the funny son of a bitch, has stolen my line. Or perhaps I've stolen his. Either way, he's delivered it better. "Any bigger, I carry with two hands," says the waiter, a different Asian man from this afternoon, but equally as friendly.

I keep looking at my dad, wondering if he's fooling around with my mother's life. I'm also thinking about my trip to Buckingham Palace today, and those two fucking construction workers, and my stupid, stinging face. All afternoon I've been playing the scene out differently, concluding it in far less embarrassing ways.

Even under the best of circumstances, though, dining with my dad is stressful in its own right. He's not Leonardo DiCaprio, but in cities like this he's enough of a celebrity to get attention. Reading the menu with Allie, helping her sound out words, he's acting oblivious to it all, but he's well aware of the table of middle-aged women next to us whispering. And the young married couple in their hipster sneakers and glasses doing the same thing. And, of course, the weirdo outside, leaning against a parking meter and peering in through the window. There's always at least one weirdo, it seems, some reclusive book nerd with goofy hair who's probably got a gun jammed into his soiled underwear.

Allie sees Anna before I do. She sets her kid-size root beer down with a bang. "Over here, Mommy!"

I'm shocked to see that Anna is wearing the brown corduroy jacket I bought her all those months ago. "Hi everyone," she says. "Curtis, what do you think?" She opens the jacket revealing her yellow "What Would Curtis Violet Do?" T-shirt. It's a little tight. It looks good.

"Well, apparently I chose the perfect size for you," he says. "Any bigger would have been a crime."

"Dad," I say, tired.

She slides into the booth next to me. "Ouch. What happened?" she asks, touching my face.

"A stockbroker fell on him," say Allie, my little parrot girl in her oversize T-shirt.

"What?"

"No. I . . . I'm an idiot. I was reading something on the way out of the office, ran right into a sign." She seems to accept my idiocy in stride. "I thought you didn't like that thing," I say, touching her sleeve.

She shrugs. Her hair is wet and she's still flushed from her workout. She smells like soap and cool air. "So, who do you think it'll be tonight?" she asks. "My guess is the creepy guy outside. I saw him when I came in. I think he's on his way to go shoot John Lennon."

This is a game we play when we're out with Curtis. We try to predict who will be the first to approach the table. I glance again at the twitchy guy outside, leaning now against a big Mercedes that clearly isn't his. "Nah, he's harmless. It's gonna be Oprah's Book Club over here. They've been giggling since we sat down. Guaranteed."

I touch her thigh, thin and firm in my hand. She was right about the jacket when I gave it to her. It's wrong somehow, a little too wide, a little too short in the arms. It's just not her.

"Did you know that chicken fingers are made from *real* chicken fingers," says Curtis. "They pull them out with giant tweezers."

"Gross, no they don't," says Allie. "Chickens don't even have fingers. They're birds."

"I'll be honest," he says. "I preferred you when you were younger and not so smart."

Anna orders a plain chicken breast sandwich and I continue the day-long assault on my body with another cheeseburger.

"Everyone at work was talking about you on *Letterman*, Curtis," she says. "You're a natural. You should have been an actor. Or at least a talk show host."

"You wouldn't believe how cold he keeps that place. Some of the women on his staff wear mittens. I guess he's got this sweating problem, and so it's in his contract that he gets to control the temperature at all times."

"What was he like? Was he nice?"

"Of course. He's a nicer man than people think. He just doesn't like stupid people. Do they serve alcohol here?"

"I don't think so," says Anna.

"Well, clearly that won't do," he says. For a moment, he plays it cool, toying with the napkin dispenser and reading the kids' tablemat with Allie. And then he points across the room. "Sweetie," he says. "Look at that over there. It's probably the biggest milk shake I've ever seen."

Allie whips her head around to gaze at a teenager in unlaced Air Jordans sipping a huge chocolate milk shake at the counter. As her eyes light up, Curtis sneaks a flask from his jacket pocket, spikes his Diet Coke, and then winks at my wife. I feel like my dad committed to a certain kind of behavior about thirty-five years ago and has gone with it ever since. There's something admirable in that.

Talk at the table turns to the economy, and my attention drifts. Some more people have discovered Curtis, others are completely oblivious—the readers versus the nonreaders. And then I get this strange sensation, as if the lights in the diner have dipped, like I'm having a mild stroke. There's a familiar girl standing at the door with three other people. I blink and look again. Amazingly, it takes me a moment to realize that it's Katie. That's the miracle of context. Outside of our office or 7-Eleven, I hardly even know her. There's another pretty girl, too, and two guys, one of whom is Todd the Idiot. Katie's wearing a short denim skirt, a Rolling Stones T-shirt, and, of course, her corduroy jacket. The same jacket, more or less, that my wife is wearing right now.

I've been married long enough to know that this has the potential to go badly.

When they sit at their booth on the other side of the restaurant, our eyes eventually meet. I smile barely and then watch her go through the same weird process of identifying who I am—her boss. *Hi*, I mouth, and she gives me a surprised little wave. I'm not sure how long to hold this, to look at each other across the room, and so I look away, but not before catching a chilly glance from Todd. It must be very tiring to give men like me scowls day after day.

And then my wife's saying my name. "Work. Tom?"

"What?"

They're all looking at me.

"How was work, Tom? We're just trying to keep you involved here."

"Work . . . was good," I say, a little dazed, as if somebody's shaken me awake. "I negotiated a peace treaty. Saved a baby seal. Standard day."

She gives me a strange look, perhaps because I've said this very quickly and I am now sweating. Across from me, my dad's expression changes, too. Smiling, his eyes are downcast as he prepares to say hello to the beautiful young fan walking toward our table.

"Hey, boss," says Katie.

Curtis looks at me, momentarily confused, and I look at Katie. "Well hey there," I say. "What's up?" I have no idea why, but for some reason I'm pretending to be surprised to see her, as if we haven't just said hello from afar thirty seconds ago.

"Just getting some dinner," she says. "I've got that Bright Eyes concert tonight at the 9:30 Club. Remember?"

"Oh yeah, right. That's tonight."

"How's your face? It doesn't look all that bad. Does it still hurt?"

I look at my family as if one of them might decide to take over, but they're all just staring at us.

"He saved me from bullies today at work," Katie says, laughing. "It was like a junior high flashback. My hero."

Anna looks at me and then back at this girl—this girl who, apparently, knows me. "How do you guys," she begins, touching my arm, "know each other?"

"Oh, yeah, forgive me. I'm rude. Everyone, this is . . . Katie. She's my coworker—the other copywriter at the office." I go around the table and introduce everyone. My wife smiles and shakes the girl's hand politely, but I see a storm cloud approaching along the ridges of her brow.

"Wow, sweet jacket," says Katie. "You've got good taste."

"It was . . . a gift, actually."

"And this is Allie," I say, too quickly, breathing too hard.

"You look just like your mom, Allie," says Katie.

"Your bracelets are awesome." Allie is wide-eyed, staring at a series of colorful bands running up Katie's arm.

Without hesitation, she slides one from her wrist, a pink one, and hands it to my daughter. "Here, you can have one. It'll look pretty on you."

"Really?"

"Oh no, no," says Anna. "That's sweet, but she can't possibly—"

"Seriously, it's totally cool. I was on this bracelet kick for a while, and so I've got about a hundred of them."

Allie holds her arm up, the pink bracelet sliding all the way up to her knobby elbow. "Look, isn't it cool?"

"What do you say, honey?" says Curtis, tugging gently on her ponytail.

"Thanks!" says Allie. "I'm going to wear it to school tomorrow."

"That was very nice of you, Katie," says my wife. "Thanks."

For about two seconds no one knows exactly what to say to anyone. "Well OK then," I say. "Have fun at your concert."

The look on Katie's face then is sudden hurt, like a girl slapped. "Oh. Yeah, OK. I will. You have . . . a good night, too."

Across the table, my dad's smile fades to intrigue, and I avoid his eyes, focusing instead on a picture of Buddy Holly on the wall. I see Katie five days a week. She's read my novel, and we've shared cigarettes on the roof of our horrible office building. I know she's allergic to cats and that her landlord made her cry last month because he accused her of lying about paying the rent. She knows that I've been offered a promotion and that I find it embarrassing sometimes to be my father's son. I know that her mother is on antidepressants and she sometimes implies that Katie needs to lose five pounds. I'm a little bit in love with her, I think about her at night, and I wonder what her skin must feel like. And I've just brushed her off in front of my family as some girl I work with.

Katie recovers and smiles again, this time at Curtis. "Congratulations on the Pulitzer, Mr. Violet. I think you probably should have won it like three times already."

He laughs hard and loud. "My dear, I couldn't agree with you more. You should write acceptance speeches for a living." As she walks away, he follows her back to her table with his eyes. "Well, she's a lovely thing."

A Beach Boys song comes on, far too chipper and summery for any of this. Allie fiddles with her new bracelet, and my dad smiles at everyone. Anna is now fascinated by the plastic dessert menu, reading it intently.

In one of his novels, my dad compares a beautiful girl to a wrecking ball—a force that destroys everything in its path. Like most famous, white, male authors of the last hundred or so years, he's sometimes criticized for being misogynistic, but you can't argue with his logic as we sit here quietly at this destroyed table.

"Excuse me. I hate to interrupt. But are you Curtis Violet?"

One of the middle-aged women is standing at the head of our table, wringing her hands together. She's self-conscious and shy and bold, wearing a sweater with a yellow cat on it.

Curtis clears his throat and smiles. "For better or worse, I am indeed."

"I knew it. I just wanted to tell you how big of fans we all are. You're just . . . you're just great."

I try to catch Anna's eye, but she continues to study the milk shakes and assortments of ice cream sundaes. Across the restaurant, I find Katie again, sitting with her friends. Our eyes meet briefly, and then she turns away, too. .

Anna and I maneuver through our small bathroom, going about our nighttime routines of brushing and moisturizing. Tonight, we've managed to do it in complete silence. Married silence is a specific kind of silence, typically one in which the woman goes mute while the man pretends as if it's perfectly normal that she hasn't spoken in hours. In the face of conflict with their wives, most men choose to remain oblivious and passive, and I'm no different. Our shoulders touch as she scrubs her face with these little medicated pads. I say excuse me and drop my used floss in the garbage bin. We could be traveling salespeople, sharing a bathroom for some strange reason.

The family walked home from Johnny Rockets, watched television, looked at some of Allie's drawings, and watched the news, all with a glass isolation shield between Anna and me.

"Good luck, kid," my dad said as we all broke for the night, retiring to our rooms. After dinner, Curtis found another bottle of kangaroo wine and took care of it all by himself.

As she rubs cream under her eyes, I decide to try words. Perhaps some shock and awe. "I think Curtis and my mom might be having an affair." Things sound strange in bathrooms, like lines from a play.

Her hand stops applying for a second, but then continues again. "What?"

I tell her about my lunch with Gary, and as I do—as I commit it to words and sentences—it all sounds stupid and made up.

"Your mother isn't sleeping with Curtis, Tom. That's ridiculous. She's just lonely." Our eyes meet in the mirror, which seems like progress. "Believe it or not, wives can get lonely. It happens."

I follow her into our room, and as she climbs into bed, I busy myself moving my laundry from the basket to my drawers. On Friday nights, we can hear M Street from our bedroom, a dull buzz of music and cheer, and I think of the word "lonely." How could my mother be lonely? And, for that matter, how could Anna be lonely? Because clearly, that's what she's telling me. I consider Dr. Charlie's pills, hidden in my side of the bathroom, and I think of Anna fucking some imaginary guy in her sleep. But the thought of the real me and the real her having sex right now is, at best, improbable, and, at worst, exhausting.

At a certain point, weeks actually become months. The distance between the last time I had sex successfully with my wife and this very second can actually be measured in months, plural. My penis picks up on what I'm thinking about and shrivels in my night shorts. If my penis were a writer/director, it would be Woody Allen—small, neurotic, and, frankly, hit or miss.

"That girl tonight," says Anna. She's staring into her *Runner's World* so she doesn't have to make eye contact with me. "She was very pretty."

"What girl?" I ask.

"How about we don't do that? We're not children. You've never mentioned her before. But she sure seemed to know you pretty well."

"Katie? I've mentioned her. Of course I have. She's the other copywriter at work."

On the television, they've gone to sports, and there are men jumping and running and tackling. It all seems irrelevant now. The financial world is collapsing and I haven't had sex with my wife in months.

"You haven't told me about her," she says, little inflection. "Wives know every other woman in their husbands' lives—at least the ones they're allowed to know about."

"She's just a girl at work. There are lots of girls at work, Anna.

Hundreds of them. I could print out an org chart for you. We could go over it tomorrow."

"That's sweet. I like it when you're sarcastic."

"It's my only defense against irrational." I'm leaning on an old guy trick here, claiming my wife is being a typical irrational woman right as she begins saying things that I don't want to hear.

"So, how did you do that to your face again?" she asks. "A sign? You were reading something . . . right? Very clumsy."

Hank hops off the bed to hide out on his dog mat. He sighs heavily, letting us know that he's not happy with where any of this is going.

"It was *nothing*," I say, gripping my laundry. "It was . . . we went to get sodas at 7-Eleven by the office. On the way back these two jack-off construction workers started giving her trouble. Catcalling and stuff."

"Catcalling?"

"Yeah. And so I told them to back off and—"

"You got into a fight?"

"No. Nothing like that. It was stupid. I just tripped, and I hit my head on their truck."

She's left her magazine behind for the moment, and her eyes move back and forth across my face, studying it. It'd be nice if, at least in this scenario, the truth actually sounded like the truth. "You hit your head on their truck? But you told me you ran into a sign. Why would you do that, Tom? Why would you lie about something if it was nothing? Seems like a wasted lie."

"It was embarrassing, and I didn't want to get into the whole . . . I don't know, backstory."

She smiles, but then returns to dutifully pretending to read her magazine. "Backstory," she says. "A narrative used to provide history or context."

This is why two English majors should never argue.

She turns a page so hard that I hear it tear. "I'm gonna let you in on something, Tom. When a young girl wearing a shirt that's two sizes too small—a young girl whom I've never met or heard of—walks up to me in a restaurant and starts making eyes at my husband . . . context matters very, very much."

"Jesus Christ, Anna. It was nothing." I fidget with more laundry, busying myself in the hopes that this conversation will end. I empty some loose change into a dish on the dresser and take off my watch. It's important to keep moving in situations like this.

"It's kind of sad what passes for attractive these days," she says.

"What?"

"I know the Violet men have a tendency to be distracted by shiny new things, but really? Seems a little obvious, doesn't it?"

"What are talking about?"

"I'm talking about Katie, the *other copywriter* from your office. The one you insist you told me all about. All that eyeliner? Or the little skirt . . . and that shirt? You think she's really into the Stones, or do you just think she likes having a giant tongue across her tits?"

"That's a little petty, isn't it?"

"You're telling me, in good conscience, that you honestly believe that she didn't stand in front of the mirror tonight in that stupid shirt and know exactly what she was doing? Oh, maybe I won't look like a whore if I put this thrift-store jacket over it."

"A tight shirt? That's all it takes to be a whore?" I find her shirt from tonight, the yellow Curtis shirt. She's left it in a little unfolded pile on our dresser. "You seemed pretty pleased with yourself tonight, showing off in this."

"Don't be an asshole. That's not the same thing at all, and you know it. Curtis gave me that shirt. I wore it to be funny. Your little copywriter wasn't being funny. She was just being a whore."

"Oh, I see, she's good-looking, so that automatically makes her an idiot and a whore?"

Somewhere along the way, men all got together and agreed that we'd all pretend not to understand women. For the most part, this is bullshit. Right now, as the first signs of hurt betray this façade of feminist anger, I know that she's interpreted what I just said as me telling her that she's not good-looking . . . or at least not as good-looking as Katie. But I'm so mad at her that I let her keep thinking it.

Her voice is different now when she finally speaks. "I don't care how good-looking you think she is. She's just like your stepmother. She leads with tits and ass because she doesn't have anything else. Is that what you want Allie to grow up to be—a girl in a tight shirt calling someone else's husband her hero."

"First off, leave Ashley out of this. This isn't about my goddamn stepmother. And, secondly, you don't know anything about Katie. Nothing. You think you're the only female in history born with a brain, Anna? Is that what you tell yourself? The fact is, she *is* smart. And she's talented and she's funny. You're not calling her a whore because of some concerned-mother bullshit. You're calling her a whore because you know that however many fucking Body Pump classes you take, you're never going to be her age again."

I slam my underwear drawer shut and the dog yelps.

"Would that make you happy, *Curtis*?" she says. "Being with someone young?"

"Don't call me that."

"No, tell me, *Curtis*. Would you actually be able to sleep with me if I was some young girl with stupid bracelets and a—"

"I said don't call me that."

"Why not?"

"Because I'm not."

The emotion that's been shaking at the back of her throat is front and center now. "But you wish you could be. Admit it."

I'm done with this, and so I turn off the overhead light, leaving Anna sitting there, bolt upright, the blankets pulled to her waist and her hair back in a sloppy nighttime pile. There was a time when we promised we'd never go to bed angry. There was a time we were making homemade pasta in her little apartment in Dupont Circle and we had sex in her kitchen hallway while garlic bread burned because we couldn't *not* be touching each other.

I'm lying on my back, and she's lying on her side, turned away from me. The TV is flickering blues and greens, and even though it's late for people our age, M Street is still wide awake. If I listen closely, I can hear laughter, and somewhere in the city Katie is awake, too. I imagine what it would be like to be at a concert together, just the two of us. Maybe we're holding hands. Maybe she's leaning against me.

"Have you ever thought of her like that?" says Anna, facing the wall, reading my mind.

"What?"

"Have you ever thought of being with that girl?" she asks.

But I don't answer. Instead I turn off the television and roll onto my own side. Outside, somewhere, a glass breaks and someone is yelling, and we're lying together in this room with our backs to each other.

## 16

I**t's very, very** early—too early to be awake, and so I pretend that I'm not. Zippers are being zipped, and things are being stuffed into other things, sorted. Anna is packing for something. Where is she going? She's going to Boston. That's right. A conference in Boston. The Northeastern Conference on Literacy in Schools, or something like that.

"Tom," she says.

I hear her, but I sort of don't hear her. This could easily be a dream.

"Tom. I'm leaving."

When I open my eyes, she's sitting on the bed, looking down at me. She's in her gray suit, her hair back, with heels and makeup and the whole works. "Wow. How long have you . . . been awake?"

She doesn't respond, and I think about how I must look—a sleepy man in old gym shorts and a T-shirt, my face and hair a wreck. It doesn't seem fair. She should have told me she was going to dress up for this particular departure.

"Do you want a ride to Union Station?" I ask, knowing that she won't. She prefers the Metro.

She's looking at me, and she looks sad.

"I'm sorry about—" I start to say, thinking about last night. But

I stop because I'm not actually sure that I am sorry. Again, I've had no time to prepare.

"What's happening to us?" she asks.

"I'm not sure," I say.

She makes a go at straightening my bed hair. I want to take her hand and hold it, but I don't. I simply let her flatten away in vain, and I realize that I *am* sorry. I feel like I should take a quick shower and go with her. Curtis could handle Allie. He wouldn't mind. If we were alone together somewhere else, it might help. I could roam around Boston while she attends her nerdy conference, and then we could do whatever people do in Boston at night. We could quote *Good Will Hunting* and I could be charming. "How do you like them apples," I'd say, over and over again in a bad Boston accent until she laughed. Maybe that would fix things somehow.

This momentary surge of energy is fleeting though, and I sink back into our sheets. "That's a big bag," I say.

She looks around our room at the walls. She's wearing perfume, and the bedroom smells like the nape of her neck. "You never know what the weather's gonna do up there."

"I *am* sorry," I say.

"Are you going to be OK?" she asks.

"If I run into trouble, I'll just take Allie to Johnny Rockets."

"I'm not worried about Allie, Tom. She'll be fine. I'm worried about you." Hank leaps onto the bed and settles between us. He's making this little weeping noise that he makes when he sees luggage. Sometimes when we leave a suitcase open overnight, he'll climb inside and burrow down beneath sweatshirts and boxer shorts. She pets his head absently, fiddling with his misshapen ears. "The last few weeks you've been acting like someone who's about to do something stupid."

I pretend to be mystified by this, but it makes perfect sense. It sounds like something a character would say in one of my dad's books—books that often feature men sprinting toward their own, entirely self-orchestrated demise. "I'll be fine," I say.

"I'm taking your book with me."

From the side pocket of her giant roller bag I see the dog-eared pages of my manuscript. "Don't call until you've read it, OK?"

"What?"

"Well, I mean, don't call until you've at least read enough to have an opinion about it. If I talk to you tonight and you tell me you dozed off on the train and you're only ten pages in . . . well, just don't, OK?"

As reasonable as this sounded knocking around in my head, the original meaning has gotten scrambled somewhere between my mouth and my wife's brain, and she stands up. "I'll read it. Don't worry. Good-bye, Tom." And then she's gone, and I'm alone in our bedroom.

"Jesus," I say. "What *is* happening to us?"

Hank licks my face in one foul-smelling little swoop. And then he turns and looks at the window, his ears tense, as Anna's foot-steps on the sidewalk outside get quieter and quieter.

## 17

*L*ater, after I've showered and shaved, I realize that I have no idea what to do with myself. For a while, I simply roam the house, considering various projects—alphabetizing the bookshelf or perhaps watering all of our dead plants. Saturday mornings I usually write, or at least I sit in the office/extra bedroom and pretend to write, staring at the blinking cursor. But I'm done with my book. *The Son of Hollywood* is finished. And so now what?

I decide to conduct a fictional interview with myself.

"Who are your most significant influences?" asks a journalist whom I've made up. He works for the *New York Times*, and he is very serious. This seems like such a clichéd question. I expected more from a made-up journalist.

Down in the kitchen, I watch Allie eat the peanut butter toast I've prepared for her. As she chews, I think of my book. By now it's likely sitting in Brandon's office in Soho, buried beneath other books from unpublished hopefuls like me.

Allie has a glob of peanut butter on her cheek. "I'm all done, Daddy," she says, holding the plate out to me, her manservant. She's in her pajamas still, and Katie's bracelet, which she insisted on wearing to bed. "You use way more peanut butter than Mommy does."

"That's how I roll, sweetie."

When I toss her crust in the garbage under the sink, I notice a patch of brown corduroy sticking up from the coffee grounds and paper towels. I push things around a little and discover that it's the jacket I bought for Anna—the one from last night—now soggy and probably ruined. Maybe it could still be saved, given to the Goodwill or perhaps cleaned and replaced in her closet for when she's feeling less dramatic. But, then again, maybe it's better off here, never to be spoken of again.

My dad shuffles into the kitchen with Hank at his feet. He's wearing his wrinkly chinos and one of my Washington Nationals T-shirts.

"Morning, Grandpa," says Allie, holding an orange juice box.

"Nice shirt," I say.

He looks like a guy in a weight loss commercial, parading around in his old clothes. "I'm swimming in this thing. Are you gaining weight?" he asks.

"Is your bald spot getting bigger?"

"Well, there's no reason to be uncivilized," he says.

By my count, my dad's been upstairs writing for three hours, and I admire his energy. When I'm writing, I work in short, distracted, twenty-minute bursts, but Curtis has always been a marathon man, spending hours on end with his men upstairs. There's probably no other way, and the rest of us are just kidding ourselves.

"When are you gonna write me my story, Grandpa?"

"Patience, darling," he says. "How about you run upstairs and put on some big-girl clothes?"

"Why?" she asks. "It's Saturday."

"Yeah, Dad. It's Saturday. The Violets lounge on Saturdays. And sometimes we give Hank a bath. He's got a bit of an odor problem."

"Not today," he says. "We're going on a family outing. I need some clothes of my own. I can't keep borrowing your things. You dress like a hungover college student. Who's up for a ride in the car?"

"Yay," says Allie, although, to be fair, she's a sucker for pretty much anything proposed with enthusiasm. Beside her, Hank is spinning happily in a little circle. "Car" is one of the dozen or so words he knows. If I tell him he can't come, there's a chance he'll hang himself in the bathroom.

"Put your shoes on, Tommy. We'll give the dog a bath later. I'm driving, and you're in charge of the radio."

Once, when I was in the fourth grade, our principal's elderly secretary came into our room, interrupting religion class. While she talked to the teacher, we all waited and I pretended not to notice that I'd heard her whisper my name.

As I followed her slowly down the long hallway, I wondered if I'd done anything wrong, and then I started thinking about those Publishers Clearinghouse commercials. They had an enormous effect on my expectations as a child, and I convinced myself that a group of people with balloons stood giggling in the principal's office, waiting for me and holding a giant cardboard check for a million dollars. Waiting instead was Curtis Violet. He stood leaning against the wall in jeans and an old sweater leafing through a school bulletin. He'd been in New York for a while, and I couldn't remember the last time I saw him. His hair was a little long, and he was working on sideburns of some sort. "Hey, Tommy." The tone of his voice was weird and sad.

Our principal and his secretary told my dad how sorry they were and asked if there was anything they could do in this difficult time. "No, no. We'll be OK. I appreciate it. We have a lot to take care of—family business."

Outside, the Porsche was parked illegally in front of a statue of St. Robert Bellarmine. It looked a little dirty from the road. There were dead bugs all over the windshield. When I asked him what was wrong, he told me to just keep walking. I was too young to be all that concerned, and so I just walked, pulling my backpack along behind me.

When he turned the key and revved the engine, the little car shook beneath us. "Your aunt Lisa died," he said.

"Oh. But who's Aunt Lisa?"

"Well, she doesn't exist, Tommy, but it's a tragedy nonetheless, and she deserves our respect."

"What?"

Curtis slapped my knee. "The Orioles game starts in an hour. I got us some seats right behind home plate. I'm driving. You man the radio. Find us something good."

If he tried a stunt like that today, there would be an Amber Alert across the entire Mid-Atlantic region and he'd end up in jail. But, back then, no one seemed worried about a grown man with sideburns and a deliriously happy little boy speeding up I-95 on a sunny spring afternoon.

The car's smaller now, or so it seems, and I have to crouch so my head doesn't touch the ceiling, but it still pushes me back into my seat when my dad hits the gas to speed by a lumbering SUV on the George Washington Parkway. I touch the dashboard and think about how much more awesome this car is than every other car on the road.

"Where are we going? Pentagon City? They've got some good stores there."

"Nah," he says.

"OK, so, where then?"

"Can we get ice cream?" asks Allie from the minuscule backseat. "I want some ice cream."

"I think that's a fabulous idea," says Curtis. "But I need some clothes first."

The car smells distinctly of dog, so I crack the window. I find a pop station on the radio and Allie yells for me to stop. It's an old Christina Aguilera song. Allie sings along about how she's going to get dirty. This goes on for a while.

"It's catchy," says Curtis, and then he starts singing along, too.

After a while, we pull off the parkway and he navigates the obstacle course of senseless D.C. roundabouts and one-way streets while sipping his coffee and smiling at the occasional female motorist. Curtis has always driven as if it's about the third or fourth thing on his mind. I've forgotten how stressful it can be.

"Is there a store around here? Where are we going?"

"I know where *I'm* going, Tom," he says. "So don't worry."

He's being coy about something, and I've learned not to like that.

"Is there ice cream by the place we're going, Grandpa?"

"Are you kidding? Loads of it."

We're passing along the outskirts of the George Washington University, winding through a large neighborhood of brownstones that have been converted into shops and little apartments for students. My dad's office is a few blocks away in one of the English buildings. His position there as chair of the MFA program requires about four hours of actual work per week five months a year, and for that he earns about three hundred thousand dollars annually. This seems reasonable.

Allie is gazing at Katie's bracelet in the backseat, considering it from different angles, "I bet that place over there has ice cream," she says, quietly, as if talking to the dog.

At a stoplight, Curtis watches a young blond girl jog through the intersection. She has a G and a W on either side of her ass and her long hair trails behind her, yellow and whipping in stride. The light turns green, but Curtis just watches her hop up over a curb and glide down the street until the van behind us honks.

"Come on, Dad, let's stay focused here."

"Oh relax, it's just a Saturday drive, Tommy. You're beginning to sound like your mother. She always hated the way I drive."

"Or maybe she hated the way you stare at teenage girls. Wives can be unreasonable like that."

"Well, she hardly looked like a teenager. Early twenties, I'd say."

"Yes, because that's definitely the point I was trying to make."

"Why are you mad, Daddy?" asks Allie. I can feel her watching the back of my head.

"I'm not mad, honey. Your grandpa and I are just discussing the word 'appropriate.'"

For a while, Curtis weaves through traffic. Allie starts singing another song. She's saying some of the words wrong, mumbling past others.

"So, you're sure that's the stance you want to take on the subject of young girls?" Curtis asks.

"What's that, Nabokov?"

He likes this, a reference to, ironically, his favorite book. "I just think that holier-than-thou might be a bit of a stretch. You may have some credibility issues there, if we're being honest." Sometimes when men like my father smile—learned, successful men—it comes off as something sinister. He checks his blind spot and passes a woman biking along the shoulder in a Hillary Clinton T-shirt. "I wasn't going to bring it up, but perhaps you'd like to tell me about the girl, Tommy?"

"What girl?"

"You know, I think I've actually used those exact words before. 'What girl?' A little advice, son, they don't work, so you might want to try something more original."

"You mean Katie?" I ask.

"Katie, that's right. I couldn't remember her name. When she started walking toward our table, I thought we were going to lose you. You looked like you were about to make a run for it. I know that look."

"She's just a girl I work with," I say.

I wish Allie would take off that stupid bracelet. It's not doing any of us any favors.

"Tom, I'm not proud of some of the decisions I've made in my life. I think you probably know that. But let's both agree that I've got some experience in this particular genre. I know when a girl is more than *just a girl you work with*. Trust me."

Outside, as the city passes, things look familiar, even though I'm not exactly sure where we are.

"How long has it been going on?" he asks.

"It isn't, Dad. I just told you that. I'm married, remember? Believe it or not, some of us are able to manage our lives with control and forethought. You should try it sometime."

He smiles. "She's a very pretty girl. I know the type."

"She's a friend. And she's a nice person, she's not a type."

"Oh don't be naïve. You know better than that, Tommy. That's what I tell my students. I see these young writers struggling to make their characters unique—going on about the color of their hair or pitch of their Southern accents or what have you. But sometimes generalities suffice just fine. Everyone is a type of something."

"God, you're so full of shit."

When the car stops, Allie claps and says, "We're here!" She says this whenever she's in a vehicle that comes to a stop.

"Where are we?" I ask. But this is a stupid question. I know exactly where we are.

"I need you to do me a favor," says Curtis. "I need you to pack some of my clothes. As many as you can get."

"Pack?"

"Yes. From my house."

I look around. "Why can't you pack your own clothes?"

"Well, it's not that simple. There's about a fifty-fifty chance Ashley's there."

"Ha. Well, hell no, then. Are you out of your mind?"

"Come on, Tommy. Let's just say she's not my biggest fan right now. And she's always liked you. At least as much as Ashley can like someone. She's probably not even there, anyway."

"You said fifty-fifty."

"Well, I meant forty-sixty. I don't know. I'm not a statistician."

"Are we getting out?" asks Allie. My daughter hates stalls in narrative drive.

"Just pack some clothes. Underwear, some shirts. In and out. It'll be easy. Oh, and I need you to get me the green bag on my writing desk. Just a little carry-on thing. Don't forget that."

"No, Dad. That woman is certifiable. She's probably got a gun."

"Oh you're being ridiculous. In fact, you're being a bit of a baby." He hands me a set of keys on a Dickens key chain.

"I don't believe this," I say. But, actually, I *do* believe it. My father has lured me here. And to do it he needed little more than the prospect of a ride in this goddamn car. What am I, ten?

"That place over there has ice cream, Grandpa," says Allie. "See, look at that sign with the cone on it. We should get out here?"

He winks at Allie's reflection in the rearview mirror. "No, baby. You and I are staying put for a minute. Your daddy's gotta run an errand for me."

"I hate you," I say.

"Oh, you don't mean that. Thirty-seventy. I promise. There was a fund-raiser up in Manhattan last night. AIDS or Obama or something. Maybe it's tonight, I can't remember for sure. You know Ashley. She never misses that sort of thing. Come on, I'll buy you some ice cream when you get back."

"Seriously. I hate you."

As I open the car door, he grabs hold of my arm. "Don't forget. The green bag—on my writing desk. I need that."

"Whatever."

"Bye, Daddy," says Allie.

Curtis and my daughter are disproportionately cheery about all of this, which is infuriating. Even Hank doesn't seem to give a shit that I'm walking into a potential buzz saw. Curtis, the coward, didn't even have the balls to park closer than two blocks from his own house. I'm the star of a public service announcement cautioning viewers of the horrors of infidelity.

*This is your brain. This is your brain when you're a hopeless, skirt-chasing philanderer.*

*Any questions?*

Pedestrians seem to be looking at me strangely, as does a woman sitting on her front porch beneath another Obama sign. Everyone knows that I'm up to something. I might as well be wearing a ski mask. It dawns on me though that it probably doesn't count as breaking and entering if you've got keys. Or if the chickenshit owner of the house has given you permission to enter. Or if you ring the doorbell first.

Maybe I *do* hate Curtis. Lots of people hate their fathers now. It's very in fashion. It doesn't have the social stigma that it used to. I'm in my midthirties anyway. I doubt if I even need a strong male figure in my life.

There's no answer at the door. I ring the bell a few more times and clank the knocker like a fool, but there's nothing still. I put my ear to the door. I don't know what I'm expecting to hear, but it sounds like the ocean. Ashley's Mercedes is parked in the street, but this doesn't mean much. She rarely drives it, opting instead for a wildly expensive executive car service.

"Fuck it," I say.

When I step into the house, I'm greeted by cool, comforting silence. "Hello?" I say. "Ashley?"

This house has endured three of my dad's four wives, and so over the last few decades it's been a home-size mood ring, changing to the styles and temperaments of its female inhabitants. Ashley's tastes are very New York minimal, with open spaces and bold, white walls. Above the fireplace, there's a black-and-white photograph of a younger version of Ashley from a shoot sometime in the nineties. She's heroin-thin and angry, sitting on a wooden chair in a dark, ill-fitting dress. I remember seeing that picture before, back when she was just a sort-of-famous chick who showed up occasionally in tabloids, and not my stepmother. She met Curtis on the set of a movie based on one of his books. She played a beautiful girl at a cocktail party.

"Ashley?" I say again.

Along the walls there are more pictures of her. Some from her old job as a frowning model, and others from her new job as a cause-celeb. She's arm-in-arm with Melissa Etheridge at something, and posing with Sean Penn at something else. In another picture she's got her arm around Al Gore, who looks a little frightened. Quietly, still, I head upstairs. Ashley has reserved the wall space leading up the narrow stairwell for my dad's most noteworthy literary accomplishments: two National Book Awards, two from the PEN/Faulkner, and three from the National Book Critics Circle. I stop, straightening one of the plaques, running my finger along a film of dust. If these were mine, I'd have them bronzed and mounted outside my house like the memorials in left field at Yankee Stadium. I'd force my neighbors and people passing by to stop and behold them on a daily basis.

Upstairs, the door to my dad's office is open, and the room looks exactly like it's always looked—dim, cluttered, and written in. The rest of the house smells like nothing I can identify, but this room smells like my dad. There are some plaques on the walls—some of his lesser awards—and a few framed book jackets. One of Allie's pictures has made the wall as well. It's from perhaps a few years ago, smiling stick people, before she'd started really putting in effort. There's an old, yellowed Polaroid of my dad at a writers' conference somewhere. He's smiling in a parka, standing in front of an old brick building with some other smiling people I don't know. If I'm not mistaken, one of them is a younger Nicholas Zuckerman. It must have been before my dad declared them to be rivals. Next to that, there's another Polaroid. It takes me a minute to figure it out—the familiar woman in a long, black sweater. It's Sonya, smiling shyly. It must be twenty years old. I'd forgotten how lovely she was.

Of the four walls in the room, one has been made into a giant bookcase that houses copies of all of Curtis's publications. There's a picture of Anna, Allie, and me, unframed, propped up against a row of books. I hold it close to my face, examining these people, a little surprised that it's here. It's as if this were a prop, something my dad planted here knowing that I'd see it when I was pissed at him.

A full row of the shelf is dedicated to *The Bridge That Wasn't There*. Among the copies are three duplicate versions of one I've never noticed until now. Leafing through the first few pages, I see that it's a first hardcover edition of the British printing. I think of Ian Barksdale in his plush office, arrogant in his appreciation of Curtis, and I make a note to take the book with me.

My dad's desk is a mess. There are papers strewn about, a few tattered notebooks, and a copy of a very old book about the birds of the Northeastern United States. A few years ago he told me that the title of his new book was something about birds. There's an old bronze marijuana pipe, and bottle of Jack Daniel's is serving as a paperweight, empty aside from maybe a finger of brown liquid. I'm looking for a manuscript, which is usually in the top right-hand corner of this old desk. This is where whatever it is that he's working on goes. But today there's nothing, and I wonder if he's smuggled it into our house. Maybe he's hiding it from Ashley. I probably would, too.

I open one of his notebooks to a random page in the middle. Curtis's handwriting is all but illegible, but I'm able to make out something:

*He arrived to find that she'd left, discovering then that he was all alone. Even the birds had gone. They'd abandoned their nest on the windowsill, and he was somehow certain that they'd never come back.*

"Wow," I whisper in the quiet room, sad suddenly. These words seem worthy of more than scrawled ink in the middle of a notebook that looks recently pulled from the garbage. Another notebook is about half empty, the other half filled entirely with drawings of violets. Slung across his writing chair, the green bag, as he said, is small, like a mini-duffel, and it rattles when I pick it up. It sounds like a tin of vitamins or Tic Tacs. I unzip it and—

"Looking for something, Tom?"

I scream, literally scream, like a woman, dropping the bag on the floor, stumbling, and nearly upending myself. My stepmother is standing in the doorway, laughing, and I'm clutching my chest. Apparently, when startled, I become a Southern woman from the 1950s.

"Ashley . . . you scared the shit out of me."

"I saw you coming from a block away. You are, without question, the worst burglar in America."

Breathing, unclutching, I recover, which allows me to fully grasp the awkwardness of what I'm looking at. "OK then," I say. "Maybe you should go put on some clothes."

Most women, especially with a full block's warning, would think to get dressed before terrifying a visitor—even an uninvited one. But not Ashley. She's standing before me smoking a cigarette in nothing but a white towel. I can feel my face turning red. Her hair is heavy and wet, and her long, narrow feet have left damp indentations in the carpet. Ashley is the most beautiful woman I've ever seen, but that beauty is as frightening as it is impressive, like looking at a tiger at the zoo pacing behind a thin shield of glass.

There's a big, scratchy laugh, and she flicks ashes onto the floor. "Oh, don't be such a prude, *son*. We're family, remember? Plus, this is *my* house. I'll wear whatever I want. You think you can handle it?" She sounds drunk and, for some reason, vaguely foreign. She's not at all foreign though—she's from a suburb of Cleveland. My wife is convinced that Ashley stays so thin by doing cocaine, and so I look for signs of this. I really don't know what I'm looking for, though, because, for me, cocaine only exists in movies like *Scarface*. Perhaps the bags and bags of cocaine are kept next to the machine guns, wherever those are.

I give up the looking-away routine and shrug. I've never been particularly cool in the face of barely clothed women, but I should be able to fake it for a few minutes. My reward to myself will be punching my dad in the face when I finally make it back out onto the street.

"So, what?" she says. "The fucker's too scared to show up himself? He had to send a henchman."

"Well, I'm not really a henchman, Ash. I mean, he's my dad. I'm just here to pick up some clothes."

She inhales deeply and crosses her arms. This pushes her breasts together and lifts them up and half out of the top of her towel. She sees me look, but has very little reaction. She bites her lip, shifting her weight like a sullen teenager. "I can't believe it. He hasn't even had the decency to return my messages. Does he really not even want to see me? Where is he anyway?"

The truth here would send her screaming down the street barefoot in her towel. As much as I'd like Curtis to have to deal with that, Allie would be there to witness all of it. And so I lie. "He's back at our house."

"Well, isn't that sweet? One big, happy family."

She takes another drag of her cigarette, and, thankfully, cinches her towel a little tighter. I wonder how this is going to play out. She could chase me off like a rodent, of course. But there's also the chance that she'll behave like an adult and we'll get through this. After all, maybe she does like me. Last year she threw up behind my house at Curtis's birthday dinner. I told her it would be our little secret, which she seemed to appreciate. That's gotta be worth something, right?

"Take it easy, Tommy. I don't bite. I'll get you his stupid suitcase."

In a short, white robe now, Ashley is sitting in a small reading chair at the corner of the bedroom. Her crossed legs look like a marvel of nature as she watches me fold my dad's boxer shorts. I'm packing like a blind person, randomly pulling things from drawers and folding them. At Ashley's insistence, we're drinking glasses of very expensive-tasting bourbon.

People always drink bourbon with their robed stepmothers in the bedroom on Saturday afternoons, right? Why not? I might as well, considering there's a framed photograph of a naked Ashley over the dresser. She's stretched out in a hammock near a beach, looking directly at the camera through wisps of windswept hair.

"That picture never made it into the U.S. version of *GQ*," she says. "It's embarrassing how uptight Americans are about the female anatomy, isn't it?"

I take a look. One arm is draped across her stomach, the other back over her head. Her breasts, subtle and marvelous, are placed at the photo's optical center, impossible not to see. "I think it's very tasteful," I say.

"It's his favorite picture of me, you know, his dumb, naked little showpiece. He surprised me with it last year for Christmas. You believe that? The man bought me a naked picture of myself for Christmas. Like I need an oak frame to see my own tits."

If I had a week alone in a room with nothing to do but think, I doubt if I could come up with an appropriate response to this, and so I concentrate on a green pair of my dad's underwear as if it holds the secrets to the JFK assassination.

"You know what, now that I think about it, the old fucker really should have it."

Ashley leaps from the chair and pulls the photo down and then disappears from the room. I hear her rustling around my dad's office, making a noisy spectacle of herself. When she returns, she drops the photo on the bed and smiles. "I've left him a little message."

Not bothering to take the frame apart, Ashley has written directly on the glass with a black marker.

Good luck with the new book, asshole! Love Ashley.

"Nice. I think he'll like it."

I fill the rest of the suitcase in silence as Ashley finishes another cigarette and her glass of bourbon. I'm about to make my getaway when she tells me, as if her inscription wasn't clear enough, that my father is a fucking bastard. "I've never met a more selfish, more ridiculous man in my life. That's right, *ridiculous*. The *brilliant* American writer. Oh, give me a fucking break. And that *stupid* little car. All those adoring, talentless little wannabes he calls his students, constantly kissing his ass. You ever notice how none of his little protégés are ever men? He's a fucking cliché. And he can go to hell for all I care."

Is it odd that the only thing about all of that I found offensive was that she called the Porsche stupid?

"I bought into it at first, you know. Jesus, we all do. Who wouldn't? That's his little trick, Tom. He lures us in. We think we're marrying the guy on the back of all those books, you know, the man behind the words. But there's really nothing there. Just a desperate little boy who's so insecure he can hardly get out of bed in the morning without someone telling him how fucking talented and brilliant he is. Gag me."

Tears now are making her eyes shiny. The arc that is Ashley Martin's range of emotions swings from outright nastiness to vulnerability in nanoseconds, and I feel myself take two steps backwards. She's a complex bomb in a movie about terrorists, ticking steadily toward zero in a crowded train station full of children and nuns.

"Do you know what he told me once?" she asks. "He told me that I'm a silly person—that I'm not serious enough for him." She drops the empty tumbler onto the floor, which rolls under the bed. "How could he say that? Do you know how much money I've raised for AIDS? For Africa? For fucking Al Gore's fucking polar bears?"

"A lot?" I say.

"Yeah, a lot! A fucking ton! Still, he talks down to me because I haven't read every boring book ever published, like I'm just a stupid piece of ass for him to fuck and toss away when he's done."

"Well, Ashley, if it makes you feel better, he doesn't take me all that seriously, either. I don't think he takes anyone seriously."

She diffuses in front of me, her face falling from frightening sneers to calm, angular beauty again. This entire event would make a good scene in a trashy tell-all. Brandon would love it. I wouldn't even need to sensationalize it. I mean, seriously, she's almost naked.

"You know what makes it all worse?" she asks, conspiratorial now. "You look exactly like him."

"What?"

She pulls a copy of *The Stories of Curtis Violet* from an end table. "Look at him. He looks like you if you were pretending to be a college professor. I don't know if I wanna kill you or fuck you."

The oxygen streams steadily out the window like a quickly deflating balloon. "Well," I say. "How about . . . *neither*?"

She smiles, setting the book on the bed. "How'd that be for revenge? Fucking his son in his own bedroom? Would that be irony? Is that what Curtis would call it?"

I consider this—the literary question, not fucking my stepmother. "Actually . . . yeah. That would definitely be pretty ironic. Difficult to explain at Christmas, but ironic as hell. If this was a book or a movie, that'd be pretty good."

With just the slightest shift of an arm, a move that I only notice retroactively, the front of her robe opens, revealing a trail of skin from her clavicle down between her breasts and ending at a thin, flesh-colored line of underwear a few long inches below her olive-shaped navel. My bowels and the things within loosen, and I fear that my insides are pooling on the floor between my feet. "Ashley, this isn't a book . . . or a movie."

She touches my arm. The skin there, muscles and tendons and bones, takes notice. "Maybe it could be," she says. But there's no sex left in her voice, none of the hostile Ashley from before with all her curse words and bitterness. She's begun, quietly, to cry.

"I think I should get going now, OK?"

"Do you think I'm beautiful, Tom?"

This is such a shocking, stupid question that I actually laugh.

"You think I'm more beautiful than her, right?"

"Than who?"

But it's too late. She crumbles, sobbing, and because I have no idea what else to do, I hug her. Buried in my shoulder, her face feels damp and warm, childlike, my daughter after a spill on her bike and not a boozy terror in a bathrobe.

"I'm beautiful," she says.

"I know," I say, glancing at her photograph on the bed, so crisp and vivid that her skin looks palpable.

"And I'm interesting."

"OK," I say. "I know you are. I know."

"Then why doesn't he love me anymore?"


My hands are full when I get back to the car. I'm rolling my dad's suitcase and carrying Ashley's naked portrait, Curtis's green duffel bag, and my stolen copy of *The Bridge That Wasn't There*.

"Hi, Daddy!" yells Allie. She's moved to the front seat, and they're both eating ice cream cones and listening to the radio.

"Are you kidding? You people couldn't have even waited for me?"

Curtis pops the trunk and steps out of the car. "Well, you did take a long time. We're only human. Was she there?"

I really *should* punch him right here on the street, or perhaps break this frame over his head. "Fifty-fifty my ass."

"Oh jeez. How was she? Was she angry? Did she yell at you?"

I fling his suitcase into the car and hand him the R-rated portrait. "No, not at all. We had a lovely time. See, she sends her love."

He holds the picture out, examining it. "My little Ash. I'm going to miss her."

"Yeah, she's a delicate flower."

"Oh, don't be mad. Think of it as a life experience. Did you get my bag?"

I toss it loud and rattling into the trunk on top of his suitcase. "What's in there anyway?"

"Just some vitamins and things. Nothing important."

As traffic and pedestrians and dog walkers pass, we stand together, father and son, looking at Ashley Martin's beautiful naked body.

"Are we going now?" asks Allie. There's a ring of chocolate around her mouth. Hank seems restless, too, smiling at us through the windshield.

"She *did* write 'Love,'" my dad says. "I guess that's something, right?"

"I don't know, Dad. The tone seems sarcastic to me. But what do I know?"

"Perhaps," he says, setting the picture carefully in the trunk. "Now, an agreement is an agreement. I believe I owe you an ice cream, right?"

"Yeah."

"OK. Here's five dollars. Go pick one out for yourself. And would you mind getting me a bottled water, too? Mint chocolate chip always makes me thirsty."

## 18

*T*_*he next day,*_ Allie and I are on our own road trip—the dog, too—off to see another one of my dad's wives. My mother.

It's illegal to talk on cell phones while driving in D.C., but outside the city, I do so flagrantly. "I'm on my way there now, Pop," I say.

I can hear Gary pacing, wherever he is, probably the dealership. "What are you gonna say? Don't be too obvious about it. Try to be . . . you know . . . casual."

"She's my mother. Don't worry, I think I can handle her."

"Tell her that I miss her. And that I'm sorry."

"You don't even know what you're sorry for."

"Well, yeah, but that doesn't matter. At this point, I'll be sorry for whatever she wants me to be sorry for."

The contrast here is distinct. Twenty-four hours ago, my *real* father sent me blindly into the wild to help him escape my fake mother. Today, my fake father has sent me on a mission to retrieve my *real* mother. My family's delicate architecture is cracking, and for some reason its men are all counting on me. From my perspective, this seems, at best, unwise. "We'll get this figured out," I say. "OK?"

Gary wishes me luck and I set the phone on the seat next to Hank. In the back, Allie is reading *Jonah and the Whale*, a book my dad bought for her in New York. It might be a little advanced for her, but she's doing her best. She moves her lips when she reads, silently to herself, and love flutters through my chest, causing me to grip the steering wheel. There's a fully formed image in my head of Allie as an adult. She'll be one of those lanky, scatterbrained women you see reading paperbacks as they walk down the street, stumbling over curbs.

"Is Grandma mad at Grandpa Gary?" she asks.

"Not at all," I say. "She's just taking a little vacation from him, that's all, visiting with your aunt Bernice. Adults do that sometimes. Perfectly normal."

"Is that what Mommy's doing now? Taking a vacation from you?"

Well played, little girl. Well played.

"Baby, come on. Who'd ever wanna take a vacation from me? I *am* a vacation."

Allie used to think I was the funniest man alive. All I had to do was make a fart-y noise and she'd laugh for twenty minutes. Now I get little more than a polite grin. In just a few more years, she'll think I'm a total embarrassment.

"Well, Hank agrees with me, right, Hank?" The dog looks at me from the passenger seat, and then turns back to the window and the blurry Maryland suburbs. One ear is cocked, and I can see that he's wondering whether this is a good car trip or a bad one.

I'm wondering the same thing.

My aunt's neighborhood is a small, wooded hamlet outside Rockville, Maryland, with yards and garages and mailboxes, and it all seems so exotic and foreign. This is how most people live, right? In suburban neighborhoods like this across America. The realist and the urban snob in me are constantly at odds when it comes to the suburbs. One thinks they seem like paradise, the other is convinced they're a monochromatic, cultureless cesspool of fidgety boredom. Like most things, they're probably somewhere in the middle.

When I pull into Bernice's driveway, she happens to be standing there on the front lawn in jeans and a denim shirt, watering a patch of flowers, like a modern-day Willa Cather. She waves, but she does so suspiciously. "Hey, handsome," she says.

"Are you talking to me or the dog?" I ask.

"I've always been more of a cat person." She gives me a rough hug and I can feel her callused hands on my back through my sweater. Her hair is gray and scattered across her head, and she pushes it back with her hand. Hair to Bernice is something that gets in the way. My father has long suspected that she's a lesbian. However, in fairness, he suspects this of all women who don't like him.

"You look good," I say.

Allie sidles up to my leg, looking shyly up at my aunt.

"Well, hello there, little missy. That's a pretty bracelet you've got."

Allie tugs Katie's bracelet and quietly says thanks. She's turned shy in front of this big woman.

"So, I hear you've got a stowaway," I say.

"Prefer to think of her as a houseguest. One with an open invitation."

I smile, just to let her know that no woman in Birkenstocks is going to scare me. "I'm just here for a visit, B. No need to worry. I brought her a present actually, some reading material." I show her a rubber band–wrapped copy of my book. "I think you might like it, too. It's very antiestablishment."

Bernice doesn't laugh. She has always liked me, but her fear that I'll someday transform into my father is never very far below the surface. Standing in her driveway with a manuscript in my hands probably isn't helping. "Your mom's in the back. So, Allie. Let's talk about lemonade. What's your stance? Pro or con?"

Allie looks at me and then admits that she likes lemonade.

"Well good. Come with me and we'll see about making some. I have a special formula. But it's a secret, so no telling your daddy."

As Allie and Bernice head off to the house, both stop short when they see that ugly little Hank is crapping triumphantly in the middle of this perfectly manicured lawn.

"That's gross, Hank!" says Allie.

Bernice looks at me and shakes her head.

"Thatta boy, Hank. Good dog."


My mom and dad met at the University of Iowa Writers' Workshop. This mythical program in the middle of the middle of the country is to the American fiction writer what Harvard Business School is to people with real jobs. It also happens to be the place where I was conceived. I've never stepped foot into that sprawling square state, but I'm proud to say it's where a good bit of my brain and circulatory system were formed. At the program, my mother was a star among all the stars there. Her stories were regularly published in the *Iowa Review* and then on the national scene, finding their way into the *Paris Review*, the *New Yorker*—back when it published three stories an issue—and a few anthologies of young American writers. Conversely, my dad was one of those young men who exists in every arts program: an unnecessarily good-looking guy who tells everyone how talented he is but never seems to finish anything.

When they graduated, my mom was offered a teaching job in D.C. and her thesis, a slim collection of short stories that is no longer in print, was published to glowing reviews and very few sales. With me busily floating and growing inside her stomach, Curtis and Maryanne got married. My dad tagged along to D.C., eventually finding a job at the American University library, where he toiled away in the stacks fiddling with his first novel, and the midseventies continued.

When I was two, that book, which he eventually finished, launched one of the most decorated writing careers in modern American letters. My mom, aside from the occasional exquisitely crafted letter to the editor of the *Washington Post*, has not published a word since.

Shortly before my dad left her—I was about Allie's age—I overheard her talking to a friend on the phone. I was on the floor beneath the kitchen table rolling Matchbox cars across the linoleum when she said, "A family can only support one writer. It's as simple as that." I don't know who she was talking to, but I remember thinking, even then, that she was probably right.

Hank and I come around the side of Bernice's house, and I find my mom on her hands and knees in the back garden. She's in a pair of her sister's soiled overalls and work gloves, and I stop and watch her for a moment. Anna contends that she's a lonely woman, my mom, but to me, she looks like she's always looked, a little too thin and serious. She smiles when she sees Hank, who charges into the yard like his name's on the mortgage.

"Look, Hank, it's Mother Earth," I say.

There's a streak of dirt across her face, and she's working a little miniature shovel, tilling the ground. There's a mess of flowers in plastic bowls sitting in the grass. I know nothing about flowers, but I can always identify my namesake, violets. Somehow, they've remained among her favorite flowers, all purple and heart-shaped.

She's small in my arms when we hug, this little person in a bigger woman's clothes. Hank sniffs the flowers and she shoos him away with her foot.

"This is my penance for not returning your phone calls, driving all the way to Maryland."

"What happened to your face, dear?"

"Allie's kindergarten teacher and I got into a fistfight," I say. "You should see her. She's like a linebacker."

She studies the wounded side of my face and shakes her head.

"I like the choice of flowers," I say. "Would a violet by any other name be so . . . *purple*? Shakespeare wrote that. You can look it up if you'd like."

"They're prettier and more vivid in the wild, I suppose, but domestic violets are nice, too. The Greeks believed they symbolized fertility and potency, you know."

As I quietly let the irony of this knee me in the groin a few times, we settle into two of three wicker chairs. I set my manuscript on the third chair with a satisfying thump, imagining that I've written dozens of them, but the world, for some reason, has been waiting for this, my career-defining masterpiece.

"That's it, huh?" She flips through the first few pages, leaving little brown fingerprints under the title. "You know, you've never even told me what it's about."

"It's a period piece. A team of crime-fighting lesbians travel back in time to assassinate Hitler."

Like her sister before her, my mom's reaction is no reaction at all. She stopped finding me funny when I graduated from high school. "I'm sure it's about you," she says. "All first novels are autobiographical. In spirit, at least."

"I threw in some sex. And a car chase. And a rabid St. Bernard. And a vampire. I'm going for marketability *and* critical acclaim. And I would also like to buy a Lamborghini."

Hank is sitting in the grass between us, and I notice a book there at his paws. My mom is a remover of dust jackets, and so it takes some squinting to see that it's *The Stories of Curtis Violet.* "Doing some light reading?" I ask.

She worries some dirt beneath her fingernails. "His stories aren't even that good, you know," she says.

"A little sentimental maybe, but they have their moments."

"I'd forgotten about his problem with endings. They're too rushed and pretty, like he's writing for TV. His contribution is the novel. Novels can end pretty, but not stories. That's the rule." Decades of teaching high schoolers about reading and writing have left my mother very concerned with rules, and there's a territorial edge to her voice. Awarding Curtis the Pulitzer must be a slap in the face of my mother's lovely, long-forgotten little collection.

"Sonya says they gave him the Pulitzer as like a lifetime achievement thing."

"Literary awards are completely arbitrary, Thomas. They always have been. I think the only reason Nicholas Zuckerman didn't win this year is because all of those awards committees are tired of giving him awards. You can be penalized for being brilliant sometimes. Curtis was a nice, popular choice."

"Well, according to him, it's long overdue."

She laughs, finally, looking into the middle distance of Bernice's yard. "He's always been his own most dedicated fan."

There's no point in telling her that he's crashing at my house. Another symptom of Child-of-Divorce Syndrome is the rationing of information. In truth, the fact that I have any relationship with Curtis at all has always made me feel like shit when I'm around my mother. I could've disavowed him when I was a little kid and never spoken to him again. A better son probably would have. Instead, I allowed Curtis to continue being my dad. This is perhaps my greatest sin against my mother.

"I hear you two have been chatting," I say, venturing. "That's certainly a development."

She scratches Hank's ears, buying herself a few seconds. "So, I suppose Gary sent you. I should have guessed that."

For the second time this weekend, I've been accused of being sent in the name of a father's bidding. "Let's avoid melodrama, Mom. He didn't *send* me, and I'm not a hit man. He's worried. He doesn't know what's going on."

"Ha," she says. "Of course he doesn't know what's going on. He's been calling here two or three times a day and leaving messages with Bernice. 'What'd I do, Maryanne? What'd I do?' It's very tiring having to explain things to him all of the time. He thinks people are like his cars—like they can just be fixed and everything will be fine."

"Is that really so wrong? Wanting to find out why you're un-happy and make it better? Would you prefer he didn't care at all? You of all people should understand that maybe that's not the best quality in a husband."

She looks at me, a little annoyed. "This isn't about him caring or not caring. Don't be intentionally dense. You try to pretend some-times that you're more like Gary than you actually are. You're a Violet, and so you know that things are always more complicated than that."

My mother has gone back to her post in the lawn again, digging away at the ground, a plastic container of little violets at her side. She rarely lets me off the hook, holding me to a different standard of emotional intelligence than the other men in her life—even my brothers. She allows them to behave like Gary, docilely going about their lives, content and happy and completely oblivious to the sticky, ugly things just a few inches below the surface of ev-erything.

"You ever wonder if it's really *not* more complicated than that?" I ask. "That maybe everyone else is right, and people like you and me just need to quit looking for stuff to be depressed about?"

She looks up, and then back at her dirt, dismissing this stu-pidity without comment. When I was little, I read books because I thought that's what people were supposed to do, because that's what my mom did and what my dad did. While I stumbled and squinted my way through math and science and everything else useful in the world, I was always confident in words and stories and the things lurking in the brains of the characters who wandered in and out of my life. Sometimes I wish I'd been born to normal people—people to whom a book was just a book and people could be fixed like Fords.

"So, how are things?" she asks. "I'll pretend you haven't been avoiding me and just assume that you're busy."

"They offered me a promotion at work. Vice president of . . .

I don't really know . . . something mildly important." This must sound as silly to my mother as it did to Katie, because she just laughs. It's very telling when your own mother finds the prospect of you in charge of something to be a joke.

"We're getting off track here," I say. "We're talking about Gary. He's a mess. I don't think he even knows how to use the appliances. It's probably dangerous to have him in your house by himself."

"Helplessness isn't necessarily an attractive quality in a husband, either," she says.

Across the yard, Hank makes a halfhearted run at a few squirrels. They scramble up their tree and glare down at him, barking in that weird squirrel way. I pick my dad's book up from the grass and run my finger over the raised "CV" on the spine. Every sentence and passage I see is familiar. In "Macy's," I read my dad's brief description of the fictional version of me. I'm frightened of the escalator and of being alone for the very first time. I'm about to put it away, to toss it back in the grass and continue watching my mother hide out here with her plants, but then I notice the title page. *See, Maryanne*, Curtis has written. *I told you it would happen.*

"Did he send you this?" I ask. "Did you . . . *see* him?"

She shakes her head. "He actually left it on our porch one night a few weeks ago. I saw him from the bedroom. I think he was drunk."

"What does it mean? 'I told you it would happen'?"

"When my book came out, when we first got married, he took me out to this little restaurant in D.C. to celebrate, down on East Capitol Street. You were actually there, too. We couldn't afford a babysitter back then. He told me how proud he was of me, but he said I'd have to work hard to keep up because he was going to win the Pulitzer someday. I told him he was being an ass."

There are very few memories for me of them together. This would have been a nice one to have. "Wow, so he was intolerable even *before* he was famous?"

She sits back down next to me again, leaving her little shovel in the grass. I'm sure there's a name for it, and it's not just referred to in the gardening world as a "little shovel." There are tears in her eyes even though she's smiling, and I get that panicky rush of feeling that men get when their mothers are about to cry. "We've talked on the phone—just two or three times—not that much. He actually told me he was sorry, for everything, and that he wishes things had gone differently. It took him more than three decades to say that, and all it did was piss me off. All these years, I've been watching him from afar, making mistake after mistake with those stupid, silly girls. His life could have been so much better. He would have been happier if he'd never left."

"But you wouldn't have. You know that, Mom. He *left* us, but Gary never did. Gary has been there the entire time."

Her face looks raw, and I wonder how long she's been out here in the yard. "Curtis left *me*, Tom. But he never left you. I think you're the only thing he actually likes about himself. I imagine that's why he's staying with you. He just wants to be with you guys for a while."

"So, you know about that, huh? I wasn't sure if . . ."

But she nods, forgiving me.

"Why are you talking again *now*? He wins a Pulitzer and suddenly that changes the last thirty years? It's just a gold stamp on a book, Mom. It has nothing to do with you, or with me, or with Gary. You're better off now. As long as I've been alive, I've watched everyone give him get-out-of-jail-free cards. He doesn't deserve it—not from you."

She pats my title page and smiles. "Who's being melodramatic now? If you really thought the Pulitzer was just a gold stamp on a book, you wouldn't have spent five years writing this when you could have been doing anything else in the world."

When she's right about something, my mother knows it, and she enjoys it quietly. Through the sliding glass door into Bernice's kitchen, I see Allie. She's holding a glass of lemonade and waving at me.

"I've been thinking about your father a lot lately, and I've realized something. I married Gary specifically for the fact that he *wasn't* Curtis. If your father has an opposite, it's Gary. I just need to decide if I want to spend the rest of my life with someone I married by default."

I miss Gary now, the constant underdog. I wish he were here to tease my mother about reading so much and ask me about the oil in my Honda.

"So, what's your book about? Really?"

"It's about a teenage boy who finds out he's adopted. He thinks that his real dad is this famous actor, so he steals his adopted dad's car and runs away to Hollywood to find him."

"He's idealized the image of his father, then?" she says, frowning at my pages. I imagine her standing at a blackboard staring out at a bunch of sleepy-eyed teenagers.

I tell her maybe, but then her face changes when she sees what should be my name on the title page. "Who in the world is Thomas Ferris?" she asks.

"That's me. It's my pen name."

"Pen name? Why? And where did you get Ferris?"

I consider lying, or coming up with some interesting, intellectual response. But I've got nothing. "*Ferris Bueller's Day Off* was on TBS a few months ago. I liked the sound of it."

"Well, that's certainly literary."

"I thought he was totally kick-ass when I was fifteen."

Dear HR:

My son, Tom Violet, is an idiot. It's as simple as that.

"What's wrong with Thomas Violet?" she says. "I like that name."

The answer seems so obvious, like one of those lines you cut out of an early draft because you don't want to hit the reader over the head with it. "Come on, Mom. A family can only support one writer, right?"

Sadly, this pitch-perfect piece of circular storytelling is wasted. My mom hasn't even heard me. She's too busy reading, and I'm left to stare at a dozen unplanted violets moving gently in the breeze.

## 19

*M*onday mornings are usually tiring, never-ending affairs of infinite sadness, like watching *The English Patient*. But on this Monday, I'm energized with a sense of purpose. Because I am a professional copywriter, allow me to draw up my agenda using bullet points. This morning I plan to:

- Tell a frightening multimillionaire from the UK to shove it.
- Inform my boss that he is about to lose his job.
- Apologize to Katie for my behavior at Johnny Rockets.

This third bullet is the one I'm really dreading, mainly because I have no idea how I'm going to do it. On the surface, I've done nothing wrong at all. I've had a friendly, short exchange with a coworker in a restaurant and introduced her to my family. However, as my mother reminded me yesterday, I'm a Violet, and so the surface means nothing.

I've arrived at the ungodly hour of 8:10 a.m. I didn't even know the building was open this early, and Cubeland is a lonely ghost town. Upstairs though, en route to Buckingham Palace, worried executives are hard at work, doing whatever it is that executives do. There's hand-wringing, and a few overextended souls are pacing about their offices while MSNBC blares in the background.

"I'm here to see Ian," I tell Lauren. Even though it's hardly dawn, she looks foxy today.

"Oh, are you?" she asks.

"Indeed I am, Lauren. We've got some pretty important business to discuss. It's all very complicated."

"Hold on, Mr. Trump. I'll give him a buzz." A moment later, she seems surprised to find that her boss—*the* boss—is available to see me. "Well, apparently you're as important as you're pretending to be."

"I tell you what. When I make my first billion, you and I'll sneak off to the Caribbean somewhere. Say good-bye to the corporate thing forever. How does that sound?"

"I'll look forward to that," she says, boredly waving me toward Ian's closed door. When my hand hits the knob, all of my posturing crumbles and I am 100 percent uncertain. This could turn out to be a profoundly stupid move. Jesus, the least I could have done was wear a tie. What's the matter with me?

He's sitting at his desk, his suit coat folded neatly on a chair, his own tie slack on his neck. This is how the titans look before securing their armor for the day. "Hello, mate," he says. "Just the man I wanted to see. What've you got there?"

I sit down and slide the British edition of *The Bridge That Wasn't There* across his desk. "Just a little something."

His eyes grow wide when he sees the title page. On the way home from my encounter with Ashley this weekend, I had my dad sign it and write, *To Ian, All the Best in the World of Business.*

"I ran into my dad this weekend. He owed me a favor."

"Well then, this is quite lovely, mate. Cheers." He flips the book over and looks at the picture of my dad, and I can see that I've made him happy. I've regressed, back to pleasing authority again like a kid, and this sudden levity only brings more uncertainty. My wife, up north with her librarians now, is almost certainly right. I am not Curtis Violet, and Brandon will probably call me this week and advise me to look into a career in accounting because my book is a festering turd, not even worth the MSW-stolen paper on which it's printed.

"This is a gift of celebration then, I presume?" he says. "If it weren't before 9 a.m. I'd suggest a toast."

"Well," I say, because this is often how people start sentences. I change my mind, and then I change it back again. And then I look at Ian's desk. Scattered there, from side to side, are trade magazines, folders with complicated names, spreadsheets, and piles of papers with numbers and figures on them. For most of my adult life, I've had no idea where I belong, and maybe I'll never know. But I do know one thing. I sure as hell don't belong in this place. "Think of it as a gift of appreciation. I appreciate the offer, honestly, but . . ."

Ian Barksdale's smile fades into an expression I'm more accustomed to: the executive perma-frown.

"The thing is, I don't think I'm the man for the job."

"Tom, if this is about Doug, I appreciate your loyalty, really, however—"

"No," I say. "That's not it actually. I wish that it was, because then at least this would somehow be noble. But, I just don't think I can do it. I want to be a writer. Actually, I *am* a writer—I just want to start being a *real* one."

Ian leans back in his chair, eyeing me carefully. He seems about to perform an Executive Mind Trick. "A writer?"

"Yes," I say. And then I say it again, trying to make it sound like something I'm not apologizing for.

He nods at my dad's book. "A writer like this?"

"Well, more or less. Most likely less."

A long breath, and then a glance out the window. "When I was at university, I wanted to teach English," he says. "It was my dream job."

"Really? Wow."

"Turns out English teachers are poor, and I actually don't like most children. They're really quite dull."

"Oh."

"You're aware of the financial opportunity that you're about to pass up, correct? The bonus structure and the improved benefits and all of those details?" His accent makes this sound very grave, but the die is cast, and we both know it. He pushes my dad's book to the middle of his desk and tightens his tie into a perfect Windsor knot below his Adam's apple. His interest in me is waning by the second.

"Yes," I say. "I am."

"Very well then. Now, if you'll excuse me."


As I head back toward my department, away from the executives, I realize that my hands are shaking. I'm exhilarated and a little sick to my stomach. I'm a writer, and I've admitted it to this powerful stranger. Forget the other shit—the drinking and bad husbanding and wildly prolific philandering—*this* is what Curtis Violet would do.

But there's no time for self-congratulations. I need to talk to Doug right away and let him know what's going on. By now, he should be in his office with his papers piled neatly beside his Washington Redskins coffee mug. I'll tell him what's about to happen. We'll shake hands, and he'll be grateful for the heads-up.

Breezing through Cubeland, I notice that Katie hasn't arrived yet. She's my third bullet of the day, though, and so I press on, sticking to my schedule. As I turn the corner toward Doug's office, though, I see that for the first time in as long as I can remember, his door is closed. On a normal day, this would be meaningless, but today, somehow, I know that it's not good. Through his door window, I peek in, and I see just enough to know that I shouldn't

have waited until today. I should have looked him up on the in-
tranet site or Googled him and tracked him down at home, or at
least sent him a goddamn e-mail. But I didn't, and now, with a
stunned, wounded look on his face, he's trapped behind his desk
staring at Janice Stringer, the head of HR, and one of her pasty-
faced lawyers.

Our eyes meet briefly through the streaked glass. "No," I whisper.

With the world's slightest nod, he tells me yes.

Before I can escape into my own office, Greg stops me. He's
holding a perfectly toasted bagel that smells of fish and an obnoxious cup from Starbucks. "Doesn't look good for Doug in there,
huh? Strange, I thought they only fired people on Fridays. Maybe
that's a myth."

"Go fuck yourself, Greg," I say—and I'm not smiling.

When I slam the door to my office, it feels so good that I nearly
reopen it so I can slam it again. At my desk, I sit and stare, contemplating some harsh realities. After my stunt up at Buckingham
Palace a few minutes ago, the only person in the building with any
authority or clout who doesn't actively dislike me is currently getting fired across the hall. The tsunami is coming—there's no way
that it isn't—and I'm a lonely little boat adrift at sea.

My computer beeps, telling me that I have a new e-mail. It's
from Katie, and the subject line reads, simply, "Sick."

She's not feeling well, and so she's taking a sick day, but that's
not true at all. She's staying home because she hates me. Because
on Friday afternoon I was her hero—at least kind of, in an asinine
way. And then on Friday evening I was a married father in a restaurant who didn't even want to talk to her. And now she's not going
to be here today. And Doug just got fired. And I just turned down
a promotion. And it's not even 8:45.

I fucking hate Mondays.

## 20

*he next night,* I'm in my bedroom leafing through my novel. This is not helping my shitty mood. As instructed, Anna hasn't called yet. She sent me an e-mail shortly after getting to Boston, just to let me know that she'd arrived safely, but there's been no talk of the book, and now I can see why. She tried to read it, but she had to put it down, stunned that she'd married a man who is so bad at writing books. On almost every page, there's something egregious to change. There are typos, clichés, errors in logic, rambling sentences, and narration where there should be dialogue. This is why Brandon hasn't called yet . . . and neither has my mom. Even my own mother wants nothing to do with it. I should flush it down the toilet, or set it on fire, or maybe both, just for drama's sake.

Today at work, I would have discussed this with Katie and asked her point-blank if she was just humoring me before when she claimed to love it, but I couldn't. She called in sick again. Two unscheduled days away from Katie have made me realize that I miss her. A lot.

I read a sentence aloud—a random sentence from a random page in a random chapter—and think instantly of ten things that are wrong with it. Perhaps tomorrow I'll go to Ian again and throw myself at the mercy of his British accent. Hank is at the foot of the bed watching me, his ears bent at weird angles as he tries to read my mind.

When I get up, the house is absolutely silent, and it dawns on me that I should check on Allie. My dad is out, doing whatever it is that he does when he's not here, and I've been held up in my room for a while now. She's so freaking quiet, my daughter, that sometimes I have to remind myself when I'm the only one in charge of her well-being. This is something that a wonderful father probably wouldn't have to admit to, even in his inner monologue.

"Allie!"

She's not in her room, and so I call her name again. There's no response from anywhere. The dog nearly trips me as I head down the stairs, which is something he does so often that I'm convinced he thinks of it as a sport. The silence downstairs is even more absolute than upstairs. It's the type of silence that I imagine would occur after a tragedy of some sort. "Allie!" I call again, this time louder, thinking about all of the things that can happen to child who's been neglected by her father for hours on end. "Allie!"

When I do find her, of course, she's fine, lying on the floor, coloring a picture and listening to Anna's old iPod Shuffle. "Hi, Daddy!" she yells over the music in her head.

"Jesus, baby, you scared me."

I sit on the floor next to her and she pulls her ear buds out. "Why?"

"You're very quiet, that's why. Daddies need noise. Try to knock over a vase or something next time. Kick a hole in the wall, maybe."

"OK," she says, "I will."

I give one of her bare feet a squeeze. They're like exact, scaled-down replicas of Anna's feet, with high arches and the fourth toes just slightly longer than the third toes, all asymmetrical and human. She's drawing M-shaped birds in the sky above a drawing that contains herself, me, Anna, and some little smiling boy.

Allie is taller than the boy, and so I assume she's imagining a little brother, perhaps, in blue pants. For some reason, she's given me blond hair.

"You know, baby," I say. "My hair is actually brown."

"I know, Daddy. Duh."

"Well, why did you make my hair yellow then? Do you want me to go blond?"

She laughs, because, of course, I'm an idiot. "No. I know how to draw your hair. But that's not you."

"Well, forgive me. Who is it then?"

"It's David."

"David who?"

"David, Mommy's friend. See, this is David, and this is Mommy. And this is David's son Conner, and this is me."

The air is a little harder to move in and out of my lungs suddenly, heavier somehow. "Allie, how does Mom know David?"

"They're friends. He's very nice and very funny. He has blond hair, see. He works at a bank, and sometimes he goes to Body Pump with Mommy, and me and Conner play together in the play room at the gym."

I lie back on my elbows and think of his name—David— wondering if she's mentioned him before. But, of course, she hasn't.

"What's wrong, Daddy?"

"Nothing. Nothing's wrong, sweetie."

"Don't you like my picture?"

"Yeah. It's a good one."

"Do you think it's fridge-worthy?"

"Maybe," I say. "I'll have to think about it."

My mind has a way of beginning with the worst case and working backwards from there. When the phone rings past ten, someone is dead. When the stock market crashes, it can never uncrash. And when your daughter says a man's name you don't know, then something is wrong.

"I'm getting better at drawing people, I think. I'm probably going to be an artist when I grow up."

In the kitchen, there's this little desk by the phone where we keep mail and bills. When she's gone, Anna leaves all sorts of information there in case of an emergency, like hotel names and phone numbers. But not this time. Our phone bill. A cousin's wedding announcement. A reminder from the vet that Hank is due some kind of shot. But that's it. Anna's gym bag is in its usual spot, and before I even realize what I'm doing, I've set it on the kitchen table.

"What are you doing, Daddy? That's Mommy's bag."

I don't know what I'm expecting to find in here, but I've never been suspicious of my wife before and it feels like mounting desperation. Her running shoes are gone, but there's her damp gym towel. There's a dented water bottle. A copy of *Women's Health* magazine, an Under Armour sports bra that smells like Anna, and a stick of deodorant. And there's a book. A thin, hardcover little thing. *How Children Read: Essays from Kids on Their Favorite Books.* To some people, this would mean nothing, a strange little book in a bag. But Anna and I are book people, and I know what she's reading and she knows what I'm reading at all times. Somewhere toward the middle, there's a business card.

DAVID ANDERSON
*Senior Branch Manager*
BANK OF AMERICA

Allie has replaced my dad and his Porsche with her new picture— Allie, Anna, David, and Conner. She's bypassed me and deemed it worthy of the fridge. "Look, Dad. We have to keep it up for a while so Mommy can see it when she gets home."

On the back of the card, there's a note.

*Thought you might like this.* —D

"I think it's my best picture yet."

I can see that he's written something else—something smaller, like a secret, but for a moment I keep it out of focus, like the last line in a book as you read your way down the final page. "Looks great, baby," I say.

*P.S. I can't stop thinking about you.*

*Part III*

## 21

**D**r. *Charlie and* I are at the driving range next to Reagan National Airport just across the Potomac River in Virginia, and my lunch hour has turned into a lunch two-hour. I wanted to talk to someone, but didn't want to look like I wanted to talk to someone. And so here we are, two guys hitting golf balls on a chilly fall afternoon into a fading green field as jets roar over our heads every few minutes.

The rest of the world is at work, apparently, aside from two old ladies in matching visors over on the putting green.

"Maybe you should aim that way," I say, pointing at the landing strip.

"Maybe you should shut your mouth," he says.

I'm not a good golfer by any means, but Charlie is the next level of shitty. He tries hard, and amateurs like me are always telling him what he's doing wrong, but still his balls leave the tee and about one hundred yards later make an impossible right turn toward forests, clubhouses, and windshields.

"Aren't doctors supposed to be good at golf? How do they even let you practice medicine?"

"That was back in the old days," he says. He takes another swing and we both watch the ball's mysterious trajectory. "Now, with all the malpractice insurance we're paying, we can't really even afford to golf."

I miss-hit my own shot and it skitters across the grass, barely getting off the ground.

"You know," he says. "I seriously think you might be making too much of all this."

I've told him about Allie's drawing, the business card, and the bruise on my face, which is now faded to a mere smudge. He listened like a doctor, nodding, his face a blank slate of objectivity.

"Really?" I say. "OK, then tell me this. Have you ever bought a present for a woman outside your family on a non-holiday or birthday whom you didn't want to have sex with?"

"Certainly a valid point. However, you, dipshit, are failing to recognize something very important. *You* may not want to have sex with your good-looking wife lately, but other guys do. Those are the facts. But the good news is, just because a guy *wants* to have sex with a woman doesn't mean he gets to. Remember college? It's God's way of ensuring that we all show up for work in the morning."

I drag a few balls over with my three-iron.

"Hell, think of it as a compliment," he continues. "As the old saying goes, the only thing worse than having a wife who lots of guys want to fuck is having a wife who no guys want to fuck."

"That's classy," I say. "You need to stand closer to the ball. You're reaching too much."

"Have you tried calling her, you know, like an actual adult, and asking her about it?"

"No. She's supposed to call me. I told her not to until she'd read my book. Crazy me, I thought maybe she'd want to read it."

He looks at me like I'm an idiot. "Junior high rules don't apply when you're married, especially when your daughter starts drawing portraits of strange blond dudes you don't know."

Another range ball vanishes into the parking lot. We listen for the crash and the car alarm, but there's nothing, so we continue.

"What really bothers me is that she's never told me about him at all. Not a word."

"Yeah. And I suppose you went home every night after work and chatted her up about your little junior copywriter obsession, right?"

One of the annoying things about friendship is that there are these people in your life who can call you on your bullshit at any given moment. I skull a few more balls before switching to my equally ineffective seven-iron. The old ladies are working on their chipping now, and Charlie seems contemplative, looking at his tattered golf glove. It looks like it's recently been chewed by raccoons. "Do you think I'm breaking my wrist too much?"

"I don't know. Probably. Your stance is pretty fucked up, too."

He looks at his shoes.

"I feel like I could write the whole goddamn scene," I say. "This guy, David Anderson, sees her on the treadmills and so he starts timing his workout so maybe he can get the treadmill next to hers. Then he strikes up some conversation about bullshit, her running shoes or something, and then before you know it they're in the parking garage getting it on in his Land Rover."

"That'd be quite a scene. But I don't buy it. This is Anna we're talking about, remember? She's one of the good ones. What's wrong with my stance? This is how you're supposed to stand, right? This is how they say to stand in *Golf Digest*."

A plane lands with a loud roar, and we watch it because it's impossible not to watch a plane landing. "Your feet are too close together. You're all arm. You should've seen that book, man. Kids writing essays about how great reading is. It was like something out of a John Cusack movie. He'll probably show up at my house next week in the rain holding a fucking ghetto blaster over his head."

"I bet he looks like a total goon. Some harmless dork with a crush. Lives in his mother's basement, masturbates constantly, sells *Lord of the Rings* action figures on eBay."

A few hundred yards away, an old man drives a ball-retrieving machine back and forth along the field. It looks like a giant lawn mower with a Plexiglas cover, and so it might as well have a bull's-eye painted on it. We both try to hit it for ten minutes or so, neither of us coming even close. I want to ask Charlie about his affair, but I don't. We haven't talked about it in two years, and I've made an agreement with myself never to bring it up unless he does first. Four years ago, when he was finishing his residency, he and another doctor had an ugly, destructive fling that ended with the girl's husband punching Charlie's front teeth out. He did this on Charlie's front porch in front of Charlie's wife and one of their kids. Charlie lived in a dreadful apartment in Crystal City for a while, and she hired a lawyer. But they eventually made it through, somehow, and now they live together like survivors of some awful tragedy, quietly going about the business of forgetting, smiling, and raising their children.

"Can I ask you something?" he says. His metal basket of balls is tipped over now and nearly empty. "Do you ever think maybe the reason you're suddenly so convinced your wife is fucking around is that you actually want her to be fucking around?"

"What are you talking about?"

"Come on. All this erectile dysfunction shit? This mystery guy, David What'shisface? Your little high school crush? It's like you want out or something, but you're too afraid to be like your dad and just leave, so you're trolling around looking for things to do it for you."

When I don't say anything, Charlie addresses his ball, takes a smooth, slow swing, and hits his first straight shot of the day, a long, soaring monster of a drive that bounces hard past the 250-yard sign. Obviously, he wants to celebrate, but that would somehow weaken his point, and so he just stands there, looking out across the field.

"Nice shot, dick head," I say.

"I don't think I've ever hit one that far."

"Your feet are still too close together. And you should really rethink that shirt."

Back at our cars, as we hoist our clubs into our trunks, my BlackBerry rings. I check my watch and count backwards to see how long I've been away from the office. I don't really have a boss right now, and so it doesn't matter one way or the other. I check the caller ID and do my best to smile.

"Tom Violet," I say.

"So, are you planning on coming into the office today or what? I was just wondering."

"Hi, Greg," I say. "It's 2:15, shouldn't you be crushing the souls of the innocent and blacking out the sun?"

"You're in another important meeting, I assume, right?"

"It's called lunch, Greg. I eat it almost every day. It gives me the energy I need to be so witty and good-looking."

"Well, I thought you might like to know, Ian has called a meeting for the whole department at three. Just in case you were interested in dropping by."

"Are you serious?" I ask, and then curse myself for this unforgivable show of weakness. "What's it about?"

"Why would I even bother telling you? You're just going to pretend you don't care."

"Ahhh, Greg. I'm touched. After all this time, you finally get me."

"Funny as always, Tom. You're a real riot. Just be here, OK? It would look bad if you weren't. You should at least pretend to be part of the team."

"Good talk, Greg, but you're not my boss. I know you're not, because if you were I'd have already gone ahead and had my friend here back over my head with his car."

I hang up the phone and ask Charlie to rate my exit line on a scale of one to ten.

"Who in the hell was that?" he asks. He's sitting in his doctorly Acura SUV now, looking at me through his open window.

"My nemesis. Do you know any trained assassins?"

"Try Craigslist," he says.

Before my friend drives away, he honks twice, and, for good measure, throws a Wendy's soda cup at me, spraying ice across the pavement and all over my shoes. Hopefully he's looking in his rear-view mirror. If so, he'll see that I'm giving him the finger.

## 22

*A* *side from Ian* himself—and whichever of his underling lackeys shows up—I'm the last person from the department in the conference room. It's not big enough to hold the whole group comfortably, and so many of my colleagues are left to lean on the walls or stand while the early birds enjoy their spots around the big wooden conference table.

"Nice of you to join us, Tom," says Greg.

Despite the fact that there are a number of women without seats, Greg has planted himself in a chair at the head of the table. A quick burst of hatred seizes my face, but I manage to wrangle it into a smile. "Wow, Greg, the Brooks Brothers tie today, huh? It must be a special occasion."

He clenches his jaw, but chooses to despise me silently.

Dear HR:

Tom Violet insists on making fun of my ties, despite the fact that it clearly states in the employee handbook in Section 3B that all male employees should wear ties Monday through Thursday unless otherwise announced. It's essential to create a constant environment of professionalism. One never knows when an important client will be on-site. Tom undermines this every day, and I believe he does so quite intentionally.

Like any department, ours is full of cliques, and each of them is represented here. The IT and database people are huddled together. They think the rest of us are idiots and we think they're socially retarded dweebs, but we tend to live in harmony. There are the Gregory People, of course. They dress more formally than necessary and sit in a constant state of alert, waiting for an opportunity to use a word like "leverage" or "facilitate." And then there are the people like me. I'll call them Tom People. They don't really care about any of this, and some of the younger ones, the graphic artists in particular, look hungover. It's the first time we've all been together since Doug got the ax, and, for the moment, everyone seems united against one common enemy: anxiety of the unknown. There is one person in the world with the power to fire us all at once, and that person called this meeting.

I sidle in next to Katie, who's standing in the corner. I haven't seen her since Johnny Rockets, and she's the loveliest thing in the room times ten. I smile and she smiles, but it's strained.

"Are you feeling better?" I ask.

"Yeah," she says. "The flu, I think."

I begin to apologize, but I can see from her look that she doesn't want me to. Especially not here. "What do you think this is about?" she asks.

"I heard we were here to pick the company softball team," I say.

A few people in the room laugh. This seems to be my gift, making a handful of bored, nervous people laugh in a quiet room.

"I hear they're shipping all our jobs to London," says Denise, a tiny woman in a plaid skirt who is a liaison between Sales and Marketing. "All of them."

"Where did you hear that?" I ask.

Denise shrugs, apparently unwilling to reveal her sources.

Alan, one of the dreadful Gregory People, is swiveling in his chair, nervous. He's wearing a Dartmouth pin on his lapel even though he's in his forties. "With the exchange rate the way it is, that's probably what's happening. There's a big movement over to the UK right now. I read about it."

Nerves, in the form of murmuring, flare up around the room. Not since the 1700s have this many Americans been so terrified of the British.

"Nah," I say. "He's probably just checking in to see how we're all doing."

Everyone looks at me, unconvinced. I don't blame them.

"I'm sure it's something a little more substantive than that, Tom," says Greg. "I doubt if a man as busy as Ian would just . . . *check in.*"

"Good point, Greg," I say. "Are you comfortable in that chair? Can I get you a soda or a foot massage or anything?"

"I'm quite all right, thank you."

Usually in meetings, our coworkers watch us with morbid curiosity, wondering how long it'll take me to make Greg blow up and turn all red. But today we're a mere distraction, and everyone goes back to muttering doomsday scenarios among themselves. A woman named Gail asks if companies are legally required to pay severance. None of us knows, but the consensus is that they're not.

"How are you?" I whisper touching Katie's elbow.

She bites her lip. "Nervous is how I am. Half the country's getting laid off right now. I need this job or I'm screwed."

It takes physical effort not to place my hand on her lower back and tell her that I'm sorry. I may not have the words to articulate exactly what I'm sorry for, but I *am* sorry. I'm like my stepdad, no cards to play other than contrition. "You'll be fine," I say. "Trust me. This isn't going to be anything big."

She takes a sip of her Diet Dr Pepper. "Have you heard from that agent yet about your book?"

Before I can tell her no, the door swings open and our collective breath is held as Janice Stringer and Ian Barksdale glide into the room. Janice is in a gray, shapeless thing, but Ian looks like he's just stepped off the James Bond sound studio, sliding his BlackBerry into the pocket of his pin-striped suit. " 'Ello, thank you all for coming."

We make the briefest bit of eye contact, but there's no expression there, not even an acknowledgment that we know each other. Greg springs to his feet, freeing his chair for Ian, and this whole thing really should be on a television show about how awful offices are.

"I wanted to have a chat with you all today about the future of this marketing organization. I know your team's future has likely been top of mind as of late. So, to start, I want to ask you all a simple question. And I want each of you to take it very seriously. What is the definition of insanity?"

Oh brother.

Silent panic flares up among the Gregory People. They don't know if they're supposed to answer this or just sit there blinking. To spite them, I consider blurting out the answer, but I've probably done enough damage to my career this month already.

"Insanity is, quite simply, continuing to do the same thing over and over and expecting a different result. For some time now, MSW's marketing organization has been behaving insanely. You have done the same things, put out the same materials, reached out to the same market verticals, and set the same goals for yourselves. All whilst expecting continued success. In light of current economic events, I have decided that the old way of doing things is no longer viable, and I'm here today to infuse some *sanity* into this team.

"Doug Miller is a good man, and he served this company well. But I'm quite certain he was ill-equipped to take you all to the next level. You can go further, *all* of you."

This last sentence, with its "you" and "all," seems to reverberate, and all at once that collective breath is released. To varying degrees, everyone is relieved—some bordering on downright giddiness—that our shitty jobs in this shitty company are safe.

"Today is the beginning of new things for your team. New messages. New audiences. New media. New promotions. New products and ideas and responsibilities and opportunities for success. As I see it, the possibilities are endless for this department. Together, you're going to take some risks, you're going to think outside the box, and you're going to unlock your personal and collective potential."

He sounds like he's running for something, and around the room, people are watching this British millionaire with wide, thankful eyes. But one person isn't: Greg. Instead, he's watching me and he's smiling. This is creepy, but I play it off, winking at him like I'm Cool Hand Luke. But, the truth is, I know enough about the world to know that Greg's happiness can mean only my *un*happiness. Set against the Imperial Death March, realization arrives in a slow, sinking weight at the back of my neck.

"I thought long and hard about who I would task with taking charge of this newly empowered group. I looked through the ranks overseas and at our sister companies, and even among our competitors. However, at the end of the day, I settled on one person, realizing him to be the ideal, most qualified candidate. And that person is sitting in this very room."

The fact that I haven't predicted this is shameful, and it shines the light on my own crippling stupidity. I've feared the Brits and the unknown. And I've agonized over my own identity and my crumbling marriage and my stupid novel and this girl standing at my side and my father's meddling in my mother's life. I've let all of this block out the most obvious thing in the world, and now I'm truly fucked.

"So, without further ado, it gives me immense pleasure to announce the new vice president of marketing, and the newest member of my management team, Gregory Steinberg."

The Gregory People erupt in spontaneous applause and good-will. The others just look at each other and shrug.

"I don't believe it," says Katie, not even bothering to whisper.

But I do. This really couldn't have gone any other way. And that's why it takes me a while to even realize that I'm laughing. It's a dark and unhappy laugh, a man laughing who's just come home from the grocery store to find that a wrecking ball has taken out the front of his house by mistake while he was gone.

Watching everyone react, enjoying it, Greg smiles and then shakes Ian's hand. When our eyes meet again, mine and Greg's, I know that he's hoping for some sign of defeat—a clenched fist, tears, me punching an intern and storming out of the room. Instead though, I just keep laughing. "Congratulations, Greg," I say. "You've earned it."

On the way out of the room, I pass Ian. He's switched from Rallier of the Common People back to executive again, tapping away at his stupid BlackBerry. I wonder how long it'd take me to run up to Buckingham Palace, dodge Lauren, and steal back that copy of *The Bridge That Wasn't There*. According to eBay, the damn thing is worth five hundred dollars. I checked.

"Had your chance, mate," he says, barely looking up from the little screen. "Good luck with the writing though."

"You just promoted the Antichrist," I say, and then I step out into the grim, soul-crushing beige hallway.

# 23

**D**o you think it's a good idea to have that many stimulants going into your body at once?"

Katie has a Diet Dr Pepper in one hand and a cigarette in the other. Squinting from the sun, she's like a live wire, skittering and shaky on the roof of our building. "He hates me," she says. "I mean, he *seriously* hates my guts. Don't you understand that? I'm completely dead. Completely."

"You're not dead. Greg doesn't hate you. He hates me."

"Well, yeah, everyone knows that. But I'm still screwed. He's gonna fire me and I'm gonna have to move to Fairfax to live with my parents. Oh my God. I'm gonna jump. Do you think it's high enough to kill myself? Here, hold my cigarette."

"Nobody's getting fired. He's not just gonna take over and start canning people. It'd be a mess. Besides, that's not his style. I think he'd rather just keep us on and make our lives miserable." I inhale from Katie's cigarette and look down on the street below. People are just wandering down there on the sidewalk, worried about their own shit, completely oblivious to the heinous war crimes that just occurred in this big ugly building.

I've been in corporate America long enough to know that if Katie did get fired, even in the middle of all this, she'd be better off in the long run. She's young enough to bounce back unscathed, and good-looking and talented enough to get on somewhere else and forget all about her time here aboard the Death Star. I should tell her that right now. I should advise her to get the hell out of here and live with her damn parents if she has to. But I don't, because, the fact is, I don't want her to be gone. And that's exactly where she'd be . . . gone.

"What about you?" she asks. "I mean, he really does hate your guts. It's not a joke."

I smoke some more, not enjoying it, but being reminded how much "The Man" hates me while smoking makes me feel kind of like a badass. "Well, let's review, shall we? My wife works for a nonprofit. I've got a seven-year-old, and we're technically trying to have another one. The check-engine light in my car has been on for three months. And my new boss has lodged twenty-five formal complaints against me with HR in the last three years. If they gave people Pulitzer Prizes for being screwed, it wouldn't even be close."

Katie studies the pointy toes of her shoes, sad suddenly. In many ways, for a long time now, Katie and I have been playing house for forty-odd hours a week, carefully constructing our own chaste strand of intimacy. By talking about Anna, even in passing, I've taken a step outside of our little world.

"She's prettier in real life," Katie says after a while.

"Who?"

"Anna. Your wife. She's prettier in person than in the picture on your desk. She looked good at Johnny Rockets. That's quite a feat."

Katie's right, of course. I'm sure it took David Anderson a few trips to the gym to notice her, pumping away on the StairMaster or treadmill. But once he did, he probably couldn't get enough of her. "Yeah, she's not bad," I say.

"She looks really smart, too. I wish I looked smarter. I don't think people think I'm smart when they see me. I think they just think I'm . . . I don't know. I thought about getting glasses once, like those fake ones. That might help."

I finish the dreadful cigarette and vow to make it my last. I'm a goddamn adult, what in the hell am I doing smoking? "You're very smart, Katie. At least *I* think so."

"Yeah, right."

"I'm sorry about the other night, you know," I say. Her hair falls across her face before being swept back by the wind, and I feel a little weak in the knees. "You're just . . . you're just a difficult person to explain. I guess I didn't know exactly how to introduce you to my family."

"I'm sorry, too," she says.

"Why?"

"When I saw you guys, I got really jealous. Like teenage-girl jealous. I know that's stupid, 'cause they're your family. But I wanted to mess it up for you, because you were with them and you weren't with me. So I said that thing about your face, about how you'd gotten hurt protecting me. I knew that'd make Anna mad at you. Does that make me a horrible person? Because it definitely sounds like something a horrible person would do."

"No, it doesn't. Whenever I see Todd I want to punch him in the mouth. And I've nicknamed him Todd the Idiot."

She laughs, and then so do I.

When we're up here, we're rarely alone. There are usually randoms doing the same thing we're doing, escaping for a few minutes to smoke or vent. But right now, there's no one else. It's just us. We're all alone.

"Do you ever wonder what it'd be like," says Katie, and then she takes one of my hands in hers. At first it's just playful, like a handshake, but then it's something else. I'm holding Katie's hand and we're alone.

"What *what* would be like?" I ask.

"If we kissed?"

I've imagined a conversation like this, in which, somehow, everything before it would culminate—all of our trips to 7-Eleven and our cigarettes and our goofing around in the office and the funny forwards we send back and forth and our secret, complicated investment in each other. I'm not ready though. Not today. "Katie, I have to go."

"What? Where?"

"I have to go to the bank. It's actually kind of important."

"You're leaving? Right *now*? Are you crazy? You can't leave. Do you know how pissed off Gregory's gonna be?"

I put my hand on her shoulder, turning her toward the door to walk her back down to Cubeland. "It'll just be one more complaint, Katie. How bad could it be?"

## 24

**W**hen *you're sitting* outside of a Bank of America looking for a white man in his midthirties with blond hair, you realize how many white men there are in their midthirties with blond hair. I thought America was a melting pot, but from my vantage point it's like some Aryan dream of pale-haired, blue-eyed domination. My car is on, and a Beatles song is playing. Passersby must think I look suspicious, a man sitting in an idling car listening to "A Day in the Life." Perhaps I'm the getaway guy. My partners are inside robbing the place, and I'm waiting out here, ready to speed off down K Street with bags of money.

Charlie doesn't think I have anything to worry about. If I called him now and told him where I was, he'd ask me, quite simply, what exactly I was planning on doing.

Dear HR:

My best friend, Tom Violet, who is the world's stupidest man, is constantly asking me for my advice on things and then doing the exact opposite. He also thinks I should change my golf stance, as if he has any idea what in the hell he's talking about.

Yet another blond guy walks out of the building. He's wearing a brown suit and a striped tie. That could be him. Another guy whose hair is more sandy than blond walks into the bank carrying a file folder and eating an apple. That could be him, too. Another blond guy, this one in nice pants and a polo shirt, leaves smiling, and he holds the door for a couple of elderly black ladies. I think of these guys from Anna's perspective, wondering what it is that women are even attracted to. It's hard to tell with women, especially the smart ones. You ask a girl what she likes in a guy and she'll say something completely immeasurable like eyes or hands.

I'm compartmentalizing the events of the day so far—seeing Darth Gregory promoted and standing on the edge with Katie are both faraway thoughts, buried somewhere. For me, anxiety has always manifested itself in nausea, and so it wouldn't be out of the question to roll down my window and throw up on the street.

When I finally get up the nerve to go inside, I'm taken aback by all the activity. Since the advent of ATMs, I can't even remember the last time I was in a bank, and it's surprising. I expected a sleepy little room with plastic plants and old ladies filling out deposit slips with pens on chains, but what I see instead is American commerce at full tilt. Tellers are speaking to customers from behind a long counter. There are dozens of little offices lining the perimeter of the lobby, each manned by an official, professional-looking person. The employees are trained to smile, but many of the customers seem worried. I wonder how many are here to simply visit the money in their accounts, just to see if it's actually still there.

On the wall, CNN is showing a clip of Obama doing a Top Ten on *Letterman*. Barack Obama and my father are doing the late-night circuit, and I'm lurking in a bank scoping out guys and trying to figure out whether or not my wife would like to sleep with them.

"Can I help you, sir?" says a girl. She's maybe Katie's age in a smart little suit-looking thing.

"Oh. No, I'm just looking." It's what I say on reflex to people in stores, but of course I'm not in a store, I'm in a bank, and the poor girl looks a little alarmed behind her smile. "That's actually not what I meant. I was looking to speak to someone in private wealth management." I point at the people in the glass offices. "Is that . . . them?"

She shakes her head. "Nope, those are our personal bankers. The wealth managers are down the hall a ways. Did you make an appointment? They usually see people by appointment only."

I have absolutely no business visiting someone in the business of wealth management, and I'm sure this girl is thinking that same thing, but she's being really professional about it. "No, I didn't," I say as we walk through the lobby. "I guess I should have. But with the markets the way they are, I figured I should stop by and . . ." and what? ". . . touch base."

"Absolutely. We've had all sorts of walk-ins these past few weeks. It's not a problem at all."

We move down a corridor past a room lined with safety deposit boxes before arriving at a quiet waiting room. There are more offices here, but the walls aren't glass and the doors are closed. There are a few people ahead of me, guys older than me reading *Time* and the *Economist*. She guides me to a podium where there's a sign-up sheet. "OK, here we are. Who do you usually work with?"

"I'm sorry."

"Your adviser. Who's currently managing your . . ." she trails off, smiling.

The version of Charlie in my head from earlier had a point. What am I planning on doing? I guess I imagined strolling in like it was a Banana Republic and I'd see a guy with a big "David Anderson" name tag on and then something would happen from there. Or maybe nothing would happen. But I'd know what he looked like, and I'd know right away if there was a problem. I'd know if he was some nerd with a crush on my wife or if he was the guy I've heard her dream about. "I'm not actually working with anyone specifically," I say. "Kind of a free agent."

I'm so obviously lying that the men sitting in their chairs waiting look up at me over their magazines.

"Oh, well, no worries. What's your name? We'll jot it down here and someone will see you shortly."

*Paul Hewson.*

"Tom Violet," I say.

She starts writing my name in a little box, and then stops. "You're not related to Curtis Violet, are you?"

"No. Different Violet."

"That's too bad. He's awesome. Just have a seat here, OK, Mr. Violet? It shouldn't be long."

As she walks away, I see that I've cornered myself, agreeing to sit and wait for a random Bank of America employee to find me and discuss the money that I don't have in this bank. "Oh, wait," I say, stopping her. "I remember now. I was actually supposed to talk to David Anderson? Is he in?"

Her smile falls and she makes a disappointed cluck with her tongue. "Well that's just bad timing. Mr. Anderson's at an investment conference this week. How about I leave him a memo with your name and contact information? He can get back to you right away when he's back."

"A financial conference?" I look down at his business card in my hand, his name and title all crisp and sans serif.

"Yeah. Up in Boston, I think."

"Boston?"

"Wait a minute?" she says. "Are you sure you're not related to Curtis Violet? Because you really look a lot like him. It's kind of freaky actually."

"Boston, Massachusetts?"

## 25

**A**s I walk toward my house, I feel like my limbs aren't quite connected. My nerve endings have been rewired somehow, and they're all tingling. I'm a head floating atop a detached body of parts. I bump into a pedestrian, and I don't even have it in me to say excuse me.

I've got Charlie on the phone. He's been listening to me ramble on. "I thought you said I didn't have anything to worry about?" I say. I've chosen to take this out, at least partially, on my best friend.

He sighs. "Here's the thing. I know it looks bad. But, before you go on some Violet quest of stupidity, just stop and think about it. It's Boston, man. Right? It's a huge city. It could be a coincidence."

This seems sensationally naïve—especially coming from Charlie.

The sun is setting as I walk. It's getting darker earlier and earlier now, fully committing to fall. I imagine my marriage ending in the middle of the winter when everything is drab and slate-colored and depressing.

"Remember when Hillary cornered you?" I say. I know that I'm being a dick right now, but I can't help it. "She said she thought you were having an affair, right?"

"Yes, Tom, I remember."

"Well, were you having an affair?"

Charlie's right. Boston is a major American city, and there are things happening there all the time. But what Charlie doesn't realize is that there's no way this can be a coincidence. There are no coincidences in these sorts of narratives. Every writer knows that—even shitty ones.

As I let Charlie go, I walk right by Gary's Ford Excursion without realizing it. But then I turn around and take in its sheer bulk. It shouldn't be here, parked illegally on my street, yet there it is, jutting out into the intersection. In this neighborhood of sensible German and Japanese vehicles, Gary's truck looks like something built by the Department of Defense to root out terrorists in Afghanistan. I feel like turning around and walking in a different direction. I haven't spoken to Gary since talking to my mom. I didn't know what to say to him before, and I sure as hell don't now. But then, as I'm finally home, I see something unexpected—Curtis and Gary standing together in front of my house. Curtis is leaning against his Porsche. He's holding a small towel and Gary is in his Ford shirt. Both of them are smiling—I think they're even laughing. My dog is sitting by the front door. He gives me a look that seems to say, *Seriously, do you believe this shit?*

"Hiya, Tom," says Gary.

I suppose there's a chance this isn't actually happening. Maybe as I lurked outside of Bank of America, I fell asleep in my car and now this is the end of a strange, meandering dream. In a minute, my old grade school gym teacher will walk by and ridicule me for not being able to do chin-ups when I was twelve.

"What's going on guys?" I say.

"Your dad here was just telling me about his new book," says Gary.

I look over at Curtis, who's smiling. "Oh really? Well, there are quite a few people who'd have been interested in that conversation."

By the look on my dad's face, I can see that he's just been toying with Gary. He's an arrogant man—a man who'd use a duller man for sport. "Turns out Gary's been reading some of my work."

"That's what I hear."

"I finished the short stories, like I told you, Tommy. But then I read the Vietnam book. The *Bridge* one. When those guys opened Davey's rucksack after he got killed and they pulled out all those old unsent letters. That part wasn't in the movie. I almost got emotional. I never saw that coming in a million years."

Curtis is smiling. Glowing praise has always been one of his favorite things about being a famous writer.

Gary is still talking, ringing his big hands together. "It's kinda funny, you don't get to read a book and then actually talk to the writer very often. Believe it or not, I don't know a lot of writers."

"Really?" says Curtis.

"I met Lee Iacocca once, at a big trade show."

"That must have been fascinating."

Gary doesn't seem to notice that Curtis is being an asshole. "I liked his books on leadership, but I don't have a lot of experience with fiction. I had no idea it takes so long to write a novel. Tommy, did you know your dad's been working on this new book of his for five years—and he's not even done, yet."

"Well," I say. "It didn't used to take him five years."

Curtis brushes this off in passing. "So, Gary thinks I need to get rid of the Porsche. Trade her in for something newer."

"Don't get me wrong, Curt," says Gary. "She's a beautiful old automobile. A classic. But the things they're doing with sports cars now—out of this world."

"He doesn't trade in cars, Pop," I say. "Just wives."

"Well, someone's feeling some pent-up aggression today," says Curtis. "Trouble at the . . . office?"

The quick stop there before the word "office" leads me to believe that my dad actually had to pause midsentence to confirm in his mind that I actually work in an office, and so I take some pleasure in seeing that he's missed a big spot on his car. A long water streak is running down the windshield, breaking my reflection into two unequal parts.

"The thing about trading in wives," says Gary. "It's what I tell guys down on the lot. It's a helluva lot cheaper to just go ahead and trade in cars instead."

Curtis laughs, genuinely, which pleases Gary. "Well, when you're right, you're right, my friend." He gives the Porsche's fender one last stroke and leaves Gary and me alone, scooping Hank up on his way into the house.

Instinctively, we start walking together, drifting back in the direction of his truck, just two men ambling through Georgetown. We acknowledge the chill in the air and he tells me about how things have been tough at the lot since the economy turned. And then: "So, I haven't heard from ya, Tommy," he says.

"I've been meaning to call you, Pop. I just . . . well, I don't have a lot of answers. I'm sorry. When was the last time you talked to her?"

"Last night. But . . . it didn't go so well. She wouldn't return any of my calls, and so I just kept calling. Persistence, you know. I'm a salesman. Bernice told me she was going to call the phone company and get my number blocked. I didn't even realize you could do that. But then finally your mom *does* answer, but it's obvious she doesn't wanna talk to me. I keep asking her questions, like how she's been doing at school, but she keeps giving me one-word answers."

"Yep. That's kind of her thing."

"I told her I loved her. I told her that she can be mean to me all she wants and not return my calls, but I'm still gonna love her, and that nothing's ever gonna change that. And then, do you know what she said? She told me that I might want to start thinking about the possibility of a life without her. I'm not even really sure what that means."

"Shit," I say. "It's not about you. None of it is. This whole thing with my—"

"But that's where you're wrong."

"What?"

"Well, I've been doing a lot of thinking. I've determined that it *is* about me. See, you know your mom. She's a romantic, right? She's got an artist's heart. That's why she reads so much. Me, though, I've always kinda been a by-the-numbers guy. Right down the middle. Black and white. But I've got a plan now. Your dad kinda helped me out with it, believe it or not."

"My dad?"

"Well, not directly. It's not like we talked about it. That would have been embarrassing. But he helped me with his writing. You know that one story of his, 'The Skywriter'?"

"Gary—"

" 'The Skywriter.' Just hear me out. You know, the one about the doctor who hires the skywriter to write 'I Love You' in the sky for his wife?"

"Yeah, I know it. But, you're not thinking of doing that, are you? I don't think my mother—"

"No, no. Don't be silly. I'm not gonna to do that *exactly*. The story just got me thinking about being romantic. Sometimes a guy has do something big to get a woman's attention."

"You *do* know that the skywriter dies in that story, right? He crashes into power lines." I stop short of reminding him that the doctor's wife also leaves anyway and takes their three daughters with her, leaving the narrator alone in a gazebo with nothing but a mint julep and a partially blind bull terrier.

"Sure, but that's just for the drama. It's the gesture that's important. That's what the story is about, being romantic. Your dad just had to put that plane crash in there to get people to keep reading."

It strikes me then, walking in a daze up my street, that Gary may have just accidentally discovered the secret of a thousand years of compelling fiction writing.

"I just think your mom needs to be reminded of how it used

to be with us. Back when we were younger, I think she loved me more. It's easier to love someone at first, when you're young and you don't know anything about anything. But it gets harder as you go along. Love is tough today. There are a lot of distractions."

"So, what's your plan then?"

"No, I don't want to say anything just yet. Some stuff still has to come together. But it's gonna be good."

I'm glad he's opted for secrecy here. I don't think I have the energy for the details, or, more specifically, for telling him that those details are either insane or completely implausible. "Well, it sounds like you've got it all figured out then."

And then he nudges me with his elbow. "Hey, looky there. It's a pretty girl at three o'clock."

I look just in time to see a blond ponytail disappear behind the steering wheel of a shining black Mercedes. It's parked between a Land Rover and a BMW. Cars like this are common here, but this car is familiar. As we get closer, it becomes even more familiar.

"Come here for a second," I say.

Gary follows me across the street. "What are you doing, Tommy? You gonna talk to her? You can't do that."

"I think I know her."

"What?"

I peer in through the passenger window, which is cracked a few inches, and I find my stepmother crouched there, hiding behind the dashboard. There's pair of binoculars on the seat beside her. "Jesus. Ashley, what in God's name are you doing?"

She remains perfectly still, even when I tap the window, like one of those animals that pretends to be dead when a bear approaches.

"Are you OK, miss?" asks Gary. "Are you broken down? Maybe we can help you out." He hasn't realized yet who we're talking to. She's wearing a tight black sweater and dark jeans.

"I can see you, Ashley. I'm literally looking at you right now. The jig is up."

Her ponytail shifts, and she's thinking of an escape plan, perhaps contemplating teleportation. "I'm not here," she finally says. "Go away. You weren't supposed to see me."

"Well, sorry, but I did."

Gary looks at me and then back at the beautiful hiding woman. "This is a really nice car," he whispers. "We got a trade in on one a few weeks ago down at the lot. Sixty thousand at least, depending on the mileage."

"That's good to know, Pop. Thanks." I tap the window one more time. Slowly, she rises to a normal sitting position, her hands at ten and two on the steering wheel. "OK. How about you come on out? I can get my dad for you, if you want? He's just inside."

"No," she says. "I hate him. I don't want to see him."

"Well, the binoculars seem to suggest otherwise," I say.

"Does your car have the sports suspension, honey?" asks Gary.

"Pop, I'll take care of this. Ashley, this is really pretty stupid. Just come—"

She turns the car on quickly and slams it into gear. Gary grabs my arm and pulls me away as she revs the engine, looking frantically over her shoulder. In reverse, she hits the gas too hard and bumps the Range Rover. Then she throws it into drive again and bumps the BMW. The tires rub loudly against the pavement as she twists the wheel back and forth.

"Ashley, seriously."

"I have to go!" she yells. "You didn't see me. I'm not here. Don't tell him you saw me."

When finally she makes it out of her spot, three cars damaged along the way, she gives us one vivid, desperate glare before peeling out. We watch her rear bumper and a little cloud of burning gray exhaust.

"Wowee," says, Gary. "That thing can really move! Who was that girl?"

"My dad's crazy-assed wife. She's out of her damn mind."

"What? Ashley *Martin*? That was her? Holy cow. She's beautiful. She almost ran you over. That's the thing about lady drivers—they're not so good in those tight situations."

"I guess her driver wouldn't bring her here for a stakeout."

"She's skinnier than I thought she'd be. They say the camera adds ten pounds."

"We should go inside," I say. "She might come back with a bazooka."

"Yeah, I think you might be right. She looked pretty mad."

Back in our driveway, Gary stops at the Porsche and uses his shirt to wipe away the spot on the glass that Curtis missed. "I wish I'd have known it was her," he says. "I'd have taken a closer look."

I think about this and wonder how close of a look Gary would consider to be *too* close of a look. "Do you wanna see a naked picture of her?"

"A what?"

"I have a framed picture of her topless in the house. It's pretty nice. I keep one of all my stepmothers."

There's a water stain across his belly now, and he's standing in the driveway looking at me, unsure of what to say. In Gary's defense, though, he's among a long list of people in my life who have never fully embraced my sense of humor. "Really?" he asks.

Hank sees us from his spot at the window and starts barking.

"I'm kidding, Pop. Come on inside."

"Are you gonna tell your dad about her?"

"I don't think so. I'm sure she'll turn up later anyway. That's kind of what she does. Right now I think I might need to start drinking."

Unable to hide his enthusiasm for this idea, Gary cuffs my ear and gives me a one-armed hug that nearly lifts me off the ground. When we get inside, I crouch down and Hank leaps into my arms, welcoming us home to the House of Exiled Fathers.

## 26

**A**nna is supposed to be home in two days, but it's impossible not to wonder if that's going to happen. When she left with that overstuffed bag, was she . . . leaving? I was just lying there, half conscious in our bed. Was she looking down on me, her husband, one leg kicked out from the comforter, and moving on with her life?

I called her an hour ago, breaking my own rule, and it went to voice mail. I didn't know what to say, and so I said nothing. In the rooms adjacent to mine, Allie and my dad are in their beds, and downstairs Gary is asleep on the couch. Instead of going to Johnny Rockets or anywhere else, we ordered pizza, and my two dads and I drank whatever we could find in the house while Allie watched *The Lion King* twice.

There's a young starlet on *Letterman*—one of those celebrities who's famous even though she's never really done anything. She's dressed like a prostitute and talking about how all of the things they say about her in those magazines aren't true and that she's just a totally normal girl. If Anna was here, we'd be making fun of her and bitching about the downfall of popular culture.

For the last half hour, I've been taking inventory, focusing on the things she's taken with her and gauging their importance. Her favorite jeans are gone, and so is the shawl she takes to restaurants and movies in case she gets cold. If she were leaving, she'd take them with her for sure, along with the orange headband she loves, which I can't seem to find, either. Her important jewelry is here, and so is her passport, and her flip-flops and the blue sweatpants she wears when she's feeling bloated. And, of course, Allie is here, too.

When the phone rings, I know that it can only be her. Still though, I let it ring a few times, like a teenager trying not to seem too anxious.

"Hi there," she says.

I wonder if he's there. Or maybe he's gone to get ice, agreeing to leave her alone for a few minutes. She tells me that I sound miserable and asks if I've had a tough day.

"You don't even want to know."

There's a knock at my door and Allie appears, smiling. "Is that Mommy?" She bounces over to me and snags the phone, flopping onto the bed next to me.

"Guess who's sleeping on the couch. No, Grandpa Gary! I think Grandma is mad at him still. He ate a whole pizza all by himself—the whole thing!—and Grandpa Curtis drank all of your guys' wine. I drew a picture of a helicopter. Grandpa Curtis took me for a ride in his car. He went soooo fast. Ashley gave Grandpa Curtis a naked picture of herself as a present. I saw her boobs. Today at school, Stephanie was sick and so I didn't have anyone to work on my art project with. Mrs. Rosemary helped though, so it was OK. Do you like Boston? Is it cold there?"

And so on.

She hasn't mastered the phone yet, and she forgets to breathe sometimes, which ends up making her sound like she's having a conversation in the middle of a set of wind sprints. Who does she like more, I wonder, when it comes right down to it? Anna or me?

"Gary's staying at the house?" Anna asks me. Allie has run back down the hall to bed.

"He's not *staying* at the house, he's just here for the night. He stopped by, and I didn't have the heart to send him home. My mother isn't being very nice to him."

She asks about work, and I tell her nothing about Greg. Nor do I tell her about visiting my mother or breaking into my dad's house, or about seeing Ashley lurking on the street with binoculars. I don't say any of this because the only thing I can think about is Anna naked in her hotel room. The sheets are pulled up between her legs and over her breasts. This is how it goes in movie scenes when actresses have no-nudity clauses. Her hair is a tousled mess from bed. It's the worst kind of fantasy.

"How's your *conference*?" I ask, hitting the word a little harder than would be natural under normal circumstances.

"It's pretty much the usual. It's basically a bunch of librarians talking about getting kids to read. There's this education company in the Midwest working on turning kids' books into video games, like for PlayStation. They turn the pages with their controllers. This is what it's come to, tricking kids into reading with video games."

"Anna," I say, and I feel sweat emerge on my forehead.

"Yeah?"

I say her name again, stalling, hoping to be interrupted or proven wrong. "Allie drew a picture of something."

"Oh? Of what?"

"It's of you and someone else. You and a man and a little boy, actually. She told me his name is David."

"OK," she says. It's a small, simple word, but her tone has changed, dramatically so, along with the temperature of the world.

I stand up and start pacing, my thoughts are all heavy and blurred from drinking all night. "Anna, who is David Anderson?"

My dad told Charlie Rose once that when writing dialogue, it's not necessarily the words that are important, but what happens right before or after those words, and for a two full seconds she doesn't say anything, and that's all I needed to hear. My heart squeezes in my chest, a clenched fist. "He's a guy from the gym. And Conner is his little boy. We see them there sometimes. Tom, what is this . . . what's going on?"

"You were all together in the picture, the four of you. You were holding hands, like a family."

"Tom, she's a little girl. I think she has a crush on Conner. They play together."

"I know that he's there. In Boston. I went to his office today and they told me. I found his business card in your bag. And the book he gave you. I found that, too. Gotta admit, it's a pretty good move."

Silence.

"Tom, it's not what you think. I don't know what you're thinking, but it's not that. OK?" She's talking fast, like Allie, breathless on the phone. I can't believe how quickly this has happened.

"Well, what is it then?"

"I didn't invite him here."

"What?"

"I didn't invite him. He surprised me. He just . . . showed up."

"He *surprised* you?"

"I promise you, OK? I had no idea. He just showed up at my hotel the first night I was here. Tom, you have to believe me."

"If someone was going to lie in this situation, Anna, do you know what they'd say?"

"Tom."

"Exactly what you just said."

"Tom."

"Is he there now?"

"No."

"Did you—"

"God, no. Jesus, Tom. I told him to leave. I told him to go away because I couldn't see him."

For a while we're silent, and I know that she's lying. Not because of how she's acting, or because I don't trust her, or because in a million years I ever thought we'd be having this conversation. I know that she's lying simply because I can't imagine it. If I were in a hotel room by myself and Katie showed up unannounced, and I was far from my real life—my other life—there's no way I'd be able to tell her to leave.

Anna's crying now. "I've been lonely," she says. "It's been hard with us, Tom, you know that, right?"

There's another knock at my door, smaller this time, and Allie's head appears. She's holding one of her books, the one about the boy and the penguin again. I hold up one finger and she disappears. How does a conversation like this end? In movies, difficult conversations, the life-changing conversations that mean so much to the characters and their stories, simply fade to black.

"Tom, are you there?"

"Did you read my book at least?"

"What?"

"My novel, Anna. You weren't supposed to call me until you'd at least started it."

"I know I was supposed to. But I haven't yet. I just wanted to talk to you. I wanted to hear your voice."

"Jesus. Why does nobody wanna read my fucking book?"

She's sitting up in bed, her book on her lap, smiling. "Hi, Daddy. You wanna read?"

"How about we read something different tonight?" I say.

Allie hugs her book, her thumbnail moving to her lower lip. "Why? I wanna read this one. It's about the penguin. Remember?"

I sit down next to her, the small bed sinking from my weight. "Honey, we've read that one a hundred times. The boy and the penguin sail back to the North Pole together, and then they realize that they miss each other because they're such good friends, right?"

"Yeah. That's OK. Don't you like it?"

"I do like it. But I was thinking that for a change maybe we'll read a *new* book." I set my manuscript on her lap, which to a child must look like nothing.

"That's not a book."

"It is. Well, it's a book before it becomes a book."

"What's it about?" She looks so much like her mother that I look away, and it scares me a little that I'll be looking at this beautiful face for the rest of my life and that it will always look like Anna's.

"It's about a boy. He goes on a long car ride all by himself to find his dad because he thinks he's lost him. And he doesn't know who he's supposed to be. He goes through a personal crisis."

"Did Grandpa Curtis write it?"

"No. I did. It's my secret book."

She scoots closer, leaning into my shoulder, and I love the way she smells, like things getting better. "OK. We can read your book if you want to."

As I read the first sentences aloud, and then the first paragraphs, and then the first pages, it's as if I'm hearing them for the first time. It's as if they are someone else's entirely and I've just stumbled across them here with my daughter, and I trust the way they sound. I believe them. And so I keep reading and reading, even after Allie has drifted off and the sound of her slow breathing falls in time with my own steady voice.

## 27

**W**hen the alarm goes off, I feel like I haven't slept at all. And maybe I haven't.

After reading roughly two hundred pages to my sleeping daughter, I stumbled back into my room and lay down to watch the ceiling, analyzing how the light looks at various points in the earliest moments of morning.

Today is the first day of Osama Bin Gregory's unholy rule, and I'm already running late. The office is the last place on earth I want to be, and so, in the shower, I look at the oncoming water for a long, long time. Outside, the sheer injustice of Greg's promotion is profound enough to have affected the jet stream, and so it's raining like it's the end of the world.

By now he's probably sitting in his office in another Brooks Brothers tie, drumming his fingers, and perhaps I should swing by Walmart and pick up a hunting rifle. As the shampoo runs into my eyes, though, I'm struck with a less violent fantasy. I'm sleep-deprived and edgy and a little hungover, but I'm not afraid to admit right here in this tiny shower that I have come up with a brilliant idea.

I'd planned, of course, on *not* wearing a tie today. But what kind of protest is that—doing the same thing I always do? *That's* insanity.

No. This particular day calls for something new, something truly stupid and childish—a futile gesture of which I can be proud.

Downstairs, I find Allie already dressed for school. She's gently poking my stepfather with a LEGO block. Gary is snoring as he spills over the couch from every conceivable angle.

"Wake up, Grandpa Gary," she whispers.

"I think it's gonna take more than that, hon," I say.

"Is Grandpa Gary gonna live with us now, too? Two grandpas in the same house?"

The thought hadn't crossed my mind until now, and I consider it. It'd be like a terrible, terrible sitcom. Or worse—it'd be *Three Men and a Little Lady*, but instead of Magnum, P.I., Sam Malone from *Cheers*, and that guy from *Police Academy*, it'll be my two dads and me, drinking until one of the neighbors calls Social Services. "No," I say. "I don't think he'd fit in the house."

"He seems kinda sad. I could tell last night. He watched *The Lion King* with me for a while, and I think he almost cried, but it wasn't even at the sad parts."

I distract her with cereal, which I prepare in her favorite bowl. Once she's settled in the kitchen, I head for the basement to execute my brilliant idea. It takes a good ten minutes of digging, but eventually I find the box marked "Halloween Costumes." In there among the masks and wigs is a long, stringy cowboy tie from a few years ago. The shiny metal knot is engraved with a scorpion. It is the most dreadfully awful thing ever.

Back upstairs, I look at myself in the mirror. Against my light blue oxford shirt, the tie makes me look like an extra from *Brokeback Mountain*. It is exactly the right amount of stupid-looking, and I can't wait to show Katie.

"Yeehaw," my dad says. He's at the table next to Allie now, rubbing his temples.

"I hear prop comedy is making a comeback this year," I say. "Wow, you look awful, Dad."

He rests his chin on his hand, picks a marshmallow character from Allie's bowl, and pops it into his mouth. "That gigantic man over there can drink," he says. "I felt like he was challenging my masculinity."

"Well, you're awake first, so I guess you win."

"It wasn't worth it." Curtis is thin, shaken, old, and tired. The hollows under his eyes look drawn on by a makeup expert.

"You'll get Allie to school, right?" I ask.

He sips his coffee and squeezes the bridge of his nose, considering this. "OK. But she's going to have to drive. I think I've got vertigo."

"That's a silly tie, Daddy," says Allie. She's looking at me the way people look at you when they're not sure whether or not you're joking. I have some experience with this look.

"I know it is, honey. But your daddy has a very silly job, and sometimes that means he has to do very silly things for reasons he doesn't quite understand."

"Should we wake Sleeping Beauty over there?" asks Curtis. "I don't think that sofa is going to survive much longer."

Gary's legs hang over the armrest as though he's been dropped there by a passing helicopter. Hank is investigating now, torn between sniffing from a distance or just getting it all over with and jumping on his chest.

"Pop! Hey, Pop! You want some coffee?"

But Gary remains perfectly still, and Allie can't keep her eyes off of my awesome tie.

"Be honest? Do you think it's funny?" I ask her.

She thinks for a moment, and then, eventually, she admits that it is. I take this to be a good sign. Because if a seven-year-old thinks it's funny, then surely an office full of miserable adults with all-but-worthless 401(k)s will, too, right?

※

Instead of going directly to my office, I opt to head immediately to Cubeland so I can parade my anti-Gregory wardrobe to the troops. My plan is to pop into Katie's cube and stand there quietly until she notices me. "Ma'am," I'll say, tipping an imaginary hat like an idiot. She'll laugh, a sound I've heard far too little lately, and I'll forget, if just for a moment, the rest of my life.

Several of my colleagues are out wandering about the office, en route to wherever. None of them seems to want to look at me, though—in fact they're avoiding looking at me. There isn't a single acknowledgment of the fact that I'm here at work dressed like a hillbilly. I turn into Katie's cube, smiling, and I actually yelp when I see that the person there isn't Katie. Instead, it's someone from HR, Judy maybe, or one of the other five interchangeable middle-aged women who work in HR. She's stacking Katie's things into a cardboard box.

I'm a child knocked from a tree, his breath pulled from his lungs in one painful heave.

"What the hell are you doing?"

"Tom," says Judy. She looks sad holding Katie's I'm a Pepper sign.

A few sets of eyes and foreheads pop up over the gray cube walls around me. "Where's Katie? What's going on?"

"You have to talk to Janice, Tom."

"Jesus, what the hell? She's my direct report. Where is she?"

"Janice's office. But you can't go in there."

"Oh yeah?" I say, and with the two strings of my novelty tie swinging like little arms, that's where I head in earnest. A few more disembodied heads appear, but vanish fast, off to send IMs or e-mails to friends in other departments. I pass the kitchen, copiers, supply closet, and fax machine in a blur. I told her that she was going to be fine, that she had nothing to worry about. Without even knocking, I throw Janice's door open hard, and it thuds against the wall. Janice looks up, unimpressed. Katie looks up, too, and so does one of the pasty assistant lawyers. Apparently Katie didn't even warrant a full pasty lawyer. I can see that she's been crying. The young ones—the girls—always cry.

"Tom, I need you to leave," says Janice. "We're in the middle of a private meeting."

The streaking rain drums against the window, distorting the world outside. "What the hell, Janice? This is ridiculous. I'm her boss for Christ sake, and she didn't do anything wrong. Why didn't anyone talk to me about this?"

"You weren't here to be notified, Tom. Now, I need you to leave immediately." Behind her there's a framed picture of a Dalmatian puppy. This is the fucking world I live in—a world where villains have pictures of puppies and smiling babies in their cramped, dank offices.

"Is this Greg? Is this his bullshit?"

"Tom, this is a private, budgetary matter, and I need you to leave. I *will* call Security."

I laugh out loud at this. Our security team consists of two old retired cops at the front door of the building reading *AARP Magazine*. "Jesus, go right ahead. Katie, this isn't right. This is *my* fault, OK? This is my fault and I'm gonna fix it right now. I promise."

She's bewildered, staring up at me. She has no idea what's happening—that there's a process, and it's going on right now while she sits here. Fat Judy is cleaning out her desk while IT deactivates her entry keys and disables her passwords from the network. She sees my tie, and for an instant there's realization there, maybe even the slightest smile, and my heart breaks.

"It's gonna be all right," I say.

"OK," she whispers. But for all the things in the world she doesn't know, she knows enough to know that I'm completely full of shit, and that there's nothing I can do to help her.

"Tom," says Janice. "This is neither the time, nor the place."

I close Janice's door as dramatically as I opened it and head toward Greg's office. A few of his minions have come down to HR to see what's going on, and I tell them to get the hell out of my way. My heartbeat is louder in my ears than my own footsteps on this horrible, trampled industrial carpeting.

His door is partially open, and so I shove right on through to find him sitting, smiling at his desk, waiting for me. They've discussed this—the Tom Factor—and set up a plan for how to deal with it. "What do you think you're doing, you asshole?"

"Good morning, Tom," he says. "I was actually reviewing this brochure copy you wrote yesterday. Not bad at all—once we cut the contractions out."

"Don't be a dick. You know exactly what I'm doing here. You can't fire Katie. She's my direct report."

"And now, Tom, you are *my* direct report. Were you not at the meeting with Ian? I stopped by your office last night to discuss Katie's removal, but you weren't there. We should probably talk about your attendance one of these days. It's not very good. Pretty unacceptable actually."

"This isn't right and you fucking know it. What did she ever do to you, Greg?"

Greg wheels back from his desk and I see that he's wearing a fucking pin-striped suit—I shit you not. "This isn't personal, Tom. This is the real world. Do you think I'm a child? We're in the middle of a financial meltdown. We have to cut costs to the bone. It was a business decision. Two copywriters is just one too many."

"Well then fire me. Because that's who it's about—*me*—and you're taking it out on a twenty-three-year-old girl. Why can't you just admit it?"

He smiles still, as big and awful a smile as I've ever given him. "Well, don't think I didn't considering firing you. But, despite our differences, you're good at your job. I think we can give this a go, you and me. Especially now that you've come on board with the dress code. It's not exactly regionally appropriate, but a tie's a tie, right?"

"Fuck you," I say, and then I heave my stupid tie across Gregory's office, burying the scorpion into the drywall and sending chunks and chips of white dust to the ground. I turn to leave, but then I turn back. "Oh, and just so you know, Ian offered me your bullshit job first, and I turned it down. So, have a good time with that, you fucking empty-suit, jargon-spilling, worthless corporate prick."

His little smile deteriorates, and the fact that I've said this loudly enough for anyone within two hundred feet to hear leads me to believe that these might be the last words I ever say to Gregory Steinberg.

My exit line.

I crash around my office for a while, knocking some things to the floor and pacing around.

Before coming back here, I tried Cubeland, but Katie and the contents of her desk were gone. By 2 p.m. the office vultures will have come and gone, peeling away whatever staplers, business card holders, or tape dispensers remain. She's gone, and there's a chance I'll never see her again. Of all the people who've left this place, fired or otherwise, I've never seen any one of them again, even by accident.

"This is Katie," says her voice mail when I dial her cell phone. It's a happy, chipper version of Katie. "Just leave a message and I'll call you back."

What I'm feeling now, sitting at my desk, goes beyond emotion into the realm of physical pain.

Many of the items atop my desk are on the floor now, except, somehow, for my plastic in-box. There at the top sits a copy of a press release I wrote the other day—some trumped-up bullshit about our clients in Asia. Gregory has made his awful little notes in red, and so have a few other stakeholders. It's due to Lyle over at the *Post* this afternoon, and I consider just ripping it up, knowing that I probably won't last that long anyway.

And then I'm hit with my second brilliant idea of the day. "Mother . . . fucker," I say.

The tie was brilliant, but it failed. I see now that is wasn't bold enough, and certainly not stupid enough. This idea though, potentially, could be my masterpiece.

I've spent five years writing a coming-of-age novel that may very well never see the light of day. I've spent more than seven years writing corporate propaganda and bullshit so hollow and meaningless that it has haunted my dreams. Today though, I'm going to make up for all that. Today, I'm going to win my own fucking Pulitzer Prize.

**For Immediate Release**
Contact: Ian Barksdale, President of MSW
ibarksdale@msw.com
202.555.7875

### STUPID AMERICAN COMPANY, MSW, NAMES
### EMPTY-HEADED, OPPORTUNISTIC, UTTERLY UNCREATIVE DOUCHE BAG
### AS NEW VICE PRESIDENT OF U.S. MARKETING

(Washington, D.C.) MSW, who absurdly and completely without merit, claims to be the world's leading provider of business training, performance development, and consulting services, has named Greg Steinberg as its new Vice President of U.S. Marketing.

Steinberg, one in a long line of spineless, jargon-tongued morons currently employed at the company's headquarters aboard the Death Star, was promoted after the CEO, eccentric British millionaire Ian Barksdale, found himself too busy managing his many other shady, overvalued companies around the world to give the issue more than one nanosecond's consideration.

"I'm excited about the opportunity," says Steinberg. "It just goes to show you, all you really need to succeed in this stupid country is a collection of meaningless corporate buzzwords, clichéd ideas, and a complete lack of tangible ability."

MSW, which has been offering largely useless, criminally over-priced services to its swollen, apathetic clients since 1977, has recorded marginal profit gains year after year by employing questionable accounting practices, underpaying employees, and stamping out any and all signs of creative or innovative thought. For more than thirty years, the company has remained a beacon for all that is wrong with corporate America, shining its light on the populace's willingness to sell its collective soul for the privilege of a laughable health care package and mind-numbing, soul-crushing daily monotony. Steinberg says he plans to continue this spirit and tradition in his new role, even as the company inevitably crumbles beneath the weight of the current financial crisis and its own uselessness to society.

"You see, I have absolutely no talent and no ability or vision beyond that of a neutered corporate sheep, blindly following the herd that is this entire fraudulent industry. Because MSW adds no real value to the world around us and is where the hopes and dreams of good, honest people go to die, I feel that I'm a perfect fit."

Steinberg adds, speaking through his ominous breathing machine and black mask, "Oh, and please call me Gregory and not Greg. It makes me feel important, and it helps me forget that I'm forty-three, paunchy, and completely intolerable to be around. My breath smells constantly of stale coffee, and I have a tiny, tiny penis. Please God, save us, because I suck so badly."

The phone at the *Post*'s business section picks up after half of one ring. "Business, this is Lyle."

"Lyle, my friend. Tom Violet from MSW here. Did you get my news release?" I'm surprised at how calm I sound.

"I sure did, Mr. Violet. We got a big kick out of it down here in the bullpen. It's a joke, right?"

"Interesting choice of words. In actuality, I think it's the first press release I've sent you that *isn't* a joke. Let's just say we're taking our branding in a whole new direction."

There's a long pause, and I hear newsroom sounds in the background, typing and chattering. I can imagine Lyle sitting at some cluttered desk, just an underpaid kid with a journalism degree wondering if he's being put on. "You mean, this is real? You want me to send this up to the editors?"

"Send away, Lyle. You might wanna hustle though. I've sent it to a few other places. Fifty-three, to be exact."

"Whoa. Really?"

"See, you've been telling me for months that eventually I'd send you something good enough for the front page. Well, here it is."

Lyle laughs, but he also sounds a little sad. "I should probably ask you, Mr. Violet. Have you been drinking?"

I look at my watch, which is an act of physical comedy that is completely wasted over the phone. "No, not yet."

"And, have you recently been fired from MSW?"

"Well, again, not yet. But the day is young."

"OK then. Well, good luck, Mr. Violet. I think you're probably gonna need it."

"I appreciate that. You take care, Lyle."

I may never see Katie again, and I may have said good-bye to my marriage, but this moment, an awkward parting with a kid I've never even seen in real life, has me nearly choking up. I look around my office, suddenly sentimental. It's how death-row inmates must feel, gazing at their little cells one last time as the clock approaches midnight. I'm saying good-bye to my real life, and my other life, too, and everything else I know in the world. Slowly, in no particular hurry, I start taking Allie's artwork down from my bulletin board. Pictures of me, Hank, Anna, Curtis, an elephant, a blue pickup truck, Simba, a smiling bear, and a wide-eyed fish. These things, I want to keep. Everything else, as far as I'm concerned, can go straight into the garbage.

## 28

*My press release,* sent to more than fifty trade pubs, business journals, online news sites, and newspapers around the country, went out from my desk just after 11 a.m. EDT. Through the lunch hour and into the early afternoon, as I sat at my desk with my door closed, the industry wires were silent. There are people at MSW whose job it is to monitor these wires and the press in general. This seems like a worse job than mine, trolling random industry blogs and sites and Google alerts, searching for any and all new references to this stupid company. This monotonous task is given to either the interns or the right-out-of-college crowd— usually philosophy and English majors who've graduated to find themselves otherwise unemployable.

Then, just after 3 p.m., one of those poor interns heard a beep on his computer. And then another. And then another after that. "Dude, check this out," he said to another intern.

"Dude. Holy shit."

Anyone who's ever worked in an office for more than five minutes can imagine what happened next. At least half of the average work person's day in corporate America is spent forwarding funny shit to colleagues and friends. Intern number one e-mailed the first media hit, a blurb on *Employee Development Weekly*'s Web site, to a guy upstairs in Receiving who he plays fantasy baseball with. That guy sent it to his buddies in Accounting. They sent it to the girls they're secretly hooking up with in other departments. And so on.

At 4:20 p.m., when there was a knock at my door, pretty much everyone in the company—even the satellite workers and the ladies on maternity leave and the telecommuters at home watching *Oprah*—knew that the shit had hit the fan in a huge way. I opened the door to find Janice standing there blinking at me, fresh from her *Crisis Management Handbook*, with our two old-timer security guards. She sighed and the men girded themselves for the unknown, wondering how much trouble I was going to be.

"What seems to be the problem, Officers? Was I speeding?"

On my way out, not quite handcuffed, but definitely *escorted*, I invited everyone within earshot to the Front Page Bar and Grill a few blocks away for a happy hour. This seemed like a good thing to say, and by "good" I mean flamboyantly inappropriate.

"I hope it was worth it, Tom," Janice said to me in the parking garage on our way to my car. "You know, if you just would have kept your mouth shut and played it straight, you could have gotten pretty good severance out of this. You know he was going to fire you eventually. It was inevitable."

Through my overwhelming, irrational pride, there was a pinch of regret. "How do you do it, Janice?" I asked.

She looked at me, considering whether or not to take my bait. She's probably a nice woman deep down, and I'm sure she loves her Dalmatian. "Do what, Tom?"

"Sleep at night."

In the low light, two floors underground, I could see the shell of what Janice once was before becoming a corporate assassin. Maybe, on some level, she respects me. Or, then again, maybe the Dark Side has overwhelmed her, and I'm just a social security number with a cardboard box—a problem that's been eliminated. "We've all got bills to pay, Tom," she said. "It's just a game anyway. A game that, I've gotta say, you're not very good at playing."

Well, as Curtis would say . . . when you're right, you're right.

As I sit unemployed and drunk at the Front Page Bar and Grill, I'm pretty sure that it *was* worth it. For the first hour or so, I drank alone, scanning the classic news clippings posted around the bar. Then, slowly, people began to trickle in, and they just kept coming. Some of them I knew, the Tom People, but some of them I didn't know—people I barely even recognized from elevators and conference rooms.

But they all knew me.

I've done something today that everyone dreams about doing. The difference is, I had the balls to do it, and so I am, at least for the moment, their hero, and my money is no good here. Shots and beers and stiff drinks have accumulated in front of me at a rate I haven't seen since my twenty-first birthday. I take out my cell phone and call home.

"Where are you?" asks Curtis. "Sounds like Paris in the summer."

"Grabbing a drink with some coworkers. You think you could take care of Allie-Cat tonight? Maybe get her some dinner, make sure she gets to bed OK?"

For a moment, he's thoughtfully quiet, on the verge of chastising me, but then he realizes that he's Curtis Violet and lectures on fatherhood probably won't go over well. "OK, sure. I can do that. But . . . be careful, Tom. You sound like perhaps you might need to be careful."

I hang up the phone and I'm instantly being hugged by an Asian guy from IT. "You're fucking awesome," he says. "You crazy bastard." We do an Irish Car Bomb together and then he runs off and tackles some other IT guy at the bar. When the doors open, a familiar figure comes in, a woman wearing Jackie O glasses, like a celebrity trying not to be noticed. It's Lauren, Ian Barksdale's assistant. She's a defector from the other side and the bar greets her with good-spirited boos. "Well, if it isn't the most unpopular man in Washington, D.C.," she says.

"What, are you kidding?" I say. "Look at me, I'm beloved."

She nods at the bartender and smiles. "Well, let me tell you who doesn't love you. Ian was in a meeting with the lawyers when I snuck out. I've never seen him so angry. And he's almost always angry."

And there it is, anxiety, budding full in my stomach. My fans are energized though, and there's a round of encouragement and anti-establishment rhetoric. I'm like Nelson Mandela. I'm persecuted— a martyr. I imagine a judge's sentence being drowned out by the chants of love from the parking lot outside the court house.

*Free Tom Violet! Free Tom Violet!*

"This is still America, isn't it?" I ask. "Isn't comedy protected under the First Amendment?"

"Is that what that was?" asks Lauren. "Comedy?"

"Ooooooo," say three guys from the mailroom that I kind of know.

Lauren raises a colorful little drink. "To the stupidest guy in town," she says, and then we knock shot glasses and drink something that burns.

This disparate group here, all united under strange, exciting circumstances, has the mood of New Year's Eve, and all around me people are declaring that they're going to start doing things differently, to start letting their own voices be heard at work. Some are even discussing how to make their résumés more attractive— financial crisis be damned—or to start thinking about new careers altogether. Some guy from Product Development gives me a knuckle bump, and a lady I don't known at all gives me a surprisingly handsy hug. The jukebox, which we've commandeered, amazingly, starts playing "9 to 5" by Dolly Parton. I haven't heard this song in years. No one has. Still, though, we sing along like it's the 1980s and scream the chorus and hug and commiserate. *SportsCenter* begins and ends on the TVs behind the bar. There are clips of Obama giving a speech, and then Bush, and then McCain, and then some guy from one of the auto companies, and no one notices a thing. A new bartender shows up to replace an old bartender, and then a girl bartender shows up to help him, and they're pouring drinks and shots and beers. We're all here because we hate our fucking jobs. Well, *they* hate their fucking jobs, and I hate my old one. Even people from other companies who have no idea who I am start joining in because they hate their fucking jobs, too, and everyone is happy together. Because for these few fleeting hours, at least we're somewhere other than work.

"Who wants a shot?" I yell.

And everyone does.


Drunkenness, I've found, has a way of becoming sadness pretty quickly. Things stop being as funny as they were before, and everything that you thought was good is suddenly spun in the other direction. Tonight, it's my mother's voice-over doing the spinning.

*These people are laughing and having fun, Thomas,* she says. *But tomorrow they're going to go about their lives and forget all about you. What are you going to do tomorrow? You have no job. And as far as I can see, dear, your wife is about to leave you. She's in another city with another man. She's going to take your daughter, too. That's how it always goes. And what will you have to show for it? Other than a bitter, hastily written press release, I mean.*

I shut my eyes and try to let my mom fall back behind the blaring stereo. And then there's another voice, and this one isn't in my head . . . and it sure as hell isn't my mom.

"I heard you did something really stupid today."

I open my eyes, and there she is. My insides flutter, and then it feels like I'm falling. Before I got married, I spent as much time as any other guy in bars like this, going from drunk to sad, and in all those lonely nights with my friends, never did someone as beautiful as this even acknowledge me. She is my youth—or, at least, the youth I wish I'd had.

I say her name and we hug, which lasts a moment.

"Are you OK?" I ask.

"I've never been fired before," she says.

"Me neither. I've fantasized about it. I thought it'd be more liberating."

She's wearing no makeup that I can see, nor is she wearing her corduroy jacket. Instead, she's in jeans and a simple black shirt. It's been a hard day for her, but her only tell is her eyes, still a little puffy from crying. A few people see her and give her hugs and high fives and words of encouragement. But then, gradually, they turn their backs or wander away and leave us alone.

"You're better off, you know," I say. "The Death Star doesn't look as good on a résumé as you might think. You're too good for that place."

"That's what my dad said. He said any company you can't describe in one sentence isn't worth working for. I still don't even know what MSW really does. It's like company in that one movie, *Office Space*, where everything is kept intentionally vague so anyone can identify with it."

"I think it might actually be one giant money-laundering scheme. Or maybe a Ponzi scheme, whatever that is."

"I'm gonna send out résumés. I hear the job market is pretty strong, so I should find something right away." She laughs a sad laugh. "I'll be standing in an unemployment line in two-hundred-dollar Kenneth Cole heels listening to my iPod Touch." She points at the five or so drinks currently sitting at the bar in front of me. "Are all of those yours?"

I offer her one, and she selects what appears to be a watered-down vodka soda that a chunky lady named Doris from Research gave me a while ago. She squeezes the lime, takes a long sip, and looks up at me. "So, did you write that press release because of me?"

"I think most people would agree I wrote it because I'm an idiot."

She rests the palm of her hand on my chest, over my heart. "I didn't come here to see *most* people. I came here to see you."

"In that case, yeah, I did write it because of you."

"Lauren says they're going to sue you, you know."

"For what? My Honda? The house that's in my dad's name? Maybe they'll garnish my wages. I'm currently making zero dollars a year."

"I'm still glad you didn't take that stupid job."

I take a sip of whatever is in this glass, something in the tequila family, and I wince. "Oh yeah? Why's that?"

"Well, the way I see it—if you had taken the job, I probably wouldn't have gotten 'let go' today. So, I'd have a paycheck, which would be nice. But, if you were still my boss, then I wouldn't be able to flirt with you at this bar right now. *Cosmo* says you should never flirt with your superiors at happy hours. It gives you a bad reputation."

"Is that what you're doing? Flirting with me?"

She brushes her hair back from her forehead and her eyes are as vivid as ever. Her face is serious and vulnerable. "What? You can't tell?"

"Oh yeah. Flirting. I remember what that looks like."

We both turn back to our drinks for a moment. Then Katie reaches into her purse and tells me to close my eyes and hold out my hand. And I do, and for one thrilling second I have no idea what's going to happen. And then she sets something against my palm, familiar and practically weightless. When I open my eyes, I see my long-lost squeeze ball, shaped like a heart.

"I wanted you to have it back," she says.

I take a breath and my eyes are stinging like I might actually cry. "Remember that question you asked me?" I ask.

"When?"

"On the roof yesterday? After we found out about Greg?"

Embarrassed, she twirls a red straw, moving ice around her glass. "Yeah. I remember."

"The answer is yes. All the time."

need to go** home!" she yells.

I hear her, barely—the Beastie Boys are blaring—but I decide not to say anything. Pretending to be deaf has bought me a moment to think.

Barry from Accounting has taken off his work shirt and is spinning it over his head. Lauren is barefoot—her heels cast aside—and she's dancing with some guy from another company with a comb-over. A couple of the admins are dancing with the interns who first discovered my press release. And then there's me, Tom Violet, dancing with a beautiful, too-young girl. She's grinding her hips into mine and holding my hands and stepping on my feet. She's laughing and her breath smells like sugar and she keeps looking into my eyes.

"It's time to go!" she shouts.

"Are you sure? I think I still have like nine more drinks over there on the bar. You can have four and a half of them if you want."

"I've got drinks at my apartment, you know. Four beers and a bottle of white wine that may or may not still be good."

"I don't think—" I begin, but then I stop there. Strangely though, this sounds like a full, declarative sentence, as if I'm standing in a bar shouting out one of my most obvious character flaws. *I don't think!*

"You owe me, remember? You got me fired." She laughs and squeezes my hand again. "Well, indirectly, at least. So, you have to do what I say. There are rules here."

"Let me get you a cab." This seems like something that a reasonable man—married, with a child at home—would say and then do.

But she shakes her head, and she's not smiling anymore. "Tom, I want you to take me home."

In the cab, speeding toward Arlington, Virginia, I tell her that I'm just making sure she gets home safely. The cabdriver gives me a look in the mirror and shakes his head. I look out the window, and I have no idea where I am. It's just after midnight and things outside are blurry and I'm not in D.C. anymore—I've crossed the river. If I'm just making sure she gets home safely, then why did I just turn off my cell phone? I should turn it back on and check in with my dad . . . but I don't. Katie's hand is on my leg. I don't remember her putting it there.

*This is a really bad idea, Thomas.* It's my mom's voice-over again, and she's not happy. *You know why they invented the phrase "the point of no return," don't you?*

Next to me, Katie smiles and then blows a string of hair out of her eyes. This makes her laugh.

At Katie's little brick apartment building, which is tucked off a busy street called Washington Boulevard, I give the driver fifty dollars and ask him to hold on a second. Katie has already started a zigzag walk toward the front door, her keys jingling. She looks back over her shoulder. "What are you waiting for, Tom Violet?"

Above me, the streetlights are pulsating. "I'm waiting to come to my senses. That's what people do in situations like this."

She laughs again and then she's walking back toward me, and I wonder if Anna and David Anderson had a moment like this, when any number of things could still happen—or *nothing* could still happen. She plants her feet firmly in front of mine and hooks a finger to my breast pocket, pulling me forward.

"You can come to your senses inside. It's warmer in there."

"Katie," I say.

"Come on."

Apparently this is all too much for the driver to handle. There's a revving engine, a squeal of tires, and then the cab is gone, off into the night, eliminating what is left of the illusion of free will.

"Too late now," she says.

Like her cube, her apartment is small and disheveled. There are empty Diet Dr Pepper cans stacked in a Jenga pile atop an overflowing recycling bin. She kicks off her shoes and pads over to the tiny kitchen, pulling a Brita out of the fridge. I scan her walls, and there's a picture of Katie and some girls on a beach in their bikinis and a picture of an old lady holding a baby. I feel like I'm spying, like I've broken into this place. Flowers, arranged in a dying bouquet, sit on the kitchen table. It's like the apartments everyone lives in when they're young, like Anna's cramped one-bedroom in Dupont Circle when we first started dating. The first time I spent the night there, I got up at four in the morning to use the bathroom and tripped over her ironing board.

Katie sips her water, and I see that she's wearing a silver ring on one of her toes. "Is this totally weird or what?" she asks.

"Not at all. Lots of people have pictures of old ladies on their walls."

For a moment she's confused. "That's my grandma, stupid. I mean, is *this* weird, you being *here*, in my apartment?"

She hands me her glass of water and I have a drink. It strikes me that this is an intimate gesture, more so than dozens of shared cigarettes and arm punches. She's so much smaller with her shoes off, and my heart is settling into a steady rhythm in my chest. We're just talking. It's going to be OK. I'm just having a glass of water and that'll be it. In movies, scenes like this begin differently. Characters don't enter the apartment carefully, hang up keys, and drink from a water purifier. Instead, they burst through the front door pawing at each other, their bodies conjoined at the tongue, stepping on the cat en route to the couch. I finish the glass of water and set it on the table. "Well, you seem safe and sound. I guess I'll—"

I'm stopped by Katie's mouth, which has come crashing into mine. She stands on my feet, on her tiptoes, her arms around my waist. At first, my mouth simply doesn't know what to do, but then it eases into its role, opening and closing in time with hers. Her tongue finds its way between my lips, and her mouth is chilly from the cold water. Our lips pop when she pulls away.

"So, that's what it's like to kiss you," she says. "It's kind of hot."

Before I can say anything, we're doing it again. This time, I'm ready and we kiss like two people kissing in secret, holding and biting. She untucks my shirt and her hands are on my chest and stomach. Bitten off, jagged little fingernails leave grooves of heat across my skin. When we come up for air, we're in the hallway. She's guided me here, and I've followed. When we break again, the light is different, darker, and we're in her bedroom. The backs of my knees meet something soft and we're falling onto her bed. Her body on top of mine is light and hyperactive, moving and grinding against me. I hold her lower back and pull her close to me and she moans into my mouth. I'm hard—without even realizing it—and her hips rubs against me and the room tilts on its axis.

Maybe this is a sign. This is what my body wants, to be here with her in this unmade double bed. Our chemistries are aligned, and it's not a matter of what's right or wrong, but simply what *should* be.

"Oh my God," she says as I kiss her neck. She sucks air between her teeth and giggles. I feel goose bumps at the backs of her arms.

Katie's shirt comes off in a flurry of elbows, and before I can even take in what I'm seeing, her mouth is on mine again. My own shirt is unbuttoned and I'm struggling out of it, our lips never unlocking—it's an act of desperation. If we stop kissing, if we take a breath and look at each other, we'll both realize that this is actually happening and that could very possibly derail everything.

When her jeans and my khakis are discarded onto the floor, she rolls me on top of her. I prop my weight on one elbow and run my hand down her body, and it's like someone else's hand, beginning at her clavicle and passing the silky mound of her bra. Her belly button, just a soft crater along the smooth topography of her abdomen, is exhilarating beyond imagination, this forbidden little thing, and I have to kiss it. My tongue fits perfectly into its hollow, and I allow my mouth to explore the honey-colored expanse above the waistband of her underwear.

Her hands knead my scalp, pulling my hair as her body tenses below me. As I move my mouth back up toward hers, I discover that her bra has come off. My tongue finds one firm, candy-shaped nipple and I hold it gently between my teeth. She arches her back and says my name and I have never felt desire like this, like something that hurts.

"I want you," she says. And then she says it again.

"I've wanted you for so long," I say.

"Really?" she asks, her eyes glazed and sleepy. Her hand is on me, holding me gently over my boxers, and I can hardly breathe. "Do you really?"

I bite the warm spot where her biceps and forearm meet. "Of course."

"OK. Hold on a minute."

"What?"

She wiggles out from beneath me and hops onto the floor. Upright, she steadies herself and runs down the hallway into the bathroom. "I'll be right back," she calls, and then the door shuts.

Alone, my eyes have adjusted to the low light, and I look around the room for the first time, listening to the hum of water through pipes. A cheaply framed Van Gogh print. A teddy bear wearing a

Virginia Tech T-shirt. A pile of workout clothes in the corner. Her corduroy jacket slung over the back of a hand-me-down desk chair. And, on the other side of the room, a bookshelf. And I scan it, because that's what I do, wherever I am—like a compulsion. Among her uneven collection of mismatched paperbacks and hardcovers, there's *Bridget Jones*, some Grishams, Stephen King's best, Kurt Vonnegut, a few female Indian writers who got a lot of press, Alice Munro, David Sedaris, and, of course, Curtis Violet. I fold Katie's pillow into two halves and sit up, looking at six of his books.

"Hello, Dad," I whisper.

Water is still running in the bathroom, and I can hear Katie moving around, opening and closing drawers. Five paperbacks and one hardcover, each worn, creased, and read. I could recite the important passages from all of them, and I remember where I was the first time I read each one. When I was younger, I used to wonder why my dad couldn't just control himself. I wondered how he could give up so much—like my mother and me—for what seemed like so little. I understand it now, and I understand how he could forget me in that department store and leave me to drift alone among the clothing and Muzak. The world outside of this lovely girl's tiny bedroom feels vague at best, like something from the distant past.

When I turn away from the shelf, I'm startled to see myself. In her full-length mirror, I look drunk and somehow too old for this bright duvet cover and these cream-colored walls. My cock is absurdly hard, lifting my underwear into a tent like a prop. I try to push it down, but it springs back up, ridiculous.

Beside the alarm clock there's a framed picture that's been turned upside down. I pick it up and look, even though I'm already fairly certain what it's going to be. Katie and Todd the Idiot are smiling. They're wearing Nationals T-shirts and holding big ballpark beers. They're young and sunburned and in love with each other. While I was kissing her belly and hipbones and forging ahead blindly, Katie must have reached over and flipped it, the very beginnings of regret already creeping in through the haze.

I look at Curtis's books again, side by side, and then I look at myself. I think of Allie and Anna, and I'm suddenly ashamed of all of this. My pants are on the floor—one leg turned inside out. My shirt is hanging from the bedroom doorknob somehow. One of my shoes is under the bed. The other is upside down under her jeans. I'm half dressed before it dawns on me that Katie's been gone for a long time.

"Katie?" I say.

I walk down the short hallway to the bathroom and knock lightly. "Katie?"

When there's nothing, I knock a little harder and say her name again. The force of my third try actually opens the door a crack. The only sound is the faucet, blasting away into the porcelain sink.

"Are you OK?" I say, pushing my way in. Steam, like smoke, has fogged the mirror. At first, what I see is frightening, and I immediately imagine the worst. But then, it's OK. Naked, aside from her pink and blue underwear, which is now stretched delicately between her knees, Katie has fallen asleep on the toilet.

I take a towel from the wall. Her body, which moments ago was all I wanted in the world, is obscene now. I drape the towel over her shoulders. "Come on, honey," I say.

"What?"

I help her to stand, but can see that she's asleep on her feet. I look away as best I can as I carefully pull her underwear back up, securing it in place with a little snap of elastic.

"Todd?" she says, her eyes closed. "Todd, I'm sleeping."

"I know. Let's just get you back to bed, OK?"

"I got too drunk. Are you mad at me?"

"It's OK," I say, tucking her hair behind her ear. "You didn't do anything wrong at all."

"Please don't be mad at me. I'm so stupid."

Back in her room, I ease her into bed. I should dress her, at least put a T-shirt on to cover her breasts, but that feels like even more of invasion now, so I pull the sheets up to her shoulders instead. She's just a girl. She's someone's daughter, and someday she'll be someone's wife. As I watch her sleep, I know that she deserves better than any of this. Her lips part and she begins to snore gently. Tomorrow she'll wake up hungover, embarrassed, and confused, and that's all my fault. She'll wonder what happened and she'll wonder where I went. If she's lucky, she'll never see me again.

"Good night, Katie," I say. And then I kiss her smooth, perfect forehead.

## 30

*A guy can get* a cab pretty easily in D.C., provided he doesn't look like Hannibal Lecter. This is not the case, though, once you cross into the Commonwealth of Virginia. Frankly, I'm not even sure what a commonwealth is. It's 1:15 a.m., the streets are horror-movie silent, and I'm loitering outside a shady 7-Eleven drinking a Big Gulp and trying not to draw attention to myself. Leaning against a brick wall, I'm replaying the last hour in my head over and over again. The nerve endings in the palms of my hands still remember the texture of Katie's skin. I can still feel her hair across my face and there's the taste of her mouth, sweet and cool and completely new.

I look at the clock on my cell phone and wonder if it's too late to call. Of course it's not. The guy I want to talk to lives on a different timetable than the rest of us. And besides, he deserves a semidrunk dial. The bastard has been ignoring me.

Brandon Ross answers immediately, and it sounds like there's a continuous car accident occurring beside him. "Tommy!" he yells. "What's up, brother? Isn't it Late Night in Married Land?"

"Where the hell are you?"

"Book party. These things always run late. One of my writers has a memoir out this week. I *think* it's a memoir. That's how we've packaged it anyway. It's pretty good. Usual stuff. Teenage druggy. Uncle Bobby touched my boobies. I danced because I hated myself. Cha-ching."

"Sounds great. Listen, I was wondering. Have you had a chance to check out my manuscript yet?"

Brandon starts laughing. "Your manuscript? Sweetie, you sent it to me like twenty minutes ago."

"Oh. Well, yeah, I guess it hasn't been that long. I'm just kinda—"

"Wait. I'm sorry. That was bitchy. Vodka makes me insensitive. I actually have it on the fast track. My hot intern checked it out and said it was solid. He just put it on my desk yesterday. I've gotta get through a few things tomorrow and then I *promise*, I'm on it, OK?"

"You're not sticking me in the slush pile are you?"

"Bitch, please. The slush pile's for ugly people. I'll read it ASAP, and then we can chat about it at the Pulitzer awards dealio. Scout's honor. We'll talk, get some drinks, then maybe we can make out a little."

"We'll play it by ear," I say.

"Cheer up, Thomas. You sound depressed. I'll see you in New York."

With my BlackBerry back in my pocket, I try to calculate the odds of Brandon actually reading my manuscript before Curtis and I go to pick up his Pulitzer. Then I wonder what "solid" means, and who in the hell Brandon's hot intern is. Does "solid" mean good, or does it just mean it won't be a complete waste of Brandon's time? I should have asked more questions. Why am I so afraid of looking uncool?

"Hey, man, you got any change?"

A homeless guy has shuffled up to me from behind the Dumpster. Normally, I'm on the move when I see homeless people, which makes it easier to ignore them. Now though, I'm pretty much just standing here, and so I dig in my pockets and give him a handful of random change.

"Thanks, man. God bless."

We stand there for a while, side by side. He smells like fish and leather and his eyes are bloodshot, and I wonder if his path to this point in his life has been anything like mine. I'm in nice khakis from a department store and a Ralph Lauren shirt, but, at the end of the day we're just two out-of-work guys outside a 7-Eleven in the middle of the night in a country that's teetering on financial ruin.

"What's so funny?" he asks.

I hadn't even realized I was laughing. "Nothing. It's just been a weird day."

"Tell me about it, man. Days just keep getting weirder around here. But it's gonna be all good soon. Obama's gonna be on the case, making shit happen."

The Excursion arrives then like a battleship docking. The pavement actually shakes from the rumbling of the Ford V8 engine. It's bigger than the parking spot, dramatically so. The homeless guy and I shield our eyes from the blazing headlights.

"I gotta go," I say. "My ride's here."

"Shit, man. We getting invaded or something?" If he says anything else, I don't hear it because Gary honks the horn. This couldn't be less necessary considering I'm standing five feet from his front bumper and we're actually making eye contact through the windshield.

"Hiya, Tommy!" He looks both happy and wide awake even though I know he was dead asleep when I called him a half hour ago. After four long rings, he answered not with "hello," but with my mother's name. *No, Gary. It's me. It's just Tom.*

"Hey, Pop. You mind cutting the headlights? I think my eyes are melting."

"Oh, sorry. So, you need a ride or what?"

"I sure do."

I love Gary for a lot of reasons, one being that when I called him, he didn't even think to ask what I was doing in Virginia in the middle of the night by myself. He just knew that I needed him.

He opens the door and hops down out of the truck. "OK, but give me a second. I wanna get a soda, too."

I talk Gary through the best legal place to park, which, at this time of night, is about six full blocks from my house. And then together, each of us finishing the last of his large soda, we walk slowly through my neighborhood.

"How about that one?" he asks, pointing at one of the most beautiful houses in town, a white, half-brick monster with a garage and a perfect black fence around the garden.

"Three point five," I say.

"Christ almighty. And it doesn't even have a real garage."

When Gary's in Georgetown, he likes to look at the big old houses and have me tell him how much they're worth. I don't know, of course, especially now that their values are plummeting as we speak, but I deliver my answers with authority, and Gary gets a kick out of it. A young couple walks by, hand-in-hand and drunk, on their way back toward campus. I envy them and their wonderful lack of complication.

Gary shakes his icy cup and sips at the bottom for remaining soda. "So, remember what I was telling you before, about my big gesture?"

I tell him that I do, but, the truth is, I kind of don't. My brain feels like it's been cleaned out and everything moved around. Something about a skywriter.

"Well, it's all systems go. Your mother's gonna be blown away. Got it all planned out for this weekend. Things really come together fast when you start throwing money at a situation."

"That's great, Pop," I say, even though it sounds more than a little ominous.

When we walk into the house, Hank leaps up from the couch where he's apparently been waiting. He yelps and wags his tail and smiles up at Gary and me. I catch him in mid air and hold him so he won't wake the whole house, but it doesn't matter. Although it's nearly 2 a.m., Curtis and Allie are sitting at the kitchen table, wide awake, playing Connect Four.

"Hi Daddy and Grandpa Gary."

"Allie, what are you doing up?"

"Grandpa Curtis and I have *in-som-nia.*" She sounds the word out slowly with great care. If I were a betting man, I'd guess that Allie heard Curtis roaming the house and came to investigate. When he's late into a book he works at odd hours, and he looks like he hasn't slept in a while. I make a mental note to become a better father. My daughter's life the last few days has been very much like the beginning of an *E! True Hollywood Story.*

"Looks like you two have been having fun," says Curtis.

"It's been a long night, Dad."

"Well, apparently it has indeed. You got an interesting message this evening. Maybe you'd like to do some explaining."

"Oh God," I say. "From who?"

"Whom, Tom." he says. "From *whom.*"

I generate a quick list of possible callers. Katie? Darth Gregory? A lawyer? Ian? The police? Curtis pushes the blinking button on our little answering machine. "When Allie and I returned from Johnny Rockets, we heard this."

From the very first word, I know that it's no one I know. It sounds like a telemarketer.

"Hello, this is for Tom Violet. I'm Andrew Brown from the *Washington Post.* We're considering doing a piece on your dismissal today. Your press release caused quite a stir this morning when it came up the chain from Business. We couldn't do anything with it, obviously. Your company would have sued us into the Dark Ages. But it definitely got a lot of us over here talking. Very funny stuff, actually. Really timely. In light of who your father is . . . well, let's just say we'd be interested in talking with you."

My family and I listen to Andrew Brown's contact information and then there's a click and some robot noises from the machine.

"Who was that, Daddy?"

"What did you do, Tom?" asks Curtis. "Did you . . . write something? Something funny."

"Yeah, hilarious. It got me fired."

"Fired?" says Gary. "Oh no. Tom, you didn't say anything about that."

"Pop, don't worry, it's a *good* thing."

"Good? How can being fired be *good*? You been watching the news?"

He's the only person in the room with a real job, and, apparently, any sort of grasp of reality. But before I can explain the inner workings of the Death Star, the answering machine makes another click and another beep, and then my wife is talking.

"Tom? Are you there? Anyone?"

"Mommy!" says Allie.

"Oh," says Curtis. "She must have called during Allie's bath."

"Well, I guess you guys are out," she says. "I just wanted to say . . . good night, I guess. I miss you."

Both of my dads look at me. Anna's voice is strained and tentative. She sounds scared even. I ignore them and curse myself for not getting voice mail on our home phone like everyone else in American younger than seventy.

"I'll be home tomorrow night. Hopefully not *too* late. Tom, maybe we'll get some time to talk before you and Curtis go to New York. I want to talk to you about your b—" She stops herself, but, of course, she was about to say "book." "I just really want to talk to you, Tom. OK?"

"Mommy sounds sad, Daddy."

Gary touches the top of Allie's head. "No, baby. I'm sure she's just fine. Don't worry."

But Curtis is well aware of what a woman sounds like when

things have gone wrong, and he frowns at me over the Connect Four board.

"Say good night to Allie for me, OK?" says Anna. "I'll see you guys soon."

"Good night, Mommy!"

With a click, a hum, and a beep, Anna's voice is gone.

I want to go upstairs, lie down, and not wake up for a month. I want today to have never happened, or yesterday for that matter—or the day before that. I want everything to be the way it's supposed to be.

Gary pats me on the shoulders. "You know, if you need to, you can come work over at the dealership. We could find something for you to do, no problem. We're always looking for good people."

I consider myself in one of his Ford polos, selling Explorers to people in Virginia. Part of me—most of me even—wishes that could be me. But it isn't.

"That's the problem, Pop. I don't think I'm actually that good of a person."

## 31

**A**llie holds her hand out for me and I take it, squeezing her wool mitten. It's chilly today, and so I pushed for the gloves and the stocking cap and her heavy coat. As I look around at other parents escorting their bareheaded children through the parking lot, I feel overprotective and silly.

"See, Daddy, it's not as cold as you said."

"Well, you look good in a hat regardless. It's a rare quality in a woman."

She scratches her head with one mitten. "It makes my hair itchy."

It's my first full day of unemployment, and despite the searing headache, I'm up and showered. Getting Allie to school today is my only real responsibility, and I'm lingering a bit, not sure how I'm going to fill the rest of the hours. The other parents are dressed for work in nice office-appropriate attire. They're going to drop their children off and head to buildings like responsible adults. I've got nothing though. For seven years, I've fantasized about how I'd quit my job when I sold my novel. I would do it respectfully and professionally, but I'd be sure to let them know that I was happy to be escaping.

"Do you think Mommy's gonna bring me a present from Boston? When I talked to her, she didn't say. But she usually brings me something . . . like candy."

"Probably," I say. "She loves you very much, and she likes to bring you presents." We step over a curb, and her backpack is almost as big as she is, weighing her down. How could someone so young have so much to carry?

All around us, children I've never seen before smile and wave at my daughter—little girls and boys, her friends. "Hi, Allie," says a black boy with a mini-Afro in a Redskins parka. "I like your hat a lot."

Allie looks at me and she's blushing in the cool air.

"See, honey, what'd I tell you? The hat's totally money."

"Daaaaad," she says.

The other parents are stopping at the front door, but I'd imagined walking her all the way to her pastel-colored classroom. Hell, if I could, I'd stay with her all day, help her draw pictures and do math problems, and chase her around at recess. But she stops me. "You can't come in," she says.

"Why not?"

"We're supposed to go in by ourselves. Mrs. Rosemary says it's good for us. It makes us feel *independent*."

"Oh. Well, if those are the rules." I squat down on my haunches and give her a hug. She's a tiny thing among all these silly layers I've made her wear, and I squeeze her in my arms.

"You know what, Daddy?"

"Hmmm?"

"Mommy loves *you* very much, too."

"What?"

"You always tell me that mommy loves me very much. And you always tell me that you love me very much. But you never say that about each other. You should. It's a nice thing to say."

I hug her again, hug her for so long that she tells me she has to go or she's going to be late for Reading. I pull her hat off and hand it to her and she tells me good-bye. Through the window, I watch her walk away, her backpack tugging her coat down over her shoulders. She talks to her friends and gives a little girl a hug and then disappears through a door. I love her so much that it's actually hard to breathe.

Back at the car, I sink into the driver's seat and give myself a minute. I close my eyes and scratch Hank's ear. He's sitting in the passenger seat wondering what we're going to do next and why I'm in jeans and a sweatshirt as opposed to my usual khakis and blue or white work shirt. Admittedly, this is assuming a lot of thought for a dog. It's more likely that he's wondering if, by chance, I have bacon hidden in my pocket.

For a long time I've been very breezy about coming and going at work, and now I have to actually remind myself that I'm not supposed to go at all. That I don't have to ever go again. If it weren't so terrifying, it'd be the most wonderful day of my life.

My BlackBerry rings and it's probably Anna. Whatever happens, I'm going to need to explain this to her somehow. But when I see the caller ID, I feel a surge of panic. It's not Anna. It's Katie. All morning I've been trying to decide if we should ever talk again—if I should call her and see if she's OK, like a gentleman, or if I should simply not and allow the circumstances of last night to somehow be their own form of closure, which seems incredibly cowardly now.

"How are you?" I ask after awkward hellos.

"So this is what unemployment feels like," she says. "Funny, it feels like a hangover."

She sounds awful and a little nervous. I wonder if she's still lying there topless and I wince. All of that tension and desire has dissolved into this overwhelming shame and regret. "Yeah, same here."

For a moment we say nothing and I turn off my radio. The bottom of the windshield has begun to cloud over. "So, a lot of girls when they get drunk try to play the amnesia card and say they don't remember anything."

"But you're not a lot of girls, right?"

"Nope. Some of it's a little sketchy, I'll admit. But I pieced things together enough to know that you're a pretty good guy after all. And that I'm a little sluttier than I thought I was."

"I don't think either of those things is true."

We chat about last night, and about how drunk everyone was. It's one of those conversations that hover outside of the conversation that you should be having. We could be chatting in my office or goofing around on the roof of the building, a cigarette between us.

"So, what do you think?" she asks, finally.

I run my hand along the steering wheel, wishing I'd thought about this more, about what to say to this girl. "I think that in a few years, I'm going to be a story that you tell your closest friends. About how you almost screwed up your life. And I think that's probably for the best. For *you* especially."

"I was thinking you might say that. So that's it then, huh?"

Last night, when she called me Todd, it wasn't merely out of force of habit. There was hope there; it's who she wanted me to be. "I think you love Todd, Katie," I say.

"When I woke up this morning," she says, "I didn't know what to do. Yesterday sucked. It was one of the worst days ever. But I had so much fun with you last night, because it was like everything else was gone, and it was just us. And I knew that that's how it could be if we ever let it."

"But it's not just us," I say. "It isn't that easy."

"I wanted it to be though. I *do* love Todd, I think. Maybe. But I know that if it was just us—if I'd met you first and you'd met me first—we would have loved each other. But the world got it in the wrong order. And so when I was dialing your number just now, I decided to roll the dice and see what you thought. If you chose your family, I'd get it. And I do. But if you chose me, then I'd have waited and gone through everything we had to go through until it *was* just us. I know that sounds so passive and awful, and I'd smack one of my girlfriends in the face if I heard her say it. But deep down I knew what you were going to say anyway, so it was easy. Because you *are* a good guy."

A few mothers and fathers hustle their children past, running late.

"Katie," I say. "I'm sorry about—"

"Don't be. And that press release. It really was the nicest thing that anyone's ever done for me. I don't know. Maybe that's a sign that I need to find some nicer guys." She laughs, sort of.

I tell her that she's wonderful, and that she's going to be fine, and that I'm going to miss her. All of these things are true, but they sound trite, like what people always say. She accepts it dutifully, though, and thanks me for not letting her do anything last night that she'd have regretted doing. Perhaps I am a good guy, and perhaps I really *did* choose to leave. But, frankly, I don't really know what would have happened if I hadn't run across the dog-eared shrine to Curtis on her messy bookshelf, or if she hadn't fallen asleep, or if she hadn't called me Todd. Things could have gone much differently.

"One thing, though," she says. "Do you remember what it felt like to kiss me last night?"

"Of course."

"Does it feel like that when you kiss Anna?"

I think of us—of Anna and me when we were younger—kissing those first few times when that's all there was going to be. I'd wanted to kiss Anna so badly, and when I finally did, it *did* feel like that. Maybe it can feel like that again. Or maybe it simply can't, and that feeling is what men like my father are willing to ruin their lives searching for, over and over. I haven't answered her question. I don't know how to.

"Good-bye, Tom," she says.

## 32

*A*nna arrives home that night, as scheduled. My dad hugs her, as he always does, and Allie and Hank are ecstatic, jumping around and making noise like she's been gone for months. She looks tired from the train in a T-shirt, jeans, and her running shoes. I search her face for signs of change—of revelation or otherwise—and find simply Anna, my wife. Taking my turn, I give her a hug, recognizing instantly the smell of her hair and the temperature of her skin. She never should have left. I should have woken up, leaped from our bed, and told her that she couldn't leave.

The rest of the evening, we're polite and nervous, afraid to make eye contact. At some point, Allie's drawing comes down, leaving a blank square on the fridge where art usually goes. Allie doesn't seem to notice, and I wonder if she's taken it down herself, aware somehow of what it's done.

Around 10 p.m., I knock on my dad's door and find him packing. Tomorrow morning, the two of us are going to New York together for the Pulitzer Prize award luncheon at Columbia University. Anna and Allie are staying home, so it'll just be the two of us.

"You got everything?" I ask.

He's written a list, which he's consulting now as he studies his travel bag. "I always forget something," he says. "I accepted my first National Book Award without underwear on."

I'm fairly certain that this isn't true, but my father's relationship with the truth has always been touch and go. As he fiddles with his shaving kit, I consider my stepmother's breasts. Curtis has set Ashley's portrait lovingly atop the dresser for the world to see. "I think that would be a good title for your memoir, if you ever write one," I say.

"What's that?"

"*Good Luck with the New Book, Asshole: The Curtis Violet Story.*"

"Attention-grabbing. Not sure how well it would play in the Midwest though."

"Is Ashley gonna be in New York?"

"I don't know," he says. "Honestly. I really don't know this time. I doubt it. She left me a rambling voice mail the other day saying that she's going to L.A. She's meeting with some directors or producers. I think she still wants to give acting a go."

I laugh because it seems pretty much perfect.

"She'll have an Oscar in five years," he says. "They'll be afraid *not* to give her one."

I sit down at my computer desk and watch him pack. He opens the green bag I recovered for him, and I see that it's full of prescriptions and pills. "What's all that?" I ask.

"Just some medicine," he says, "and some voodoo pills that Ashley got me on. Organic, revitalizing crap. So, I was thinking, how about we scrap the train tomorrow and take the Porsche up to the city? It'd be like old times."

I think of the two of us together coming off the Jersey Turnpike, crawling toward the Lincoln Tunnel with the entire amazing city laid out to our left. I'd been hoping he'd say this all along. I really am like a ten-year-old. "Can I drive?"

"Of course not, but the radio's all yours."

When I nudge the mouse, the computer comes to life, and I'm looking at my blue desktop. If he'd found my book on here, buried in its folders, would he have asked me about it? Would he have read it without telling me?

"You know what everyone's gonna be asking this weekend, right?" I say.

"The same thing they always ask."

"Where's the next book?"

"Exactly. Poor Harper Lee."

"Well, where is it then?" I look around the room. "Have you hidden it here somewhere? Under the bed?"

"It's done," he says. "Well, *almost* done. I can always tell when a book is done because I start to hate it. And I still love this one a little."

If I were one of his students, or some journalist, I'd have written this frantically in my notebook. There are five major universities that I know of that teach courses exclusively on this man's work. He's one of the handful of living writers that people outside of academia even care about anymore. But I'm his son, and I've been looking behind the curtain my whole life. "Have you ever considered that you're just a hack, and that maybe you've just gotten lucky now sixteen times?"

He takes a sip of his Jack Daniel's on ice, his hand shaking slightly. "I can't balance a checkbook, you know. And I don't know the first thing about how the Porsche works, or how to fix a faucet. I'm a mediocre father, and a bad husband. In the real world, I'm almost completely incompetent. But I'm one of the best writers in the world."

"Now *that* should be the title of your memoir, you arrogant bastard."

He smiles. "Maybe. But, enough about me. Why are you here?"

"What?"

"You heard me. I don't need help packing. You're obviously stalling."

Anna has read to Allie and put her to bed. And now she's in our room, waiting for me.

Curtis sits down on the bed as I lurk awkwardly. "You know, there's a point in every marriage where you either give up or march on. Giving up sounds easy, but I promise you, it isn't. All of those things that men think are better on the other side really aren't."

I think of saying good-bye to Katie this morning. A week ago, the thought of never seeing her again terrified me. Now though, it's more like relief.

He clears his throat. "There's something I've never told you."

"OK."

"One fall, a while back—you were about ten, I think. I was supposed to have you for Thanksgiving. We were going to spend the whole weekend together. It was the year there was that early snowstorm. Do you remember?"

"Of course I remember. You brought me back to Mom's because you had to go up to New York all of the sudden. Something with NPR, right?"

"Yes, well, when I dropped you off, your mother and Gary and your brothers were just sitting down to eat. There was all this great-looking food at the table and Maryanne was playing one of her Beatles records. The house smelled like cooking and it was like a painting of what a family is supposed to be. Gary was wearing some God-awful holiday sweater."

"I think he still has that," I say.

"Of course he does." Curtis looks at his hands, tugging a hangnail. "When I was about to leave, you waved at me and told me to have a nice trip. And then I watched you sit down at the table. You were with the people you loved, and you were all smiling and everyone was happy. And even though you're my son, I wasn't a part of it. It didn't feel fair at all, like I was being cheated. But I knew that I had no one to blame but myself. At that moment, I regretted everything I'd ever done that led to you sitting at that table with your real family while I stood by the door in those ridiculous snow boots."

"Dad," I say. I want to tell him that no matter what, he was always my dad and that I loved him. But that's not how fathers and sons talk in real life. And, the truth is, I was kind of relieved when he told me he had to go to New York. And so I don't say anything.

"I don't ever want you to have to live through a moment like that," he says. "And I promise you, if you're not careful right now, you will."

I lean back against the wall—the day catching up with me. "I don't even know if it's up to me anymore, Dad. I think Anna might be—"

He waits for me to finish whatever I'm about to say, but I don't.

"A woman never *wants* to be with someone else. Not really. That's the business of men, and for some reason we destroy things because of it. But not them. They're better than us. They only choose someone else when we push them away."

"So, what should I do then?" I ask.

"Don't be a fucking idiot," he says. "Anna is the sort of woman who writers write about, Tom. Somewhere in the third act, women like her save characters like you and me from ourselves. She's the loveliest literary device in the world. So get your ass out of this room right now and go tell her that she doesn't have to be with anyone else. Because you love her, and because you're not going anywhere. And mean it."

She isn't reading her running magazine or playing with Hank or laying her clothes out for tomorrow like usual. Instead, she's sitting in our bed, her eyes wide and expectant. She's wearing one of her bedtime tank tops and a pair of my old boxers. Hank is sniffing her travel bags, which are lying in heaps on the floor. I make her wait while I brush my teeth and analyze my hairline in the mirror. I look old still, and I realize that I need to start making some changes in my life.

Back in our bedroom, I see my novel stacked neatly on the comforter. "Read anything interesting lately?" I ask.

Her face is noncommittal, serious. She says my name, and when someone says your name things can go either way. "I started it yesterday in the hotel. I actually skipped a presentation I was supposed to go to. I finished it today between Baltimore and here."

I wait for her to say more, but, apparently, I'm going to have to participate in this. "And?"

"I loved it."

"What?"

She laughs, which falls away quickly. "I loved it. And I'm sorry. All these years, I didn't think I would. That's why I was afraid to read it, because it scared the shit out of me that I might hate it. But I didn't . . . I love it."

There's no way to interpret or respond to this.

"It made me feel like a bad wife because I never really believed that it *could* be good. It didn't seem possible. Does that make sense? But, while I was reading it, I realized that it could be your dad's book. It could be something he wrote when he was younger and then hid away somewhere. It's funny like him, but sad like him, too. And it has his, I don't know . . . elegance."

Uncertainty sits in for happiness here, like I'm being tricked. "I sent it to Brandon."

"Brandon Ross? Sonya's Brandon?"

"Yeah. He's an agent now."

She looks at the comforter, fiddling with the dog-eared copy of my manuscript, acknowledging that this is something she would have known—that she should have known—if we hadn't been avoiding each other for so long. I've felt the full burden of our struggles for a long time. I've been pulling away, drifting toward Katie and another life, and it's made me feel aimless and guilty.

But I can see now in Anna's hanging head that she's shouldered the burden, too, and she's sitting here sad, lonely, and, more than anything else, sorry.

Someday, maybe we'll talk more about the book. Maybe we'll eat dinner and discuss it, chapter by chapter and section by section. Maybe she'll tell me her favorite parts, and maybe she'll tell me what she thinks it all means, and maybe she'll reveal a bunch of shit buried between the lines that I didn't even know. But not tonight.

"What really happened, Anna?" I ask.

Her eyes meet mine and then return to the bed. It takes her a long time to say anything. "I knew he was going to be there. I guess I didn't know *technically*. He never told me exactly. But I knew that he was going to show up in Boston. I told him about the conference and the name of my hotel. I said it all casually, like I was just talking, but I wanted him to come."

I need to not be standing, and so I sit on my side of the bed. "What happened?"

"I don't think I want to talk about—"

"Tell me," I say.

She's a little startled by this. "Well, he used to talk to me when I was working out. We met at that 6:30 spin class I take sometimes. I could tell he liked me, and so I flirted with him a little because it was just silly. It was kinda fun, I guess—*funny* even. I haven't flirted since . . . well, *you*."

"People don't take trips to Boston because of flirting."

Anna carries on, grim. "He looked at me like he wanted me. I don't know if he even liked me at first, or if he thought I was nice or smart or a good person. He just wanted me. I'd forgotten what that feels like. And so . . . I let him."

"You let him what?"

She looks at me, and I urge her along. "I let him want me," she says, finally. "Married women have these tricks. We learn them somewhere along the way, and they let us make men lose interest in us or just go away. I didn't use any of those tricks on him though. I didn't want him to go away."

I stand up, take a few steps in several directions, and then I sit back down again. "Keep talking," I say.

"Really? But—"

"Keep talking, Anna," I say, and then I bite the skin on one knuckle. All of the tension in my body eases into a crisp shot of pain, and I'm somehow able to refocus.

"OK. That first day of the conference when I got back to my room after our evening sessions, he'd left me a message. He said he'd come to surprise me and that he wanted to see me. I was supposed to meet Tammy and Beth for dinner, but I told them I was too tired. I knew it was wrong. But it was just dinner, right? Just a drink and some dinner and nothing else—no big deal."

I wonder if she believes this, or if women are simply that naïve. Can a person be that inherently good inside to think that a man travels the length of the Eastern Seaboard for dinner and drinks with a married woman?

"And so we ate, and then we went to the bar for another drink, and it was fun to talk to someone again. We don't talk anymore, Tom. Do you even realize that? I can't remember the last time we had a legitimate conversation about something. David and I talked about our kids and our jobs and . . . just . . . our lives."

"Does he know about me?" I ask.

"I never tried to hide you—or hide anything else. I didn't talk about you very much though. And he hardly ever talked about . . . *her*. It's not like we ever agreed to not talk about you both. We just never did."

I understand exactly what she means. And I also understand that somewhere there's a woman, David Anderson's wife, in some bedroom somewhere. Right now she's lying next to a man she thinks she knows everything about. I want to know what David

Anderson looks like. And I want to know what Anna was wearing. And I want to know what she had to eat and drink. And how he was sitting next to her and what she thought was happening and when she knew that it wasn't just a drink and dinner. But I don't. I really, really don't. And I do.

"So, you were drinking," I say. I'm stern when I say this, like I'm scolding her, but I'm thinking of Katie licking salt off of her hand and doing a tequila shot and smiling at me.

"A little. I wasn't drunk or anything, Tom. But, after a while, I started to feel like it might be time to go. And so I said good-bye. But then he touched my leg. He set his hand right here on my thigh, like you used to do in the car when we were driving."

Her eyes are watery, glistening in our reading lamps.

"He touched you?" I say.

"Yeah."

"What did it feel like?"

"It felt good. It felt really, really good. But I knew that it was wrong. He shouldn't be touching me. Only you can touch me. And so I told him that I had to go. He asked me if he could go, too, to make sure I got back OK. I told him that he could."

"You knew what he wanted though, didn't you? Tell me that you—"

"Yes," she says. "I knew. And . . ." For a while, she says nothing and her eyes fill again. She wipes them on one of the shoulder straps of her tank top. "When we were waiting for a cab, I decided that I was going to let it happen. I didn't tell him that, but I knew that I was going to let him come into my room, and that I was going—"

"You were going to what, Anna?"

"Let him sleep with me."

My heartbeat has slowed—the blood clogging in my veins—and I feel light-headed and short of breath. I can see him clearly now for the first time. My brain has filled in Allie's picture, adding flesh to crayon, and there's David Anderson. He's whispering in her ear, and his hand is no longer simply resting on her thigh. It's moving up, steadily, along the contours of my wife's leg. "What happened?" I ask.

"What do you mean?"

"What do you mean what do I mean? What happened?"

"Why do you want to hear this?"

"Because I have to. You think you know men, but you don't, Anna. OK? I can't explain it, but I need you to tell me everything right now."

"He kissed me in the taxi."

"Where?"

"On my neck," she says, touching her throat. "And then just barely on the lips. Not even a real kiss—just a small one. And for a minute I couldn't breathe at all. You and Allie. This house and our life here. They didn't matter to me. I just wanted him."

"Anna, what happened?" I ask, again.

I can see that she understands now. She takes a breath and it comes out shaky, and she knows that she's going to tell me everything. And maybe she needs to say it as much as I need to hear it. A tear streams down her cheek, landing on her bare arm. "He got out of the cab with me, and he followed me into the hotel. I didn't ask him to, but I didn't ask him *not* to, either. He just did. We went up the elevator with some other people, and he touched my hand and I had to close my eyes. And all of the sudden, when I put my key card in the door and made it beep, we were kissing."

I put my hand on Anna's as she talks. I want her to stop, but I can't let her stop. This . . . *this* is the point of no return now. It's like watching a tragic event over and over again until you can feel it in your chest. I think of Katie again—of the exhilarating strangeness of her little body under me.

Listening to Anna is my punishment for that.

"I lay down on the bed and he lay on top of me. That weight, you know, it feels good. Women need that weight sometimes. It, it reminds us that we're alive. He asked me. He said, 'Do you want this?' and I told him that I did. Because I did. I wanted to be fucked. I wanted to feel that again. And so he took his shirt off, and then he took my shirt off. And he kissed me."

"Where?"

"Do you really want to know this?"

"Where did he kiss you?"

She wipes her eyes and clears her throat. "Here," she says, touching her breast over her tank top. Through the thin material, I can see the faint shadow of her nipple.

"Where else?"

She moves to her inner thigh, tracing her finger upward. Then she lifts the front of her shirt and draws a circle around her navel. "And here."

I've grown hard so fast that I'm almost unaware of it. Katie is there again, vivid against the front lobe of my brain, her back arched and her little moans in my mouth. But then she's gone, and there's only Anna sitting in this bed next to me.

"Did you touch him?" I ask.

She blinks at me. "No. I didn't want to touch him, or do anything to him. I just wanted to be taken. I wanted him to want me so badly that I didn't have to do anything at all."

"What happened then?"

She breathes again. Two big, slow breaths. "I took off my underwear and we were both naked. And I lay there with my arms back over my head and my eyes closed. And I felt his mouth on me, and I had to bite my lip because I was afraid I'd yell."

"Where was his mouth?" My hand is on her leg now, running my fingers along the back of her knee.

"You know where," she says. A small sob escapes, but she fights it back.

"And then what?"

"He was on top of me again. And I could feel him against me. And I wanted him inside of me. I was waiting for it. But then he stopped."

"He stopped? Why?"

"Because I was crying. I think it scared him."

"Why were you crying?"

She looks at the ceiling, her eyes on the thin cobwebs at the corner of the room. "I didn't want to."

"Want to what?"

"I didn't want to be the person that I'd be if I let him fuck me." She closes her eyes and my hand is resting on her hipbone. "I didn't want to be alone. I knew if I let him . . . I knew that's what I'd eventually be. I'd be alone . . . like Curtis."

"Alone," I say. I pull her shorts down and kiss her belly, biting her skin gently. I slide my hand up her shirt and run my palm in smooth, slow circles over her breast. She breathes out, just a whisper, and desire, like need, wells again in my stomach. I have seen every centimeter of her body a thousand times, but tonight I'm seeing it through the eyes of another man. David Anderson looked at her, this long, skinny thing on a hotel bed, and wanted her. He'd dreamed about her and fantasized about her as he sat in his office talking about rates of return and other people's money. He wanted nothing more than to fuck my wife, and that's what I want, too.

I kiss her deeply, and our tongues sink into each other. She pulls her tank top over her head and I'm on top of her in a frantic rush. Anna is stronger than Katie, and she digs her heels into my lower back, pressing me as close as two people can be, and it feels absolutely right.

"Get these off," she says, gripping the waist of my jeans, and I do as I'm told.

Our bodies are perfectly in sync, as perfect as they've ever been. When I'm inside of her, she calls out the way she did the first time, back when there was no one to hide from. No children in the house. No dogs watching from the floor. And no lonely, brilliant fathers in the other room.

*Part IV*

## 33

*C*olumbia University is one of those schools that make you wish you hadn't been such a dipshit when you were eighteen. Unlike the sprawling, suburban state campus of my college years, this place is tucked behind a big gray wall right in the middle of the coolest city on earth. It's difficult not to somehow idealize the students here with their iPods and cool jeans, because they all seem to look exactly the way I wish I would've looked back then—intellectual and worldly, like they might say something devastating and subversive at any second with their exotic majors and far-flung ideas about how the rest of their lives might go. Most eighteen- and twenty-year-olds don't read a word of prose beyond magazines or Perez Hilton, but these kids are obviously different—our world's final hope for literacy. As Curtis, Sonya, and I step into the big courtyard on Center Campus, there's a troop of them, maybe a hundred or so, standing together along the pathway leading to Low Library. My guess is that they represent much of Columbia's writing program.

"Uh-oh," I say. "It's a riot."

It's a beautiful fall day in New York, one of those days where all of the things you don't like about Manhattan seem silly and you wonder how you could possibly live anywhere else. In the car on the way here, Curtis and I shared some bourbon from the minibar, and we're both smiling like two guys who've been drinking bourbon before noon. Sonya squeezes my elbow. "They're here for your father, dear."

And, of course, they are. When they see him, there's a quick flurry of clicks from digital cameras and iPhones. There will probably be a few other famous writers here today, but Curtis is who got them here on a perfect Saturday afternoon. About half of them are carrying books, used copies of his novels that they've studied in class and underlined and argued about over lattes late at night.

"I should go say hi," says Curtis. "They'll probably be the most interesting people I talk to today."

"By all means," says Sonya as he leaves us standing in the shade of an impressive white building.

"Oh for the love of God. It's hardly noon," says Curtis, shouting to the small crowd. "Aren't you people in college? Shouldn't you be hungover in your dorms somewhere?" They laugh and smile and some of the kids clap their hands. He pulls a pen from his pocket and begins signing their books and notebooks. It's clear to see that he's every bit as excited to see them as they are to see him.

"Do fans always show up to this thing?"

Sonya shrugs and reminds me that she's been to as exactly as many Pulitzer Prize award luncheons as I have. I haven't seen her in a while, and she looks great. She's a year or two younger than Curtis, but it could easily be a decade. She's one of those older women in this city who remains perpetually youthful by dressing cool and lining up with twenty-five–year-olds each morning for yoga. She's in a black skirt suit and silver heels and I remember why I had such a big crush on her when I was twelve.

"Brandon's still coming, right?" I ask.

"He said he was meeting us here, but who knows? He's probably in some alley with that tattoo artist doing God knows what."

I get the sense that she's playing the part of the disappointed Jewish mother here. We all have roles to play in our families.

A girl in faded, hip-hugger jeans and a Yankees hoodie screams and hugs my dad. She's young and pretty with smart-girl glasses and so my dad hugs her back while another girl takes their picture. These kids—all of them—remind me so much of Katie that I feel myself reaching for my phone. It would take me five seconds to text her, and then she'd text back, but I've promised myself that I won't.

"He seems happier lately," says Sonya. "It couldn't be more obvious."

"He's getting the Pulitzer today. I'd be happy, too."

She gives me a look—one I've received from my mother many times. "He's *happy*, silly boy, because of you guys. *You* especially. Being your father has always been one of his favorite things to be. He was afraid to admit that when he was younger. I think he always thought it made him sound too suburban. God forbid." She winks at me and smiles.

We look back at Curtis, posing with four kids in a picture. "Maybe," I say. "But it looks like his other favorite thing to be is a famous writer."

"Yeah, there's definitely more money in that."

Over her shoulder, a familiar man catches my eye. He's walking toward us with determined purpose in a dark suit. Like my dad, he wears his suit a little faded and misshapen, more like an academic than an executive. He's fidgeting with a tuft of hair, pulling it across a bald spot as he squints against the sun in the cloudless sky. Whoever he is, he doesn't look particularly happy.

"Hello, Sonya," the man says.

"Well, how are you, Alistair?" Her voice is chilly, and now I remember. This is Alistair Stewart, the fiction editor at the *New Yorker*. By sheer lineage, I feel a culpable sense of guilt. My father has been sleeping with this man's wife off and on for twenty years.

"So, he finally won the goddamn thing, huh?"

"He did indeed. It was bound to happen eventually."

"Pretty big award for a bunch of reissued stories," says Alistair. "Did he need to buy a new condo or something?" He lights a cigarette and coughs dramatically. Thirty feet away, my dad is signing books and asking a girl about her nose ring. The look on Alistair's face is practiced hatred. "We got a few reader copies down at the office. They're great for keeping fire doors open."

Sonya smiles, above it all. "Well, they're pretty good stories, Al, even if they never quite made it into the *New Yorker*."

"We go for relevant, Sonya. Curtis hasn't been relevant in years. This award should have gone to Nicholas Zuckerman. Every literate person in America knows it."

And then Alistair sizes me up.

"My wife and I are big fans of your magazine," I say. "Especially the movie reviews and cartoons."

That tuft of hair flips up from his head again and he grunts at me before charging off with his cigarette.

"Well, he seems nice," I say.

"I doubt Curtis will be invited to the *New Yorker* Festival this year."

At the steps of the library, we're rejoined by Curtis, who smells, I realize, a little like bourbon, which means I probably do, too. "What'd old Al have to say?" he asks.

"He was just wishing you well," says Sonya. "He sends his best as always."

A few well-dressed people pass by, taking note of my dad. He puts his arm around me and gives my shoulders a good shake. "If things get ugly in there, I'm going to need you to be my bodyguard, OK? Personally, I'd hit him in the jaw . . . he'll go down like a bag of sand."

Inside the Low Library's main lobby, there are about two hundred people milling around, and it dawns on me that many of them are here to accept their own Pulitzers. From investigative reporters to local journalists from cities I've never visited to war correspondents and jazz musicians, they've all accomplished something great. Still though, the temperature in this big marble room changes as everyone slowly begins to notice that my dad has arrived.

A thin man in a brown suit identifies himself from the *Times*. "Curtis, how does it feel to finally be taking home the big one?"

Curtis looks at Sonya. "Oh, you're right. I guess I haven't won this one before, have I? We're going to have to start charging my students more, I suppose."

The reporter laughs, and as he begins asking my dad about the progress of his newest novel, I realize that this could go on for a while, and so I drift off toward a big round table at the center of the room where people are finding their seat assignments. Through the loitering crowd there's a big, open space, like an empty hall moments before a wedding reception. That's where I find Brandon, at a table near the front, sitting alone over a glass of Coke. He appears to be in physical pain.

"Waiter, I think this man has I had enough," I say. There's no waiter there, of course, I'm just being funny.

"Jesus, remind me again why this thing isn't at night," he says. "What is it, seven o'clock in the morning?"

We give each other a quick bro hug, slapping backs. "You smell hungover," I say.

"Well, you smell like bourbon, so we're even."

"Our mothers would be so proud of us. All right, let's both agree right now not to hug anyone for the rest of the day."

"Deal."

He's sporting some baggage under his eyes, and there's more forehead there than last time I saw him, but he looks nice in his black suit and open-collared shirt. I pull at my own blue tie, and, ironically, I wish I *hadn't* worn it. I was never meant to be a tie guy. "Rough night?" I ask.

"They're all rough nowadays. Acting twenty-two when you're

thirty-two takes a lot out of a girl. We're not as young as we used to be, Tommy Violet." He gulps his soda hard, as if the physical effort required to speak has left him dangerously dehydrated.

"Dude, you haven't been young in years. You're just better at faking it."

"Hush your mouth. If you knew how much I spent on eye cream you'd fall right out of that Banana Republic suit of yours."

I take a sip from one of the nine water glasses at the table. It's lukewarm and the ice has dissolved into little jellyfish-looking slivers at the brim. I'm playing it cool, like someone who doesn't want to blurt out, *Did you read my novel yet, you asshole?*

"How's work? The wife and kid?"

"I just got fired the other day. I think my old company's gonna sue me."

"It's just as well," he says. "You don't need some sell-out job anyway. If you smarten up and let me take care of your pretty little ass we'll make so much money together we'll be able to buy all the Banana Republic suits we want."

"What does that mean, exactly?" I ask. "I don't speak gay."

"What it means, Thomas *Ferris*, is that I read your book. And, aside from a stunning lack of tits or ass, I think it's pretty fucking great. But, if you want to make some *real* money, you're gonna swallow whatever overly dramatic artistic bullshit pride you're trying to cling to and let me put your *real* goddamn name on it."

Background noise has dissolved into a steady white hum as I play back what he just said in my mind. *Pretty fucking great.* It'd be more thrilling if I weren't about 51 percent certain I'd just hallucinated the entire thing. "Well, what kind of money are we talking about if I stick with Thomas Ferris?"

Brandon pantomimes sadness.

When we were kids, we used to put on little plays for his mom and dad on weekends. He'd always insist on playing whatever character was the saddest, because it was the only emotion that fit his natural aesthetic. "Let's see, a complex little dramedy lit novel with no tits or ass from a no-named white boy named Thomas Ferris? I could probably get you enough for a nice dinner out at the nearest Olive Garden. No dessert though. Is it hot in here? Why is it always so fucking hot when I'm hungover?"

I drink some more lukewarm water. "But you liked it though, right?"

"Look at you, all handsome and vulnerable. It's good, Tommy, I promise. You're a *real* fucking writer, it turns out. Cards on the table here, I was pretty sure it was gonna suck it. No offense, but lit brats can never actually write. But this, *man*, is good stuff. It's like Violet 101, all Americana and thinly veiled metaphors. And I can sell the holy shit out of it. Regardless of the name on the cover. But, if you insist on being an idiot, can't we at least change your name to something good? Maybe brown you up a little? Mohammad Bhatia? Hector Julio Hernandez maybe? Nobody's reading honkies anymore. Especially male honkies. Thomas Ferris sounds like some secondary fucker in *The* fucking *Great Gatsby*. Some blond asshole with a trust fund lounging by the pool."

"Are you finished?"

"For the moment."

"Good. Then I think we should stick with Thomas Ferris."

I'd like to run around the table with my arms up and give everyone in the room a high five. However, it's hard not to have this tempered by the fact that Brandon is the second person this week to (a) be surprised that my book isn't terrible, and (b) tell me that it could have been written by Curtis Violet himself.

"Tell me then, Mr. *Ferris*, are we still keeping this literary venture a secret from Daddy?"

"Yeah, why?"

"Then zip it, because here he comes."

Sonya has slid her arm inside of Curtis's and she's laughing. My dad found her name thirtysomething years ago on a list of literary agents at the library, and now here we are.

"Hello boys," says Curtis.

"Well, Tom, you missed it," she says. "Your dad just told the nice little man at the *Times* that his next book will effectively reinvent the novel and change the way people read fiction."

"Change the way people *process* fiction," says Curtis, correcting her. "Weren't you even listening to me?"

"Reinvent the novel?" I say. "What does that even mean?"

"I'm not entirely sure. But it sounded nice as I was saying it. Now let's talk about the alcohol situation here. I was under the impression that the bar would be distinctly more robust."

Brandon clears his throat and opens his suit jacket, revealing a shiny silver flask. Apparently this is the norm for people like us. "In this economy," he says, "you gotta bring your own bar with you."

"Oh, Brandon," says Sonya.

"I've always liked you, Brandon," says Curtis. "You're my kinda guy."


The actual event is like a distant family member's high school graduation. For about an hour, we've been sitting patiently, looking at all the interesting people around us, waiting for my dad's category to be called and listening to stranger after stranger win Pulitzers. As the president of Columbia University—a man who looks startlingly like Mickey Mantle in his late middle-age—talks about each winner, I'm thinking about my book. I decided that I wanted to be a writer when I was eleven listening to my dad read at Politics & Prose in D.C. And now Brandon, an actual literary agent, has told me with almost bored certainty that that's exactly what I'm going to be. It's been such a shitty few weeks that it's difficult not to see this all being pulled out from under me. Clearly

I'm being punked. Ashton Kutcher is about to jump out and I'm going to punch him in the nuts.

"You really liked it?" I whisper. Brandon is sitting next to me, droopy-eyed. "What did you like most? Did you think it was funny?"

"Stop being so needy. I'll tell you what it *does* need, though . . . lesbians. They're so hot right now. People love them."

"OK, maybe I'll try to work some in."

And then we hear my dad's name reverberating from the box speaker at the podium.

"The first time I read Curtis Violet, I was a very serious English professor." Mickey Mantle's doppelganger's voice has changed. He's been reading from index cards about people he's never heard of, listing credentials and bibliographies. Now though, he's talking about someone that everyone here knows, and the steady murmuring and rustling and clinking of glasses comes to a stop.

"I read a lot, of course . . . it was my job. But I'd always read with purpose. I'd read to study—to glean information that I could dissect and use to impress people later. But, about halfway through my used copy of *Tomorrow Is November*, I realized that I was just reading for reading's sake. Reading for the sheer pleasure of it. Reading the way that we were all intended to read."

Whenever Curtis is listening to something like this, he looks friendly and a little aloof, smiling politely at the nearest centerpiece. He's a guy who's finally grown too old to be embarrassed by the things he's achieved.

"I didn't know a lot about fiction then, but I knew that this young writer, Curtis Violet, was going to be somebody important. He was an author I was going to be reading for the rest of my life."

The room has grown restless and people are sitting up, looking over at our table. In this strange little world, he's a star, one of the biggest.

"Curtis Violet has won the National Book Award twice, the

PEN/Faulkner twice, and the National Book Critics Circle Award three times, along with a host of other notable prizes and honors. His novels have been made into noteworthy films and have found themselves time and again among best-of-the-year and bestseller lists around the world. Perhaps more importantly though, he has become that rare writer, like Vonnegut and Mailer before him, who has managed to be celebrated here, academically, as well as among the far more elusive reading public. For my money, he is one of our greatest living writers, and he is this year's Pulitzer Prize winner for fiction for his collected stories. He is Curtis Violet."

When I look over at Sonya, I see that she's crying, and amazingly, I think I might be, too. Only Brandon among us is unshaken. He yells, "All right, Curtis!" and claps his hands, and this begins what quickly becomes a standing ovation for my dad. On his way to the podium, as he snakes his way through the maze of tables, he shakes hands and smiles. It seems that everyone here has brought a camera, and now those cameras are fixed on him. Then I see Alistair Stewart again. The poor man has begrudgingly stood with the others, but he refuses to clap. Glaring at my dad, his arms crossed, he looks like a man with dynamite taped to his chest. My father is his nemesis, and his loathing is palpable, like humidity.

I nudge Brandon and nod at old, fuming Alistair. "Check it out," I say.

Brandon just rolls his eyes, still clapping. "Oh for the love of Christ. When will you straight people get it? It's not the end of the world. It's just fucking."

## 34

**B**etween 113th and 114th on Broadway, just a quick walk from Columbia, is where the West End Bar used to be. It was this legendary dive that was made famous by the beatniks like Jack Kerouac who used to hang out there and get drunk. The place was finally shut down a few years ago, though, after the last of many fraternity brawls and underage drinking busts. To the horror of alumni and the entire literary community, it reopened a year later as a trendy Cuban restaurant. The new owners tried to stave off some of the mounting uproar by naming it Havana Central at the West End, but the damage was done.

I remember reading about this a while ago, but I'd forgotten about it entirely until now.

"They totally changed that place, Curtis," says Brandon. He's walking arm-in-arm with his mother down Broadway, guiding her around a discarded slice of pepperoni pizza on the sidewalk. "How do you *not* know this? Everyone knows this."

"Don't be an ass, Brandon," says Curtis. "They didn't change the West End. They'd never be allowed to do that."

"All right, man. Whatever you say." Sonya tries to smooth Brandon's hair. He's doing the stylishly messy thing. "Mom, stop it!" he says, pushes her hand away like a nine-year-old.

There's a line of about fifty people behind us, all award luncheon attendees dressed in suits and ties, following blindly. Cars and buses on Broadway are slowing to look at us. We're like a funeral procession on foot. My father announced to everyone within earshot on the way out of the event that drinks were on him. Apparently this is what Violet men do at critical moments in their lives.

"I'm telling you, man, they gutted it out. It's Mexican or Spanish or something. *El lamo es muy.*"

"I think he might be right, Dad," I say.

He waves us both away, two stupid kids, but it doesn't matter. Once a troop of marching academics and writers has its orders, there's no turning back, even as those of us in the front see the bright orange awning growing closer and closer. No one wants to say anything when we actually get there.

"What in the holy shit?" asks Curtis.

"See, Pulitzer, what'd I tell you?"

Sonya shushes her son.

My father is staring up sadly at the big, tangerine-colored building. "How could this be? I played darts with Allen Ginsberg here."

"Who?" asks Brandon.

A chalkboard sign by the door advertises CREDIT CRISIS SPECIAL: MOJITOS 2 FOR 1! "What in the hell is a mojito?"

Those who've followed are now loitering on the street, looking at the restaurant with indifference. Most of them didn't seem to know where we were going in the first place. "Is this it?" someone asks. "Yeah, I guess," says someone else.

Sonya asks my dad what he wants to do. "We're here, Curtis. Maybe we should just go in. It looks . . . *festive.*"

Defeated, he nods.

The decor inside does little to appease my dad. I have to admit, though, the place looks pretty nice. I wouldn't call it subtle, with pastel walls and flowers like Starburst candy, but it's cool and open and, in the middle of the afternoon, almost completely empty. The two bartenders leaning against their counter look at us like an approaching invasion. At the very front of the assault is, unbelievably, Alistair, barking for a scotch and water. His attendance at the awards ceremony was reasonable, a professional obligation, but showing up, still fuming, to the impromptu after party seems like masochism.

For a good twenty minutes, Brandon and I wait to get drinks, and he types continuously on his BlackBerry.

"How can you type so fast on that thing?" I ask. "The keys are so small."

"It's all shorthand and symbols," he says. "It's like a whole new screwed up little language. It's even infiltrated the biz. I'm working with this novel right now. Holy shit, you should see it. Some eighteen-year-old chick from San Diego wrote it. The entire fucking thing, every sentence, is written in text speak. LOL and IDK and BRB and smiley faces and all that. It's infuriating to read. Every high school teacher in the free world's worst nightmare come to life."

"But you're representing it?"

"Hell yeah, I am. Going to auction on the stupid thing on Tuesday. Two mojitos says I get the little ho a one-hundred-and-fifty-thousand-dollar advance."

"Jesus, what's it even about?"

"Who the hell knows? From what I can tell, it's pretty much *Romeo and Juliet* set in some high school in da 'hood. Pretty lightweight stuff actually, if we're speaking off the record. But *MTV Books* wants to do it in a Podcast series. Bling, bling."

I'm a dinosaur. I'm a giant, doomed lizard in a clearance-rack suit.

"Two mojitos and two tequila shots," Brandon tells the bartender when we finally make it to the front.

"Are you serious?" I ask.

"When in Rome, Tommy."

Like every tequila shot ever taken, this one goes down like shards of broken glass, and Brandon and I wince and hiss and cough at each other like longshoreman. I slap his back and he punches me in the shoulder. "Well, that was great," I say. "We should do like nine or ten more of those."

Brandon wipes tears from his eyes and sets to work on his mojito. "We'll do that later. Right now I need you to seriously listen to me about this name thing."

"OK. Bring it on."

"I've been playing this thing for laughs so far because I'm happy to see you, but I want you to think about something. Your dad over there is one of the most famous fucking writers in the world. If you publish a book under a fake name—even one inspired by an eighties movie—you dork—people are gonna figure it out. It's just a matter of time. And what about readings? Jacket photos? Promotion? I mean, you look just fucking like him. It's not gonna take Nancy Drew to put the pieces together."

"Couldn't you have at least said the Hardy Boys?"

"Don't try to throw me off track. I'm being serious here."

"Well, what if I don't do readings or any of that other stuff? What if I just publish it and let it exist on its own? Don't people ever do that?"

"No," says Brandon, plain and simple. "Well, sometimes dead people."

It's amazing how little I've thought this thing through, logistically speaking. Until now, it's just been me and my imaginary kid in a car headed for California.

"Listen," he says. "I get what you're doing. You don't think I can relate? Nobody's gonna ask my mom for an autograph today, but she's a legend. Curtis isn't her only big client, you know. That's why I spent my entire twenties trying to be anything *but* an agent. How could I be an agent when my mom was *the* agent? Sure, some people still think of me as Ross Lite, but fuck them . . . I had my first bestseller last month. Number seven with a bullet."

"*New York Times*?"

"Close enough."

"Don't you ever feel like you're . . . I don't know . . . cheating?"

He takes a long sip and scans the crowd. "It's not about how you get there, Tommy. Sonya won't be around forever . . . and neither will Curtis. I'm an agent. A fucking good one. Screw *Entourage* . . . they should make a show about me. And you, whether you like it or not, are a writer. Now close your eyes and give me a kiss."

I try to tell him that I just might, just to make him stop talking, but he tells me to shut up. "Holy shit," he says, grabbing my arm.

"What?"

"Don't look now, Bueller, but you're not gonna believe who just walked in."

I've never been good at *not* looking when someone says, "Don't look now," and so I spin around to the entrance where a tall, distinguished older guy stands in a tweed blazer. He's hunching a little, like tall men do who are trying not to stand out, and he looks lost as he scans the crowd. I've seen him before, of course, this brilliant recluse, but only in pictures. Brought into three dimensions, it takes me a moment to realize that I'm looking at Nicholas Zuckerman. "Whoa," I say. "Look how tall he is."

"Actors are always midgets in person," says Brandon. "But writers . . . they're giants."

"Wow."

"Dude's been in his cabin in the Berkshires for about a hundred years. He's like the literary Unabomber."

"He doesn't look like a terrorist," I say. "Do you think we should buy him a mojito?"

"I don't see why not," says Brandon, but we're all talk. Neither of us has had nearly enough to drink to be delusional enough to think we can just walk up and start talking to Nicholas Zuckerman. He's pushing eighty if he's a day, but he still looks like he could kick both of our asses, and so we watch him from a distance, like some exotic old animal in the zoo.

Curtis spots Zuckerman quickly from his spot deep in the bar surrounded by people. "Ladies and gentlemen," he announces, raising his glass. "A round of applause for the second greatest living American writer."

I've taken a conservative stance this afternoon regarding alcohol. Since having two more unnecessary tequila shooters with Brandon and finishing my mojito, I've been sipping at a perfectly reasonable Corona, which has grown warm in my hand. Brandon and I have separated, and I've become the social ghost that I usually become at these sorts of things. The TV above the bar is on the YES Network, which is running an old Yankee playoff game from the nineties. From my spot alone at the corner of the bar, I watch the room. Brandon is bouncing from group to group, chatting everyone up and handing out his business card. He looks like a kid running for student council president. I catch snippets here and there, loving every second of it.

"Wait, your agent lives where? You need someone here—in the city!"

"Really? I think you could expand that into a book. I see a market for that."

"If Obama wins this thing, that could really sell. Here, keep me in mind if you decide to write it."

"Are you kidding? If I sell twenty books a year, three are novels. Stick with memoirs. Fiction is dead."

God bless his energy.

The Havana Central at the West End has had enough time to adjust to the sudden flood of thirsty writers, and two cocktail waitresses have been assigned to roam around taking drink orders. The prettier of the two, a lanky blond thing with a star tattoo at the back of her neck, has found several opportunities to chat with my dad—or vice versa. She's just brought him another glass of wine and is laughing at whatever he's saying. By the shade of reddish-pink that his cheeks have become, I'm fairly certain that my dad is officially drunk.

If I left now and simply wandered down Broadway toward Harlem, would he even notice? I squash this thought though, because it's teetering on pathetic. I'm not a little boy hiding behind a rack of ladies' dresses at Macy's. I'm an adult, and I can go an hour without my dad paying attention to me. Can't I?

That's me giving myself a tough-love speech. I'm going to start doing that more often, I've decided. One might as well put his inner monologue to good use.

I take out my phone and hold down the number one. Anna answers on the third ring. "How was it?" she asks.

"Nice," I say. "More boring than I thought it'd be though."

"Well, you know, a bunch of writers congratulating themselves."

I can hear phantom domestic noises in the background—*The Lion King*, Allie chattering about something, the steady hum of our house. I wish I was there; I'm also very aware of the fact that we don't know where we are right now, Anna and me. We're talking to each other carefully, like people who are friends but only through other friends, all guarded and superficial.

"So, I talked to Brandon," I say.

"Yeah?" she says.

"Believe it or not, he loves the book."

"I do believe it," she says. "I told you it's great."

"He's less than thrilled with the pen-name idea though. Apparently it's something like publishing suicide. I don't think he gets it."

"I'm not sure I get it either," she says. "But it's your book, and you should do what you want with it. Either way, Brandon will live."

"Probably," I say, and then we lapse into silence. It's these silences that do damage, that reveal glimpses of the distressed foundation struggling under the weight of things.

"So, where's Curtis?" she asks. "Is he with you?"

"Sort of. He's actually flirting with a cocktail waitress."

"Curtis Violet? No way."

"I don't think she has any idea who he is though, which is oddly satisfying."

And then again, just as we were beginning to volley things back and forth so well, we're quiet again. "Tom," she says. Someone across the bar laughs and I'm squeezing the neck of my beer bottle. "Are we going to be OK?"

I think of her collapsing on top of me the other night, her lower back damp with sweat. After a moment of catching our breath, we both just started laughing, and we went on like that for a while. If every moment in a marriage was as simple and lovely as that, there would be no strained conversations like this over cellular telephones and hundreds of miles.

"Do you want us to be OK?" I ask.

"Yes," she says. "I . . . I do."

I can relate to that pause—that small, barely perceptible hitch in decisiveness. She knows that this won't be easy, but she cares enough to be having this conversation in the first place. And so do I.

"I think I do, too," I say.

"Then I guess it's up to us then, huh?"

"Yeah, I guess it is."

"Do you remember when you were a kid," she says, "and you always knew how you were supposed to feel because people told you—and so that's how you felt? I miss those days. They were less complicated."

"Sometimes I think I learned how to feel from reading my dad's books."

"Wow," she says. "Then we're all in big trouble."

She laughs and so do I, and then for a moment we're quiet again. It doesn't feel as charged as those other silences. There's an ease to it—a rhythm.

When I let her go, I finish my Corona and order another, just so I have something to do with my hands. On the other side of the room, my dad and Sonya are standing beneath the only semblance of the bar's roots—a dented sign that says THE WEST END nailed to the wall between black-and-white pictures of Allen Ginsberg and Jack Kerouac. Among the pastels and jungle of flowers, they seem silly, like afterthoughts.

"This place used to be such a dump," says a voice close by.

I've been so busy hiding out that I hadn't even noticed that Nicholas Zuckerman has sat down two stools over. "Truly," he continues. "People glorified it, of course. Writers glorify all sorts of things that don't necessarily deserve it. Your dad especially. But it was definitely a dump."

I look around to see if Brandon is nearby. "Umm, hi. I'm Tom—"

"Of course you are," he says, holding his hand out. "You look just like him. You didn't so much as a child, but you do now. I guess we change as we get older."

He's not a well-looking man, Zuckerman, and his sadness is vivid, like an aura. I've read every book he's written, and he's written many, but I'm a little frightened of him. He and my father have been famous for decades, but they've largely drawn wide circles around each other, interacting most often in the abstract, by referencing one another in the occasional interview, and not always in flattering ways.

"Were you at the ceremony thing earlier?"

"No, no. I've stopped attending those things. I'm in New York for—well, for some medical reasons—and I thought I'd drop in on your dad. He called me last week and made me promise I'd come. It's quite a day for him. You should be proud of him."

For years I've been watching seemingly intelligent people grow tongue-tied and stupid around Curtis, and I never understood exactly why. But now, the part of my brain that controls talking is filled with fog and static. Zuckerman must be used to this, and so he looks at his drink, something clear with a lime wedge floating in it.

"I'm sorry," I say. "I actually didn't realize that you and my dad knew each other all that well."

"It's interesting. People always assume that we don't like one another. Your father behaves like an imbecile most of the time, that's certainly true. And I think people tend to assume that I don't really like *any*one. But I'm actually rather fond of Curtis. We've kept in touch over the years. He's the only man I know who's as bad at being married as I am."

I laugh eagerly at this. Nicholas Zuckerman just made a joke to me. This is one of those moments that I'm going to think about for years and wish I'd been more clever and interesting.

"So, what do you do, Tom?" he asks.

"Well, that's complicated. I used to have a horrible office job, but I'm currently working as my dad's bodyguard."

Zuckerman smiles. "Your dad told me once that he thought maybe you'd end up writing as well. 'He has a writer's sensibility, and a writer's flair for knowing how bad things can get.' That's what Curtis always told me. Sounds like a bit of a curse to me, actually."

I resist the impulse to ask Zuckerman to repeat himself. The idea that he and my dad have discussed me, even in passing, is shocking.

"How's he doing anyway?" he asks.

"Who, my dad?"

Zuckerman nods.

"Fine, I guess. He's trying to finish his novel. He tells everyone it's brilliant, but I think it might be giving him more trouble than he's going to admit."

"I mean, *physically*. How's he doing? He's lost some weight, but he looks well, all things considered. I have some experience with cancer myself. It's an awful thing. But it *can* be managed. I'm certainly a little worse for the wear, but I'm here. And Curtis is a younger man than me."

The drink in my hand goes heavy, and I nearly drop it on the bar. "Wait. I'm sorry, what did you say?"

"I—" he says. His face changes, the lines go smooth, and then everything snaps back into place. But before he can say anything else, my dad, Sonya, and Brandon appear, and Curtis is accusing the two of us of being wallflowers. "Come on, you reclusive bastards, this is a party. Nicholas, I see you've met my son."

"Um, I have," Zuckerman says.

I'm almost certain that he said "cancer," but that's impossible. My father is standing right here, drinking with his arm around his literary agent. It doesn't make any sense.

Sonya introduces Brandon to Zuckerman. The shortest among us all, Brandon pulls his shoulders back and lifts his chin. "I tell you, Mr. Zuckerman," he says. "I've got a lot of clients right now. But, if you're interested in a new literary agent, I could probably make some room for you."

Zuckerman forces a smile and looks at me before quickly looking away. "I'll give it some thought. I'm actually in a bit of a dispute with my current agent over some cover art."

"Cover art? Jesus, why do you even need cover art? Save the money. Your cover art should be a sign that says, 'I'm Nicholas Zuckerman, buy this damn book, you idiots.'"

Everyone laughs.

I'm still dazed, replaying over and over what Zuckerman just said. The two writers together have caused the room to shrink as people have begun shifting in our direction, and in a matter of seconds we're all but surrounded. I look at Curtis's neck and his hands and the hollows of his eyes and his belt, cinched tighter around his waist. I think about the way he looked when he showed up at my house that night and the way he looks now. There's the duffel bag of pills he had me steal for him. Did he even need clothes? He could have just bought some.

Curtis is going on about some student of his, some story about a character murdering his girlfriend with his grandmother's ancient blender, and Nicholas Zuckerman is looking at me, trying to silently apologize. He thought I knew. *Of course* he thought I knew. I'm his goddamn son, why wouldn't I know?

"Tommy," says Brandon. "Have you ever even driven the Porsche?"

"What?"

"The Porsche. You ever driven it? Or have you just been staring at it since you were a kid?"

"I . . . no. Never."

There's more laughter and then Brandon is telling my dad that he's too old for a Porsche, that men his age should drive sensible Cadillacs. People are getting closer still, and I don't even know who any of them are. It's suddenly very claustrophobic.

"OK, so he won't let you drive his car," says Brandon. "That seems a little obsessive, but at least he's told you what his new book is about, right? Come on, Violets. Give it up. Curtis, it's been five years. Give us a synopsis, at least."

Curtis laughs and takes a sip of his drink.

How could I not have seen how thin he looks?

"It's about . . . the human condition," he says. "Right and wrong. Good versus evil. I don't want to give anything away."

Brandon is about to push further, and I should tell him to back off, but someone yells "Ha!" and the room goes quiet. And then it's yelled again and again. It's a big, loud, drunken fake laugh. It's Alistair Stewart. "Ha, ha, ha, you smiling asshole!"

"Hey, Al," say Curtis. "How've you been, old friend?"

Alistair elbows his way into our circle. "Sorry, didn't mean to eavesdrop, Sonya, but I couldn't help but overhear your kid asking about this arrogant bastard's *new* book."

"OK, Alistair," says Zuckerman. "This isn't the right time."

But not even Nicholas Zuckerman can stop this. Alistair is too determined, and worse, he's shit-faced. "It's an interesting question,

Curtis, isn't it? How *is* that novel coming along? What's it about again? There's no reason to be shy about your brilliance. We're all so interested, being as the sun rises and sets out of your ass."

"You'll have to wait and see, Al, just like everyone else."

"Alistair, please," says Sonya.

His highball glass is empty in his hand and he's using it as a pointer. "I'm sorry, Sonya. I've always respected you. But no. I've had just about enough of this—our pandering to this overrated fraud. Tell us again how talented you are, Curtis. Please, it never gets tiring."

Curtis is half smiling, but all of the bravado is gone.

"Come on, the Pulitzer for *your* collected stories? It's a stroke off, and we all know it. Your little farewell award."

"Dad," I say, taking his arm. He looks at me—he seems almost confused—but he remains there, standing his ground against this little tyrant.

"Son," says Alistair. "I hate to break this to you, but your precious father hasn't written a bloody word in five years. It's his little secret. But *I* know it—and other people are starting to figure it out, too. He's finished."

Zuckerman steps forward now, unsteady but towering over Alistair. "Al, I forget, how many Pulitzers have you won?"

The editor seems stung, stumbling back a step as a smattering of laughter echoes off the pastel walls. But his anger brings him back into focus quickly, and he levels his gaze on Curtis. "You're washed up. In thirty years when people are still reading Nicholas and all the other writers who really matter, no one will even know who you were. No one will give a shit about you anymore."

Curtis sets his drink on the bar and manages still to smile. This is bad. I should get him out of here, but behind my dad's smile there's something like genuine fear, and I'm so startled by it that all I can do is stare at this scene like some car accident in slow motion. Curtis surveys the room—acknowledging all of the eyes on him.

"You shouldn't believe everything that comes out of your wife's mouth, Al. Unhappy women have been known to tell tall tales. I can't say I blame you though. It's a lovely mouth."

At the mention of his wife—and worse, her mouth—Alistair goes rigid.

"Those lips are really something. All pouty and damp. It's amazing the things she can do with them."

Sonya covers her face and lets out a sound I don't think I've ever heard before, like a sob and a scream.

Alistair slams his empty glass down and it shatters into a wide circle of broken glass as a lime skitters across the floor.

"Can I get you another drink, Al?" Curtis says. "That one looks empty."

And then Alistair Stewart is lunging at my father. The rest of us, Sonya, Zuckerman, and I, are frozen. We're statues in a movie about people who can stop time. Everyone except Brandon, that is. One quick step and my would-be agent's fist catches Alistair's weak jaw, sending the editor sprawling to the floor atop his own broken glass.

"Brandon, no!" yells Sonya, too late.

When Alistair scrambles back to his feet, he inspects his hands. Blood, even in trace amounts from dozens of tiny cuts, leaves everyone stunned. And so no one has the presence of mind to stop him as he charges, flinging himself and Curtis Violet over a table of empty mojito glasses.

## 35

*I t couldn't have* lasted more than two minutes, even though it felt much longer. Of all the brawls in the history of that bar/restaurant, I doubt if ours ranks among the best. With its scratching, name calling, flailing elbows, wild, virgin punches, a split lip, two bloody noses, and a bunch of wrinkled shirts, it was all definitely more Havana Central than West End. You'd think that the New York City Police Department would have more serious problems to deal with, but it must have been a slow afternoon, and they showed up so fast that I wondered if they were waiting outside, peering in through the windows just in case this gathering of American writers got out of hand.

To say that we were arrested would be an overstatement. However, since we were all legally drunk and some of us actively bleeding, we were rounded up, loaded into the backseats of two squad cars, and taken not to jail, where real, legitimate criminals go, but to a detoxification center about seven blocks from Columbia in the middle of East Harlem.

Thank God this didn't include Nicholas Zuckerman, who did little more than stand in our ridiculous swarm and tell us all how asinine we were being. I could see that he was trying to protect my dad, but Alistair was too much and kept pulling Curtis back onto the floor where they rolled around grunting at each other.

"We've got some fighters here," one officer said to another officer, a heavy man with a mustache sitting behind a Plexiglas window. He looked up from a crossword puzzle and frowned. "You fucking kidding me? These guys?"

"Seriously, can I, like, talk to a lawyer or something?" asked Brandon. Everyone ignored him. "Umm, hello?"

That was about an hour ago. Now we're sitting in a long, narrow room with padded walls and about thirty rubber benches, each just wide enough for one person to lie down on. There's a water fountain and a toilet toward the back of the room, and the walls are a dingy beige color. It's an ominous, soothing, emotionally devastating color, and it's almost identical to the hallways and conference rooms aboard the Death Star. Aside from a few snoozing bums in the corner, we're the only people here. The fact that they've shoved us all in together, with our bruises and bloodstained collars, is testament to just how unthreatening we are as a group.

"Do you have any idea how long I've wanted to hit you?" says Alistair. He's been steadily sinking into his bench, his eyes at half mast.

"Probably fifteen years, I'd guess," Curtis says.

"You're such a dick."

"If it's any consolation, Al, I haven't seen her in a long, long time."

Alistair folds his arms, petulant. "It's not. Not one bit. You ruined my marriage. Do you realize that? The only good thing in my life."

"Well, let's call it even, because my fucking eye is killing me." He touches the side of his face, which has begun to swell. "I'm probably going to have a black eye for a month."

"Good," says Alistair.

"I can't believe they took away my BlackBerry," says Brandon.

"What the fuck do they think I'm gonna do with it? Make a bomb? Who am I, MacGyver? At least let me check my Facebook."

My dad coughs, holding his ribs. I saw him once with Alistair's wife a few years ago. It was his birthday and I stopped by his office at the university to say hello. When he finally answered his door, he was harried, and his shirt was unbuttoned. Through the crack in the door, I told him I was taking him out for a birthday drink, but he said he couldn't go because he was working on a scene. He told me he had two characters right on the brink. You can never leave them when something is just about to happen, he told me. As he closed the door, I caught a glimpse of her naked on his couch, her arms crossed over her breasts and her long bare legs on the armrest.

"I'm sorry about your lip, Tom," says Alistair. "I wasn't aiming for you."

There are traces of insincerity there, but I appreciate the effort. "It's OK. I probably deserved it for . . . something."

"What about me, Alistair?" says Brandon. "Where's my apology? Look at my nose. I look like a coke fiend."

"You hit me first, you little queen."

"Well yeah, but I got all caught up in the moment. You were being a real asshole to Curtis. We don't take that shit where I come from."

"Where's that, the Upper East Side?"

"Ha-ha!"

I study a yellowing water stain on the ceiling, wondering if it's urine. If so, I'd like to know how it got there.

A few minutes pass, and then Brandon perks up. "So, Alistair. Before you went all apeshit and got us throw into San Quentin, I was going to ask you—did you read that story I sent you last week?"

Alistair squints. "What?"

"You know, the one about the Iranian family at the Thanksgiving Day parade? It's a good story, Alistair. His novel is slated for the spring at Random House, and it's freaking awesome. Like *Kite Runner* after few Red Bulls. I think it'd be good to debut him in the *New Yorker*. He's got an exotic last name and everything. I know how you guys love that shit over there. Think about it—you can take all kinds of credit when he blows up and goes on *Oprah*."

"Christ," says Alistair. He lies down and throws his arm over his eyes. "I don't have time for this right now."

"That's interesting," my dad says. "Does the *New Yorker* still publish fiction, Al?"

"Screw you, Curtis!"

"Really? I thought it was just movie reviews now."

I've been denying it to myself for a long, long time, but I am my father's son. Asking the fiction editor at the *New Yorker* if the *New Yorker* still publishes fiction is exactly the kind of thing I would have proudly asked Greg. Looking back, things might have gone more smoothly for me if I'd just learned to keep my goddamn mouth shut.

More moments pass, an hour, maybe more, and Alistair has fallen asleep—or passed out, depending on how one classifies these things. His breathing has trailed steadily into a little whine, and for a while, it's the only sound in the room. Brandon has gone into a sort of pouting trance as he pines for his BlackBerry and stares at his expensive shoes. Curtis is quietly examining his bruised knuckles.

What Zuckerman said—that word he used—is abstract and unformed. It still exists only in the realm of the impossible. But what Alistair said, about Curtis's writing, that's different. "Is it true?" I ask.

He knows what I'm asking, of course. He looks over at Alistair, checking for signs of consciousness, and then he simply nods.

"How long has it been?"

He puts one knuckle in his mouth and rubs it. "About what Al said. Five years. Give or take. But it's complicated." He leans toward me, lowering his voice. "I've started more things than I can count. I've got so many damn beginnings. But everything just fizzles out. At first I thought I had Alzheimer's. That's how arrogant I am, Tommy. I've never had writer's block in my life, so it had to be something else, right? Some deterioration. I saw this specialist in D.C. He stuck these little suction cups to my head and had me solve puzzles and do math problems. But my brain . . . apparently . . . is fine."

"Then what is it?"

"There just aren't any more words."

He looks smaller than he's ever looked to me, slight and worn on this rubber bench, and that's when I'm able to grow up and admit to myself that it wasn't a mistake, and that I didn't misunderstand Zuckerman. I should have known, but I didn't. This has been my mantra lately—I should have known, but I didn't.

"Who else knows?" I ask.

"Well, before tonight, just the women. Sonya. She knows. Al's wife, Veronica, knows, too. And Ashley, kind of. As much as Ashley can truly know something that isn't about herself. That's my problem, Tommy. I've always told women too much. Oh, and I told your mother, too. It seemed like she should know. Like poetic justice."

"Mom knows?" I say, and right then, somehow I know that she knows everything else, too. Curtis closes his eyes for a long time and coughs. I should ask the cop with a mustache for some water—or for . . . the last several years back.

"I don't even remember what it's like not to be a writer. It's who I am—it's *all* I am. I've alienated everyone in my life, and I've pushed everyone else away. But it didn't matter because I could always count on the men upstairs. But now they're gone, and I have no one."

Brandon is listening now, and I can see him looking at me, wondering how Curtis could say this to his own son, that he has no one. But I know that he's right. The most important people in this man's life—the people who have mattered to him most—aren't my mother or his wives or me or Anna or Allie. The people who matter most are the people in his head. *That* is loneliness.

Curtis takes my forearm, squeezing it for a moment. His eyes, blue and bloodshot, are fixed on mine. "Tom," he says. "Do you have any idea what it's like to be me?"

One of the two bums murmurs something in his sleep. Up above us, at the thin row of dusty windows near the ceiling, I see Danny outside, the boy from my novel who lives in my head. He's peering in at me, waving sadly. He's wearing a jacket and he's got a backpack over his shoulder, like he's ready for us to go somewhere.

"Do you ever see them, Dad?" I ask.

"Who?"

"Your characters."

He smiles and looks up at the beige ceiling. "I used to. All the time. Especially the ones I killed. I always felt like they held it against me. I bet that's how God feels."

Across from us, Alistair is curled in the fetal position, sleeping soundly. He's kicked one shoe onto the floor and there's a hole in his sock. I wonder if any of my dad's imaginary people are here now, too, maybe lying on these benches beside us, or maybe just watching, waiting to be told what to do, like ghosts who never existed in the first place. But I doubt it. The room feels cold and empty, and I'm pretty sure that they're all gone.

"You're sick, aren't you?" I say.

He looks surprised, but only mildly. Today has been a day of revelation and of things unraveling. "Your mother told you?" he asks.

"No. Nicholas. He thought I knew."

Curtis shakes his head. "Zuckerman," he says, and no one says anything else for a long time.

## 36

I t's a little after 10 p.m., and I'm walking through my dad's neighborhood by myself. West Twenty-ninth at this time of night is eerily quiet, and I keep looking over my shoulder like a tourist. I'd wanted to live here so badly when I was younger—anywhere in Manhattan—but I never made it. It's one of those cities that work so much better in the abstract. The romantic house of cards crumbles quickly when you start to do the math.

A half hour ago, an officer who none of us had seen yet opened the door, pointed at the four of us, and said, "You turkeys, outta here." On our way out, we passed a few rough-looking guys cuffed to a wooden bench. One of them wore a T-shirt covered completely in blood. Apparently those in charge didn't think we'd all get along very well. Outside, I was astonished to see Brandon and Alistair climbing into the same cab. When they closed the car door, they were talking about that story that Brandon was trying to sell. Turns out Alistair *had* read it, but wasn't completely on board yet. Brandon was listing off other publications that he was sure would be thrilled to publish such a "kick-ass story."

"I don't have what it takes to be an agent," said Curtis.

Up at the corner, stopped at a light, there was an open cab and I held my hand up. "Come on," I said. "Let's get you home."

Curtis shuffled his feet, toeing a crack in the sidewalk. "Well, actually, you think you could make it back to my place on your own? I sort of owe someone a nightcap."

"A nightcap? What are you talking about? Dad, we just got out of jail."

"Detox, Tommy. Not jail. Legally speaking, there's a pretty big difference."

"But you're—"

"Alive," he said. He turned his cell phone back on, which had been kept in a plastic bag while we were detained, and began dialing a number. My cab pulled up to the curb, reggae music blaring through the windows. "You take this one," he told me. "I've never been a fan of Bob Marley."

The overnight doorman in my father's building gives me a sleepy nod, and the entryway smells like the same mildew and dust and curry that it did when I was a kid. In the elevator, along the wood paneling below the numbers, I find my own name, carved with a twisted paper clip, when I was maybe twelve. Upstairs, I flip on some lights and the loft comes into bright, minimalist focus. He bought the place before he was rich, and even though it's now worth millions, it doesn't look a lot different than it did in 1984. The fact that it has survived Curtis's many terminated unions is a feat worthy of a feature article in *Divorce Lawyer* magazine.

My travel bag is on the couch where'd I'd left it, and our dishes from breakfast are in the sink. Something seems different though, rearranged somehow. But how could it not look different? The last time I stood in this apartment, thirteen hours ago, the world was a different place and Curtis was healthy and finishing his novel.

When I call Anna again, she answers quietly.

"Were you sleeping?" I ask.

"Yes, but I didn't mean to be. I was reading. What's up?"

"It's been a strange night, Anna."

"Good strange or bad strange?" she asks.

Anna waits for me to respond, but I don't know if I can. I'm tired and all I want to do is wash the detox from my face and go to bed on this lumpy couch. If I begin talking, I'll start crying, and I'm not up for that now.

It started where it always starts for men, in his prostate. Amazingly, it was his penis that had alerted him first. After years and years of steadily balling almost anything in his path, things had become problematic and tricky down there. But by the time he thought to actually see a doctor, to accept that his own shriveled manhood might be a metaphor for things more serious, the illness had begun its slow, steady migration elsewhere. Writing had been difficult for a while by then. Nothing seemed to be taking hold, and his men upstairs were, for the first time ever, unsure of themselves. But since this, the idea that whatever it was he was trying to say might be the last thing he says made the blank screen insurmountable.

"Just strange," I say. "That's all."

"You weren't arrested, were you?" she asks, making a joke.

"No, not . . . technically."

There will be time to tell her everything later, and I will.

"Gary called earlier," she says. "He forgot you were up in New York. Looks like everything's going to be OK with your mom."

"Seriously? What'd he say?"

"Not much. He said he'd explain later. Said something about a big gesture and started quoting one of your dad's stories, the one with the skywriter. He sounded happy though. So, I guess that's good news."

After I say good night, I get a drink of water from the sink and inspect the loft. I step out of my pants and take my dress shirt off, leaving them there on the kitchen floor in a ball. In my boxers, undershirt, and black socks, I could be a businessman, home from another stressful day at the office.

In the bathroom, the light is already on. When I look up into the mirror, the first thing I see is my stinging, split lip. The second thing I see is a hand hanging limply over the side of the tub behind me. There are crimson droplets on the floor and one red footprint against the stark white bathmat. And then I see my stepmother, Ashley, floating naked in red water.

I clutch the sink to keep myself from tumbling to the ground. Then, in one painful heave, I throw up. Her eyes are closed. A delicate red trail beads up along her wrist and another drop of red falls to the floor. "Oh fuck," I say. "Fuck."

I have no idea what to do. I'm shaking so hard my vision is blurring. The police will come, and our names will be in the paper. My God, Ashley is dead in the tub. I throw up in the sink again, everything I've eaten for days. And then—

"Oh shit. Tom, it's just you." Back in the mirror, she's looking at me, and she's annoyed. "You were supposed to be Curtis."

"Ashley? What the fuck?"

"I'm not dead, Tom, don't worry. I'm just trying to make a point. Now, unless you need to barf again, would you mind handing me that towel?"

I'm sitting on the couch, and my hands won't stop shaking. Back in my wrinkled suit pants, waiting for this lunatic to come out of the bathroom, I'm all jittery and wired from the adrenaline surge. My mouth tastes like vomit. Better men would have sprung into action, scooped naked Ashley from the tub and gone about the business of bringing her back to life. But not me, I puked in the sink.

"Thanks a lot for spoiling my little show." She's wearing a pair of oversize pajama bottoms and a tank top. I look away from her nipples, which press against the thin fabric like things trying to get out.

"Sorry. I should have seen it coming. The situation had 'fake suicide attempt' written all over it."

"What the hell happened to your mouth?"

"It's a rough city," I say.

She strolls into the kitchen and starts making a drink. It's a safe bet that she's already had a few this evening, but you can't fault her manners, as I can see that she's making two. "I know you think I'm crazy," she says.

"What? Not at all."

"I need to show Curtis exactly what he's done to me. I need him to feel what it'd be like if I was gone. *Really* gone—not just *divorced* gone." She hands me a drink, which tastes like it's about 90 percent vodka. Either that or gasoline. "Here, this will settle your stomach," she says.

"When I was little, my mother always gave me vodka when I had a stomachache."

She settles next to me on the other side of the couch, pulling her long legs beneath her, resting her drink on her knee. In detox, my dad told me he hadn't said anything to Ashley about being sick. He said he didn't think she could handle it, and I believe him. There's still some pink around her wrist where she's gone heavy with the food coloring. "He would have looked at me, and he would have realized how big of a mistake he'd made. Right there in that bathroom, it would have hit him like a ton of bricks."

"But then what?" I ask. "You wouldn't have been dead, Ashley. Eventually he would have figured that out."

"That's not the point," she says. "It's the first five seconds that would have mattered—the five seconds that made *you* sick. A lot can go through a person's mind in five seconds. But you had to go and ruin it, and now you're gonna rat me out, aren't you?"

This emaciated thing in her nightclothes is like a schoolyard bully, daring me to tattle. She throws an arm over the couch cushion and glares at me, her eyes set above two gray half circles. Nothing I say now to her or later to my dad is going to keep this beautiful maniac out of his hair. If she's not lurking outside his home with spy equipment or floating fake-dead in his bathtub, she'll be doing something else. Probably something worse.

"I wouldn't even know where to begin," I say.

She takes a sip of her drink, swallowing like Kool-Aid. "So, where is he anyway?"

I say nothing.

"You're such a pussy, you know that? Don't worry, Tom, I know where he is. He's screwing that old hag. Grosses me out to even think about it. I don't know how he does it."

"What?"

"Oh, don't patronize me."

"Ashley, I don't know what you're talking about. He didn't tell me where he was going. He just . . . left."

"He left you behind, huh? Well, now you know what it feels like. That's what he does, you know. That's what he's always gonna do—he's gonna leave people like us behind, because he's awful. But little old you and me are too stupid to do anything about it."

I begin to tune her out as she goes on and on, and as I sink further into the couch, a fog lifts. It's the fog I've put around this new woman in my head, the newest woman in Curtis's life. Before being flung across the bar, my dad made a snide comment about Veronica Stewart's mouth that had made Sonya literally cry out. It had hurt her that badly. "Sonya?" I say.

Ashley studies my face. "Hmmm. Well, so you see what I'm talking about then. But I'm not worried. When he's done rediscovering his old age, he'll come back. She's just a passing phase. An identity crisis."

"You know that's funny," I say. "My last stepmother said the same thing about you."

The room is as silent as deep space, and I feel like a dick as a tremor of hurt travels the length of her pristine face. She sips her drink some more and looks at me, this woman I've seen in magazines and once on the side of a bus in D.C. while I was buying a hot dog. "*I* am the woman men leave women for, Tom. Not the other way around." She shifts her weight to free one leg, which she stretches the length of the couch until the arch of her foot is resting on my thigh. She's watching me as I look down at her long, ornate toes. "Ever since I was thirteen years old, every man I know has wanted to fuck me. All of my teachers. All of my dad's friends. Every photographer. Every director and producer and agent. Curtis is no different. None of you are."

"But what if he loves her, Ash? Does that even matter?"

She cocks her head as if talking to a small boy or a dog. "Do you love your wife, Tom? Sweet, brainy Anna with her split ends and clunky shoes?"

"Yes."

"Well, if you love your wife so much, then why did you want to fuck me at my house when you came to collect Curtis's underwear? And why do you want to fuck me right now?" Her toes, like fingers, grasp my thigh, and little fireflies of what can only be desire flutter in my groin. "Curtis can love anyone he wants—just like you can love your smarty-pants wife. But at the end of the day, all of you follow your dicks over your hearts, and Curtis is always going to want to fuck me. That's going to lead him right back here, whether he likes it or not."

I grab her foot and hold it, feeling its weight and texture in my hand. She breathes in, watching me from across the couch, waiting to see if I'm going to prove her right. She doesn't know what I know, that Curtis, wherever he is now, is no longer the man she thinks he is, the man we all thought he was this morning. And I guess I'm not, either.

I set her foot on the cushion. "I think you should go," I say.

Her laughter is loud and jarring. "*I* should go? You moron, I live here."

She has a point.

For a fleeting moment, I consider simply taking the keys off the hook by the door and going across the street to the parking garage and sleeping in the Porsche. That would be poetic, and I make a mental note of it for later—for some book that I may someday write. But my back hurts from the bench in detox and I'm too old to be sleeping in German sports cars from the 1980s.

She laughs again, and I freeze as she climbs onto all fours. I watch her crawling toward me, and I try to pull away but there's nowhere to go. "Relax, *son*," she whispers. Her breath on my face is hot and boozy. With a quick snap of her head, she licks my scabbed-over lower lip and smiles. "Enjoy the couch."

Her bedroom door closes and the loft is bright and silent, and I'm all alone. The next morning when the sun from the uncovered windows wakes me up, she's gone.

## 37

**M**y dad's Pulitzer is in the backseat along with a few shop-ping bags from some of his favorite stores on Fifth Avenue. It's Monday afternoon, and after fighting through some traffic get-ting out of the city, and the usual mess on the Jersey Turnpike, we're humming our way south down I-95. There's this phantom pull of anxiety in my gut. I wonder how long it'll take my brain to fully embrace the fact that I don't have to be anywhere other than wherever I am.

I keep glancing at myself in the mirror on the sun visor. My lip has turned surprisingly ghastly. It's like *Fight Club* all over my face, which makes me proud. I'm so antiestablishment and danger-ous. Curtis's black eye is similarly impressive. Maybe we're not two helpless book people after all. We're real men who occasionally tear up posh Cuban restaurants just for the hell of it. Kerouac would be thrilled.

Curtis has assured me that he's perfectly capable of driving. In fact, his doctor has told him he can do anything. It could be six months. It could be a year. It could be two years. But I keep look-ing over at him anyway. He looks like himself, like Curtis, but then the light will hit him a certain way and he'll look like a sick person.

Near Delaware now, he shifts in his seat and takes a sip of a soda he bought about fifty miles ago. "So," he says. "I'm moving back to D.C. permanently."

"Really?"

"I've liked being near you guys very much. Allie in particular. When you were her age, I missed some things that I shouldn't have missed. And even when I was there, well, I was often not really there. And even though you're thirty-six, you could still use a father, right? Everyone needs a dad."

There's sentiment and finality in his voice, and so I don't remind him that I'm actually thirty-five. "Maybe once you get settled in, you'll be able to—"

"No," he says. "I've been trying to write one last book for years. I'm done with that. I just wish my last one had been better. It would have been nice to go out on a crescendo. But, so be it."

"You can stay with us, if you want. I'm sure we can work out a reasonable agreement on rent."

He smiles at the steering wheel. "That's nice, but I think it's best I get out of the way. I'm giving Ashley the loft. She actually deserves it, and she hates D.C. anyway. There aren't enough people there to tell her how beautiful she is."

Somewhere in the Lincoln Tunnel about an hour and a half ago, I gave Curtis the *Reader's Digest* version of Ashley's performance in the tub. He just shook his head and apologized, completely and utterly unsurprised.

"What about Sonya?" I say. "What's she gonna think of D.C.?"

He looks at me and then back at the road. It's very telling that in this narrative, so many of my father's secrets have been revealed not by him but by the women in his life. His confidantes.

"You could have told me, you know. I could have handled it."

"If I had, you'd have lumped her in with the others, and you wouldn't have taken it seriously. Who could blame you? I haven't exactly given you much to take seriously over the years."

"True."

"But Sonya's a real person, like your mother. Thirty years ago, that was your mother's biggest flaw in my eyes, and now that's the thing I love most about Sonya. It's funny how things end, isn't it?"

He's talking about his life the way he would one of his books, something that has drawn to a slow, inevitable conclusion.

"Sonya and I are both ready for a change. It'll be easier in D.C. Easier to just be normal and together."

I consider Sonya, dressed in black, sitting at Johnny Rockets with my family, and it's ridiculous. If ever there was a woman who belongs in New York, it's Sonya Ross. Her moving south will be like disassembling the Chrysler Building and putting it up in Georgetown. The fact that she's agreed to this must mean she's got a lot of faith in my father, faith that I'm not sure he's earned.

"I just thought of something," I say. "If you guys ever got married, Brandon would be my brother."

The New Jersey station we've been listening to finally turns completely to fuzz, and I fiddle with the knob, settling on a classic rock station. There's a song on that I used to love, and now it's an oldie.

"Red states, be damned," says Curtis. "We're the modern American family."


For the first time in a long time, I'm dreaming about my wife. It's a husband's dream. We're on the couch together and Allie is on the floor between us, her crayons scattered at random. Hank is there, too, beneath the coffee table, making sure we don't go anywhere without him. It's our house, but a little different—an idealized version of home without dust or cobwebs or those little scratches on the wood floors.

The terrain beneath the Porsche is changing. My dad is driving over gravel maybe, turning around or stopping, and I'm half asleep and half not. He speeds up and then slows down and then stops all together. My body is used to motion, and now, totally still, I open my eyes. Outside my window, there are trees and a mile marker and an empty fast food bag skittering along the overgrown grass. I'm looking at the side of the highway. Next to me, my dad has taken off his seat belt, but we're still idling. He's quietly smoking a joint. Over his shoulder, cars are whooshing by at a million miles an hour.

"Dad?" I say.

He laughs. "I don't believe it."

I have a horrible taste in my mouth from sleeping in the car. "What's the deal?"

He nods ahead and I follow his gaze, but I don't know what I'm looking at. There's an exit ramp, and over a hill there's a McDonald's sign, and we're maybe twenty-five yards from a billboard. I'm about to ask him what in the hell I'm supposed to be reacting to when I notice that the billboard is one of Gary's. There he is, giant and smiling next to the Ford logo. "It's Gary," I say. "He's got them all over the place. It's not a big deal."

"Yeah, but look what he's saying."

I rub the crusty things from the corners of my eyes, and then I laugh, too. In the place where there's usually an advertising message about low financing or a new model of some Ford vehicle, there's something else entirely. In big, bold letters, it reads: MARY-ANNE, PLEASE TAKE ME BACK. I LOVE YOU!

"Holy shit."

Curtis exhales through three open inches of window. "It's very subtle. Not sure if the exclamation mark is necessary though."

"Now *that* is a big fucking gesture."

"What?"

"Remember your story, 'The Skywriter'?"

"Yes."

I take a breath, breathing in secondhand pot, and I'm not even sure where to begin. "Never mind. Where are we anyway?"

"Maryland. About twenty miles from home."

An eighteen-wheeler rockets past and the car shakes hard and then settles. "The man is a freaking idiot," says Curtis.

"What, are you out of your mind?" I say. "The man's a genius."

## 38

*I've been unemployed* for about ten days now, which means I've gotten to know Regis Philbin and Kelly Ripa pretty well. I could be using this time to start another novel. Or maybe I could write a short story first. I haven't written one of those since college, but it seems like writing a twenty-page something would be easier than writing a four-hundred-page something, right? Or I could try to write a résumé. Or, I could just keep watching *Live with Regis and Kelly*. I've also heard good things about *The Young and the Restless*.

I check my watch, trying to look like I'm not checking my watch. It's funny, for ten days I've done virtually nothing, but today I've got two appointments. My mother has given me strict instructions to meet her in her office at my old high school at 2 p.m. But right now, I'm sitting in a Starbucks on Fifteenth Street talking to Andrew Brown from the *Washington Post*.

The *Post* actually ran a story about me the other day, or, more specifically, about my famed press release. When my colleagues were forwarding it back and forth to each other on the day I got fired, it somehow made it out of the building and began spreading like some sort of virus. Within a few days it'd become what the article called "a minor Internet sensation."

LOL . . . I guess.

Andrew Brown is a good-looking guy in his forties with salt-and-pepper hair. He looks like a newspaperman as he drinks his venti latte with a double shot. One of the weird by-products of unemployment is the inferiority complex you develop around people with jobs. I found a parking spot right out front, and I can see Hank sitting in my car, looking out the passenger-side window at the building, wondering what I'm doing in here.

"So, you enjoyed the article then?" asks Andrew Brown.

"I did. It made me look like less of an idiot than I thought it would."

He smiles. Up until now, we've been talking about baseball, and I'm beginning to wonder why he wanted to see me.

"Never underestimate the power of humor," he says. "People can get away with saying a lot of interesting, poignant things when they're pretending to be an idiot. I have a feeling you're one of those guys who gets a lot of laughs by being self-deprecating. Maybe by pretending you're not quite as smart as you actually are?"

"Perhaps," I say. "Also, I'm not afraid to fall down in public, either. People laugh at that every time."

Andrew Brown seems to be enjoying this. He's been laughing a lot since we sat down together, which makes me happy. I instantly like people who laugh at my jokes. It's a weakness of mine. "Listen," he says. "I wanted to talk to you about an opportunity."

The word "opportunity" makes me immediately suspicious. It's one of those once-harmless words that corporate America has ruined. Like "task" as a verb or "facilitate."

"Right now, the country is a mess. OK? That's obvious. People are getting laid off everywhere, in every industry. McCain and Obama are talking about a bazillion-dollar stimulus package, but that might as well be Monopoly money to people on Main Street. Fair or not, nobody thinks they're gonna see any of that.

"There's a lot of anger right now. It's palpable. I think that's why your press release caught on so much. People kept forwarding it to their friends because you could have been talking about *their* company—*any* company really. Let's face it, people are afraid. But . . . of what? Sure, they need to work and they need to have paychecks, but a lot of people *hate* their jobs. Most of the things people do for forty hours a week is drudgery at best. A *lot* of people feel a *lot* of resentment toward their employers right now. And why shouldn't they? Companies go on about teamwork and synergy and investing in *you*, and they have happy hours and employee appreciation day and career tracks, but that's all bullshit. The last few weeks have proven that no matter how long you've been there, or how good of a job you've done, if they need to get rid of you to maintain profitability or appease stockholders, they sure as hell will. In a heartbeat."

I feel like I should yell out an "amen." "You're right," I say. "My wife helps kids learn to read, and my best friend is a doctor. But I don't think I know anyone who works for an actual company who doesn't wish they could show up with an Uzi most days."

"Exactly," says Andrew Brown, slapping his knee. "And that's why I want you to write a blog for our Web site."

"A what?"

"Think about it. You worked for your crappy company for what, seven years? My God, think about how much pent-up frustration you must have stored in that head. I bet that press release was just a taste. Here's how it'll work. You follow the week's business news, you draw on your personal experience, and every Thursday you give us five or six hundred words on how it's all garbage."

"You want that in your *business* section?" I ask.

"Hell yeah. Opposing viewpoints. You're a man of the people, Tom. Every day we'll run articles about mergers and acquisitions and stock prices and new products and hostile takeovers. And we'll quote CEOs and CFOs and PR spokespeople with their spin and hyperbole. And you'll be right there to give the everyman's perspective. And we'll all love you for it."

I look out the window again at Hank in my car, and then all the people in line for their teas and coffees. They're wearing slacks, ties, jackets, and heels. These people have all managed to keep their jobs, somehow. At least for now. Maybe there's hope for the world after all.

Andrew Brown takes a sip of his drink, his pitch complete. "Will you think about it at least?"

But I already have. Before he was even done talking, I'd mentally gone through my "Ass Face" file of Greg's complaints. Thankfully I'd managed to e-mail it to myself before IT shut me out of my computer. Writing about my loathing for that awful place will be the easiest thing I've ever done. Greg will be my muse, Ian Barksdale and Janice Stringer my Lolitas. My insubordination, rampant and grossly unprofessional, has given me the chance to blow up the Death Star once a week until the *Washington Post* tells me enough already, and I say, "I'll do it" so fast that Andrew Brown actually laughs at me.

"Wow," he says. "You should probably work on your negotiating techniques."

I park in the visitors' lot and enter my old high school through the main lobby. On the way here I've written a blog in my head about how stupid it is that no one says "call" or "e-mail" anymore. It's "ping" or "reach out."

```
Can you reach out to Stephanie in Marketing
and see if she can give you a download on our
plans for Q3? Can you ping me later, after your
meeting?
```

My God, this thing is going to write itself.

I've only been back in this building a handful of times since I graduated 250,000 years ago, but I'm always struck by how small it seems. There's a big trophy case front and center, and I stop at the little placard that says CROSS COUNTRY. Sure enough, my name's still there. When I was seventeen, I ran a 5K in 16:22, which at the time was the fifth best in school history. Since then, I've fallen to tenth. A kid named Rash Lahari ran a 15:12 in 2002 to take over number one. God bless him.

There are some students roaming the halls, and each eyes me with suspicion, a stranger among them dressed too casually to be anyone of any authority. I do my best to look like I'm not here to murder them all, but this is harder to do than you might think at my age in a building full of teenagers and lockers. There's a big blue poster announcing a dance on Friday.

I find my mom exactly where she said she'd be, sitting at her desk in the main English office. She's eating a salad from a clear plastic container and looking through a stack of essays. In a thin cardigan sweater and looking a little disheveled, she's all English teacher. I lean down and kiss her on the cheek before falling into the uncomfortable chair across from her old desk. We've been playing phone tag, halfheartedly, and exchanging e-mails. I've told her the vaguest possible version of my current employment status. To be honest, though, I've been avoiding her. It's taken me a while not to be mad about all the things she hasn't told me.

"Honey," she says, giving me an unhappy look. "You really didn't have to go and get all dressed up."

I'm fiddling with a paperweight bust of William Shakespeare. "In my defense, Mom, these are my most expensive jeans."

"What happened to your lip?"

My wound is barely there anymore, no more ghastly than a cold sore. "The fiction editor at the *New Yorker* punched me in the face. I'm thinking about suing him. Nicholas Zuckerman is my star witness."

She rolls her eyes and pops a baby carrot into her mouth.

"So, I saw an interesting billboard the other day. I was meaning to ask you about it."

She hides her smile behind a forkful of iceberg lettuce. Along with the one that my dad and I saw in Maryland, Gary arranged for the conversion of seven other Ford billboards across Southern Maryland, D.C., and Northern Virginia. "Ridiculous," she says. "A complete waste of time and money."

"Seems like it worked though, huh?"

"If you define *working* by making me realize that Gary cannot be left to his own devices without terrorizing the entire city, then you're correct, it *did* work. I've moved back home as a service to society. Some of my honors students saw it. They've been giving me a hard time about it."

For a long time, my mom has hidden behind a façade of pessimism when the subject of happiness comes up. I imagine other women have done this, too, in the wake of men like my father. But I can see through it now, and she's beaming. She is as loved as any woman can be—a fact that has been demonstrated now to the entire D.C. metropolitan area.

"Consider yourself lucky. It could have been a lot worse. I had to talk him down from a skywriter."

"You knew about it?" she asks.

"It seems you and I have been keeping some secrets from each other lately," I say, thumbing Shakespeare's goatee.

She ignores this, setting her salad aside. "I saw something interesting the other day, too, now that we're on the subject." From a drawer full of pens, she pulls out a newspaper, which I recognize proudly. It's the article the *Post* wrote about me and all of my snarky, immature brilliance. She smooths the wrinkles and clears her throat. " 'It's like day care for adults, says Tom Violet, of corporate America,' " she reads. " 'We sit in meetings and we use important-sounding, utterly meaningless words to impress each other, but so few of us are actually doing anything to improve the world in even the slightest way. Sure, we may be able to buy iPhones, but we're handing over our souls and our happiness in the process.'"

Over the top of the paper she gives me a very specific look. Many have sat in this same chair before me and received this same look. In their defense, though, most of them have been, legally speaking, children.

She continues: "'It is a world in which followers and yes-men prosper, the suits at the top get richer and richer, and anyone with any semblance of creative or innovative thought is either cast aside as a non–team player or slowly beaten into submission. It's just an awful, awful place.'"

"It's like poetry," I say.

"A little self-righteous, perhaps?"

"I think I made a compelling argument."

"Yeah, a compelling argument for why to not *ever* hire you. What are you going to do for a job, Tom? You've successfully burned every bridge in your industry. In *every* industry, really. It's probably the most impressive example of irresponsibility I've ever seen."

As excited as I am about my brand-new professional blogging career, I feel like telling her about it will not get me very far here, especially considering I'll be making one dollar per word, before taxes. But, in truth, I didn't come all the way here to listen to a detailed analysis of my shortcomings as an adult.

"Why didn't you tell me he was sick, Mom?" Startled, she looks around the room. A few of her coworkers are eating their lunches at their desks. It's the educational community's version of Cubeland. "I had to hear that my dad has cancer from Nicholas Zuckerman? *Nicholas Zuckerman.* Do you have any idea how weird that was? That's not normal. Why is our family so strange?"

Zuckerman's name perks the ears of some of the other teachers in the room, and we instinctively lean closer to each other across her desk.

"Tom, I'm sorry. He asked me not to tell you. He said he was going to tell you himself. Nicholas Zuckerman? Really?"

"Well Curtis *didn't* tell me. And I seriously don't know if he ever would have. I stumbled across everything on my own, Dad being sick, the writer's block, Sonya."

"Sonya? What about Sonya?"

"Oh . . . well. He's with Sonya now."

As she suddenly makes her hands busy straightening her pile of essays, I see an old kind of pain there. "Well, that figures. She's been waiting around for him for thirty years."

"Mom, you're the responsible one. The actual *real* parent in this scenario. I just wish you would have told me." Even as I say this, whatever irritation I have for my mother is dissipating fast. Maybe it's because I can see that this Sonya thing has wounded her. Curtis has the ability to hurt my mom still, from a world away. But more than that, it's impossible to be angry with her because I know that it's not her job to be my father.

"I'm sorry," she says again, and I can see that she is.

I set Shakespeare back on her desk next to some correcting fluid. "You're prettier than Sonya, you know," I say.

She smiles. "I have something for you. There's something I want to talk to you about." She slides a piece of paper across the desk, a printout from the careers section of the school's Web site. She's highlighted one entry in yellow, "Writing and Composition Teacher Wanted."

"What's this?"

"It's for next school year. Mr. Gilmore is stepping down and we need to fill his space. We haven't officially put out an announcement yet. When we do there will be a lot of applications. But, if you took some teaching courses, your real-world experience would make up for never having taught. Since this is a private school, you don't need to be certified. It could be a great opportunity."

There's that word again.

"Mom, I'm not a teacher."

"Well, according to this article, you're not a businessman. If you're not a teacher, then exactly what are you? I think that's a question you might want to start trying to answer for yourself."

"I've got an agent," I say. "And he's getting my book ready to send out next month. He thinks he can sell it, and I believe him. I'm gonna be a writer. A *real* one."

She leans forward further still, weaving her long, narrow fingers together. "You will be, dear, *some*day. But not yet."

"What do you mean?"

She opens yet another drawer and pulls out my manuscript. With all that's gone on this past month, I'd forgotten she even had it. "It's not you, Tom," she says.

"No kidding. I told you that, I'm not using my *real* name."

"It's not about your name. It's the writing—and it's not yours. This *book* isn't you. Do you know what a pastiche is?"

I tell her yes, but, of course, I have no idea.

"It's when you write something, a story or an essay, but you do it in someone else's voice and style. You mimic their aesthetic. A lot of my students respond to Salinger, and so as a writing exercise, I'll have them do pastiches of him in their own words. Your novel is wonderful—but it's a wonderful imitation of Curtis. It's his book from start to finish." Her face is compassionate, but stern.

"What are you talking about?"

"The themes. The tone. The little details and metaphors—the baseball glove and the ashtray in that old car. These are the things that made your father famous, Tom. It's obvious. People are going to recognize that."

I suddenly don't like her, this skinny old woman who could never write her own novel. I don't like her because somehow she's opened up my brain, sifted through all the muck there, and found the one thing I've been worried about most—the one thing that no amount of name changing and denying will ever fix. She's telling me exactly what Katie and Anna and Brandon told me, but it's not a compliment. "You don't know what you're talking about."

"Sit down, Tom. I didn't mean to make you upset. I just wanted to be honest with you. You're very talented. This proves that. And you're going to find your own—"

"I've gotta go."

"You just got here."

"Hank's waiting in the car."

"Thomas Michael, please."

As I storm out, behind me, the printout about her silly teaching job blows from her desk onto the floor.

## 39

*A few more days* of unemployment and daytime television have passed. Much of that time has been spent opening my novel to random sections on my computer and then comparing them to equally random sections of my dad's books. Much of that time has also been spent eating a startling number of Chips Ahoy chocolate chip cookies and wearing sweatpants.

It would be easy to write my mother's criticism off entirely, but I can't, because, of course, she's right. And she's been telling me as much in voice-over form for about seventy-two hours now.

I know what I have to do to make this right. It came to me in a moment of pure clarity this morning when I was standing over Hank, plastic bag in hand, waiting for him to go to the bathroom. But the thing that I need to do is going to be difficult and foolish and far-fetched. And so, as a last-ditch effort, I've decided to ask Anna what she thinks.

"I hate to say it," she says. "But I think she might have a point." Her face is still flushed and her breath is slowing now to a regular clip. She's unapologetically naked and beautiful, lying on her belly beside me.

"Really?" I ask.

When you're having sex again, it makes you wonder why you

weren't before. What could possibly have been bad enough to make you stop doing *that*? The cement barrier down the middle of our bed has gone away, and being with her has become, well . . . effortless.

"Maybe," she says.

When people are worried about delivering bad news, the word "maybe" almost always means "of course." She's read as many of his books as I have, she's got a master's in comparative literature, and she's smarter than me by leaps and bounds. And so that settles it. Today is the day that I officially admit to myself that I've been slowly and quietly pretending to be my father for almost five years.

She rolls onto her side to face me. "Maybe it doesn't matter," she says. "Maybe every writer is *like* some other writer. They say Hemingway influenced everyone—even writers who've never read him."

I smile, wondering how many other couples reference Hemingway immediately after sex. It's purely academic though. We both know that it does matter. A lot. And so I climb out of bed and find some underwear.

"Where are you going?" she asks.

I kiss her lightly on the forehead. "I'm gonna stay up for a while, OK? You get some sleep. You actually have a job to go to tomorrow."

She smiles at me, and it gives me flashbacks, like a flurry of highlights from when we were young and she had no reason to think that I was anything other than exactly what she wanted me to be. I tell her that I love her. A simple, unpolished word. I've made an agreement with myself to start saying this more—to say it for no good reason and to avoid assumptions.

In boxer shorts and an old T-shirt, I slink out into the dark hallway. It's 10:45, but unemployment has made time merely a concept. The extra bedroom/office is just an office again since my dad left, and it's a little chilly in here. The computer screen lights up when I nudge the mouse, and I open up the document on my desk that I've named "Untitled." This afternoon I started working on something. It's not one of my blogs—there will be plenty of time for those. But it's something else, something that might become something. I can practically hear the men upstairs, working and squabbling and plodding. I read the first few lines, and they're pretty good—smooth, like the first few strides of a cross-country race when I was a kid.

I dial Brandon's number, a little exhilarated by what I'm about to do.

"What's up, gorgeous? Are you done watching *Murder, She Wrote*?" I like when he finds creative ways to call me an old person, considering we're basically the same age, at least geologically speaking. Wherever he is, it's quiet.

"I'm having trouble sleeping." I say.

"Do you want me to talk dirty to you? I can. I'm what you call a full-service literary agent."

"Not tonight. What are you doing home anyway?"

"It's the middle of the week, Tommy. Even the beautiful people need a night off sometimes. Blaine and I are catching up on *Lost* on TiVo. Why is it that Sawyer has so much trouble keeping track of his shirt? The rest of them don't seem to have that problem."

We chat about random things, like how he's begun to grow less and less enchanted with thirty-nine hundred dollars a month for an apartment the size of an inner-city school kid's gym locker. And, of course, we talk about Curtis and Sonya.

"I've always wanted a big brother," he says. "Someone to beat me up and show me *Playboy*s."

"I've been thinking about the book," I say. "I've got an idea, and I want to run it by you. It's . . . a little dramatic."

"Oh, thank God. You've pulled your head out of your ass and you're letting me use your real name, aren't you? This is great news. First thing tomorrow, I'm going to Fifth Avenue and I'm going to buy the biggest fur coat I can find. Suck it, PETA!"

I let him go on for a while, simply because I enjoy listening to Brandon talk. When he's finished, he's actually a little out of breath. "It's not about my name," I say. "Well . . . not exactly."

## 40

**A** *few days later,* I open my dad's front door carefully. "Hello, hello!" I say, announcing myself thoroughly. For fear of what or who might be lurking there, I will never again walk quietly into my dad's house. I've brought Hank along for the ride, and he skitters through the front door and immediately disappears into the kitchen.

"Oh no!" cries Sonya. "It's a rat! Get out of here, rat!"

There are some suitcases scattered in the main room, and the photos of Ashley are gone from the walls. The house is in the midst of its umpteenth stylistic reimagining, and it's hard to say what it'll eventually look like, because right now it looks like a big peaceful mess. Sonya Ross's journey out of New York City has begun.

She appears from the kitchen, carrying the rodent in question, who welcomes her to our nation's capital by trying to French kiss her. She's wearing jeans and a bright blue T-shirt, and her hair is pulled back off her face. I've only seen her in New York colors, and the effect is startling. As are her sneakers. I'd have never guessed Sonya even owned sneakers.

She sets Hank on the ground and we kiss the air near one another's cheeks. "So, you're here," I say.

"In the flesh. I was just working in the kitchen. You know they didn't have but four dishes here between them?"

"Well, Ashley gets most of her nutrients from the sun . . . and vodka."

"I keep thinking that if this had all happened sooner, then maybe I could have been here to . . . to look after him."

"Well, you're here now," I say. "That's what matters."

In the kitchen, I step over some discarded Crate & Barrel boxes and lean against the counter. A new spinning spice rack sits next to a shining toaster, and a bright yellow dishrag hangs from the faucet, still creased and unused. This is the first time I've seen Sonya since New York. She's known me for most of my life, but I can see she's nervous. "I'm sorry that everything had to be so hush-hush. He didn't want to put you in an awkward situation. He just felt it'd be best if you—"

I stop her, touching her wrist, determined to help her from feeling like she doesn't belong here. In the face of vulnerable women, I've found there's always the one right thing to say. I've decided to dedicate myself going forward to actually saying that thing whenever possible. "Sonya, I promise, there isn't anyone I'd rather see here. I mean that."

The overhead light reflects from her eyes. I've caught her off guard. "Tommy," she says.

"All right, enough of that. If you start crying, then Hank will start crying, and there's nothing more pathetic than a crying dog."

"Deal," she says, and points me upstairs. Apparently, my father is up there playing with a new toy. I have no idea what this could mean. "He's just taken some medicine that makes him a little stoned. He rather likes it actually."

The Pulitzer is on the wall, hanging beside his other awards, and it's a staggering sight, this completed wall. So much so that Hank runs into the backs of my legs on my way up the stairs as I stop to look. I can hear hushed voices and quiet applause, literally, and I imagine a small crowd of well-read people clapping for his achievements. And then I realize that what I'm hearing is actually just televised golf.

Curtis is reclining in his leather reading chair facing the most enormous television I've ever seen. It's sitting on the floor next to the box it came in and what appears to be some sort of wall-mounting contraption. If there's a less physically capable man on earth than me, it's Curtis Violet, and I get the feeling it'll be staying there on the floor for a while, wearing grooves into the carpeting.

"That's a pretty freaking big TV," I say.

"Do you think it's too much?"

"No, I've always wanted to see the inside of Tiger Woods's nose."

"The high-def really makes everything pop, doesn't it? I called Gary. He said he'd come by tomorrow and help me get it up on the wall, unless you wanna give it a go right now."

Hank jumps on Curtis's lap and sets up shop there, and I agree to come by tomorrow and give them a hand. Curtis and I will offer Gary no value whatsoever, but it's one of those events I don't want to miss. Across the room, his computer is dark, turned off, and the symbolism, set against this flat screen monster, is as vivid as the TV's perfect picture. He's never allowed a TV up here, even on the second floor, for fear that it would be just one more distraction, and a writer isn't someone who should invite distraction into his life.

"It was an impulse buy," he says. "I was there buying extension cords, and it caught my eye. This is what people do, right? They watch televisions like this with surround sound and everything. There's this package you can buy where you can see every baseball game that's being played on any day. That sounds like fun, doesn't it?"

"Yeah, Dad," I say. "It does."

He's lost a little more weight, just in the last few days, and there's a pharmacy of orange prescription bottles on his desk. When none of us knew he was sick, I think it was easy for him to pretend that he simply wasn't. But now, he's accepted it, committed to it somehow. "The guy at the store told me these TVs have come down in price considerably.

Apparently I got a very good deal. I could get one for you guys, maybe have it sent over. It would be great for Allie's *Lion King*."

"I think we're good," I say. "But thanks." I drop the big manila envelope on the chair next to him.

"What've you got there?" he asks. His voice is slow, spoken through a small tunnel of narcotics. "Is it a present for me? If you're bringing me presents, at *least* let me buy you a television. It's the least I can do."

"I wanted to talk to you about something," I say.

Tiger Woods's ball drifts along an invisible slope in the grass and falls neatly into the hole, and everyone claps. Curtis shoves Hank to the ottoman and removes my manuscript from the envelope. He frowns at the title page for a long time.

"What is this, Tommy?"

"I wrote a book, Dad."

"You what? When did you do that?"

"Over the last five years. Slowly. You've always made it look really easy. But it's the hardest thing I've ever done."

He touches the crisp corner of the manuscript. His hands are shaking, a steady, unending tremor. "Why didn't you tell me?"

I look down at the floor, studying our shoes. "It felt silly that I was even trying to write a book. So I kept it a secret."

"But I could have helped you."

"I know," I say. "But I guess I just wanted to try doing something on my own."

He seems about to ask me any number of questions, but then he sets the book on his knees and looks at me. His pupils are big and dark, blackening out most all of the blue. "But, why's *my* name on it?"

We both look at the title page.

*The Son of Hollywood*
By Curtis Violet

"That's what I wanted to talk to you about. It's complicated."

"OK."

"I think that somehow I knew what was happening to you. That's the only way I can describe it. When you read this, you'll see what I mean, because it's completely obvious that I was never writing it for myself. I was writing it for you the entire time."

He turns the TV off and asks me what that means, and I don't know how to answer. I imagined this moment differently. I'd hand him the novel, he'd read his name on the title page, and he'd just understand what was going on. For a moment, I say nothing, here in this very room where he's written so many of his own novels, and I wait for a long, slow fade to black to mark the end of this scene.

"My whole life I've told everyone who would listen that I didn't want to be like you. But that's not true at all. I wanted to be like you so much that I pretended to be you. I wrote this book the way I imagine you would, if you could have."

He opens to a random page in the middle and reads a sentence to himself. "Is it good?" he asks.

I've shrouded the last five years in a blanket of anxiety and insecurity about the answer to that very question. But I'm beyond that now. I'll channel all of that pain and neurosis into the next one, and into the one after that. But this book, my dad's book, is no longer mine, and so I can think about it objectively. It might as well be sitting on the shelf behind me. "Yeah, it's good. And if you're really done writing, Dad, if this is all really over for you, then I want it to be your last book."

His lower lip is trembling below his aging, handsome face. "What's it about?"

"You and me," I say. "I finally figured that out. Mom told me that all first novels are autobiographical. I guess she's right."

He touches his own name beneath the title. "Did you make me a bad father?" he asks.

A vulnerable woman is easy. A vulnerable father, though, is not. But I'll do the best I can.

"No, Dad. I made you a great father."

# Epilogue

**I'm the oldest** person in the room by a long shot. And, aside from a blond-headed jock named Troy wearing a Red Sox T-shirt who's about to become a P.E. teacher, I'm the only man. It's about a hundred degrees outside, but it's chilly in this heavily air-conditioned basement classroom in Building #3 at the Fairfax Community College. Barack Obama is the president of the United States, the economy is still dicey at best, and in a few weeks everyone in this room will be turned loose to do our parts at helping to shape the minds of America's youth.

I've revisited the nightmares of my childhood in earnest over these past few months. Last night I was standing naked at a blackboard holding a copy of *The Catcher in the Rye* over my penis. The night before that, two faceless bullies with braces and acne were trying to wrestle my head into a urine-splattered toilet bowl, and I can't believe I let my mother talk me into this.

Diane Griffin, the instructor for this course in educational psychology and my mom's friend, is going over a list of proven techniques for effectively communicating with teenagers.

"So, just to, like, clarify," says Troy. "We're not allowed to choke them, right?"

Everyone in the room laughs, even Diane, at least begrudgingly.

Troy is the class cut-up, and it's been a running joke throughout the summer that the first opportunity he gets, Troy will beat his students without mercy. He looks like the guy in every after-school special who smacks his girlfriend around, but everyone in the room has decided to assume that he's only joking.

The point of the lesson is that teenagers are a complicated, volatile bunch who process information differently than adults. I, of course, wouldn't know. Aside from Danny, the teenager I made up and who doesn't exist, I haven't had so much as a conversation with anyone younger than twenty in about fifteen years. This is among the myriad reasons I am in no way qualified to be anywhere near this room. Everyone knows it, even, I fear, Diane. My mother, though, has more pull in the Northern Virginia teaching community than I imagined. And so here I am, a now-thirty-six-year-old former corporate propagandist turned snarky blogger who's been fast-tracked to teach English Composition and Literature thanks to the desperate need for what my mother calls "warm bodies in the classroom."

I may not be a businessman or a teacher, but I am, at least, a warm body.

Mr. Gilmore, whom I'll be replacing, has agreed to stay on for the first month of the semester this fall to coteach my classes in lieu of my student-teaching requirement. But then, after that, I'll be on my own. The first book on my syllabus is *Lord of the Flies*, which makes perfect sense. At some point, maybe halfway through the semester, when they've identified my many personal and professional weaknesses, the students will rise up against me. They'll paint their faces and do unspeakable things to the nerds among them and act like animals, and there will be nothing I can do to stop it.

What frightens me most is the actual attention and work that seems to be required to be a teacher. During my stint on the Death Star, I could phone it in. I could blend into the unholy beige walls and turn my brain off and look at CNN.com and kill hour after hour without anyone even noticing. Not so in the teaching world. For a fraction of what I made back then, I'll have twice the work and responsibility and I'll never be able to escape at random, smoke on the roof, or wander the streets goofing off.

"But you'll be doing something worthwhile for once," my mother said. We were having dinner at her house the other night. "*And* you'll be fulfilled."

"I think you'll be a great teacher," said Gary. That's his role in my life: blind encourager and ambassador of false senses of security.

As the class ends, everyone stands and gathers their things and a little circle forms around Diane. My young classmates have so much freaking energy to do something good and righteous and meaningful. They probably could have made more money selling sandwiches out of the back of a van on Connecticut Avenue, but they've chosen this, and they're fully committed. Sometimes I feel like I should warn them that things often don't turn out the way you think they will, but they probably wouldn't listen to me anyway. I know I wouldn't have, either, when I was their age.

Troy punches my biceps. "See you next time, Gramps."

This is what he calls me, Gramps, but I like him anyway. Despite his propensity for violent humor, he's the only student in the class who really talks to me, and it's nice to have a friend. The rest of the class is made up mostly of young, pretty girls. One in particular, Jessica, whom I have a small crush on, is standing at Diane's desk now asking about the reading assignment. The first day of class she asked me if I was related to Curtis Violet. We haven't spoken since, and if I can help it, we won't. She reminds me too much of Katie and of how things can spiral out of control.

I have never loved my wife more than I do right now. Somehow, all of this has jolted Anna and me back into the breezy mix of comfort and desire that was our youth, despite our occasional bouts with silences and trepidation. A few times now since her return from Boston, I've thought of telling her about Katie. But I haven't.

I listened to my father give a lecture once to a group of young writers. He told them that by the end of a novel, their main characters should have had to answer to each of their sins. In terms of fiction, he's absolutely right. Unfortunately, reality is more complex, and each of us has to live beyond that final page. And so I've allowed her to believe that she took our marriage to the brink all by herself. It's not honorable, of course. It's a lie of omission at best, but I know that it's the way it has to be. I've thought about her and David Anderson a lot, together in her hotel room and the things they did and almost did. Somehow, I'm able to compartmentalize it, to bury it somewhere in the murk. I don't think Anna would be able to do the same thing. I've been married long enough to know that the image of me nearly naked with a beautiful young girl in a tiny apartment in a different state is something we'd never be able to recover from, and all of this would be undone. I think of Dr. Charlie, exiled from his home a while ago, fighting to reassemble the pieces of something nearly destroyed.

"You'll be as bad a teacher as you are a golf instructor," he's told me, several times, in fact. That is his role in my life: manager of expectations. I asked him to review my dad's file a few months ago, and he did so at a bar. And then the three of us got drunk—my dad, my best friend, and me. Because that's all that we could do.

I'd be lying if I said there isn't still a small, Katie-shaped hole in my heart, this little nook that hurts during those fleeting, less-and-less frequent moments when she crosses my mind. Two afternoons ago, I got a call from a smart-sounding lady from one of the ad agencies downtown. "Is this Tom Violet?" she asked. The remaining corporate synapses at the back of my brain fired and I immediately recognized her as an HR person. I felt a sudden welling of shame. After all, it was the middle of a weekday afternoon and instead of working in some office somewhere I was eating a peanut butter and jelly sandwich over the sink and watching *Judge*

*Judy* with my dog. She asked me if I wouldn't mind chatting about Katie Montgomery, who was a candidate for a junior copywriting position. She'd listed me as a job reference.

"What was your relationship with Katie?"

I suspect she was interested in the shorter version. "I was her direct supervisor."

"How would you describe her as an employee?"

"She's wonderful," I said, complete with a pang of melancholy. "A great person and a really gifted young copywriter. If I were you guys, I'd hire her in a second."

In real life, nothing concludes without a few loose ends, and some are more glaring than others. My feelings for Katie and what they say about me as a husband and a man are clearly unresolved. I'm less worried about that, though, than I am about the troubling matter of logistics. Katie read my novel, and toward the end of this year that same novel will be published by Curtis Violet. She'll figure this out, of course, and what she chooses to do with that information has kept me up more than a few nights this summer. I know it sounds romantic and ridiculously naïve, but maybe when she hears about Curtis—if she already hasn't—she'll understand. At least I hope so. Either way, it'll be up to her to draw her own conclusions and to make her own decisions. Contacting Katie, even something as simple as an e-mail, will open a door that's best left closed.

I'm absolutely certain that she's going to marry Todd the Idiot. It's one of those cosmic facts that I simply know to be true. David Anderson will stay with his wife and their boy Conner, and Anna and I will be married until one of us dies. And Todd, who's probably not as much of an idiot as I've claimed him to be, will buy a ring and she'll accept his proposal, and that will be the life she has. In our hearts, we all wish we were unforgettable to the people in our lives and the companies that show us the door. But, in truth, for a while Katie will think of me from time to time, and then, gradually, she'll begin not thinking of me at all. And MSW, in all its horridness and empty, meaningless bullshit, will weather this economic storm and trudge on, and someone else will write their crap for them and no one there will even remember that I exist. Not even Greg.

The circle of students with questions dissipates and Diane smiles at me. I've known her casually through my mom for years, and so, without ever actually discussing it, I've volunteered to walk her out to the parking lot after each class. Like my mom, she's one of those people who can be identified instantly as a teacher. A tiny woman, she's dressed in a long, flowing skirt and a loose-fitting blouse of random, mismatched color, as if she dressed this morning with the lights off. She smells like the inside of an old book.

We step into a swamp of heat, and I start sweating instantly. It's dusk, but still unbearable. A group of male students is playing hacky-sack with their shirts off.

"You think these kids are ready to be teachers?" she asks. She's well into her sixties, but she likes commiserating with me like we're peers.

"I don't know. Hell, do you think I am?"

"Probably not. But I'd give you an edge over them. These young ones, right out of school, are too idealistic. The job can't possibly live up to their expectations. The first time a father shows up at a parent-teacher conference drunk or one of their students says, 'I hate you,' they'll be devastated."

"Well, fortunately for me I've learned to embrace people's hatred of me. You learn that where I used to work. Everyone hates everyone, for the most part."

She grins at the pavement as we walk. "I've been reading your blog, you know. I look forward to it each week. I used to sometimes wonder if I made the right choice all those years ago, and if I would have been better off giving the business world a try. Your blog makes me feel good about where I've ended up."

"Well, if I can save just one person's soul each week, then I've succeeded."

As Andrew Brown predicted, my blog has done pretty well. In fact, it's one of the most popular features of the *Post*'s Web site. Last week, my blog, "Life After the Death Star," received 112,000 unique hits. I'm not exactly sure what this means, but Andrew tells me it's very good. I'm currently working on a blog called "40-Hour Sentence" in which I make an argument for why inmates in maximum security prisons have it better than the average cube dweller. It's not Shakespeare, but it keeps me off the streets.

"And how is your father?" she asks.

I look away, off at nothing in particular, the way I always do when people ask me about Curtis. Most of the world doesn't know that he's sick, but people like Diane do, teachers and readers. There are stories here and there about him and his illness, but I suspect most news outlets are waiting until he's actually gone to pay their tributes.

"Not great," I say.

"I'm sorry to hear that, Tom. It's good, though, that he finished his last book. I think a lot of writers don't get that opportunity. Have you read it? Does he let you read his books before they're released?"

"Not usually," I say. "But I've read this one."

"And?"

I still get an odd little charge of anxiety when faced with questions like this. I guess I haven't fully embraced the lie yet. "It's not bad," I say. "I think you'll like it."

There's a lot of symmetry to what we've done, which makes it feel not quite so wrong. In the weeks after giving the book to my dad, part of me was never actually convinced that it would work. But, somehow, it did. Brandon, taking over from his mother as Curtis's agent, delivered the manuscript to Curtis's publisher in person, showing up at their offices downtown in his best suit. He even wore a tie. They were surprised, of course, considering they'd heard the same rumors that Alistair had, that my dad was done. As Brandon predicted, though, any suspicions or trepidations that they may have had were trumped by the thought of blinking dollar signs.

"They fucking love it," Brandon told me over lunch in Georgetown shortly after our literary heist. He'd come to D.C. to check out his mother's new place in my dad's house. "They called me the next damn day. 'A new and invigorated Curtis.' That's what they called it."

"I wonder if they'd have liked it if they knew it was by me?"

"I guess we'll never know," he said. "It's a good fucking book, though. I don't care whose name's on it."

"Oh shit . . . what about your hot intern?" I said, startling the child in the high chair one table over. The intern . . . another loose end, of course. There could be dozens of them scattered around the country. People I haven't even thought of yet. People I don't even know.

"What about him?"

"Brandon, he read it when it was by me . . . or, well, Thomas Ferris anyway."

"Oh, right. Dude, this isn't amateur hour. I'm way ahead of you. I gave him and his handsomeness a full-time job, complete with the all-important nondisclosure clause. It's funny, I don't think it had even dawned on him what kind of power he momentarily had over me. He's very pretty, but, well, you know."

"Do you think this whole thing is even illegal?" I ask. "Like we could get into trouble?"

Brandon smiled at his sandwich. "Yeah. Maybe someday the book police will come and take us away."

I see Diane to her Volvo station wagon and head to my own sinking Honda. On the way home, traffic is mysteriously lighter than it often is, and I think about my book. I've started writing a new one—a book of my own—and I think about it almost constantly now, lying in bed, in the shower, walking Hank. The men upstairs have left my father behind and come to live with me in my head, and they've been working nonstop for months now to the tune of 133 double-spaced pages. There's an office in my book and a man in trouble there. He's driving the car next to mine right now, staring ahead grimly, his tie loose around his neck, his collar yellow from sweat. He looks at me and then back at the road. He has no idea who I am. I'm going to do everything I can to make sure he ends up OK. But I guess it's not really up to me.

If there really are dozens of loose ends to this story, my mother is decidedly not one of them. I expected her to loathe everything about our plan and be convinced that it was a literary travesty, but, somehow, she was very Bohemian about the whole thing. "Anything is better than Thomas Ferris," she said. And the case was closed.

I park the Honda and begin my trudge through the heat toward home. I can hear Hank barking as he always does when I get to this place on the sidewalk where the sound of my footsteps can reach the spot where he sits, waiting. He hops up and down when I come through the door, pawing at my knee and smiling in his ugly little dog way. "Hey, buddy," I say. He leads me to the kitchen where Anna and Allie are sitting at the table. Their identical sets of eyes look up, and I feel so much warmth for them, these two beautiful females who I don't deserve. They're splitting a bowl of tortilla chips and drinking Crystal Lights.

"Ladies," I say.

I touch my lips to Anna's neck and squeeze Allie's head, running a hand across her hair, which is frizzy from the heat. "What are you working on?"

"A picture of Mommy. It's a *portrait*."

In the picture, Anna, for no reason that I can identify, has a giant nose and one of her ears is larger than the other by about 50 percent. Anna and I exchange a little smile. Our daughter is failing to develop as an artist, which is fine by us. Anna and I are both quietly rooting for her to be good at something reasonable. Someone in this family has to be. But I tell her that her picture is wonderful because this is what fathers say—or at least it's what they *should* say for as long as they can.

She smiles, agreeing with me.

I set my bag of textbooks and pamphlets next to Anna's Adidas bag and open the fridge to stare.

"Oh, could you do me a favor?" Anna asks. "Could you take the garbage out? Something in there has gotten kind of nasty."

"I'd love to. Anything else, madam?"

"No, that'll do for now."

The garbage bag is only half full and I can't smell anything particularly nasty, but who am I to argue? I step out the back door, back into the heat, and before I can close it behind me, I hear them giggling at me, the women in my life. Anna and Allie are like a little team sometimes, and I think of the possibility of someday having a son. We could form our own team, and there would finally be some equality in this house.

The garage out back is where we keep the garbage to hide it from the drunks and rats of Washington, D.C., and when I open the door to the dank little place, like I've done hundreds of times, I instantly know that something is different. That something happens to be a silver Porsche. I exhale, staring, with the bag of garbage in my hand, for a long, long time. I don't need to look back to know that Anna and Allie are at the kitchen window looking out at me. I can hear my daughter cheering from behind the glass.

There's a simple index card beneath the windshield wiper. It's Sonya's handwriting. She's been taking dictation from him lately as he's gotten more and more tired.

*Tommy—This car doesn't belong to me anymore. It's meant for a young writer, and you've got your whole career ahead of you. My only request is that you come over tomorrow and take me for a ride. Believe it or not, I've never actually sat in the passenger seat before. I'll man the radio. Just remember . . . no matter what happens, always listen to the men upstairs. They're never wrong. Dad.*

Sonya has done her best to draw a violet, but it's not the same. It's too small, wilted, like an old sunflower.

Anna, Allie, and Hank are outside now, and Anna is holding a set of keys. "Sonya brought it over a few hours ago. Curtis wanted to wait until you were gone. He said it'd be more dramatic that way."

"Hop in."

The clutch is soft and releases higher than I've imagined it would, and so I stall three times, one for each stop light on M Street. Pedestrians glance in our direction. People have been looking at this noisy little car for years, but never with me in the driver's seat, and I don't care how many times I stall it, I feel like the coolest man alive. I'm Paul Newman. I'm James Bond. I'm Tom Cruise before he jumped on that stupid couch. I'm . . . Curtis Violet.

"I think I might sell the Honda," I say.

Anna mans the radio, flipping to our favorite station, and the stoplight turns green. I release the clutch in time and we move forward, the engine humming and whining behind us. I shift into second and then into third as we move across the Key Bridge into Virginia and toward the closest open road I can think of.

"Go fast, Daddy!" yells Allie from the backseat as we come off the entrance ramp to Highway 66. Rush hour has come and gone and both lanes are wide open. I hit the gas, still in third, and the beautiful little car roars forward, shoving us all back into our seats. Anna holds her armrest and laughs and screams.

"Daddy," Allie says. "Are you sad?"

"No, baby," I say. "Not at all."

"Then why are you crying?"

Anna puts her hand over mine on the gearshift.

She doesn't have to be with anyone else. Because I love her. And because I'm not going anywhere.

I should really slow down. I'm responsible for my wife, my daughter, and an easily frightened dog, and we have our entire lives ahead of us. And I will . . . in just a second. But right now I wanna see what this baby can do.

# *Acknowledgments*

Thanks to my dedicated agent, Jesseca Salky, for so much support. Thanks to my editor, Emily Krump, for making this book a lot better. Thanks to Ryan Effgen, for always wanting to talk about writing. And thanks to my parents, for more things than I can list.

## About the author

## About the book

## Read on

Insights,
Interviews
& More...

# Meet Matthew Norman

Trang Dam

MATTHEW NORMAN works as a copywriter in Baltimore, Maryland, a city that once declared itself "the City That Reads." Born in Omaha, Nebraska, in 1977, he attended the University of Nebraska where he studied advertising and English, and where he was, briefly, a DJ on the campus radio station. While earning an MFA in fiction writing at George Mason University, he published a number of short stories in various literary magazines, including *Phoebe: A Journal of Literature & Art*. Norman lives with his wife and daughter, and posts sporadically on his blog, the Norman Nation. *Domestic Violets* is his first novel.

**www.thenormannation.blogspot.com**

# This Book May or May Not Be Completely Autobiographical

LIKE A LOT OF PEOPLE who are totally cool and not at all nerdy, I'm a big fan of author readings. For those of you who have never attended a reading, it's a little like going to a rock concert, except there's a lot less alcohol, and instead of dancing, you're encouraged to be very still and quiet. Another difference is that almost everyone in attendance suffers from some sort of social anxiety disorder.

Of the many readings I've attended, two have stuck with me over the years as being truly memorable. This is because both authors were very famous, and because both readings were highlighted by moments so awkward that the simple act of committing them to type is making me feel like I need to take a mood-stabilizer.

When my wife and I went to Politics & Prose in Washington, D.C., to see my all-time favorite writer Richard Russo read from his book *The Bridge of Sighs*, things started out great. We listened as he read and politely answered questions, and then we lined up to have him sign our book. It was a lovely evening, I was in a great mood, and there were no signs whatsoever that I was just moments away from being emotionally scarred forever.

But then, as we stood there making married-couple chitchat, my anxiety level began to rise. My wife, who was pregnant at the time, could sense this ▶

**This Book May or May Not Be Completely Autobiographical** *(continued)*

and encouraged me not to humiliate her in public. Her concern, admittedly, was valid. I have an impressive history of getting nervous around celebrities (and often non-celebrities) and blurting out really stupid things. This was not only a Pulitzer Prize–winning author, this was the guy who created Hank Devereaux, the narrator of the novel *Straight Man* and my favorite fictional character ever. For people like me—super-cool people and wannabe novelists—this kind of thing is a pretty big deal.

So, when our time finally came, I stepped up to the little table and handed Mr. Russo our new copy of *The Bridge of Sighs*. He smiled up at my wife and me, friendly as could be, and said "Hello" and asked us our names so he could inscribe our book. And then apropos of God knows what, I said/ shouted, "Hi, if we have a boy, we're going to name him Hank!"

Now, allow me to defend myself for a moment. In my mind, informing Mr. Russo that he'd created my first child's potential namesake sounded like something that a perfectly reasonable person would say—it's a compliment! Turns out, it actually sounded like something that a serial killer would say, similar to, "Hi, I have a lamp shade made of human skin in my den," or, "Hi, I brought you my mailman's head as a souvenir of this blessed occasion."

For about five seconds, the awkwardness was staggering. Thankfully my wife, who is *not* an idiot, was prepared. She swooped in and said something charming about upstate New York and totally diffused the situation. I didn't actually hear what she said, though. By then I'd burst into tears and run out into the parking lot.

The second awkward reading moment was also in D.C. This one involved another of my favorite writers, Jonathan Franzen. But this time, I'm pleased to report that the awkwardness, although equally as soul-crushing, didn't involve me at all.

After Mr. Franzen's impressive reading, during the Q&A portion, a young, nervous-sounding guy asked, "How much of this book is autobiographical?"

Whenever this question comes up at readings—and it comes up a lot— authors are almost always annoyed. Most of them simply shrug it off and give a canned, unfulfilling answer. But not Franzen. For a moment, he looked down at the podium and fiddled with his hair. And then, obviously irritated, he asked the guy why he wanted to know. A few people in the audience laughed, assuming that this was a rhetorical question. But, as his gaze remained fixed, it became clear that he wanted an answer. "I'm genuinely curious," said Franzen. "Why does it matter to you?"

What followed was awkwardness so devastating and so unspeakably profound that I imagine it was visible ▶

from space, like the Great Wall of China. There had to have been two hundred people there—which is the equivalent of a football stadium in the world of author readings. I don't even remember the poor bastard's answer, but I remember my heart breaking for him as he struggled to dig a hole in the floor with his program and disappear forever.

In *Domestic Violets*, my main character's mother, a high school English teacher, tells her son that all first novels are autobiographical. As a blanket statement, I doubt that this is completely true, but there's usually some truth to comments like this, otherwise people wouldn't make them—even fictional people. Now that I have a first novel of my own, though, I find myself wondering the same thing that that random guy in D.C. wondered—right before getting bitch-slapped by a *New York Times* bestselling National Book Award winner.

*How much of this book is autobiographical?*

I'm not going to lie, the evidence against me is pretty damning. My main character, Tom Violet, is a white male copywriter in his thirties with a wife, a daughter, and an emotionally needy dog. Me, too. And, when the book starts, Tom is at a job that he believes is slowly killing him, like asbestos. OK, I've been there myself. And, like Tom, my inner monologue consists almost entirely of movie references.

I guess if I'm being completely honest,

all I've done here is taken someone who's a lot like me and made him better looking, less afraid of authority, more at ease around women, a little taller, much more charismatic, quicker on his feet, more self-destructive, a cooler dresser, and hopefully a hell of a lot more likeable. And then I unleashed him on our nation's capital during a full-blown financial crisis.

All right, fair point. But allow me to defend myself again. In real life, my dad isn't famous, neglectful, or a philanderer. My parents aren't divorced. My daughter wasn't even born when I started this book. I've never been anywhere near important enough to have my own office. I don't live in D.C. My dog isn't really *that* needy. And, well, none of the things that happened to Tom in this book ever actually happened to me. At least not exactly. For the most part. Give or take.

So . . . how much of this book is autobiographical?

I guess you've probably figured out by now that I don't really know. Unlike Tom, I was never an English major, so all of these labels are frightening and confusing to me. Maybe all of it's autobiographical. Maybe none of it is. Either way, if you ever happen to see me at a totally cool and not-at-all-nerdy author reading, you sure as hell better not ask me if it is. Because if you do . . . I promise that I will embarrass the living crap out of you. How's that for a canned, unfulfilling answer? ◠

# A Conversation with Matthew Norman

*You've said that the book may or may not be completely autobiographical. Where did the idea for the book originate?*

I saw a documentary a while back— I think it was on HBO—about the children of the super-wealthy. It was really fascinating. There were all these young adults who were smart, highly educated, and hyper-articulate, but most of them were completely aimless. For some reason, it really stuck with me, and I started thinking about it again shortly after grad school when I found myself being a little aimless, too, at least writing-wise. This got me to thinking about what it'd be like if my dad was a famous novelist. And then I wondered how that would make me feel, and then how those feelings would manifest themselves into entertaining, self-destructive behavior. That seemed like a book I'd want to read.

*Do you think that Tom would have made his own leap to leave MSW if he had not been fired?*

Sadly, I think the answer is no. In fact, I'm pretty positive. In my experience, there's this strange, bastardized version of the Stockholm syndrome that sometimes develops in people who have soul-crushing jobs. You may loathe your job, you may bitch about it constantly to your friends, and you may lie awake on Sunday nights paralyzed by dread, but you somehow rationalize that suffering year after year, or, worse, you convince yourself that the suffering you know is worse than the potential suffering you don't know. It's an ugly, unhappy cycle, and Tom was caught dead in the middle of it. Having him get himself fired wasn't just a plot device. It was a gift, from me to him. I just couldn't stand seeing him suffer anymore.

**Do you think that the book would exist without the financial collapse?**

Well, for a little while, it kind of did. I had a completed draft of the book all printed out and sitting in an impressive pile on my desk. The basic plot and characters were the same, give or take, except there were very few references to the "real" world—and certainly no references to the financial world, of which I have only a childlike understanding. Then, pretty much over night, the world got flipped upside down. As I started going back through the manuscript, I realized that it had become laughably irrelevant. The world had changed, and I couldn't just ignore it. So, after a few days (perhaps weeks) of anxiety and low-level alcohol abuse, I decided to open a new Microsoft Word document and just started typing. It turns out that balancing the stuff I'd made up with the drama that was unfolding nightly on the news was really exhilarating. So, yeah, a worldwide financial crisis . . . lucky me. ▶

### A Conversation with Matthew Norman
*(continued)*

*Allie is very precocious for a young child and very aware of her parents' lives. Is she "gifted and talented," or are Tom and Anna simply not that discreet about their marital problems? Do you think kids generally know when something is up?*

Little kids are tough—even fictional kids. I think as a writer, you can only go one of two ways: you either make them really bright and perceptive or you make them complete idiots. Anything in between is just kind of boring. If you go the smart route, they can end up being your little truth-tellers, and that's exactly who Allie is. She isn't old enough to know about neurosis or subtext yet, so she just calls things as she sees them. Adults spend a lot of time not saying what they should be saying because they're afraid of the consequences. Having a little kid lurking around to do some strategic blabbing is a great way to make people actually deal with their problems.

*Tom mentions that the word "ironic" gets misused a lot. But, in fact, many of Tom's experiences are ironic. What's this all about?*

Hmm. That's actually a pretty ironic statement. At least I think it is. I have a theory on irony, which I've been halfheartedly working on since junior high. I sincerely believe that when irony shows up in fiction, it's almost always completely by accident—just like in real life. That's certainly the case with *Domestic Violets*. I'm nowhere near organized enough to plan irony, so I had to trust that if I was diligent enough, I'd eventually stumble blindly into it. Admittedly, Tom's worldview helped. He's a person who's always prepared for the worst. So, when the worst inevitably happens, he just sort of looks at you and says something sarcastic. I think it's why most people who actually know him find him infuriating.

***If you could choose a dream cast to play your characters in a film, who would you include and why?***

I absolutely love movies and I quote them incessantly, so you'd assume that I have an entire cast list typed up and laminated. But the truth is, I really have no idea. The only character in the book who I casted with an actual actor was Gary, who's played in my head by Brian Dennehy, Chris Farley's dad from *Tommy Boy*. Everyone else was just an amalgamation of random people I've known over the years or people I just made up. I imagine it's sort of like the complete strangers who show up as extras in your dreams. Where do those people come from? Does your subconscious create them, or are they just sort of . . . there? (Side note: I think I just blew my own mind.) ▶

**A Conversation with Matthew Norman**
*(continued)*

*If there was a playlist for* Domestic
Violets *what would be on it? Do you
listen to music while you write?*

Silence kind of freaks me out when I'm
writing. It makes me overly aware of the
sound of me not typing. So, I've always
got something on in the background.
Here's a list of songs that had varying
degrees of influence on the book.

**"I'm Always in Love" by Wilco**
It's a joyous song, but also kind of manic.
And it was actually the working title of
the book.

**"Street Fighting Man"
by The Rolling Stones**
This song was in my head during the
absurd bar fight, and then again in the
very last scene of the book.

**"Arc of Time" by Bright Eyes**
Katie is the type of person who goes
crazy for Bright Eyes. I imagine her
listening to this song in her little
apartment while she's putting on
makeup.

**"Where Is My Mind" by The Pixies**
This feels like it could be Tom's theme
song. I am aware, however, that the lyrics
don't really make very much sense.

**"Some Days Are Better Than Others"
by U2**
It's always reminded me of that
moment somewhere between youth